BRE

:an Au

N.J. Hallard was b   ngland in 1975.
He lives with his wife and child in
Worthing on the West Sussex coast.
He enjoys cooking and telling tall tales.

Follow @NJHallard on twitter.com
or NJHallard.wordpress.com,
for details of what to do with
your own autozombiography

BREAKING NEWS
:an Autozombiography

N.J. Hallard
Baron of Cissbury

Cissbury
Publishing

Breaking News: an Autozombiography :

ISBN 978-1-4457-8538-7

N.J. Hallard gratefully acknowledges the assistance of
Ordnance Survey®; West Sussex County Council Library
Service; and the staff of Worthing Library

Cissbury Publishing uses paper formed from the
mashed-up brains of the infected undead.
Gloves are recommended.

Cissbury Publishing
65 Downlands Avenue
West Sussex BN14 9HE

Contents

Illustrations

For Lou

Act II Scene I
Richard II
William Shakespeare

"This royal throne of kings, this scepter'd isle,
This earth of majesty, this seat of Mars,
This other Eden, demi-paradise
This fortress built by Nature for herself
Against infection and the hand of war,
This happy breed of men, this little world,
This precious stone set in the silver sea,
Which serves it in the office of a wall,
Or as a moat defensive to a house,
Against the envy of less happier lands,
This blessed plot, this earth, this realm, this England..."

[prologue]

I was asked to be as accurate as I could when writing my account of the events of that summer, to include as many seemingly inane details as possible.

The writing came easier to me than I thought it would - I never read many books before all this happened, and I certainly hadn't sat down and written anything since I was at school. But even though we could raid the burnt-out shops for all the pens and paper I needed (while dodging the bloodied fingernails and bared teeth), finding the time to sit and write proved more arduous.

I hoped I had done the tale justice, but reading back over the wad of sheets neatly bound with green garden twine, and picking over my tiny handwriting I can now see that this, my own account of the last twelve months, is as close to a life story as I have ever read.

Breaking News
[day 0001]

I remember the exact time it broke: thirteen minutes past eleven in the morning. It was all a bit of a rush after that point - I didn't even have time to press the record button on the video.

For three days the item had been climbing up the running order of the news. On television it was getting close to the 'top of the hour' as they used to say, and closer still to the front pages of the daily printed papers. It was always a good gauge of how serious they thought a situation was when the rolling news channels threw away their scripts and tried valiantly to improvise, devoting hour upon hour to a story as it was developing.

Al and I had settled down for a day lazing about in front of the television, but the news channels weren't on our agenda. He'd managed to scrape a day off work and had arrived at my house early to make the most of it - my wife Lou had already been at work for hours, but like Al I was my own boss. We had yet to decide on whether it would be a day of PlayStation 3 or zombie films (I kid you not) when the news broke. He'd plonked himself down in my front room and started rolling a joint as I made a couple of brick-orange cups of tea; milk and two for me, milk and none for Al. He sipped it kettle-hot, his nose-ring clunking the mug as he nodded his thanks. His tattoos, shaven head and goatee gave him an air of menace, but in all the time I'd known Al I'd never seen him so much as raise his voice. I, on the other hand, would go purple-faced with rage at the drop of a hat, mostly leveling my venom at the television; seething and spitting until my wife stroked my arm and made it go away, telling me that I was born fifty years too late. Maybe I should have done what all my friends did and not watch the news, effectively ignoring it out of existence. As it turned out, the news really would disappear before that summer day was done.

As the TV warmed itself into life we could hear the newsreader's voice before we could see her face. The government was apparently in the process of performing a huge and elaborate U-turn, now admitting that the epidemic wasn't necessarily due to terrorist activities as they'd been insinuating that it was to a panicked public. What was it then?

Breaking news. The health minister - a midget tit-witch with unrealistic hair and a rictus smile - appeared in front of a pack of cameras and microphones. She had a breathtaking ability to answer her own questions no matter what she'd been asked, and had famously been on the business end of Jeremy Paxman as junior farming minister the year before. She smiled as she confirmed that some sort of virus had hit Britain and that it was 'right and proper that we are keeping an open mind about the source of the outbreak', but that the public were to be reassured that everything was definitely well in-hand. She even had the nerve to suggest in a roundabout way that terrorism had never actually been suggested by her party as a cause for the illnesses. She said she was 'pleased to be rolling out an immediate and wide-ranging raft of measures that had been put together aimed at tackling the issue', in a news conference at midday.

Questions came at her like shot from a gun, making her blink for the first time. She grinned that she simply couldn't answer anything at this stage, but before she could finish the sentence her hackles rose visibly at the tone of one question, and like an impatient child with a shattering secret she blurted out that it might well turn out to be a new and virulent strain of bird or even swine 'flu. Then, like the Cheshire cat, she was gone. She actually seemed pleased to have spouted such a torrent of wet drivel. I hated the way management-speak seemed to have crawled its way up the arses of politics and journalism. Cue purple-faced howling.

'What about all that stuff about poisoned reservoirs they've been banging on about all week? They're saying that it's not the Al Qaeda ninjas after all?' asked Al after my tirade had lost some steam.

'It sounded like that, but it was rather hard to tell,' I said. It wasn't the first time someone had mentioned mutating animal 'flu. Chatrooms and public houses alike had been bubbling with rumours and alternative theories to explain the spate of sickness that had swept through England and beyond. Some said that those infected had rabies; others suggested an experimental swine 'flu cure that had gone bad; some suggested yet another deadly leak from a government germ-works. Obviously lots of excitable citizens rejoiced in the imminent end of civilisation; boiling seas, brimstone, trumpets etc.

As the newsreader began to talk of 'new concerns about the on-going situation', I remembered an interview with a nursing home staff member we'd seen on the BBC the night before, when Lou and I had been hosting the regular Sunday poker game. The nurse had snorted when they put the bird 'flu theory to her. She seemed genuine, even though I didn't like what she had to say. I hated any outbreaks of any sort - any epidemics, any unknown diseases, or new viruses that had to be dealt with in a panic. I had to leave the classroom when we covered the bubonic plague, and had nightmares for weeks after they first worked out what Ebola was. What she said gave me the creeps.

Old people had been the first to get infected, she'd explained, and her workplace in the north of England as well as other rest homes up and down the country had been overwhelmed. The symptoms were all the same; splitting headaches, cold sweats and - worse still – violent, fitful fevers when the patient would become uncontrollable and aggressive. Apparently some people had been scratched or even bitten by the afflicted. Hospitals had only been able to cope with the numbers by cancelling operations and non-emergencies. In amongst the confusion of the public, the near-collapse of the NHS and the strong hints from the government's spin-surgeons that the country was under large-scale biological attack from lonely god-botherers, two things were obvious to the nurse - it was spreading fast and it wasn't 'flu.

It was something much more ghastly, which became clear when many of her patients starting vomiting blood. The newsreader - one of the silver old-guard - all but begged the nurse to back up his much more exciting germ warfare theory. Instead she recounted how she'd finally fled the building and her patients and those colleagues of hers that had become infected. She said that some of them had even slipped into a coma, developing rashes, boils and horrific skin lesions. The newsreader was almost jumping up and down in his seat as he put forward the idea of a deliberate smallpox contamination, then Lou grabbed the remote when I wasn't looking and stuck the *Eastenders* omnibus on.

Even though no-one had died at that point, I started to herald triumphantly the rising of the dead, telling anyone who would listen that we'd soon be overwhelmed by the groaning, fetid, walking corpses that would soon come bumbling up the street - mostly because I hated *Eastenders*, but partly because zombies scared the living shit out of me and that's what I always said was the cause of any new disease. Even if anyone had been listening to me, back then zombies registered understandably low on the scale of what the British public should be scared of. We had the news to tell us exactly what the establishment's approved threats were: terrorism; paedophiles; hooded youths; climate change; climate change deniers; bird 'flu; swine 'flu; the upper classes; the middle classes; the working classes; drugs; guns; identity theft; rap music; cancer; nuclear war; anorexia; obesity; AIDS. All of these registered high on the scale. But not zombies, that was just daft.

As Lou shushed me to find out what Dot Cotton had to say about something or other, Al leaned over to me. 'S'definitely zombies, chum,' he grinned. 'What do you think?' He was taking the piss out of me, but that was when I first suggested cramming as many George A. Romero movies into our Monday off as we could manage, for maximum freak-out effect. At that stage I hadn't actually seen anyone who had been infected – if I had done I wouldn't have been so keen to indulge myself.

In the end, that morning I flicked on the PlayStation instead of getting out my George A. Romero boxed set, and we contented ourselves with rampaging through city streets, leaving a trail of burnt out cars and corpses behind us, occasionally getting wasted by the Feds, constantly getting wasted by the rather strong doobage Al had brought with him. I loved that PlayStation game like a favourite album, but in equal measure loathed those people who came on TV calling for it to be banned and wailing about the children who would be damaged for life by playing it. I would hiss through gritted teeth that games had certificates just like films, and maybe the cheeky little monkey might be better off playing hopscotch outside instead of spoiling my fun.

It had been at least half an hour since we'd had the TV on, but maybe the skunk was slowing things down a bit for Al.

'No 'flu makes you violent,' he snorted. 'I had 'flu last year, I could hardly move.'

The skunk had taken its effect on me too - I couldn't feel my feet, so I paused the carnage and stood to stretch my legs, make a cup of tea and maybe a sandwich.

'Tea,' I stated. Al nodded.

'It sounds more like rabies or something,' he suggested. 'Getting all bitey and that.'

'I had the 'flu too, at college,' I shouted to Al from the kitchen. 'I shat water and sweated like a nonce on a school bus. But I didn't bite anyone,' I filled the kettle and got the bread out for a couple of tuna melts. Floyd - my ten-month-old beagle pup and a serious contender for my wife's affections – was stretched out with his front paws on the worktop looking at me like he would just die if I didn't let him have just a little cheese, but I batted him away with my leg. He was a tricky little bugger, a destroyer of shoes and paint brushes. He'd pooped out a whole hiking sock recently, I didn't know whether to flush it or put it in the bin.

It was nearly midday by the oven clock, so I pulled out the tuna melts as the cheese bubbled. Al ate his too quickly, burning his mouth. He had some melted cheese in his little beard, but I didn't point it out. As mine cooled, I rolled another joint - we didn't pass them to each other any more. It's just what happens when you've been smoking for a long time and all of a sudden you wake up and you're thirty-something. The buoyant, generous nature of the smoking sessions of my youth had given way to a feeling of bread-and-water necessity and all the bland practicalities that came with it, including not sharing.

'Turn it up,' I waved my lunch at the remote control near Al. The news conference was starting. The backdrop sported the logo of the Metropolitan police, and boasted the words 'Working Together for Safer Communities' as if that was a new idea, or a luxury we should be bloody grateful for. There was a policeman with mutton chops who looked like he hadn't seen a street for a decade; two doctors; and someone from DEFRA who appeared to be about sixteen years old. As the NHS Direct telephone number scrolled across the bottom of the screen, I noticed that the government's grinning little bridge-troll wasn't present. After the standard shuffling and coughing, the greyest of the two doctors - a moon-faced man with a bad suit - jumped in feet-first and told the assembled press that the disease was a killer, and people were dying right now. Al and I looked at each other.

Because the emergency services were 'stretched' as he put it, full use was to be made of the list of symptoms and accompanying images on their website. He held up a piece of A4 paper with a telephone number written on it in thick black marker pen. His hand was shaking. He said everyone who had contracted the illness must be reported and to call the number even if in doubt. He said people who had 'sadly passed away' should be wrapped in bed sheets and isolated in a locked room to prevent further contamination.

'Why put dead bodies in a locked room?' I muttered.

'Why is he shaking so much?' Al frowned.

'Where's the poison dwarf?'

It soon became clear why she had excused herself, as Moon-face's chum said that (strictly departmentally of course) they definitely didn't think it was any type of 'flu, bird or swine, mumbling into his tie that they were still keeping all options open. It made some sense – it was the middle of summer after all. However it also didn't mean that they actually knew what it was, which became evident as he ran through the wide-ranging list of symptoms to watch out for. The early stages were certainly 'flu-like, with sweaty, clammy skin and feverish slips into unconsciousness. Lesions or bruising developed next, along with rashes around the nose and mouth. The disease took between one and three days to fully develop.

Mutton-chops took over, shouting down some questions and adjusting his microphone. He started by requesting that people contact all elderly or infirm relatives and neighbours, and to make sure they were looked after. Those at work should stagger their journeys home, drawing lots and leaving on the hour. It seemed they might have to ask non-essential workers to stay at home for a few days, and everyone should keep their televisions and radios on to stay up-to-date with any developments on travel restrictions. There had been light law-and-order issues, mainly in or around hospitals. Non-emergencies were being turned away at most hospitals in England, and operations had been cancelled across the UK. They had already begun setting up 'event control hubs' (what did that even mean?) in open areas around the country where people could seek medical attention or advice and report cases of the disease. As soon as it seemed the officer was running out of steam, the journalists started flinging questions at him.

'What's the death rate – how many people have died already?'

'Will it affect Premier League fixtures?'

'Is it spreading through cuts and scratches?'

Moon-face pipped in again at this point, holding both his hands up as if in surrender, suggesting that it was a very unpleasant and uncomfortable condition which wasn't helped by the hot weather. Even though it was pure speculation that it spread this way, any scratches or cuts should be thoroughly disinfected as a precautionary measure.

'Is it true it started in a meat packing plant?'

'Have you thought of smallpox?'

'Who spent the bird 'flu prevention kitty?'

Everyone laughed, except moon-face and his pal. Even Mutton chops stifled a smirk. The young lad from DEFRA seemed to be more interested in his mobile phone. Looking cross, the other doctor went to stand up and the officer held his hands out to the journalists, stating that there were to be no more questions. It didn't look like they had any answers anyway.

I felt a bit sick, and needed to hear Lou say something nice. I also wanted to let her know what had just been said about leaving work, so I started to look for my phone. Eventually Al rang it for me, and I retrieved it from the mound of poker chips and cards still scattering the dining table from the night before. The newsreader – one of the new ones; bright orange with a peroxide bird's nest on her head – announced with more than a hint of glee that the NHS website with the list of symptoms on it had already gone down, 'overwhelmed by traffic'. I called Lou but her mobile just rang and rang, as did the reception desk in her building. She was an administrator for an insurance company in a monolithic ex-civil service building, with no air conditioning and a gloomy mid-70's paint job. I tested my Jedi capabilities by leaving it as long as I could before her answer phone kicked in. I never leave a message for people, chiefly because I get cross when I have to pay to hear someone I almost certainly don't want to talk to tell me they'll ring me later. I tried again and stared down at Floyd who was laying full-stretch on his back on the sofa, his reedy legs splayed, showing his pink belly and his tan freckles and his little black bollocks.

Bird's Nest introduced a helicopter shot of a London hospital and a huge crowd stretching away down the road. They were crammed in pretty tight, all facing the building. It had none of the co-ordination of a demonstration, or the activity of a marathon. There was no ticker-tape, no open-top bus. I shuddered.

'It looks like *Day of the Dead*,' I said, just as Lou answered her phone. Al nodded sagely as he re-lit his doobie. Lou had heard me.

'Hello baby. You're not still on that zombie nonsense are you?' Lou chuckled. It was good to hear her voice, even if it was delivering a low-level nag.

'What? Listen, Sweetpea, you've got to come home now. Have you seen the news? They're saying to come home now.' It was worth a try, I thought.

'Ooh you fibber. They're saying to stay put,' she said firmly. 'Jan had the local radio on in the office. They're telling people to draw lots and stagger their journeys home by an hour, actually.'

'Oh alright then, they're saying to stay put, but I'm saying I want you to come home now.'

'Well, I'm not going to. I drew nine o'clock in the evening, and if everyone left at once there'd be madness.' She always thought she was right. Most times she was.

'I know. I know. But I want you to come home,' I pleaded.

'Well, you'll have to wait. Look, I'll be alright. I love you.' With that she was gone.

'She won't come home,' Al stated, rather than asked.

'No.'

I could never get to sleep at night without the BBC news channel burbling away self-importantly to itself in the background. It was like a comfort blanket to me, no matter how discomforting or uncomfortable the news actually was. One of my old college friends couldn't fall asleep until the shipping forecast came on, and if he found himself awake at the end of it he'd have to wait until it came round again five hours later, so I considered myself quite lucky. It provided a rhythm, from the self-regarding, orchestral techno of the countdown to the hour (based unsubtly around a sample of the original 'pips'), through links to items studded with quarter-hourly headlines, through the weather and back to the techno-pips again. Pips-headlines-stories-headlines-stories-sports-weather-headlines-stories-headlines-stories-sports-weather-pips. It was like an hour-long heartbeat. The two main benefits were an absence of adverts and a subliminal intake of the names of world leaders, which proved less useful in conversation than I would have liked. I had also developed a sixth sense for when things were going wrong in the newsroom, and now was one of those times. A young chap – not quite so orange as his colleague, but still with unfeasibly solid-looking hair – was linking to a reporter as she got jostled in amongst the crowds outside a large white inflatable tent in a London park. She stood with a finger hovering by her ear as Haircut asked her with delicious anticipation whether she'd seen anyone get bitten yet. I knew she couldn't hear him, and as her eyes darted to one side, she mouthed 'Are we on?' to someone off-camera.

'No, we've lost Julia,' Haircut smoothed. 'But we can cross over live now to Jeremy, who is inside New Cross hospital in New Cross. Jeremy?'

Jeremy didn't appear but the weatherman did, being tended to by a news-fluffer with headphones and a clipboard who fiddled with his collar. As he caught sight of himself on his monitor his jaw dropped, but he was quickly substituted for the park Julia was in, minus Julia. Then the black-and-white clock-face came onscreen – the one that leads into a report, but is never meant to be seen. This quietly counted down to itself, but we could hear Bird's Nest stuttering 'Have we got…? Are we…?'

Al laughed, enjoying the sticky embarrassment of it all, but I was just getting more unnerved. Haircut's voice got severed mid-sentence as the vision cut to a shot of a building interior (presumably Jeremy's hospital) in almost total darkness. I could just make out the silhouettes of people crowding the foyer. At first I assumed there was no sound to go with the pictures, it seemed too quiet for so many people, but then I heard the scrape of metal on tiles. It didn't come from the sound-dampened BBC studio – it was echoing around the inside of the hospital. I scrabbled for the remote control and turned the volume up as high as it would go. There was moaning but no talking. Feet shuffled.

Haircut's voice thundered through my television and as the bright colours of the studio came back onscreen again I jumped and dropped the remote, spilling the batteries across the living room floor and out of sight. The volume was still up full and continued to blast us both with news as I fumbled under the sofa. Al was looking at me with one eye shut tight against the wall of sound until I opted for the root cause and leapt to the TV, jabbing at the standby button. Instead of blissful quiet, I heard two things – my phone ringing, and glass smashing in the street outside. Al leapt out of his seat and to the window, joined swiftly by Floyd with his front paws on the sill. Lou was calling from her office phone.

'What the fuck was that?' I asked Al. 'It's a bit early for the chavs over the road to be having a barney. Hello? Lou, what's up?'

'My car's gone,' she said calmly.

'What?'

'Someone's taken my keys out of my bag and nicked my car. I saw the news, and I'm coming back now.'

'What?'

'Neil's giving me a lift, he lives in Southampton. I'm waiting for him now,' Lou, always calm and practical, gave the impression she'd come to terms with the stolen car situation already. I suspected she was boiling with rage however, as she was pronouncing the ends of her words very crisply.

'Who's Neil? Southampton? Who drives that far to work?' Lou's sixty-minute rush-hour commute was incomprehensible enough, so sixty miles was beyond me – I made old fashioned pub signs in a workshop at the end of my garden a thirty-second commute away - but if our house in Worthing was on this Neil chap's route home who was I to argue?

'He works in my department,' Lou explained. 'I called the police about my car, but it was engaged all the time. We've been trying the ambulance for Clive too. Hang on…' Lou's mobile started ringing.

'Check this out,' Al was looking through the blinds onto the street. I could hear Lou talking on her phone.

'Curtain-twitcher,' I said, lifting a slat and peering out with my mobile still pressed to my ear. Standing dead still on the pavement over the road was an old man in a dressing gown: I could have sworn he was staring right at us. Floyd started barking.

'Neil, where are you?' Lou was shouting. 'I've been waiting ages. No I haven't. No, well thanks a lot. Thank you very much.'

'Lou?'

'Neil's gone,' she explained. 'He's already in his car on his way back down to the coast. Cock. The trains aren't running either. Look, I drew nine pm as my slot to leave, so that gives me plenty of time to find an alternative. Someone's got to look after Clive anyway. I'm staying here.'

'No no no. Absolutely not. No way. Who's Clive, and what floor are you on?' I didn't like it when she sounded so determined.

'Floor six, but I'm staying here.'

'Yeah, and I'm a lady chimp's chuff. We're coming to get you.' I cleared my throat and put on my best American accent. 'When we get there, don't make me come looking for you.' I waited for an answer, but the phone was dead.

'*Dawn of the Dead*?' Al asked me as he sat back down. The old man was still outside.

'Well spotted sir. Have you got reception on your mobile?' I asked him.

'"No Network Coverage",' he read. 'That happened on the millennium, do you remember? The system got jammed up by every twat in the country texting 'Happy New Year', or 'HPY2K' or whatever.'

'Well what were you doing to know that then? Texting someone?' I asked, trying to hide some light smugness.

'Fair point, smartarse', he said as I checked the landline – also dead. Not static but deathly silence, as if it had been unplugged.

'Look chum, we've got to go. Lou's car's been nicked.' I said simply. Al pointed over his shoulder towards the window.

'Mine's still there,' he countered.

'I know you dippy stoner, and we've got to get in it and go now! Come on!' I made wafting hands at him.

'Alright, we're going now,' he said, leaping off his chair. 'Look at you there, holding me up. Fuck's sakes,' he grabbed his car keys, rolling tin and tobacco and headed for the door, as a scream rang out from down the road. I was already breaking out in a sweat from the summer heat, but that sound chilled me to the bone.

'Let's go.'

Breaking Out
[day 0001]

Lou and I lived in a terraced house in a fairly unremarkable seaside town in the south of England, but she worked in her office in Crawley thirty-odd miles up the road to London. If you drove east from our house along the coast road you'd soon get to Brighton, where Al ran his painfully hip clothes shop. His car was a battered old Audi four-wheel-drive estate with a crumpled bonnet and a dog grille in the boot for Dmitri, his two-year old beagle and Floyd's uncle. It was parked ten doors down the road; his dog was with his shop assistant in Brighton.

Floyd slipped through my grasp and out of the front door. I threw his lead out to Al, went back through the kitchen to lock the back door, picked up my useless mobile phone, put my keys down on the coffee table, then slammed the front door shut and joined Al on my driveway. The wall of midsummer heat stole the breath from my lungs, and I squinted at the cloudless sky through my fingers.

'Hot.'

'Look,' Al was pointing. 'He's been sick. Dirty boy.' The old man in his cord dressing gown and slippers was still staring towards us. Other than him, the street was empty. Mock-Tudor toy-town terraces.

'It must have been that silly cow screaming. *Jeremy Kyle* must have riled them up.' I ventured hopefully, looking up the road.

'He's been sick,' Al repeated. The old man had a beard of vomit.

'Should we do something?' I asked, not really wanting to do anything.

Floyd's body was arched backwards, snout skywards, and he was drooling; his nostrils pulsed like they had a little heartbeat of their own. I couldn't smell anything except the heady, slow burn of a summer that had long outstayed its welcome. Hot tarmac and rubbish. Al had an unflappable belief that Dmitri wouldn't ever run off, and assumed the same of my dog even though he was

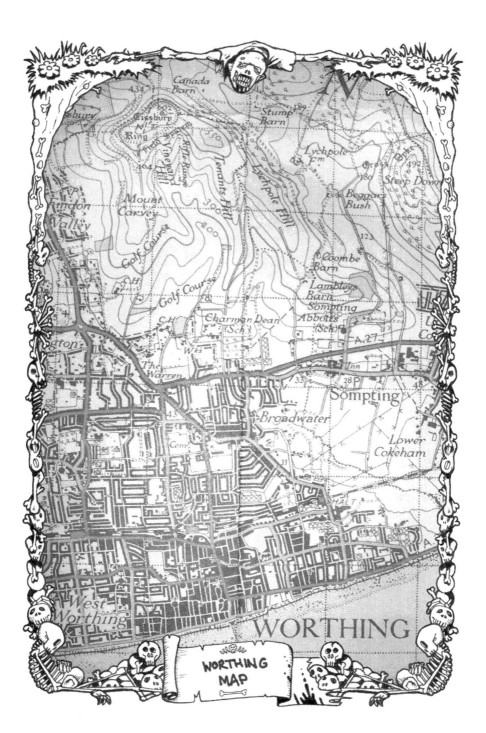

WORTHING MAP

still a young pup and therefore a foolhardy twit. He hadn't been wrong though - until that point.

Floyd bounded into the mercifully empty road, tail wagging furiously and his long ears following his head half a second later. He laid down three or four feet away from the huddled figure, whining quietly, before standing again and ducking his head, doing the half-bark, half-howl thing that beagles do. The pale old man, his jaws gurning like a camel, slowly turned to look at my dog. Floyd backed up a few paces, as his youthful baying turned into a deep growl I'd never heard from him before. I walked into the road.

'Come on boy,' I clicked my fingers. It was like a trigger.

Floyd kicked away at the asphalt with his lanky legs and propelled himself at the old man's face. His lunge only just fell short, instead snapping up a mouthful of soiled dressing gown lapel and bringing the pensioner crunching to the ground beside him.

'Fuck. Floyd, heel! You alright mate? Heel!'

Instead of heeling, Floyd started tugging at the old man's lank comb-over, spinning him on his side in a slow-motion geriatric breakdance. I grabbed a healthy handful of puppy fat and hauled him off, but he had a good grip and came away with the old man's remaining hair. I slapped his arse and he sat, chewing and looking pleased with his handiwork.

'I'm so sorry, mate. Here,' I held a hand out, which he ignored. He rolled onto his front and awkwardly hauled himself to his feet as Al walked over to join me.

'Is he alright?' Al asked.

'No idea,' I said out of the corner of my mouth. 'I think he's shat himself though, he stinks.'

'Maybe he's got 'flu,' Al laughed. Floyd started growling again but he was still chewing hair so the growl quickly turned into a hacking gag. I pulled some strands out of his mouth and rubbed his chest. The old boy slowly turned to face us again. 'Look, I'm really sorry - he's never done that before. He's a pup,' I explained. Illogically, I offered the man his hair back, but Al put my arm down.

'He doesn't want that now,' Al was backing up. 'That's not vomit chum.'

His stringy umber beard of sick glistened red in the bright sunlight. Instinctively I backed up too.

'Should we do something?' I said again, even less keen now he looked like he might be infectious instead of just ancient.

'No. That copper said to help relatives and neighbours.' Al said quietly.

'Well, he is a neighbour.'

'Not a next-door neighbour. He's over the road from you, and up a few. Let's go.'

I didn't need any persuading, and the old man seemed pretty much okay all things considered. I pulled the dog by his collar, claws scrabbling on the road. His attention span was ridiculous, and as soon as he saw Al open the boot he jumped in eagerly, the floor scattered with the rubber bone toys of his uncle Dmitri. I shut him in and joined Al in the front. I swear he had lowered his car seats somehow, making it feel like we were in a Los Angeles low-rider with baby nines under the seat and a couple of ho's in the back. But we were in a beaten-up Audi with no weapons whatsoever, and my wife was stuck in Crawley. Al performed his pre-flight checks – ignition on; CD in; doobie out from behind ear; pull away. Then maybe mirrors, but rarely signal. I looked back at the old man standing in the same spot like nothing had happened.

'He's giving you the evil eye,' Al chortled.

My street was quiet even though it led straight out onto the main road to Brighton. It was narrow and curved in the middle, and had never become a rat-run for the school-run or a detour for the rush-hour even though it did cut out some traffic lights. We didn't have to wait long at the T-junction, which on any other day took forty or fifty cars before someone let you out, or you got the chance to plunge headlong into a gap. That day, even though it was much busier than usual, we were waved out almost straight away. That great English characteristic of 'crisis-politeness' came to the fore even though I'd have bet a decade ago before that it had long since vanished. The traffic ebbed and flowed as we headed east, but remained fairly good-natured. The on-ramps were swollen, but almost everyone waved people out in front of them, even Al, but as a result we often ground to a halt. I wondered how long the mass courteousness would last as Al flicked over to the radio, to an advert literally singing the praises of a local carpet warehouse in mock Gregorian chant.

'Put Radio 4 on,' I suggested earnestly. After a bit of prodding, the sounds of *The World at One* poured forth. I always listened to Radio 4 in my workshop, even though it was often a toss-up between bladder phone-ins and documentaries about moss. It was good because music - even music I loved like The Who and Led Zeppelin - didn't help me to work, unlike almost everyone else it seemed. After a few months of working for myself I realised I couldn't get anything done without *Woman's Hour* to start my day. I was hooked.

Al pushed his antique Aviator sunglasses onto his forehead and reached into the glove box, pulling out his St. Andrews enamel Zippo. I had a St. George Cross on mine and my mate Vaughan had a Welsh dragon. Jay had bought them for us all as Christmas presents over the past few years. Lou organised a 'secret Santa' thing so we didn't all have to buy half a dozen presents each, although only Lou would have bought anyone anything anyway. We would pick a name from a hat, returning the slip of paper if we drew our own names or if we'd had that person last Christmas. Then you bought them a present under £20. Jay had completed the Zippo set with my one last year, and had almost pissed himself with excitement.

'You can be Angliax', Jay had giggled to me. 'Al's Doctor Scotland, and Vaughan's Captain Taff. I'm basically your leader', he had explained, almost certainly disappointed he'd not got a flag on his lighter. 'You're all my super-bitches,' he had explained.

Al pulled on his doobie and we listened; there was some good news – no mass graves or funeral pyres were planned, and family burial plots would not be commandeered. They read out a list of public parks and 'green spaces' where 'crisis management spokes' had already been set up, and additional medical help or advice could be sought at temporary 'community care nodes'. The health minister wasn't available to comment on the fact that there were already no hospital beds available, but had clearly left her mark on the day's jargon. It had become impossible even for the hospitals to remain in contact with each other as they became overwhelmed. Looting had been reported in some of the major cities but martial law was, apparently, a long way off. This wasn't as reassuring as I'm sure they had hoped it would sound. Apparently the situation in the hospitals had been further exacerbated by a marked increase in road traffic accidents, and it wasn't long before we saw one of our own.

The staccato rhythm had eased into a flow as the A27 moved further from the suburbs and we began to pick up speed. Al was doing something which annoys me when others do it; weaving in and out of the lanes, filling gaps by undertaking other cars. I said nothing as I was anxious to meet up with Lou, and kept forcing from my mind the thought that we might well get stranded in Crawley. Al seemed oblivious to everything except the traffic – he might as well have been holding a PlayStation controller. Trance-like, he picked his way from one side of the dual carriageway to the other towards the Southwick Hill Tunnel which cut into the slow curve of the hill up ahead. The rapeseed fields on either side of us blazed yellow, and I closed my eyes against the beating sun. I had one of those forgotten glimpses of childhood complete with sounds and smells – of the fields above Lancing burning, spitting black clouds into a blue summer sky. Stubble burning was a practice that hadn't happened in years, a cheap way to ready the harvested fields for the next year.

The sound of our tyres squealing shook me out of my daze. My hands lunged for the dash and my legs went taught, lifting me a few inches off my seat as a red Fiesta two cars in front of us veered across the road. I thought for a second or two that someone had got pissed off with Al's driving, and was blocking us off. So did Al, who was instantly apologetic.

'Sorry dude!' he waved and flashed his lights. He turned to me. 'I'm still tuned into the PlayStation,' he explained. He's one of the good ones, my mate Al – he only wants to go calmly through life, not ruffling feathers or rocking the boat. I knew there wasn't any meanness in the way Al was driving that day - he had learnt to drive on the eight-lane behemoth highways of Los Angeles, when he was out there playing college basketball. They don't do indicating there, or steering for that matter; light collisions get waved on and it is your duty to drive for your life. Such skills proved useful that day.

The red Fiesta straightened up in the path of a Range Rover in the fast lane which clipped the Fiesta's rear bumper, sending it left in front of us and over the hard shoulder towards the embankment. Car impacts never sound like you think they should, like they do in the cinema. It came to a halt at right-angles, mounting the raised verge and crumpling the crash barrier under it. Al stopped the car dead alongside them, surveying the car's body parts strewn across our lane. A fat woman fell out of the Fiesta's passenger side door and onto the verge, gripping her arm, trying to stem the flow of blood. She screamed at the driver, who was still inside the car flailing about with a passenger in the back seat.

The Range Rover and two of the cars in the fast lane accelerated, heading for the tunnel ahead. We just stared, open-mouthed. Horns started filling the hot air, and we heard screeching tyres and another crumping sound in the traffic far behind us. The fat woman stood up, staggered a few paces, and sat back down in the road. The man in the car was clearly shouting something to the figure in the back seat, but I couldn't make out what over the racket of angry horns. I watched as the colour drained from his face before he disappeared in a flurry of blanket and limbs, the vehicle rocking with the momentum. The fat woman was now lying down on the asphalt, her eyes closed. The car door opened and the driver poured out onto the road, clutching a gaping crimson hole in his throat. I was getting twitchy again.

He looked straight at us as he reached out, but I couldn't meet his gaze. I turned to look at the Fiesta and saw that the figure in the back was a frail old woman, now pressing her face up against the rear windscreen and chewing slowly. That was enough for Al who slammed his foot down. Wheels slipping we screamed away at an angle, through the debris, hot tyres on broiling tarmac. The acceleration sent Floyd skittering about in the boot.

'What the fuck was that?' I squeaked.

'Bad day if you're a Sunday driver,' Al replied quietly. Looking in the side mirror at the receding horror, I caught sight of a white convertible VW Golf bearing down the hard shoulder with a girl at the wheel, clearly impatient with the halted flow and keen to take matters into her own hands. I watched her face as she saw the red Fiesta in her path and jerked the wheel to her right, heading for the space we had just made. She rammed into the woman in the road and her car bounced two feet into the air. I saw the fat lady roll over once, before being gobbled up along with the Golf's own front bumper. I wasn't quite sure what I had just seen, or which of the two events had stunned me more. I felt nothing, as if the fat woman's jam roll had cancelled out the driver's improvised neck-hole. The radio fell silent as we punctured the ceramic cool of the tunnel, its huge fans turning listlessly.

'That was a big wound for an old girl to inflict, even if they hadn't been keeping her fingernails trim. Do you think she bit them both?' Al asked shakily.

'Bit them? He might have fallen on some glass or something,' I said quietly.

'That old boy in your road,' Al was hesitant. 'What if they're not vomiting blood like the nurse on the news said? What if that was someone else's blood?'

'What are you saying?' I asked. He couldn't be thinking what I was thinking.

'Rabies,' he said confidently. Obviously he wasn't thinking what I was thinking. I don't know what it was about zombies that used to scare me so much. Like any normal person, pretty much anything in the cheesy horror back-catalogue – demons, werewolves, ghosts – and I'd laugh. Show me other un-dead fellows of the silver screen like Dracula or Frankenstein's monster and I'd be fine. But zombies would shoot pure, unfettered, childhood fear straight through me. When I look back now, I suppose the more you learn about something the less you fear it. First hand, that is – the George A. Romero movies still scare me, when I can get my hands on a generator and a working TV. I had often thought – fantasised even – about what a zombie holocaust would be like if it ever arrived. When it really did, I was far less prepared than I gamely assumed I would be.

The radio hissed back into life as we left the Southwick Tunnel. The traffic was at least moving here, and soon we joined the A23 which connects Brighton and the coast to Crawley, London and beyond. The radio presenter was explaining how to do a citizen's arrest. London was being ransacked he said, but law and order could no longer be a priority for the police. There had been reports of shootings and rapes, and parts of the West End were ablaze. Then the weather forecast came on.

I thought Crawley was a shit-hole. I haven't been back since so I couldn't vouch for it now, although I suspect little has changed. It was just close enough to London to warrant money spending on it, on schemes like driverless buses and a monolithic leisure centre; but far enough away from London to be completely empty of style, charm and character. New-build houses sat next to bland art installations on roundabouts. There were huge glass hotels to mop up the flotsam from Gatwick Airport five minutes away: the new and even newer in perfect discord. I'd only got one of my pub signs up in Crawley – the landlady wanted to stand out from the other pubs, and from their love of printed banners and vinyl lettering.

Towns that grew organically over time made more sense to me. They had roads that went places, had parks that people visited, and a war memorial or a green in the middle, even if the village they once sat in was now a bustling civic centre. You would get traders who'd been operating on the same spot for generations - butchers, shoe-shops, even department stores - as long as an out-of-town mall hadn't sucked the blood from the community rump like a fat mosquito.

In urban areas that had grown accustomed to sudden and repeated change, the focus of people's attention often shifted to new areas of the town, leaving in its wake stagnant pools of concrete and glass. In turn these new areas of interest would become tired and useless, and the people would shift again from the bright lights to the brighter ones a mile away. Traffic would rocket along on overpasses; pedestrians would be redirected by wire-mesh covered foot bridges; huge car parks would stand empty, simply because things had moved on. Buildings get left behind. I remember years before this all happened seeing an old house teetering on the edge of a deserted ring-road around some backwater of Greater London. The house, meshed in by huge wire fence panels with concrete feet, was coated in grey dust. Fill in the blanks with your own metaphors - the black windows looking like hollow eyes, or something. Anyway, the humans had been sucked away from the area, drawn off by the capillary action of 'inevitable' change. As we left the A23 and joined the queue on the slip-road into Crawley I remembered that house, and found myself wondering for the first time what had been there before it was built.

We hit a glut of traffic towards the middle of the town, but mostly people seemed to be trying to get out. I knew roughly where Lou worked so I guided Al though the streets – busier than Worthing; tenser, with heated exchanges between angry drivers and fighting on the pavements. The traffic lights had stopped working at some crossroads ahead of us (the last time I was here they hadn't been working because of road works) and people weren't being as organised or logical as they could have been. I counted at least eight cars which had been involved in accidents; three askew on the brand-new black asphalt and the others pushed to the side. I could see people sitting on the side of the road. Al gunned the engine and forged a path through the wreckage, holding his hand up in a gesture that served as both an apology and a thank-you.

Two enormous inflatable tents were being set up on a precinct scattered with huddled bodies. Lines of people curled around the tents and out of sight, and the blue lights of ambulances and police cars turned dimly in the searing sun. Vast areas of shadow from the tall buildings around the square drew people like moths, sheltering from the heat.

'Chum,' I said. 'We should have turned left.'

'Okey-poker!'

I think Al was glad to pull off the main roads. The traffic was definitely heading out of town, so diving into the middle of the whole thing was far easier than getting out would be. I checked my mobile phone – still no reception. Before long we saw shops with their windows smashed, and people pushing loaded shopping trolleys through the streets. I knew where I was now, and pointed Al onto a small trading estate. It seemed to be marooned in the middle of a vast roundabout and boasted a drive-through fast food shack and a single-storey monochrome pub called 'MacTafferty's Again'. They both looked sad and empty, and the pub had a vinyl sign. The word "again" had been written in a different font, in italics, as if the marketing team had imagined the punters sighing and resigning themselves to another evening of fun at "MacTafferty's *Again*". It looked like there was little life about - another area where interest had moved on and things had slowed to a mouldy halt.

We pulled off the road and onto the inexplicably pink tarmac strip leading up to the office block where Lou worked. To the right of that was a multi-level staff car park with two floors above ground and more below. Ahead a lowered yellow-and-black striped barrier blocked the way in, but on the way out a second gate was raised. No-one was around. Al looked at me, shrugged, and put the car into reverse. For a moment I thought he was going to get enough distance to break through the barrier and I gripped the edge of my seat. Al pulled to the right and rather disappointingly drove slowly under the raised exit barrier instead. We were in. The little bubble-gum road led us past the front doors of the building before doubling back towards the car park.

'Go down a level or two, it'll be cooler for the dog.'

Al found three parking spaces he liked, and straddled them with the Audi. We'd be further away from the front entrance than I would have liked but I shrugged off the horror-movie chills and got out, my eyes fighting the cool underground gloom. I opened the boot and let Floyd out on his lead for a piss. He was eager to explore, but when he was finally done I lifted him back in and held his head in my hand, making eye contact and whispering 'going to the shops', which Lou had taught him. He started whining as I shut him in and Al locked the car. As I got my mobile out to check the reception again I heard Al say 'Hello?' under his breath. I looked up. No undead – instead I saw a young security guard, shouting and running towards us down the ramp. I checked behind me for zombies all the same.

'What the *fuck* are you two doing?' he yelled.

'Eh?'

'I saw you!' The guard was almost upon us.

'What mate?' Al asked, chin out.

'Through the barrier what mate, that's fucking what!' he spluttered.

'Well, I thought about going through it but I didn't,' Al shrugged. The guard wore a shirt ironed to a crisp line, but dark rings leeched out from under his arms and into his cheap green jacket. He was out of breath, and sweat glistened on his scalp between tight corn rows.

'You went in through the Way Out.'

'So what?' Al puffed his chest out. 'Haven't you seen it out there, mate? You want to get on home or you'll catch the lurgy.'

'It is mental out there mate,' I thumbed over my shoulder, 'and my wife's in there,' I said, pointing ahead.

'No-one's left, mate, only the building staff. What floor was she on?'

I looked at Al. What floor was she on? I didn't do dates or numbers. Birthdays and anniversaries; anything made from fabric; tickets and passports - that's what Lou did. I was drains; electricity; cooking and bins. What floor was she on?

'Four.' I said. 'Six.'

'Which?' He quickly unclipped his radio from a little holster which prompted Al to make karate hands at him before raising them in apology.

'Six,' I repeated.

'Hello mate, it's John. Yep. Got anyone left on six?'

The guard looked at me.

'What's her name mate?'

I told him, and looked back at the car. Floyd had his front paws up at the window, tail on automatic. The guard was gesturing us to follow him, still on his radio. We trudged up the car park ramp and into the heat, past the barriers and up to the glass front doors. I nudged Al. Fifty feet away by some weak-looking bushes there was a kid with a hooded top and headphones round his neck staring at us. He stood still, shoulders drooped, mouth open. We followed the guard inside where it seemed even hotter and smelt like cleaning products. There was a long brown and orange desk and green-flecked linoleum on the floor. John was talking to another guard, fat and pasty, who signalled for us to follow him.

'Don't drive through my Way Out again!' John said, taking up position at reception.

'I will on the way out!' Al shouted over his shoulder. Nice one.

We followed Fatboy up the stairwell. The two tone décor was even better up here —winter grey above bottle green, separated by a sticky handrail.

'Lift's out again,' he sighed. 'What's it like out there?'

'Hectic,' Al said.

'Haven't you got people at home?' I asked him. It took him another flight of stairs to gather the breath to answer.

'Yeah, but the missus is good in a crisis. She's with the kids. I've got to stay here anyway, to protect all the records - insurances and that. Did you hear they're talking about martial law on Sky News?'

'How very colourful of them,' I muttered as we climbed.

'Five!' he said with a triumphant wheeze.

'My wife's on six.'

'Fucking hell.' He pointed upwards. 'I'll wait here.'

He leant against the wall and closed his eyes as we went up the stairs towards the double swing-doors at the top.

The main thoroughfare was scattered with pot plants and chairs. On each side were cubicles with black and brown carpet tiles, and a radio was on. This bit of the building smelt like photocopier toner and proper coffee.

'Lou?' I asked, tentatively.

'Oh,' a head popped up from behind a cubicle at the back. 'You scared me. Hello!'

Lou ran up to me and squeezed me. Her hair smelt like fruit sweets, and today her eyes were ice-blue. I squeezed back.

'You took your time! Hello chum,' she beamed at Al, and hugged him.

'A27 was a bit mad. Crawley's heaving,' Al explained.

'Oh, it's been a drama here.' She lowered her voice. 'Clive's an actuary and he collapsed earlier so we tried to call an ambulance, which of course there weren't any. He's come round a couple of times and one time he grabbed at Susie's leg and it's freaked her out a bit. That's Susie, she's Lyn's PA. Susie!'

'Hiyaaa!' another head popped up.

'What?' I could feel my ears getting hotter and a knot twisting in my stomach.

'An actuary. His wife Janet, I don't know what she does, got sick yesterday with this thing and he was up all night looking after her. He fainted a while ago.'

'We don't have air conditioning.' Susie pointed out unnecessarily. I was dripping with sweat. 'Fucker scratched me. Dirty old man, he could see right up my skirt from down there.'

'I don't think that's what he was doing Susie,' Lou sounded like she'd had enough of Susie for today.

'So he's been with an infected person all night,' I rubbed my temples, 'and now he's collapsed and he's possibly infected young Susie here.'

'Young? I'm twenty-one,' Susie sneered at me.

'Oh let me guess, you think they'll all turn into zombies? You're a big boy now.' Lou scoffed. 'Give it up.'

'Anyway, what about your car chum?' Al intercepted wisely, alert to the warning signs of our spectacular tussles. Lou being sarcastic about my core values – it was a tinderbox.

'Gone.' she said. 'There was just smashed glass where it was. It's alright, it's insured. It's just a pain in the arse.'

'The paedo's woken up again.' Susie said glibly as she turned to Lou.

'You're twenty-one you silly little twat, just shut your gloss-caked gob for one minute.' Susie did as she was told.

I bounced after my wife like a puppy as she strolled over to a far cubicle, where a thin grey man with a shiny bald patch sat on the floor groaning, chin to his chest. He was wearing a sodden short-sleeved shirt and, rather bizarrely, cycling shorts.

'I've got a splitting headache,' Clive said meekly. 'Can I have some more water please? I think I lost my balance,' he looked up, squinting against the light.

Susie looked as if she might pipe up again, but Clive's head lolled forward. Lou bent down with a paper cone of water.

'Clive!' Lou was supporting his head. I wondered if she was as tempted as I was to begin slapping his cheeks. He was breathing heavily, and the sweat beaded on his gleaming dome. Lou looked at Susie.

'Can you get me some paper towels please Susie?' she asked.

'Yeah, and I'm getting security too. Fucker. Sorry, not you Lou,' she added as she headed for the doors.

It was too late for paper towels anyway. Clive hawked a string of black snot onto his shirt.

'Oh, shit. Hurry.'

More came, faster. It was vomit.

'That stinks.' Lou stood, holding the back of her hand to her nose. 'Eggs.'

As she checked her pencil skirt for splatters, I watched Clive lift his head slowly. He was gurning, his eyes watery. He bared his teeth, his eyes rolled back into their sockets, and then he fainted again.

'Look, Lou,' Al sounded weary. 'I know Clive's your colleague and that, and there's no-one else here except Abbot and Costello on the front desk, but I have to leave - I've got people to get back to. And Dmitri, but he is kind of a person. But I'm hot and I don't want to get back any later than I have to. The traffic's just going to get worse.'

'I'm getting the creeps too, Sweetpea.'

'I'm not getting the creeps.' Al said firmly. 'I just want to get back.'

Lou stood up.

'Alright. Do you think Clive will be okay?' she asked.

'I don't know much about rabies,' Al said. 'I think it's pretty serious.'

'Rabies? Who said it was rabies?' Lou asked.

'I said it was rabies. It makes sense, getting all bitey and that. I think you get feverish too and, well that's almost foaming at the mouth,' he offered, gesturing to the pool of black mucus Clive had eagerly produced.

'Well, it makes more sense than *28 Days Later*,' Lou muttered.

'*Night of the Living Dead*, if we're being technical,' I turned to Al. '*28 Days Later* was rubbish, plus they weren't actually dead.' Lou and Al just looked at me, as if waiting for more. Then we heard a sharp crack echoing around the stairwell, and the fat guard swearing as we ran to the doors. We saw him kneeling, cradling Susie's head.

'She just fell to the floor. Lucky I caught her,' he wheezed, nodding down the stairs.

'Get her in the recovery position,' Lou ordered as she put Susie in the recovery position herself. Susie rasped a phlegm-laden cough, and I scanned the back of her legs where Clive had grabbed her, without getting too close. The inch-long scratch was white and puffy with an angry red circumference, like a long, fresh mosquito bite.

'She's really hot.' Lou wafted Susie's top. 'Can you get me some water? The cooler's at the back.'

Al seemed impatient at the hold-up and keen not to reverse the small progress we'd already made. It seemed that I was on my own for this one, so I reluctantly turned to face the doors back into the office. This is it, I thought - this is where you get bitten. This is the bit in the movies where only the worst kind of bit-part idiot would double back on himself... and for what? Fetching water for a doomed girl - typical.

'You'll get bitten,' I muttered to myself, 'your wife and your best friend will try to look after you, and then you'll infect them.'

'What? Get some water, you fucking arse,' Lou snapped, 'and grab Susie's handbag, the one on the chair.'

I considered pointing out my lack of handbag-recognition skills, but my throat felt like it was swelling up. The fact that I almost certainly wouldn't get fully eaten was no comfort, although I'll admit I did have a wealth of battle apparatus to improvise with from pot plants to chairs, but Health and Safety legislation had no doubt ensured there was nothing I could lop a head off with in a modern office.

I chanted the words 'there's only one of them' very quietly as I put my hand on the swing doors. There it was – the word 'them'. The opposite of us. Reaching that stage would be a struggle for every survivor I would meet, but it came quickly to me. I say I was unprepared for that day, but my ability to dehumanise was half the battle.

'Come on, I'll show you where it is,' Fatboy pushed past me through the doors, making me jump. 'I'll get the first aid kit too, see to Clive first.' He held a door open for me.

'First aid. Right.' I said, peering inside. There were two of us now. Good. And he's fatter than me. Good. Slower, and meatier. I could hear Susie moaning softly as Lou sat her up, pushing damp strands from her pasty forehead.

'Can you take me home please?' Susie was tearful and snotty.

'She only lives in Crawley. Is that alright Al?' Lou asked, helping Susie to stand.

'No, no, no, no, no! You've got to be...' I began, but Al cut me off.

'Sure, I've got room in the back, but let's go now though.'

'But she's a...'

Lou shut me up with her icicle eyes. 'Water?' she said through thinned lips.

'Okay, you lot take her home,' Fatboy said. 'I'll look after Clive. I'm a bit rusty but I think John's done his first aid this year.'

'That sounds like an offer we want to take him up on. I'll get the water.' I followed him into the office to the cubicles at the back as he pointed me to the water cooler and opened the doors to a cupboard. I started to pour a cone of water, but I saw two full bottles stacked up in the corner just past Clive's cubicle. The guard's back was to me, so I tiptoed up to the foetal Clive. I tried not to look, but I couldn't help myself. Tiny yellow pin-prick blisters had broken out around his grey-blue nose and in the corners of his mouth. It didn't look like he was breathing. I grabbed one of the water bottles – it was heavier than it looked – and tiptoed back. Clive gurgled moistly.

'Here we go,' Fatboy said (to himself I hoped), as he pulled out a laminated flow-chart. 'Now let's have a look at you, matey-boy!'

'Cheers then,' I said as cheerfully as I could muster. I had turned my back to the guard, holding the bottle in front of me so he couldn't see it.

'Mind how you go, then.' he said.

'I will,' I was almost running for the door. I grabbed the only handbag I could see - it seemed to be in the right scale for the small Susie, who was now on her feet and leaning on Lou as I burst onto the stairwell.

'I'm alright.' I announced.

Progress was slow except for Al, who was jumping the last few steps on each level. How could it be getting hotter? I had to keep swapping the bottle from arm to arm. Susie stumbled, nearly pulling Lou down with her, so Al stopped and came back up the stairs to hold her other arm. In the foyer the younger guard was on his radio. He held his hand up, nodded a 'hello' to Lou and pointed at the closed front doors. Half a dozen dark silhouettes were pressed against the glass, and there was distinct shuffling.

'Graham. John. Yeah we've got some people trying to force entry. I have secured the doors. We have a lock-down, over.'

'Keep them locked, they'll be looters,' the radio crackled. 'I'll be down in a minute. Clive Cocker's not well but he has come round again, over.'

'There's the stairs to the car park.' Lou pointed to an archway off the foyer.

'Looters,' I muttered, looking over to the entrance. 'They couldn't loot an open grave.'

'Err, John?' the radio hissed. 'Can you come up here a minute?'

The young guard hesitated, looked at us, and then walked to the stairwell.

'Can you lot stay here for a bit?'

Al grinned and nodded enthusiastically. Lou looked at me, but I didn't give her time to think about staying anywhere for a bit and when John was out of sight I pulled her and Susie toward the car park stairs. We headed down and it was cool. Susie had now started walking under her own steam, and Lou watched her navigate the first few steps.

'Floyd's in the car,' I said. Lou didn't reply – she was still being a bit eggy with me – but I knew she'd be pleased I'd brought him with us. Someone was missing.

'Where's Al?'

'He was with us in the lobby.' Lou said.

'Okay, look. Wait here. Shout if… well, just shout.' I said, turning back up the stairs.

'We'll go down, you follow us.'

'No babe, I don't know the way. Please?'

'There is only one way – down,' she said, smiling.

'For fuck's sake woman, just wait here!' I stuttered. 'Look, please just shout if you see anything.'

I climbed the stairs again, and slowly opened the door to the lobby a crack. It was deserted, so I tiptoed out. There were now double the number of people at the glass front doors than a few minutes before; enough now so you couldn't see light between the bodies. I was just about to call Al's name when there was a noise to my right, from a door behind the reception desk. I froze, holding my breath. My heart was beginning to make my head throb as Al appeared in the doorway with a grin across his chops and an armful of radios in a charging rack. The plug trailed behind him.

'You resourceful little beggar!' I exhaled, proud as a dad on sports day.

'Radios.' He was pleased with himself too.

I held the door to the stairs open for Al as he made his way across the foyer, glancing towards the front doors. No-one was trying to force entry. They were all just standing there, facing in. Al squeezed past me, and we started down the fresh air of the stairs. It was pleasant to be in some underground car park stairs that didn't smell of piss for a change. I called for Lou, and to my relief she replied. She looked at Al and the radios.

'What are they?'

'Radios,' Al said.

'I can see that. Why have you taken them?' she probed.

'Because they'll be useful,' he said simply. I saw a sign by a door.

'This says level two. We parked on level three. We've come too far.'

'There isn't a level three,' Lou explained. Of course there wasn't – why would there be? Al pushed the door open to the echoing sound of a dog howling for England. Our beagle. Lou forced past me and into the gloom of the car park. I saw her face drop. Peering into Al's car was the kid with the hoodie and the headphones.

'Oi, Asboy!' Al shouted. The kid didn't move. My eyes were starting to get used to the light, but I could barely make out his features. Al had set the radios down and was strutting towards the young man.

'Oi, Workhouse!' he yelled again, louder. I'd honestly never heard him shout before. The kid stood up straight. He looked at Al, cocked his head slightly, and started ambling towards us. I almost breathed a sigh of relief that he was walking normally, but I was starting to make out swollen blisters that cut across his pale cheeks, under his nose and around his slack mouth. Floyd had stopped barking and was now wagging his tail enthusiastically at the sight of us.

'Dude you stink!' Al said as the youth came closer. 'Ooh, you're not right. You're all messed up.' He started to back away but the lad bared his teeth, so Al thumped him soundly on the nose which sent him spinning to the ground. He was sprawled out awkwardly, his chest heaving a bubbling wheeze as Al blipped the Audi's central locking, jumped over the kid and up to the car, waggling his right hand like it was hot before opening the door. Sitting low he turned to say something to Floyd who was bouncing about in the boot. Then he started the car, fired up a little stub of a joint from the ashtray, and looked at us.

'Come on then!'

Lou pulled Susie towards the car as I called 'shotgun'. They were soon in the back seat.

'Come on, for fuck's sakes!' Al revved, Floyd barked, Lou beckoned furiously at me.

The kid got up, and I drew a sharp breath. His eyes were dead, but his chest still gave off a bubbling sound. I was frozen. A childhood nightmare flashed in front of me; my feet sticking to the pavement as my mum and brother walked ahead. As they get further away, I am screaming but no sound comes out. They are soon too far down the street to hear anyway. I look to my right, to a high red-brick wall stretching as far up as the clouds. There is just one window, at head height right where I am stuck. Through it I see a stuffed owl perched on a branch, dead leaves scattered around. I hear huge, booming footsteps behind me. That's when would wake up, damp and tearful, scared to call out in case nothing came out of my mouth.

I found myself standing breathlessly next to Al's car, the door handle in my grip, water bottle under one arm. I got in, blinking. The lad was still facing the spot where I had been standing. Al gunned the engine and roared past him towards the exit, then stopped the car and turned to me.

'What the fuck are you doing?' Lou screeched. 'He's coming!'

'Grab the radios chum,' he jabbed his finger at my door. I looked out of my window – he could have got a bit closer.

'Fucking hell, they're miles away.'

'Well, you should get a move on, then,' Al grinned. I flung the door open, and ran to the rack of radios on the ground. I couldn't help but turn to see where the kid was, and wished I hadn't. I ran for the car but as I approached Al moved a few metres forward and waited for me to catch up, before lurching again as I put a hand to the door. Lou found it highly amusing, but when he did it a third time, I punched his roof. He got out.

'What the fuck was that for?' he asked, indignantly.

'Jesus! That's how people get eaten! Don't fuck about, not today.' I got in the car and slammed the door.

'Okay - because of all the zombies around.' Al sat back down and slipped the car into gear.

'Oh, and you think that kid's got a bad case of doggie fever? Do me a lemon.' The radios were pressing into my nuts.

'Did you see him baring his teeth at me? Rabies or not, that's just rude,' Al said as we roared up the ramp to ground level, and back into the daylight.

'Is that a Highland insult, or just in the new towns?' I asked, still miffed.

'Did you smell the eggs?' Lou leaned forward.

'The same as that old boy in my street,' I said.

'I thought Clive just had bad guts. How many people have you seen like that?' Lou said, sitting back and reaching through the grille to Floyd. 'Oh, sorry Al, he's having a little piss in your boot.'

'There's loads of them,' I said grimly. 'You'll see in a minute.'

I glanced at the building as we drove past the front entrance, and saw the huddle of motionless figures gathered around the door. Most were wearing smart clothes – ties and shirts and pencil skirts - but dusty, bloodstained or torn. Some turned to face the car.

'Oh my God, that's Dean,' I heard Lou say.

'Dean's nice. I'm tired.' Susie yawned, oblivious.

It had all got a lot more hectic outside. We crawled across town as the traffic built up around us, sometimes forcing us onto the pavements. Lou was silent. We saw frenzied struggles in thick queues and fist-fights around dented cars - and still the sun bleached everything around us ash-white. More shops had been looted, and inside them we could see dim flames picking out the silhouettes of aisles and trolleys and people. Our route was blocked in several places by lines of blazing cars, as fuel tanks sparked and spat their flames about them. Al motored on, picking his way through the debris on the wide roads. Susie had her eyes closed; her head slumped against the window. Finally Lou spoke.

'We said we'd drop Susie off, but I don't know whereabouts she lives.'

'She's been out for a while now,' I said. 'Shouldn't we just drop her off at the medical tent?' I suggested. My words betrayed my real instinct, which was to shovel her head off and get going.

'Do you really want to get out of the car and queue?' Al asked. 'I'm not waiting around to catch the lurgy. We'll get her some help in Worthing or Brighton if she still needs it, they'll be less busy down there, anyway.' Al looked over his shoulder at her slumped figure. 'It's probably just the heat.' he said, hopefully. I said nothing.

'Are you sure, chum?' Lou asked. 'There's your last chance.'

The inflatable medical tents now sat fully engorged on the precinct, with only their tops visible above the hordes of bodies and the banners advertising the medical industry sponsors. We drove on.

Al beeped people out of the way as he navigated the gaps between parked and burning cars, occasionally hitting an empty stretch. As I pointed Al to the next right there was a screech of rubber from the forecourt of a petrol station mini-mart, with broken glass and people scattering. A new-shape Volkswagen Beetle was coming to rest on top of a line of crushed fuel pumps, springing two or three foamy pink fountains behind it. I saw a curl of flame lick the underside of the car.

It felt briefly like we'd driven into a shaft of brilliant sunlight thrown between two tall buildings. The heat hit me next, tightening my cheeks and drying my eyeballs, before a breathtaking thump hit my lungs. I saw no more, as deep gold flames billowed through the forecourt, enveloping cars and customers. There was no bang, just bright silence sucking in all the noise around us except Lou whispering 'Oh, no!' as she put a hand to her mouth. Al looked in his mirror agog. The flames blossomed, quickly forming a black bubble of ink in the blue summer sky.

'Fuck off!'

Al was in full PlayStation mode now, weaving fast through the hulks of cars and people and the sprays of shattering glass. I turned to Al, deciding that now was a good time to tell him about the fat woman I'd seen getting crushed by the girl in the white Golf, when he practically stood upright on his brake pedal. The tyres screamed, and the rich oily stink of carbonising rubber filled the car. I looked forward to a small figure bound in a blanket, slap-bang in the middle of Al's racing line. As we slunk ahead in dreamy slow-motion, the little girl turned to us, her blanket falling to the road. Closer. She had the same expression as Al, who was vertical, his head sideways, his ear almost pressed to the ceiling. Closer. The car felt like it was tipping me forwards off my seat, my fingernails sinking into the dashboard. Floyd started howling, and everyone exhaled. We had stopped.

The girl ran off, into the arms of a woman who dropped a mobile phone to scoop her up. Al raised a hand and made a grimace. He checked his mirrors and blind spot, indicated and pulled away carefully. In the mirror I could see that the dome of smoke had twisted into a thick black finger.

Near the slip road down onto the A23 to Brighton we ground to a halt. People were trying to form two lanes in each direction on the single lane street, and had started honking their frustrations at each other. We sat for five minutes or so, until Lou had a brainwave.

'I've got my SatNav in my bag. Hang on. Good job I always take it out of the car.'

I took that as a dig at me, because I always left it in full view whenever I took the car out. My record on car security was not good – I'd even heard an announcement in the supermarket once, reading out my number plate and asking if the owner could go to customer services. The stout chap on the desk had told me I'd left my car open. I told him I thought it was very vigilant of someone to notice that I'd left my car unlocked, but he said that in fact I'd just left the car door wide open and went shopping. That had been a morning of Play-Station and skunk, come to think of it.

Al propped it up against his windscreen – the bracket was still in Lou's car, wherever that was – and we waited in the queue until it picked up enough satellite signals to locate us.

'I can set the destination now,' I said. 'You want to go back to Brighton don't you? What's your postcode?'

I had wanted to download the voice of Alec Guinness for the instructions but Lou had refused point-blank, instead keeping the soft, dreamy tones of the default female who told us to continue ahead for half a mile within seconds of me tapping in Al's postcode.

'Fuck's sakes, we're trying to continue ahead,' Al snorted. There was certainly no space to reverse.

'It's all good, if you take a wrong turn it will recalculate, so we can just double-back into Crawley and try another way out.'

'Useful,' Al said, staring ahead at the blocked road. A woman had got out of her tiny car in front of us and was having a to-do with a chap in a white van. She had been one of those most keen to make two lanes, so she was more in the middle of the road than anyone. She was waving her arms and screaming, but the man just laughed. Two little kids in the back seat of her car started yelling, and she ran to the passenger door and hauled a man out, white as a ghost and doubled over. She sat him down in the road, leaning his head against her rear bumper. The other chap held his hands up and got back in his van, but the woman wasn't going to let it go yet and started thumping on his door.

'Cough it up, might be a gold watch,' I murmured, transfixed by her passenger's weary heaving. Al laughed; Lou tutted. He slumped, and the black tar strung from his chin glinted in the sunlight. The man's mouth slowly fell open, and his head rolled onto one shoulder.

'Shouldn't we help?' Lou asked.

'Yes, let's travel the countryside collecting the fuckers in a big net!' I spat. 'We could start a freak show, except ticket sales wouldn't be that hot because we'd be the freaks. The tasty-smelling freaks. Sorry I shouted. Al wants to go home,'

'It's not like we're going anywhere,' Al pointed out.

'For Christ's sake, Lou, we're not getting out and helping. They're all dead.'

I'll admit it was overly melodramatic, and probably not what was called for at the time. I was in Dutch with the wife – I knew without seeing her face and without her saying anything. It was more like an imperceptible lowering of the temperature.

'He's alright anyway. Look,' Al said, pointing at the sick bloke who was now standing. He leant against the back of the woman's car, like his legs weren't ready yet. The woman was still having it out with white van man.

'I'm at least going to tell that bitch to look after him,' Lou stated, and opened her door. I swung round angrily and began to shout at her not to dare get out, but the sound of an approaching motorcycle stopped me. I saw it in the rear window careering down the middle of the road towards us, taking on a precarious wobble. Lou must have read something in my face because she slammed the door and assumed a nifty crash position. The whine of the engine flooded the car and Al's wing mirror was ripped off, spinning away into the line of traffic.

The bike slew into the woman's car which ground forwards and into the rear of the car ahead, simultaneously launching the rider clear over the top of three or four vehicles. The dry sounds of smashing glass and crunching bones were pierced by the woman's screams as her children and passenger became folded up with the motorbike inside her crumpled car. As the wreckage settled I could see that her sick passenger's torso was still in relatively the same place; pinched into the twisted roof with one arm severed at the shoulder. The woman ran with floppy arms and all the noise drained out of her, staring at where the man's lower half – and the back of her car - should have been. She took a faltering step forward.

Two things happened – a breathtakingly large quantity of guts fell from his torn torso onto the sizzling hot tarmac; and his remaining arm flailed out, clutching a handful of the woman's hair and pulling her face towards his open mouth. Al wasted no time putting the car into gear and pulling into the rubber-streaked space left behind the wreckage. She made no sound as Al pulled alongside in a three-point-turn. She didn't even resist as great wads of fat were pulled cleanly from her skull.

We accelerated back up the road. The SatNav was the first to speak, without emotion.

'Take the next left, in four hundred yards.'

'I feel sick,' Lou said. 'That would have killed him outright, but he just…'

'You want me to stop?' Al asked her. She shook her head, and closed her eyes.

'That could have been anything, couldn't it?' she pleaded. 'It happened so quick; it might have just been leftover messages reaching his brain or something. You know, like wiring a frog's legs up to a battery. When they guillotined people their eyes would sometimes move...' She gave up, knowing we had no answers.

'It's true. I saw some footage of a severed monkey head on the internet; some Russian scientist bloke had wired that up to the mains, and it still wanted to eat. Food would just drop out of its neck though.' Al stopped, realising he wasn't helping much.

After we ignored a few of the instructions to join busier or entirely blocked main routes, we opted for a terraced street which was lively but passable. Al was using his indicators now, I noticed. We did what the calm lady told us, through the screaming and the car alarms, and after twenty minutes or so we had ended up by a quiet meadow in the fields and farms still left on the southern edge of town. It was quiet; so quiet we could hear the hum of traffic on the dual carriageway a hundred metres away, on the other side of the field.

'We need to be on there', Al pointed at the A23. 'She's telling us to go through Horsham now though, which will be just as mental. I'll just keep going south.'

I wondered how to get the huge bottle of water open as we continued south on the narrow lane, towards the coast but still a good twenty miles inland. We passed another field on our left, catching glimpses of the tops of cars through the trees which were moving faster than we were. Up ahead was a dirt track tracing through the field, leading to a one-lane service bridge which rose up and over the A23 itself.

'We've got to get on the other side of the road anyway, if we're going to get on it without causing an accident,' Al rubbed his chin and looked at me. 'What do you reckon?'

'Let's do it – that bridge is probably for a farmer to get over the road to the rest of his field.' I said. 'I'll open the gate,' I offered, then realised I'd have to get out of the car to do so. It was hot; moreover, there were zombies afoot. I checked behind us; in front of us; either side of us. I waited then checked again.

'Right, I'm going – keep your eyes peeled and beep if you see any freaks.'

I got out of the car and ran the five metres or so to the gate. There was a chain, but it had no padlock and was easily pulled away from the gate – obviously a visual deterrent more than a practical one. I swung the gate wide, and Al gingerly left the tarmac for the parched mud of the field.

'Grab that chum,' Al motioned at the chain. 'We might need it.'

'You've got your magpie eyes on today,' I said, running with the gate until it shut, then wound the thick galvanised chain around my arm and headed back for the car. Al watched me sit in my seat before taking us down the track and up onto the bridge which was strewn with hay and dung. We looked down onto the A23 at the heavy traffic, sluggish but still moving in both directions, and up to the odd column of smoke smudging the blue sky above the towns.

'This is all very saucy,' Al murmured as we headed down the arc of the bridge and onto new tarmac which doubled back on itself through a gap in a high fence, under the bridge and onto the southbound lane of the dual carriageway.

'Emergency Services Vehicles Only, my arse,' Al said dramatically, heading under the bridge. 'Tell The Man his rules are dead.' He nosed the Audi down the slipway onto the hard shoulder, and forced a gap in the constant stream of cars to much indignant tooting. As soon as he could, we peeled away into the fast lane. Progress.

Al was happy to keep his head down, happy to just be making progress back home. Every so often someone would come thundering past on the hard shoulder but from what I could see from the purple faces, it seemed to be testosterone-fuelled road-rage as opposed to Armageddon panic-driving. No point rushing though - people still die from road accidents even during a zombie invasion. At points the hard shoulder at the side of the road was jammed up, with cars mounting the verge and people dotting the embankment. We saw a scrap taking place between the drivers of a minivan and a Mondeo, with wives or girlfriends dutifully pulling at shirts. In a lot of the cars people in the back seat were wrapped in travel rugs, the odd grey face staring out open-mouthed at the traffic. I did a double-take as we pulled alongside one car - a young boy was driving. He looked no more than ten and could barely see over the wheel. He turned to face me as my window drew level with his. Our eyes met, and he looked scared. The rest of the car was filled with slumped figures and duvets.

The good thing about not being a scared ten-year-old any more is that you can hide it better. The bad thing about being a scared adult is that you're the

KID DRIVER

fucking responsible adult. Why did it have to be a zombie outbreak? Give me an alien invasion or walking shrubbery any day.

I don't know where it all started. The seeds were surely planted years ago as a child: maybe by a snatched VHS glimpse of a long recorded-over splatter movie, a few frames of a disfigured face existing between cartoons taped from the TV; or by a waking daydream whilst alone and snot-nosed in a friend's field one winter, of a blue-faced figure rising stiffly from a mound of snow in front of me; or by the hazy yet enduring memory of a trick played on me one summer by my brother and his friend, who donned duvet covers and waited for me behind the shed before walking out, their arms outstretched, moaning (they thought they were being ghosts, though). Throw in an episode or two of *Dr. Who* to taste and bake in an Englishman's head for a few decades. The luxury of being scared of apparent bullshit really was a privilege that only a truly decadent lifestyle could allow.

Sirens and blue lights from behind us. A couple of police motorcycles were roaring down the centre line, cleaving the traffic into two and forcing cars onto the outer edges of either lane. They slowed to our pace and squeezed us even further to the edge of our lane, one drawing up right next to Al's window. In between them sped another two bikes swiftly followed by a dark green Jaguar, a black Range rover with tinted windows and two black cars I didn't recognise, all in a line. Al rammed his spliff into his mouth and grinned at me, then executed a particularly cheeky move behind the alternating bikes at the back of the entourage and put his foot down, easily topping a hundred miles per hour in places. One of the riders looked over his shoulder at us, but did nothing. Al held the joint in his teeth at a jaunty angle.

'Fuck The Man.'

'Why are they going south?' Lou asked.

'Ooh,' I said, quietly. 'That's quite interesting.'

'What's that?' Al said, staring ahead intently.

'Do you remember that mad letter in the *Argus*?' I had read the reader's letter about a year before in our local paper and it had tickled my interest.

'You know the Southwick Tunnel's coming up? Okay, there's this theory that under the same hill is a bunker, or meeting rooms or something. Al - you know how often that tunnel is shut, right? It's ridiculous. This chap pointed out in his letter that, even though they always put it down to maintenance work, the light bulbs that were blown before they closed it are always still blown af-

terwards. How much maintenance can you do without getting round to changing a few light bulbs? If you check out the doors they look like steel blast
doors, with covered hinges and that. Plus, chalk's pretty easy to dig into, right?

'Well here's the weird thing; and this isn't rumour, its fact. That tunnel was
closed on September 12th 2001, right; from midday when the London underground got bombed; on the eve of the war – shock and awe, remember that?
When we went into Afghanistan… and these are just what I can remember.
They guy had documented loads of oddly coincidental dates that the tunnel had
been closed on.'

'I remember you reading it out. It is closed a lot.' said Al. Lou was incredulous.

'I'm sure people have got better things to do today than play king of the
castle,' she said. 'They're probably going home, or sending cars to take people
up to London. Aren't all the MPs on holiday still?'

'Think about it, think about it. Okay, that hill is flank-on to any firestorm
from a nuclear blast over London; it's an hour – or half an hour driving at our
current speed – from London itself, so land access is no problem; Shoreham
airport's just a spit away, as is the sea obviously; there's a superstore at the west
end of the tunnel for supplies; plus there's more golf courses round here than
there are fields. That's the secret COBRA headquarters; I'll put a fiver on it.'

'The what?' Al quizzed, still focussed.

'COBRA; it's the government and police and army chiefs and that when
they all meet up for crisis talks in an emergency.'

'They might as well have called it "Cougar Force" or "The Power Squad".'
Lou could be overly sarcastic at times.

'It stands for "Cabinet Office Briefing Room A", actually.' I sniffed.

'Why would their HQ be under the South Downs, then?'

Lou was pleased with her point. I kept quiet, a touch eggy. We powered on
in their slipstream for a mile or two before losing them as they turned west onto
the A27 and towards the Southwick Tunnel and Worthing. Al continued into
Brighton, on a road that would take you to the end of the Palace Pier if you
didn't turn off. It was 5.30pm, and we had made pretty good time.

Breaking In
[day 0001]

Brighton was great. It was a place that had grown fairly organically, and as a result it made sense, at least to me. The benignly militant population had, on the whole, indignantly rejected the mindless progress that had ruined other towns yet their own brand of progress gave the city a sense of freedom that sometimes bordered on lunacy. It was so bright and breezy that a wag on the council marketing team had even plastered 'Brighton Breezy' over anything from buses to billboards. Old and new sat comfortably - almost respectfully - next to each other, nurturing tiny theatres, impossibly trendy bistros and renegade comedy clubs. Being as gay as sandals was optional. Naturally there were throwbacks from the 60's and 70's – sickly tower blocks and absurd concrete wastes – but the greedy madness had never been allowed to actually take over the place.

Withdean Park was large and open, and usually dotted with sun seekers on such a bright day – now it was packed with bodies. Some pushed; some queued towards a similar set of inflatable tents to the one we'd seen in Crawley. A line of ambulances fought with cars and pedestrians to get off the road and onto the grass. Al flicked on the local radio as the crowds spilled onto our side of the street and I watched for faces.

'We should get her some help,' Lou said, dabbing at Susie's forehead.

Al forged through the crowd, leading an impromptu line of half a dozen other opportunists. There were hardly any moving cars now; most were abandoned or contained people less bold or cheeky than Al, honking horns and gesticulating at each other. On the radio they were reading out those town halls that had made available lists of the known dead, and moved on to the longer list of places where the stricken could visit the makeshift treatment centres. I gazed over the park at the bouncy hospitals, and Al slowed as more people spilled onto the road.

In one motion, I saw a hundred people shoal outwards to make a circular gap in the thick throng. At the centre was a man in a shawl, with a crimson chin. Through the ever-increasing hole in the crowd I could see a boy lying at his feet, pawing at his own face with red hands. People were running and falling. A young man with 'FCUK you!' on his T-shirt turned to us and started hammering on the roof in sheer white-faced terror, setting Floyd off barking and making me jump. We powered through, and the lad thumped on the car behind us, and then the one after that. The road ahead was blocked by an upturned furniture van and its contents. Al knew where he was, so he simply swung a left onto a side street, and after several tight squeezes turned south onto the Seven Dials roundabout. He passed the GPS unit back to Lou.

'Save the batteries.' He said.

'It's alright; I've got a spare charger at home.'

Al said nothing, but I caught him checking his petrol gauge. We weaved through the obstacles littering the streets, slowing down and sounding the horn where humans outnumbered cars. There was more thumping on the bonnet. We passed a bus stop, seeing a man thrashing about with an umbrella, beating people away from him. A woman in a night-dress ran from her house screaming, with one handless arm raised in front of her. I saw a fight – or a beating – in an alleyway, and lots of foaming blood in the gravel. There were kids on bikes grinning on street corners and people weeping in the sun. Raging house fires burst glass onto the road in front of us; screams and sirens became muffled in the blistering heat.

Al's shop sat in the centre of an old quarter of the city called the North Laines. Its small, quirky properties made them an obvious choice for independent traders; being in Brighton in the first place leant the outlets a style which would make you rich if you could bottle it; the fact that they were in the most fashionable part of Brighton's trading district gave everything a further bohemian twist of exquisite nuttiness, which was so evident in the elaborate shop signs.

He knew a steep back road which took us down by the dark railway station with its closed shutters dotted with notices; then under a bridge, out behind a grim block of flats, and right to the top of Al's street. The roof of the Komedia comedy club was ablaze, and the few shops without grilles had their shattered windows strewn across the pavement. There were less people about than in the tree-lined suburbs, but people seemed either bumbling and slow or frantic and violent, depending on whether they were at Death's door or merely taking advantage of the situation. We double-parked, blocking the middle of the road; Al took his keys from the ignition, relieved to see his shop in one piece still.

'Wait here; I'll blip the car behind me.' He carefully selected the two shop keys before getting out. The heat poured into the car along with the sound of a dog barking - Floyd's ears picked up and he cocked his head. I watched Al sprint between parked cars and up to the side door of his shop, key at the ready. He hopped inside; turned around to blip the car then shut the door behind him. He was inside. I couldn't help noticing that we were outside.

Al sold clothes for young people – to my eyes just hooded tops, shirts and hats – and for a long time had been the sole distributor in Britain for a number of sought-after West Coast labels. He'd pretty much set up the business while still in LA, nurturing contacts with some of the independent designers and bringing the stock back to an enthusiastic UK 'yoof'. Within a few years though, his trendsetting meant those same labels could be seen in most high street stores, and he had moved on with disdain. Al would raise two fingers to the big boys whenever he could, wearing his independence like a badge of honour. He had been an avid skater when he was younger, when it was underground and dangerous. Then the big corporations had moved in, with their patronising demographic targeting and sponsorship ruses. He couldn't help but see the irony that these were the same people who would call the police if they saw people like him skateboarding in their office car parks. Something had been lost to the big boys, he had told me; something intangible but crucial. He gave up boarding soon after that.

'Is Dmitri coming? Are you going to see Uncle Dmitri?' Lou was talking to Floyd in her puppy voice, and he was whimpering in sheer excitement at the prospect.

'Don't wind him up Sweetpea; Al might be a while.'

'I hope not', Susie stretched, peering through the window at the chaos, and pinching her temples. 'This isn't Crawley.' She clearly hadn't turned yet, but she looked really rough all the same.

'We're outside Al's shop in Brighton. Still got a headache?' Lou asked loudly, fishing about in her bag. She pulled out a blister pack of pills. 'Can you open that water baby?'

I gave it a go, but Susie had pulled a bottle from her own tiny handbag and popped a couple of the painkillers from the pack. A car drew up behind us and started honking; Lou waved him off, pointing to the shop and mouthing soundlessly. Floyd just barked at them. I looked ahead, getting twitchier by the minute. Peering through the patchy smoke of the comedy club inferno I could see single slumped figures standing dead still. On the pavement a large man and a larger woman were helping a grey old lady, grasping an arm each. She was wrapped in a foil blanket and looked like the last Quality Street in the tin. They'd all been sat by the side of the road when we'd first pulled up, but they'd since pulled her to her feet and now she was taking doddery steps with sunken eyes and a slack neck - the park was a long way away at their speed. We didn't offer to help them. The shop door opened and a beagle bounded out.

'Wait!' Al roared at him, but Dmitri was more interested in the old lady. He stopped in front of her, growling and drooling. Al was calling him to the car but Dmitri started barking more impressively than Floyd could, who was now whining like a little turbine in the boot.

The half-dead old girl flinched with the sudden noise, and as the man tried to shoo Dmitri away I watched her brittle lips peeling back to reveal teeth like yellow tombstones. She buried them into her carer's arm, and the fat woman promptly fell to the pavement with a shriek. Al didn't hesitate – he jumped over the woman, pulled the driver's door open and whistled. His hound sensed the change in urgency and quickly scrambled into the car and onto my lap, and began licking my beard intently.

As the woman fitted on the floor the chap backed away from the old dear, but she sank her skeletal fingers into his shoulders and her teeth into his neck before he could get too far. A gargling screech pierced the air as she took a long deep draught before snapping her head away and chewing listlessly on the strip of throaty tubing she'd wrenched free. He joined the woman down on the pavement, silent but writhing, clutching his neck with both hands. Then the old dear locked her glassy eyes onto us. Floyd's bark became a drawn-out bay as the blanket dropped to the floor to reveal her greasy night dress. Her chin sat back into her wattled neck, and she shuffled towards us. Al wasted no time and we jerked away, tyres squealing over the noise of dogs and sirens.

'Heavy,' Al suggested.

'Okay, so it's not bird 'flu,' Lou said grimly.

'I told you what it is.' I snapped. 'What neither of you seem willing to address is that - whether you think they're common-or-garden zombies or not - nevertheless they still want to eat people and we've got one of them right here in the car.' Al was checking his clenched fist.

'Lucky I didn't break my skin on that chav's teeth,' he said.

'We'll have to be careful fighting them off,' I nodded.

'It's got to be some sort of biological weapon,' Lou muttered.

'What?' I sighed.

'Okay, that guy we watched get hit by the motorbike. If he really was dead when he bit that woman… if it wasn't electrical impulses or whatever; if dead bodies can come to life again… If all that is true, which I don't think it is, then biological weapons would make sense. You remember the gay bomb you told me about?' she asked intently. Al sniggered.

'Yes,' I said, convinced she hadn't been listening when I'd told her about the CIA weapon they wanted to make; it would, apparently, turn all enemy troops ragingly gay thus switching their attentions away from the battlefield and onto action of another sort.

'Well what if the terrorists have made a cannibal version? What if they've released a kind of bug into the population that spreads a bloodlust, a craving for human flesh?'

'Stranger things have happened at sea,' Al suggested. I frowned.

'It sounds too much like rage-infected monkeys,' I sniffed. 'It all seems a bit far-fetched to me.'

'What, and zombies aren't?' she raised an eyebrow at me.

'I didn't mean that; it seems far-fetched that terrorists would even have the knowledge to do that. I'd have heard about something similar before now if the knowledge was out there, and they never made the gay bomb anyway because it didn't work.' I turned to Lou. 'It just turned people a bit poofy. Look, what you've just described is a zombie, like it or not. If they're dead, even better, I mean even more so. In *Return of the Living Dead* a military canister of green gas turned people into zombies. It's not unexplored territory, even if that was a comedy. But we're arguing at crossed purposes here, the fine detail's not as pressing as the fact that there's one of them next to you in the back seat.' I jabbed a finger towards Susie who promptly heaved a Queen's pint of black sludge down her top. Her head fell back and she gargled.

'Aah, is that on my seat?' Al slammed his foot on the brake then got out of the car. I clung onto Dmitri's collar as he made for the open driver's door, but he's a strong dog and I got hoiked out onto the road after him, spilling radios around me. The water bottle started to run down the hill so I followed it at a sprint, jumping on it like it was a runaway pig when I finally caught up with it. It didn't take much to get a sweat going, and I wiped my eyes with the back of my hand as I looked back up the road to the car, to Lou kneeling with Susie by the side of the road, holding her up and trying to pull her soiled top over her head.

Al opened his boot, put the radios in and took out a rag for the back seats. Floyd seized the moment and bounced out. I muttered about putting Floyd on a lead as I watched him lick all the things he'd been desperate to lick since Crawley: Lou's face; Al's shoes; car tyres; Susie's top; and finally – at last – he got to lick the bit between the pavement and the road. Sated, he trotted down the road towards me, weaving, searching the tarmac with his nose as his white-tipped tail whipped the air. He ducked my head-rub with bonus ear-tug and turned instead to scratch his chin, facing the others with his tongue beating. I picked myself up, put the water over my shoulder and jumped as Floyd howled, front end down and backside in the air. Three silhouettes were shuffling from the shadows toward Lou and Susie. The ambling gait of the undead was unmistakeable, and one was almost upon them.

'Lou!'

Dmitri - who'd been cleaning up the back seats with Al - ran up to the three and began howling too, his arse in the air like Floyd but bouncing in a circle around them. Lou turned and shrieked, pulling Susie to her feet. There were five now, wandering toward my wife and my friend. One opened her mouth and rasped. I was a good thirty feet away, but the freaks were just five feet from the car. As I started back up the steep hill with the water under my arm a stench filled my nostrils, like eggs and piss - you don't get the stink from the movies, I thought. Floyd tore past me and up to the freaks which were spread out and moving at different paces towards the fresh meat. Al looked at me.

'Little help? Don't cut your hands on their teeth!' he yelled, taking Susie's arm and bundling her into the back seat after Lou. He turned and desperately waved the black rag in the closest one's face, then began towel-whipping at his legs. He was clearly running out of ideas.

'Get the fuck back, Freakboy!'

Al dodged his bared teeth, but one of the others had got a grip on his T-shirt. I ran up and brought the water bottle down over my head onto grey upturned features. He released his grasp and crumpled, but Freakboy was getting closer to Al's face with every lunge. Dmitri took the plunge and jumped - higher than I'd ever seen him do for a stick in the park - biting into a clump of matted hair and pulling Freakboy headfirst onto the road with a hearty crack. He turned to the others and snarled, his hackles raised. Floyd was soon at his side but barking at me, unsure of what to do.

I remembered the old man in my street and Floyd's reaction when I clicked my fingers, so I did it again and to my excitement it worked - the dogs each took a trouser leg of the nearest one and simultaneously pulled in separate directions, sending him to the floor in spectacular splits. I threw the water bottle through the open window of the car and onto the passenger seat.

'Floyd! Get in!' I shouted over the roof. The dogs were still on the offensive, pulling an arm from its socket in sharp gristly tugs. Then Freakboy stood up again, between us and the dogs. I whistled.

Beagles have the most ridiculous ability to hear just what they want to and nothing else, but you can trick them by getting their attention with something instinctive, like whistling. It made Floyd face me and also catch sight of Freakboy, now within a foot of the car and of Lou who was leaning over Susie and winding up the window furiously. Within a second my pup was working Freakboy's feet from under him in hearty jerks. We watched as he slid down the window and out of view with a powerless moan.

'Al, get in my side!' I opened the boot and whistled again. Dmitri was the first to break away and Floyd, who hated to miss anything, followed quickly. I shut them in, then sailed through the passenger door after Al who was now behind the wheel. Accelerate please.

'Yeah, what we said about being more careful,' I said, doing my seatbelt up. 'Lou, I don't mean to sound like a dreadful old git, but I really think you should stay in the car from now on. We have got to get some weapons too - I don't want to end up like Pukes MacGinty back there.'

'But you can't hurt them,' Lou said. 'What if they find a cure for all this?'

Brighton was on fire. Screaming drowned out the few sirens that were left. Black smoke from a Tesco Express was hanging low in the airless heat, filling the road ahead. Everything went dark for a few seconds before we heard a thud and a white face with matted hair rolled over the windscreen. The smoke cleared to reveal bleached and dusty human outlines filling the road, some lifeless, some stumbling. Arms flailed against the sun and the noise, jaws fell open slackly, heads hung loose at the shoulders. We hit another, a thin woman with braided hair. Her neck snapped forward and hit the Audi's bonnet, folding her in two. A second crunch - a black man with bone-white eyes bounced to one side. Four, five, six. There were no screams, no attempts at evasive action as we ploughed through, teeth gritted.

'Seriously, what if they find a cure?' Lou gripped her seat.

Cars were strewn across the road as we headed back north over the Seven Dials roundabout and up Dyke Road (I'd laughed on many occasions, but not that day). Weary of the repeated lists on the radio, Al put a CD on as we passed the Old Shoreham Road which heads back to Worthing through several towns. It was usually jammed, even on a good day. More freaks stood in the road ahead and I pushed back in my seat as Al picked up speed. Hot bellies swollen with poison popped like bubble wrap, swilling black fluid over the windscreen.

'No more! Please.' Lou was sobbing.

'You're stressed, Sweetpea. We've got to get back - Al's doing his best.' I judged that it was not the time to suggest we turf Susie out onto the verge. Heading out of the city there was less activity, but we still had to fight our way onto the A27.

'I knew it!' I squeaked - the Southwick Hill Tunnel was shut. The signs read "ROAD AHEAD CLOSED - ALL TRAFFIC USE A270 ½ MILE", the point driven home with flashing orange lights. There were plenty of cars ahead, their windows popped and fuel tanks smoking, but hardly any were still being driven. Al picked a course as I surveyed the rolling downland. Bodies lay in the sun. Bodies stood in the sun.

'Look!'

The hills to the north were dotted with hundreds of figures facing the city and the sea. It looked like the *Dawn of the Dead* poster, and gave my skin goose bumps even in the car's broiling heat. When we had turned off the dual carriageway and onto the detour road into Portslade Al slowed the car and pulled into a lay-by.

'I'm not going back into a town,' he stated.

'Isn't there the South Downs Way or something?' I ventured.

'What, off-road it?' Al asked, intrigued.

'I just want to get back home. I need a pee,' Lou said.

'There's a West Sussex map in there.' Al pointed to the glove box at my knees.

'Remember we've got the GPS.'

'Thanks Sweetpea – I'll have a look at the map first.' I said, finding the right page. 'Save the batteries and all that. I'm not oppressing you, am I?' Lou smiled back weakly. The sun was beginning to sink, turning the Downs a fire-gold.

'Monarch's Way.' I said to myself, poring over the map.

'Where?'

'Monarch's Way - look.'

I jabbed my finger on a point where suburban streets met the Downs about a mile to our west. A footpath led away from the houses, over the Southwick Hill (over the tunnel, in fact), and onto the rolling chalkland beyond. The route would take us in an arc over the South Downs Way, past the ruins of an old castle where I used to drop acid, over the river Adur and towards Cissbury Ring two or three miles north of our house. Lou and I would often walk with Floyd up to the ancient hill fort, with its flint mines and steep earth ramparts - modern man's contribution was a golf course at its base. We knew the bit from Cissbury Ring to our house well enough, but getting there by car from where we were was another matter altogether.

'What's the road like?' Al questioned.

'It is off-road, there's no denying it, although this says that dotted lines are a "Path, bridleway, byway open to all traffic, road used as a public path". Then it turns into "Other minor road", see?'

It was enough for Al. We pulled out of the lay-by and down into suburbia, looking for the edge of town and signs for a footpath, picking through the twisted wreckage of the day. It was uneasily calm there, a slight breeze pulling faint shouting and screaming to our ears along with the acrid smell of burning plastic and hair.

'What about Susie?' Lou asked.

'Worthing will be quieter than Brighton.' Al suggested.

'I think we should dump her here.'

'She's my friend; how would you feel if someone was talking about me like that?' Lou asked indignantly.

'Honestly? I'd want them to take your head off, to put you out of your misery,' I was pleased to see Al was nodding agreement.

'Oh, thanks a lot. That's charming,' she said huffily. 'Footpath!' Lou had sharp eyes. A heavy stile marked the entrance - I don't know what we'd been expecting, but it was so solid that we opted for destroying the rustic wooden fence next to it instead. After a few minute's heaving and wobbling, even that was so well built we thought we'd have to go through the towns after all. Then we remembered the chain I'd salvaged, and after checking the coast was definitely clear I got out and looped it around two of the thick wooden posts whilst Al reversed the car so his tow bar was in position. When everything was in place I banged on the car's roof. Al leaned out of his window.

'Don't do that. I know she's a bit battered chum, but love and respect for the motor and all that.' He sat back in his seat and gunned the engine. After some slip, his tyres gripped and the car leapt away. The chain went taut and a four-foot length of fence whistled past my head before splintering onto the road. Al got out to survey the damage. After another two attempts a whole section of fence lay strewn across the road. One vertical post was still in the way, but I loosened it out of the ground like a tooth.

'Nice one,' we both said simultaneously, and headed back to the car.

As we approached Lou asked if the gap we'd made in the fence was wide enough.

'It'll have to be,' Al said.

We nosed through and onto the field, fighting the resistance of the long grass underneath the car. Al scraped his paintwork against the stump of one of the posts to the sound of nails on a blackboard. We were into the open field but still had to break through a wire fence to actually get onto the footpath itself. Al accelerated over the grass towards a likely looking fence post, hitting it square-on and snapping it to the path, pulling down others along the line. After we ground to a shuddering halt I got out and guided Al over the wires tangling the ground so they didn't snare the axles. The sun was low now, casting long shadows like fingers over the hills.

As we made our way up the hill with hazy meadowland on either side, Lou was eager to boot up the SatNav again to see if the tracks were marked - they were, and it would certainly help later, but it was slow going and soon our path was blocked again. The track was bumpy and Susie was moaning about her headache. I looked back at her, still in her bra; Lou had draped one of Dmitri's muddy towels around her. I wondered if she'd thought that morning that by the early evening she'd be in her bra, wrapped in a dog's rag in a strange man's car. Probably not, but if you'd told her so, would her imagination have been able to find her a route from one to the other? Rape? House fire? Zombies?

When the rain hits the South Downs it finds a route on the chalk pathways and dirt tracks, gathering pace and carving out long trenches; fissures which will catch your feet and twist an ankle if you're not looking. In a car, however, anything from bumpers to oil sumps would get ripped right out from under you. We had to stop the car when Al spotted such a crack in the ground up ahead - sure we were in a four wheel drive vehicle, but it was an estate and its length could easily ground it. The track was so narrow and the fissure placed just so, that it was impossible for the left-hand tyres to go anywhere else but into it. The low sun pierced the trees, casting in shadow the deep rut ahead. Perhaps, if the sun was still high, the shadows would not have highlighted it in such a way. Al stopped, peering over his bonnet, hoping he wouldn't have to get out of the car.

'That's shat in my hat,' he moped.

'It's cool, we can fill it in,' I ventured.

We hadn't seen a soul for half an hour or more, but I still checked before I got out. I peered suspiciously at the suburbs below, and once satisfied trotted back down to the wrecked fence. I pulled up one of the broken posts but it was still attached to the thick wire linking all the posts together, running behind a horseshoe-shaped nail which kept it firmly attached. I walked back up to the car and knocked on the boot like a door.

'You got a tool kit in here?' I motioned to Al who was watching me in the driver's mirror. He popped the boot and the dogs nearly bowled me over. They must have been relieved to get out of the car and stretch their legs, and they both started pounding up and down the dusty track. They would sometimes box like hares, standing on their back legs and trying to pin the other to the ground for a good ear-chewing.

I pulled a long crosshead screwdriver from Al's meagre toolkit and went down to sit by the fence. I couldn't get the fat head under the horseshoe-shaped nail to free the wire, which had obviously been hammered into place, so I found a fist-sized lump of flint and used the screwdriver like a chisel to gouge a notch under the nail. It loosened but was longer than I'd expected so I levered the screwdriver up and down, eventually pinging the nail into the dust. The wire sprang free and I stood up.

When I reached the others I dropped the post into the gap with the flattest side facing upwards, and a chalky cloud rose into the air and caught on the slightest of breezes. I jumped up and down on it before kneeling down to wheel level, motioning to Al as the car crawled over the fissure. I whistled at the dogs and, to my delight, Floyd thundered up to the car and through the open tailgate. Dmitri followed at his own pace, and when he finally decided to get in I shut the boot and hopped aboard.

'We need horses.' I suggested.

'Susie's going again.' Lou said, opening Susie's door and holding her head out as Al drove on. She puked long bales of black oil onto the bone-white chalk, and when Susie was dry-heaving Lou pulled her back in by her arm. I could see she was dribbling a bit, and her skin looked almost blue.

'Ah, all done,' I said. 'Are you sure you want to keep her so close? Shouldn't we strap her to the roof or something?' I was ignored, as if I was joking. The track had widened and Al was concentrating on climbing the hill, weaving in second gear like a tacking yacht over the minor bumps and around the deeper holes. Small stones would make constant popping sounds under the tyres, echoing round the metallic rims of the wheels as we approached the crest of the hill, the A27 looming into view below us. Looking down onto the road I had one of those moments when you can see for the first time the actual scale of something you've been trying to judge in your mind. If I closed my eyes when I had such a moment, it felt like I was falling, but falling over a distance of mere millimetres.

'Southwick Hill,' I said. The road ran below us on both sides, impossibly disappearing under the sun-paled grass which stretched all around us and ahead as far as we could see. The tarmac looked so thin from up there; grey and im-permanent, like it would get swallowed up by the green if it was to be given half a chance. There were no vehicles on either side in either lane; in the distance I could see a line of cones, but beyond that cars were scattered and flaming. Every so often I saw the bright orange puff of a petrol tank igniting. As we rounded the summit and started to roll down the other side I caught my breath.

'Look!'

Two British Army soldiers with camo helmets and green rifles were to one side of the track ahead, one bent double and vomiting as the other slapped his back. Al didn't stop; instead we rolled past them, tyres pinging. I saw a tar-coloured mound glistening wetly at the feet of the sick soldier, and the one who was playing nurse looked up and waved us on. What would they do anyway - surely they were here to protect us citizens? We rumbled down the hill, allow-ing gravity to pick up our speed.

'I told you there was something going on in that tunnel,' I said triumphantly, looking at the soldiers in my mirror. 'Good job we hadn't wrapped our T-shirts round our heads.'

'Whatever this thing is, it's got to them too. They didn't even have those big rubber suits with the space-helmets.' Al said, looking at me, disappointed. 'You know, like bio-hazard suits.'

'We'd be better off with chain-mail,' I suggested. 'I tell you what; doing any-thing in this heat would make me puke.'

We continued down the track and into the cool green of an old overgrown wood with a low chicken wire fence running through the undergrowth on each side, and chest-high barbed wire in front of that.

'Piss-flaps,' Al sighed.

Another great dry crack split the chalky path ahead. I first checked for any movement in the trees; then got out to search in the dim light of the woods, occasional slivers of brilliant golden sunset blinding me. Al's door slammed shut and soon I heard him snapping through the undergrowth nearby.

'A log should do it.' I yelled.

I found a three-foot branch, a bit thicker than a car tyre. It was not light; therefore I assumed probably not rotten and would hopefully give good support to the car.

'Give us a hand.'

We lifted the log and carried it back to the track. Before it we could fit it into the hole in the ground we had to stamp off two or three branches, and Al put a splinter through the sole of his shoe with a pop and a hiss.

'Fuck it. These are original.'

Up until then they had been in ridiculously good condition for a pair of fif-teen-year-old trainers. They were Nike Jordan No. 4's and Al had lovingly cared for them, keen to keep in good shape what he rightly predicted would become a sought-after piece of fashion history - I liked the fact that had no problem wearing something so valuable nearly every day. He'd shown me some knack-ered ones on the Japanese eBay, and told me that the more wear and tear there

INFECTED
SOLDIER

is, the more they fetched. He hadn't wanted to sell his — he'd wanted to use them. I'd looked down at my own shabby trainers, five years old and tatty through tight-fisted neglect. Worth nothing on eBay but priceless if you've got no shoes. Al poked a finger right through his sole and through to the other side. His socked foot hovered above the undergrowth.

'I've got another pair still in the box at home,' he said, sitting in the car to put his trainer back on. I rolled the log into the hole, and jumped on it again to make it sit right, snapping off any smaller twigs that were left. I guided Al safely over our makeshift road repair before sitting back in the car. We headed for the golden light at the end of the tunnel of trees, but just before the fields opened up again Al spotted another hole.

'We're being stupid,' I said.

'Why's that?' Al asked.

'Well, I can't go looking for a suitable lump of wood each time we come to a hole in the ground, we've got to recycle. Hold on, I'll go and grab it.'

Halfway back to the log I realised that I hadn't checked whether or not the coast was clear. Safety first - people die when they get cocky, I told myself. I raced the rest of the way and prized up the log from the ground, but as I began to drag it back to the car I heard scrabbling in the undergrowth and froze. A twig snapped; then silence. Right beside me on the other side of the low chicken wire a pile of fallen branches and dead leaves rustled - and then I saw it.

It was just a pheasant, scratching around in the dirt. I quickened my pace as much as the log would let me, ears pricked. My heart was thumping; the blood hissing in my ears. Then I heard Lou screaming for the first time in ten years of knowing her, and I was impressed to hear that she had a good set of lungs on her. As I ran closer I saw a flurry of movement in the car and Al pulling Lou from the back seat with her blouse ripped. It wasn't long before Susie was out too and Al stood between them, shielding Lou and looking rather pale.

'Oi!' I shouted, catching Susie's attention. As she turned to face me Al lifted his leg and hoofed her in the arse, whipping her forward and cracking her head into the edge of the open door. She crumpled backwards into the dry leaves as Lou ran to the front of the car, turning to me with a look I'd not seen before; a look to go with her scream but just a few seconds late. Susie stood bolt upright. I ran towards her with the log out in front of me as she lunged at Al; I rammed it into her, catching her shoulder and spinning her round. I tried to hold onto the log but the momentum pulled my feet from under me; I loosened my grip too late and fell on top of Susie, who hadn't missed a beat. She was grabbing me and tearing at my clothes, pulling my head towards her face. I felt Al grab a hold of my arm and begin pulling me to my feet, but she was strong. I could feel all the muscles in her arms and hands tensing into tight little beads, and she stank. I got one foot flat on the floor and heaved myself up, Al nearly pulling my arm out of its socket.

Then the log whistled past my face and connected with the underside of Susie's chin, lifting her into the air and back against the wire fence. Lou let go of it before I had done and kept her balance; the log soared past Susie and into a fence post, the release of tension springing coils of barbed wire and thick splinters around her as she went down, tangling feet and torso. She fell backwards onto the lower chicken wire fence behind it but didn't shriek out in pain; instead she tried to get up but the more she struggled against the barbed wire the tighter it became – only her forearms were free. A strand of wire had lashed across her face and was cutting bloodlessly into her white cheeks as she reached out to us, her arms flailing as if she was treading water, her throat bubbling. Lou sat where she had stood, dropping fat tears into the dust. Her workmate wasn't going anywhere, so I knelt beside her to put an arm around her shoulders and pull her in close to me.

'She just went for me in the car,' she sobbed, every intake of breath a great shuddering effort. 'Her eyes – it didn't look like Susie. She was going to bite me. Her teeth… She would have bitten you,' Lou turned her face upwards to look at me - she hated how her eyes puffed up when she cried, but she was always beautiful. When she looked into my eyes like that it was as if everything was still and there was only us left in the world. She couldn't look at Susie; instead she buried her head in my chest and eventually the tears turned into tired little sighs. I checked her over for scratches and found no breaks in the skin; just some red friction marks. When I was happy Lou was okay Al and I sat her back in the car, then stood in front of Susie as she struggled against the barbed tangle.

'She's not feeling any pain. Look at her cheeks,' I said, my legs still weak.

'Do you think she's dead?' Al asked.

'Look at her. I just don't know. That guy who got hit by the bike in Crawley; he was cut in two and just kept going at that woman's scalp like it was a Sunday roast.'

'We could test the theory. You know, see if she's dead.' Al rubbed his chin and looked at me sideways.

'How?' I asked.

'Well, that bloke's heart wasn't helping him chew; it wasn't pumping blood to his arms if it was sitting in the road with the rest of his guts. It could have just been lucky electrical impulses making him attack, but we'll know for sure if Susie keeps going too once we've stabbed her in the heart.' Al said simply.

'Once we've stabbed her?' My legs were getting weaker by the minute.

'Well, once you've stabbed her actually. I thought of it, and I've done all the driving,' he said.

'But I already know what today's about. I don't need to prove it.'

'Yes you do,' Al was walking back to the car, 'and I need to see it.' He wrestled a muddy golfing umbrella from the dogs in the boot and trudged back. 'I haven't got a fucking clue what today's about, but if you're right we need to get ready. Go on.'

He offered the umbrella to me. I took it, and pointed the metal tip at Susie's writhing body. 'I'm right behind you. She won't get free,' he said confidently. I hesitated.

'What are you so afraid of?' he asked me. 'You said you thought she was dead already, so it won't be like you're murdering her.'

'Its still a bit grim though.'

He did have a point. I gritted my teeth and made contact with her chest, finding the centre of her bony chest-plate with the tip of the umbrella. I pushed. She sank back onto the splintered stump of the fence-post but still made no sound except a faint, determined wheeze.

'Go on, push harder. Push it through,' Al said.

I leant on the handle with both hands and pushed again - nothing, except the sound of her spine clicking as she arched over the stump. Each push ripped a little more skin, the barbs on the wire cutting hundreds of tiny lateral slits all over her body, but there was still no blood, no cry of pain.

'Right through,' Al said again.

'I can't; she's as tough as an old boot. Give us a hand.'

Al stood next to me and we put alternate hands over the end of the umbrella handle.

'You ready?' I nodded.

'One; two; three!'

It popped through her sternum and in by two or three inches; at the same time the thickest sliver of fence post poked through the front of her belly and up, a stray splinter taking one cup of her bra and poking it into the air. She looked bent, but continued to fight the tangled tension of the wire as if nothing had happened. A well of black sludge appeared in the depression left where we had penetrated her chest, and the acrid stink of sulphur made my stomach flip. We watched her squirming like a worm on a hook for a minute before Al eventually spoke. I didn't have the energy to make a joke about ramming the point home.

'Well, I'd say that's pretty conclusive. I mean, it's not scientific or anything, but it's enough for me. We need to get properly tooled up.' He pulled the umbrella out with the sound of sticky suction, wiped it clean on some dry leaves and started back for the car. 'I'm sorry I kept driving off when you were with that kid in the car park,' he ventured meekly, opening his door. 'I'll not be fucking about like that again chum.' Lou was dozing, her black hair straggling across her face.

'It was quite funny, if you were inside the car maybe.' I said. 'But you know how it is though; we watch the movies, we know when someone's going to get bitten - we sit there cheering. We can't slack off now. We should agree: no checking out any wooded areas alone; no rescuing people who should have known better; no going a bit nuts and getting careless; no pressing your ear up against a door you've just escaped through; and no more nursing people who look a bit peaky. Next time their heads come straight off. Lou nearly got scratched by Susie back there – she just got lucky.'

'Susie's had her nails filed down.' Lou murmured distantly. 'She's getting new acrylic ones fitted for her twenty-first this weekend.'

For a minute or two I could still see Susie at the edge of the woods in the wing mirror, tangled in the wire and grasping at the evening sunlight as we headed off up the track before the dust clouds pulled in like stage curtains. The next hour or so was navigated in grim silence as the sun set. I couldn't second-guess what Lou would think was worse – thinking that her husband had just killed her colleague; or knowing what Susie really was and that her teeth were still gnashing. I didn't want to use Susie to prove to Lou that I was right about what they had become. I had to wait for Lou to come to her own conclusion.

We ploughed on over the spine of the Downs, Al taking a tight left turn signposted as Monarch's Way. He turned the radio on, and we found that all the BBC stations carried a static-laden recorded message of a woman with a clipped accent repeating:

'This is a test of the national alert and information system. Stand by. Stand by. Around the ragged rock, the ragged rascal ran. Mary had a little lamb; its fleece was white as snow. Fee fi fo fum; I smell the blood of an Englishman,' followed by a string of electronic tones of increasing pitch, before the message began again. It sounded like it was recorded in the fifties and gave me the serious willies. There were one or two stations still playing music, but Al reckoned they were recorded sets. The only human voice we heard was French – we often got very strong radio signals from the continent between the Downs and the sea. He sounded frantic, desperate. A plea for help sounds the same in any language.

The night brought a clean freshness to the air up above the towns, and the road soon improved. After crossing over a properly surfaced country road and into fields again we were soon at a gate. This was Upper Beeding.

Al eased out onto a terraced street, the orange glow of civilisation clinging to the air like fog. Several cars had been pushed to the side of the road, their occupants long gone; strips of cloth hung from a bush and blankets dotted the tarmac. On our left the convent school was on fire, orange sparks dancing around the roof timbers which were splayed out like an opened ribcage. Then we heard a human voice.

'Shush! Al, stop the car.' It was a man's voice, not screaming but shouting words. Al slowed up, but continued west through the abandoned streets. Lou was the first to see him, and let out a gasp. A wire-haired silhouette stood on a street corner.

'They walk! They walk!'

We drove closer and he turned round, but not to us - he seemed oblivious to the car. In the streetlamp-orange light I saw his dusty clothes and bloodied hands and something around his neck. It was only when we were right up to him, close enough that we could see his eyes unfocused but wild that I caught sight of a vicar's dog-collar which had come loose and lay wagging like an accusing finger. I shuddered, and thought for the first time that day of my parents.

'Where are my mum and dad?' I asked quietly. Al's head snapped round.

'You alright chum?' he asked, concerned.

'Yeah fine, I was just asking Lou.' I replied.

'It sounded like you were going a bit mental there. Don't freak me out.'

'Aren't they on holiday in Bristol seeing your brother?' Lou asked, perching her chin on my shoulder. Birthdays and anniversaries; anything made from fabric; tickets and passports, I thought. I felt guilty that I hadn't phoned my old dear earlier, when the phones had been working. They should have been second on my list after Lou. Surely I wouldn't have just forgotten about them? The sickness had started up north, so if it was here in the south it was definitely in Bristol too. I felt all of a sudden like I'd lost a member of the group, like my parents had been with us all day. I wasn't used to missing them.

We found the entrance to Monarch's Way again and carried on as the track imperceptibly curled toward the coast. I could see fires pinpricking the towns, brighter than the street lights which halted at the blackness of the sea. Al had turned off his headlights a while ago and our eyes were now used to the night, with a half-moon that shone as brilliantly as the stars. The only thing we saw was a figure in a field, a man sitting cross-legged with a lamb on his lap. The animal's feet were in the air and its belly was empty, blood black in the moonlight. It either didn't care we were there due to the fresh meat in its hand; or it didn't make the connection that there was more flesh available inside our car. How would you lose a connection like that? How long would it take you to forget what cars were? What would it take for you to forget what cars were? None of us even mentioned him; we'd seen bigger things that day.

Looming on the horizon, standing over the surrounding hills, was Cissbury Ring. We'd all been walking the dogs up there just the weekend before and had found it pretty much deserted in the sweltering sun. All I could remember from school field trips up there, on the highest hill for miles around, was that people had been mining for flint on the top as far back as five thousand years ago. Iron Age settlers also enjoyed the hill's natural vantage point, and had remoulded the mile-round hill as a fort with a deep ditch and steep fortifications made from the surrounding chalk. It was used for farming and as a trading post for a bit after that, until the bloody Romans took it over for another three hundred years or so. They would have loved the golf course. Various inhabitants of my island had used Cissbury Ring ever since to escape further invasions;

from the Saxons, Angles and Jutes (who took over from the Romans); the Normans (who took over from the Saxons, but were considered Vikings only a hundred years or so beforehand); to the Allied Forces of World War Two (who in turn were descended from Iron Age miners, Roman centurions, Saxon raiders, Viking warriors, Norman barons and your pick of half a dozen other battle-hardened tribes).

My dad had once told me that during the Battle of Britain anti-aircraft guns had been put in place along the high earth ramparts up on Cissbury Ring, as well as a huge one-hundred-pound gun pointing out to sea. One day, when I was a young lad, he had walked up there from our house carrying a mirror, leaving me in our back garden with a carefully hand-drawn sheet of Morse code — he could, he had claimed, reflect the sun's rays back down to me and spell out a message. I'd waited there, watching the Downs intently for at least ten minutes before getting bored and going inside to watch television. He had returned breathless an hour and a half later, excitedly asking if I'd worked out his message, but I didn't have the heart to tell him the truth so I'd pretended I just couldn't see the flashes. This new sensation of guilt drove me to learn Morse code by heart before the end of that same week.

I loved the views of Worthing and Lancing pushed right up against the sea, and of the open downland stretching to the north, east and west. You could almost drink in the sparkling air. Crickets would drone in the summer months, and you could immerse yourself in the heady scent of meadow flowers and the green and gold of the surrounding countryside; in the winter the rain would sting your ears and the wind would tug at your clothes and push you on your way. It was one of the few places left on the south coast where it seemed we might be tamed by nature and not the other way around. High up on the top of Cissbury Ring it was easy to imagine that the glass and bricks of the town had just been poured out from a cup, glistening grey crystals flowing downhill and finally settling at the base of the valleys, clinging for dear life to the coastline for fear of falling into the English Channel. Sitting in Al's Audi that first night, the Ring was a black hump, like a rising whale against the dark blue seas of the night sky.

We were soon driving up to the familiar territory of the National Trust car park beneath the north side of the fort; really no more than a dusty patch of broken tarmac squeezed between fields at the crossroads of two chalk tracks. From that point we had three options to get back to our house: We could have taken the route we would drive on any normal day walking the dog, on tarmac streets back through Findon village; we could have taken the dusty crossroads onto an eastward track, doubling back on ourselves for a mile and a half to a proper road leading south; or, we could go straight down the footpath we always used when we walked from our house up to the Ring. The track from our house up to Cissbury was certainly thin and steep in places, but we reckoned it could take a car, so that's the way home that we opted for even though it would be slowest. It was the most direct route, and Al was getting concerned about his petrol. It took us through no towns, was downhill all the way, and led straight out onto the A27 no more than fifty yards from the top of our road.

The footpath followed the scalloped crest of a hill overlooking the golf course, but first we had a gate to get past. It was chained and padlocked, so I quietly got out of the car, alert to the tell-tale sound and smell of trouble, but the air was fresh and still. I looped my own chain around the gatepost and linked it up to Al's tow bar once he was in position. It took three attempts, as the tyres slipped on the dew-laden grass, but eventually the post was wrenched from the ground. I stood the gate post back in its hole when the car was safely through.

We rumbled down the straight track. It was tight in many places and I had to dismantle three other gates and negotiate Al though a sharp ninety-degree bend into some woods. I was also filling in the bigger cracks with my log, and it was when I was sorting out a particularly long one that I saw we'd got a puncture. Al rolled onto level ground and got out, pleased with himself that he'd encouraged his eyes to get used to the gloom. Within four minutes we'd had the spare tyre on, rounded up the hounds and set off again.

'I'm sure I've seen tractors coming down from this far up.' I said. 'We'll be alright now.'

From that point we could see the creeping urban mould of Worthing, and the notion of nature's dominance over man disappeared pretty quickly. A large business park ate into the green of the downland with vast corrugated roofs hiding a DIY store and a supermarket. I hated both, but hypocritically Lou and I used both stores; Lou understandably balking at the thought of going to a greengrocers, a butchers, and a fishmongers after commuting home at seven in the evening; me because I needed screws and paint to make pub signs and I was a lazy arsehole. We were just doing what we were used to doing; what our parents did and probably what our grandparents wished they could do. I couldn't help think that we'd been hoodwinked though – the smaller traders were being squeezed out by the big stores and their impossible economics of flying asparagus from Peru to England when it was in season here. It's not like we didn't know how to grow vegetables; we just couldn't resist cheap ones when we were offered them. Lou and I had fought back by starting a tiny vegetable patch in front of my workshop and had already had carrots, wild rocket and tomatoes out of it. "Dig for Victory" was a long-forgotten sentiment. I learnt more and more about how to grow vegetables and where and when, but all the while Sainsbury's was just at the top of our road curling a fat, cold finger at us, luring us inside like a portly Siren. Inside we all went, into the cool crisp cathedrals, oblivious to the millennia of trading history being throttled purple outside the doors. Except some of us weren't oblivious, we were just hypocrites, which was even worse.

Soon the track grew less steep as the golf course opened out to our right, and Al actually had to use the accelerator for the first time since Cissbury. The dusty chalk turned to wide, dry mud and eventually we were driving past the back gardens of houses. Some were grand old places, others were more recently built. One had a high concrete wall with ornate stone gates leading out onto the unassuming dirt track; fruit netting rose above some fences and mouldering garden waste lay to the sides, alongside the occasional long-browned Christmas tree. The odd farm building and horse field stood empty. We reached the end of the lane with high hedges on both sides and a good view onto a slice of A27, where we saw no moving traffic and heard no sound. Our house was one left turn at the end of the track, then the next right. That was it – Lou and I would be home. Al faced me.

'Let's do it.' We rumbled down the last few metres of the dusty track, accelerating all the time. Al spun the steering wheel, deliberately losing traction before taking us sideways onto the tarmac road - but then he stalled. He grinned and fumbled at the ignition, then took us haring past an overturned van as one or two figures turned to face us, skin milk-white in the moonlight. There were more up ahead. Headlights still off Al gunned towards our road, taking the right turn with a snap of the wheel and I saw three or four of them along the length of the street as we got nearer the house. Al hand-braked another right onto our drive – really a concrete front garden – and switched the engine off. Lou was eager.

'I need to pee.'

'Right, here's the plan,' I said. 'I'll open the front door, and only when it's open do you two get out. Don't forget the dogs.'

'We're right behind you baby, just hurry up.'

I did the breathing you do before you dive into water, then sprung out, slamming the car door behind me. I'd been too noisy, and down the road I saw heads snap round, open mouths slitting across pale oval faces. A groan sounded out.

'Oh shit.'

I patted my pockets for the front door keys. Front left and right, back right, back left. Nothing - try again. Front left and right, back right, back left. They hadn't suddenly appeared in my trousers, to my dismay. I went to check my coat pocket, but I wasn't wearing one.

'Are they on my seat?' I shouted to Al – no point in being quiet now they know we're here now, I thought. One was close, I could hear shuffling. Eternally optimistic, I patted my pockets again. I could see the closest one now, at the end of my path with a leather jacket and a beer belly. I didn't have the keys no matter how hard I looked, so I bounded back to the car and got in. The dead man was at my window scraping uselessly at the glass with his fingers - he had no nails and left greasy streaks. His face was a mess, with watery boils spreading down to his neck. Al popped the central locking shut.

'Great plan,' he said.

'Where are your keys?' Lou asked.

'I'm pretty sure I put them down on the coffee table before we left.' I said limply.

'Durr,' Al added helpfully.

'It's alright, let's have yours.' I held my hand out, but Lou didn't reach for her bag.

'I told you,' she said exasperated, 'someone took my keys from my bag at work, and then drove away in my car. With my keys, I should think.'

'What?'

She didn't repeat herself – she knew I had heard what she said. I watched the putrid face at my window, gurning and gnashing its teeth.

'Hello.' Al said, turning the ignition, watching the face of a young boy with hollow eyes on his side of the car, but I had caught sight of an open downstairs window.

'Wait, I can get in through the window. Look.'

'Not now you can't, not with these two outside.' Lou said to me. 'Plus, if we got to break into our own house we might as well do it round the back. We can get a ladder from your workshop.'

Al reversed into the road with a thud or two, and I saw that he was taking a distinct pleasure in not looking behind him. The two creeps were now rolling about on my driveway.

'Sorry Lou.' Al said sensitively, and thundered back up the road onto the A27.

Our back garden faced onto a thin strip of woodland; from our bedroom at the rear you could see the backs of the houses one road over peeping between the leaves. It was marked as No Man's Land on the survey map we'd received when we bought our first house together, but that sounded more exciting than it really was. Sometimes local kids would festoon the branches like monkeys, and I would lean out of the upstairs windows to holler at them. It was mostly lawn clippings and fallen twigs from the unkempt stand of trees - because no-one owned it, no-one really looked after it. Some of the trees were dead or weak, so I had paid a hundred quid to have the most skeletal specimens pruned heavily before I built my workshop under them, but other than that it was left to its own overgrown devices.

On the other side of the copse was a stretch of hard standing and some garages for the houses one road over, and this was where Al headed with the car's headlamps still switched off. We needed to circle once, because Al sensibly sounded the horn at the entrance to the garages and, sure enough, five or six dark shapes bumbled out. We waited until they were close, then reversed twenty feet or so, tooting the horn and flashing the fog lamps. They followed, so he did a three-point-turn as we begged him not to stall the engine again; we drove right round the block, approached from the other end of the road and slipped in behind them.

'I'll stay here for as long as I can,' Al suggested. 'Then I'll drive the car back round the front of the house, in case we need to leave in a hurry. Let me in when you've got the front door unlocked.'

'Good skills chum – you alright to take the mutt with you?' Al nodded. 'Come on Sweetpea, let's go!' I piled out of my side to see that Lou was already out. Floyd started barking when he realised we were leaving him in the car.

'Shush! Going to the shops!'

We clawed our way past thick cobwebs strung between the garages. I pushed through undergrowth and up to the fence around the perimeter of the parking spaces, and soon found the gap in the chain link that the kids must have used. I peeled it back so Lou could crawl through, looking down the alleyway and trying to distinguish between zombie groans and tree creaks.

'Hurry up.' I followed Lou, as she held the wire back for me to inch underneath. The weather had dried out everything and we couldn't help snapping twigs as we went, but soon I could make out the back of my workshop roof.

'Come on.' We both clambered over a pile of cuttings and fallen branches, setting down in the alleyway round the back or our house – now all we had to do was get into my garden. I had nailed the gate shut when the bin men refused to collect the rubbish from the alleyway any more, but the fence was old enough that I could punch through it, trying to make as little noise as possible. The hole ended up larger than I'd have liked, as the interlocking planks above it fell to the floor. I was being too noisy.

'I wish we had Floyd here,' I said ruefully, checking over my shoulder.

'Well you told him to stay.'

The heat of the day had given way to a cool, still night with little breeze, especially in our leafy back garden. Even though it was summer, the only window I had left open that morning was one in our bedroom, and only the small top one at that. Maui, our cat, had jumped onto the water butt we used for the vegetables in front of my workshop, and was curling round Lou's arm and gently nudging her chest whilst Lou scratched her long ears and talked nonsense to her.

My workshop was undeniably just a big shed with a pent roof and horizontal slats, but even so I tried very hard never to call it a shed when talking to a potential client. It was the same thinking that made me say it was one hundred and sixty eight square feet as opposed to twelve foot by fourteen foot. It was definitely a shed though. I had a sturdy combination padlock on my workshop doors which I'd bought in exasperation at having to trudge back into the house for the keys I forgot every single morning, effectively doubling my thirty-second commute. I could open the padlock in seconds with a plate of toast and a cup of tea in one hand, so doing it with both hands was quicker still. I silenced the pre-alarm beep and waved Lou in, followed quickly by Maui who was eager for her biscuits. I didn't turn on the light - that was as stupid as checking out funny noises in the attic. Basic rules.

'Let's get the ladder down.' I moved some plastic crates about and pulled an ancient wooden stepladder out from under my workbench, long past safe use and dangerously wobbly, but I needed it to reach the bigger one on the ceiling. As I steadied myself I eased the long ladder off its wide hooks, whilst Lou grabbed the other end. We carefully negotiated it over a half-finished Royal Oak sign and onto the floor. I glanced around, at my carefully organised tools arranged on the walls - I had spent many enjoyable hours looking around for items I might be able to put to use to fend off a zombie infestation, instead of actually doing any work. This time it didn't feel like so much fun.

I looked across the garden to the decking directly under the open bedroom window. We'd have to put it on there, moving the table and three chairs at least. Both ground floor doors looked black and hollow; the single kitchen door with a cat flap to the right and the double doors opening straight out onto the decking on the left were all definitely locked.

'Let's set the ladder up in here, under cover.' I suggested. 'Save time mucking about outside. What do you reckon that is up to the window, fifteen feet?'

'Probably.' She sounded unsure. We extended the ladder, locking the three sections together to give at least fifteen feet of height. Checking behind me to make sure I didn't knock anything over or scratch any of my signs, I pushed the door open with the end of the ladder. But I forgot a basic rule; always look through the door you're opening. Maui was recoiling and hissing at the garden behind me, her ears flattened against her head. I whipped round to see my neighbour Bill in his pants and a T-shirt, and missing a lot of hair on one side of his head.

I ploughed the ladder into his chest as he sprang at me. Lou didn't have the viewpoint that Maui and I had, so she wasn't expecting to have to move with me and the action ripped the ladder from her grip. Her end of the ladder crashed to the floor, sending my end into his chin in a superb uppercut. His neck gave out a crack which echoed off the house and back to us, and his head flopped back between his shoulders.

'Nuts. We've got to move, now!'

We set out into the garden and I pulled Lou past my neighbour's crumpled heap on the ground outside the door. I could see no-one else, so we trotted the fifty feet to the decking where I pushed the ladder above my head and guided it up the wall, as Lou bent down and fed it through my hands. It made a tinny clunk as it hit the window, but was too steep to climb.

'I've got to get a better angle. Let's move the table and chairs, but do it quietly - they can definitely still hear. Bill had heard us in the shed!'

'That was Bill? From next door? She asked quietly.

'Yeah, I think I broke his neck.'

She held her head and stared at the floor. Her brow was wrinkled and she looked like she might cry, but we had to get a move on.

'It might not have been him; his face was a bit... fucked up. Come on.'

We took great care not to make a noise as we lifted the furniture clear. When there was enough space I pulled the ladder out and re-sat its feet, giving it a wobble to test it. I started to climb up the ladder, but after a few steps I stopped, climbed back down and said with a grin:

'Ladies first.'

'That's fine. I'm thinner than you anyway,' Lou scoffed.

When she was half-way up I realised I might not actually have to climb the ladder if Lou let me through the back door but then I heard the rustle of leaves. The bushes were moving, down the side of the shed towards the hole I'd made in the fence. That wasn't the closest noise though. A dry bamboo bush just twenty feet away split apart and a straggle-haired woman fell onto the path. I started up the ladder after Lou, who was fiddling with the window.

'What's up?' I asked, trying not to rush her.

'It's a bit stiff.'

There were four freaks now, and two of them were scrambling up the path. I was racking my brain, trying to remember if they climbed the ladder up to the helicopter at the end of *Dawn of the Dead*.

'Come on.'

One fell over the edge of the decking with a thud, and looked up at us, rasping and gagging. His eyes were matte in the moonlight, deep scratches lacing across his scalp.

'Oh my God!' Lou was looking down.

'Don't look down, look at the fucking window.'

'Don't speak to me like that,' she said indignantly. 'That was uncalled for.'

'Oh for Christ's sake,' I muttered.

'I heard that.'

'What?' I asked, wondering what we were doing arguing up a ladder when zombie flesh-eaters were clawing at my feet. Well not quite at my feet but certainly too close for comfort, bumping around with the bush lady.

'Don't get in an egg with me, do something!' Lou spluttered.

I clambered back down until my feet were just above their head height. I made sure my grip was good, crouched, and cracked the man in the temple with my right foot. He hit the decking, but the ladder had an equal and opposite reaction and lurched sideways. Lou shrieked. I looked up and saw that our precarious angle was sustained only by my wife's fingertip grip. She grunted and pulled her way along the windowsill, slowly righting the ladder.

'Sorry darling,' I offered.

Two more were at the base of the ladder, one gripping a rung, staring up slack-jawed at me and gaining extra height by standing on the one I'd clobbered. I scaled the ladder as far as I could without making the thing too top-heavy and looked up to Lou – but she was already through the window. She soon had one of the larger bedroom windows open and was grabbing me by the elbow. She hauled me in and onto the floor. We hugged.

'Don't ever speak to me like that, okay?' She was furious.

'Are we still on that?' There were times when I should just say sorry and be done with it. 'Sorry. Thanks and that, you know, for the ladder.' I shifted feet.

'Just remember that when you want me to stay in the car.' she said, her chin pointing my way.

'Fair point, that's the second time you've saved me from getting bitten today. I never want to be without something to fight them off with. Or a dog for that matter.'

'It's got to be proportionate though, they're ill people,' she said.

'Oh, come on! You don't still think they're alive, do you?' I snorted.

'Oh, and you think they're dead?' she shouted, then took a breath. 'Look, I know this stuff freaks you out, and I know it's been a hard day. I've seen some stuff I... look; I'm keeping an open mind. I know it's not bird 'flu, or rabies. But I know it's not zombies either.'

Silence. I wanted to tell her what Al and I had done to Susie, but I was pretty sure it wouldn't go down too well.

'I also know that I wouldn't be here without you and Al, and, well, thanks.'

'Al!'

We both looked at each other, and started for the bedroom door.

'Hang on, shall we pull the ladder in?' she asked. I looked out of the open window.

'Wait a minute. Watch what they're doing.'

There were four or five of them now, looking up at the window, moaning and rasping. None of them were trying out the ladder.

'Let's just close these windows - we might need to get out this way in a hurry. Come on, Al must be waiting for us.'

I hopped over the bed and in front of Lou, and thundered down the stairs into the darkness. I hovered by the front door, but I could see Al wasn't there through the door's frosted glass. There were, however, half a dozen or so figures in my driveway and on the pavement in front of the house. My mobile was still out, so the only way to warn Al was to illuminate them – it was worth the risk. I knelt down by the front door to turn the security light on, but there was nothing.

'The electricity's gone,' I said, flicking the switch uselessly. We could do nothing else, so we waited, and after a few minutes we heard the crunch of tyres as Al, without headlights, rolled onto the drive and into the legs of two of the freaks, hammering them onto the concrete. The ones that were still standing rounded on the car, and the dogs started baying at them.

We had to act fast, as the noise would no doubt attract more of them from up and down the road. I opened the door a crack to see Al looking at me and shaking his head. I held my hand up, making a door-latch action with my hand and pointing to the boot. I mouthed 'release the hounds.' He grinned and leant down to the floor of the car, and I heard the boot unlock with a clunk. The dogs, though eager, weren't able to push it open themselves so Al clambered over to the back of the car, flicked a clip and pulled one of the rear seats downwards. I watched as he shuffled his upper body through the gap and into the boot, springing it open. The dogs were out and on their quarry in seconds, as Al climbed back into the front seats, picked up the radios and the water bottle, and waited until the dogs had felled enough of them on one side for him to get to the house. When he made his move I ran out and took the water from him, letting him through the front door first, which Lou held open for us.

We whistled for the dogs but they were busy pulling at hair and faces, ripping them up like they were rags. They certainly didn't seem to show any mercy, and I'll admit I was shocked at their efficient determination. It was only when they had immobilised all of them that Dmitri decided he'd had enough and sauntered inside with Floyd hot on his heels, both their white chins streaked with foul-smelling jet-black seepage.

'I don't know what all the fuss is about,' said Al, grinning.

Breaking Bones
[day 0001]

Al had sat down in the front room to settle the beagles when he realised he'd left his rolling tin in the car.

'How badly do you want a doobie?' I asked him.

'Pretty fucking badly, actually,' he said, seriously weighing up whether or not to go back out there.

'Don't go outside again; it's really not worth it. Remember what we said? You'd be the stoner who'd get eaten trying to retrieve his stash! Don't give the bastards the satisfaction chum,' I said with my arms folded.

'We can't even boil the kettle to have a cup of tea,' he said glumly.

I left him with the dogs to join Lou, who was checking out every room in the house armed with one of our heavier frying pans. She had already made her way up to the loft, and gave me an arse-quivering fright when I first saw her dark silhouette from the landing as she retrieved the camping gear from under the eaves.

'Don't do that,' I said, clambering up the ladder. 'You scared me shitless.'

'Get a grip; give me a hand getting the cooking stuff out,' she whispered hoarsely.

'Have we still got those blue camping ice blocks in the freezer?'

'I think so,' she said as she stood up to kiss me. 'I hope the milk's alright.'

'I could do with a beer, too.'

We took a box of stuff each, and helped each other negotiate the steep steps down to the landing. The electricity couldn't have been off for long, as the freezer was still freezing. The fridge was cooler than room temperature too, so the milk was fine. Al had lit some candles in the front room and stacked books in front of them to stop shadows casting on the windows.

'Cup of tea chum?' Lou set up the camping gas stove on the coffee table.

'Gawd bless you, missus,' said Al, smiling from ear to ear as he doffed an imaginary flat cap. Lou lit the stove and turned it down to a faint glow, then filled the tin kettle as silence fell and we watched. We were soon unwinding with our first cuppas since what seemed like a lifetime ago. I made roll-ups as they sat back and gingerly sipped their hot tea. My home is my castle, I thought as I reclined in my armchair and let a coil of smoke wind its way from my lips.

'No PlayStation,' I remarked.

'No doobies,' Al mumbled. I was quietly pleased that I wasn't craving a spliff as much as Al was – it was an ongoing (if fairly half-hearted) project of mine to try and stop smoking. That's not to say I didn't think a strong zoot wouldn't be useful right then, as the adrenaline of the day was still coursing through my veins and I needed to get some sleep soon. I was often disappointed by my addiction to the stuff - I don't think more than a month of abstinence had gone by for the previous twelve years or so. I should point out the fact that not only is a that a collective month but that the abstinence was imposed on me too, mainly due to foreign holidays that weren't to Holland or due to the dreaded dealer drought. The worst thing was that I felt it slowing my brain down over the years and I still didn't stop. The giggling novelty of forgetting everyday words wears off after a decade or so – but by that time smoking pot is as much a part of your life as taking a dump. It was self-imposed stupidity, but very enjoyable stupidity nonetheless.

I would still hold my own in a good argument, as long as it wasn't with my wife who pretty much cheated in our discussions back then, moving goalposts randomly until I gave up in a huff. I still enjoyed a good pub debate though, as long as fisticuffs weren't on the agenda. That's not to say I used to actually gave two hoots about other people's opinions much; I was more fascinated by how passionate they were about them, and how they went about expressing them - the opinions themselves felt pretty meaningless. I would often play Devil's Advocate with my opponents, provoking them into expressing some form of opinion. Fox-hunting, eco-guilt, corporal punishment, nationalism, Marxism, feminism - any and all were my territory. Suicide bombers could be freedom fighters or terrorists, depending on who I was talking to.

I could flit from left-wing to right-wing at the drop of a gauntlet, but even with my own personal opinions I wasn't sure-footed. I leaned to the right with my unfashionable patriotism, but I felt a lefty empathy for the underdog. Prejudging someone based on their particular DNA pick-and-mix was abhorrent, but in a country were ginger-haired people were still very much fair game I had little patience for legislating against it. Social injustice left me uneasy, but I didn't think of it as my duty to try and change it.

Was this still playing Devil's Advocate, or was I just sitting on the fence? Maybe I was just being typically 'English' in my hypocrisy, but did such thing as a 'typical Englishman' even exist any more? Had it ever? Looking back it is evident that I encouraged external manifestations of what I thought English-ness was, which I wouldn't have felt the need to encourage unless I was starting to feel a bit like the underdog myself.

However, there were distinct and undeniable traits amongst many English people which you only see in an old and close-knit culture. No-one could deny that we English had a fondness for humour which tended to be both self-derogatory and self-critical. This is all well and good but in the preceding years it had transformed into an ugly self-loathing. It had been suggested that we were as close-knit as an open sore. As a people we were pretty lost, yet no-one my age or younger seemed to care – and anyway, *Hollyoaks* was probably on.

Someone has since told me about the theory of relativism, and about how before the outbreak we weren't unified as a country by common ideals any more (the relativist in me asks 'were we ever?'). The terror felt by the general public which led to volunteering for the trenches could never happen again (the rela-tivist in me asks 'is that a bad thing?'). Thinking relatively is tiring even when you don't know you're doing it - it saps the will and takes away the stomach for a fight, things which if our predecessors hadn't proudly displayed them would have spelt a rather different (and probably quite German) future for England.

I wondered if we hadn't all somehow been hamstrung by our own hard won freedom to express ourselves, especially when we started blowing each other up on public transport - apparently you could be English and hate everything Eng-land stood for. I used the suicide bomber/freedom fighter argument less after that, not because it didn't wash with other people but because it made me feel sick to do so. I was English and proud to be so. I do hope sincerely that a bea-gle, a pair of green wellies and a few books on Winston Churchill didn't make up my entire personality, however. These were my part of my vision of Eng-lishness, but like it or not there were sixty million visions of what Englishness was - before everyone enthusiastically set about eating each other.

I had an old Ordnance Survey map of the Downs spread out on our dining table and a roll-up hanging from my lip like a General's cigar. Al was sucking on his second helping of tea, and Lou was fiddling with a little battery radio from the bathroom to find out if any stations were broadcasting. Then the dogs started to growl.

The gaggle of freaks we'd disturbed in the back garden was now a crowd, one or two of them occasionally falling off the decking into the bushes or onto the lawn. We'd watched them as their numbers swelled, drawn to the house by our activity and noise, maybe even by our smell. But when I walked into the kitchen I saw what had caught the dogs' attention. One of the original freaks had pushed his head right through Maui's cat-flap in the back door, and got one whole arm inside right up to the armpit. It looked like an impossible situation, like he had to at least dislocate a shoulder to get through. Our kitchen was long and narrow, with barely enough room for two people to pass each other. At the end was the back door, with the sink to the left and the fridge and oven on the right. His head was forced down into a position facing the fridge door, but his teeth seemed to be magnetically leading his face towards us, gnashing at the closest flesh. Floyd was right up in his face giving a shrill continuous bark with Dmitri behind him deeper and louder. I didn't want the dogs to start tearing him up, it would have made a right mess. Floyd's paws slipped on the lino as Al tugged him by his collar to hand him over to Lou, who herded both dogs into the front room and shut the door behind her. Al looked at the corpse trying to crawl into my house.

'What do you want to do?'

'I don't know.' I replied. 'Do you think he can get all the way in?'

'Well, he's got that far chum.'

I inched forward, warily feeling my way along the countertop. I stopped just out of the range of the flailing arm and torn nails, and muscles contorted in grabbing spasm. I put one hand on the counter top and leant forward to get a knife from the magnetic strip above the sink. It was only just out of reach, and my fingertips were touching the handle but unable to get a grip. I looked down at the desperate arm, and the head still straining to get to me. I could hear the sickening sound of pressure on gristle coming from his neck as I took a step forward – it would only be for a second - to grab my choice of knife, but I felt my trouser leg tightening. It reminded me of the time I'd accidentally drilled into my jeans and the material gathered up instantly and nearly cut off my blood supply. I tried to take a step back but instead I was pulled towards the door.

I felt the force in this one. He was very strong, stronger than a dead bloke should be. I was pulled to one knee, my balls dangling inside my tense trousers not three inches from the teeth. You could see him trying to twist his head impossibly towards me until, with a sickly crack, it snapped round to face me. It looked like the arm and the head of two different people were sticking through the cat-flap as his lips peeled back to show the roots of his teeth. He lurched towards my groin with a moist snap as his arm seemed to cramp up, pulling me in.

My nuts were now just an inch away from his grinding teeth when the refrigerator door slammed open and onto the top of his skull with a sharp crack. I saw Al's ruined Nike Jordan no. 4 pushing harder onto the inside of the door and popping the lid off the carton of milk. It seemed that because the fridge door was now an obstacle to the flesh available, it became more of a priority to him than the flesh itself, and his grip on my trousers loosened enough for me to pull free and jump to my feet. Al was grimacing as he pushed the door, using the fridge itself as leverage to stop it slipping. I took a step forwards and stamped on the arm with all my weight, breaking it with a splintering crack. Still it moved, now just muscles contracting an arm-shaped bag with bits of bone in it. I grabbed the cleaver - a sushi cleaver, as opposed to a butcher's - and slammed it down onto the arm as it clutched uselessly at Al's shoe. The arm lay on the floor with fingers still twitching as the stump revolved, grinding bone onto bone. A slow dribble of blood – more like it was pooled in the arm than ever flowing through it – ran down the stump and onto my kitchen lino. It was black, and stank of eggs.

'Ready?'

Al nodded as I raised the cleaver. He pulled the fridge door shut and I sank it deep into the back of the freak's exposed neck with a distinct metallic ring, where it stuck. The shoulder stopped grinding instantly. I leant down to retrieve the knife from the guy's head, and Al jumped.

'Jesus,' he breathed quietly.

I looked up at two ghost-white faces pressed into the window. We all stood there staring at each other through the glass; their jaws churning at the prospect of meat, our noses twitching at the volcanic stink of sulphur. I heard Lou open the door behind us and gasp.

'Oh, shit, the shed door's still open,' I said.

'My fault I suppose, but we were in a bit of a hurry,' Lou said, her eyes flickering to the cleaver in my hand. 'It'll have to stay open; you're not going out again. Cor, it really stinks in here.'

'At least you know nothing will get stolen,' Al said helpfully. Lou looked at him.

'So you don't think anyone's left is… normal? Remember we saw looters in Crawley, and in Brighton,' she offered, almost wishing my workshop would get pillaged as some proof of normality. I thought Al was going to say it to her, right there and then; that there were real zombies, real fucking *Night of the Living Dead* right there in your back garden, and they wouldn't even know how to steal a free gift because they're obsessed with eating your flesh. He didn't.

'I'm sure even the looters have got other things to worry about right now,' he said.

'If anyone else is actually still alive,' I added

'Okay you two, what if there really is a cure? What if they come round injecting everyone with an antidote and you're standing there with a kitchen knife in your hand? How many have you killed today?' she asked, here eyes sparking dangerously. 'Bill! You know it was Bill, don't you, and you're not telling me. Do you feel guilty?'

'When would you ever think it was zombies, Lou?'

'What?' she asked, lips thinning, sensing counter-attack.

'I mean, what will it take to persuade you that these are proper common-or-garden zombie flesh-eaters?' I asked her. 'What have you seen today? Cannibalism, that's a new one on me. What about that smell - have you ever smelt that from something that's alive? I could understand if it was the smell of pus or infection, but it isn't – it smells like carcasses, of ammonia and decomposition.' I was shouting now. 'You saw that old lady in Brighton, and the guy with the motorbike rammed up his arse. You've seen what happened to Susie after just a scratch; and people taking massive injuries, deadly ones, and getting straight up again.' Al was looking at me.

'Tell her,' he said. 'She should know. But don't shout; it's not nice.'

'Know what?' Lou asked shakily, the colour draining from her face, her eyes starting to puff up. I took a deep breath and told her how we had pierced her friend's heart with an umbrella in the middle of nowhere, and how she had just kept moving, kept clawing at our legs. We'd watched her dead eyes and her open chest, and seen how she'd still writhed amongst the rotten, skeletal leaves.

'You know when she attacked you in the car? That was the first thing she did after she died. You said yourself it didn't look like her - you said you saw it in her eyes. That's why I don't feel guilty about Bill, or Susie.' I said. 'It wasn't them inside; they'd already died. Look, do you think the security guards at your work are still alive? How about Clive or Dean? Or the newsreaders, or those soldiers we saw on the Downs? Lots of people died today Lou, but not us. I think we can give ourselves a bit of a pat on the back for that.'

There was a long silence, and the moaning and scratching from outside the back door had ceased, as if they were listening to us arguing. Lou spoke first.

'I don't know what to do any more.'

'Let's just survive. We can all try and do that, right? As far as we know, we're the only ones left until we see any different with our own eyes. There's no friends, no parents, no Prime Minister. No-one.' I stopped, feeling like I might have been a bit harsh, but it all seemed so clear to me – if people were smart they would have survived that day just like we had, but right now the only people left in the world as far as I was concerned were the two people standing in front of me.

'Look,' I said eventually, 'I'll bet a tenner that we're not the only ones who aren't... infected. But let's just look after each other for now, and concentrate on getting through the week, at least.'

'Help will come.' Al said to Lou. I wasn't so sure that help would come, but I knew it was likely that there were more people like us, surviving. I kept quiet.

'But all those people... What about poor Susie?' Lou asked.

'She's dead, Lou, but we didn't kill her. She died in Brighton, before we got onto the Downs. Look, if we get the chance, we'll go back and I'll bury her. You know - give her a proper send-off.'

That was enough cold logic for Lou, who burst into hot tears.

'So. How did they know we were here? Let's apply ourselves.' I was leaning over the dining table again. As Lou dozed on the sofa we'd levered the dead bloke out of the cat-flap with a mop, and Al had heaved the coffee table up against it.

'Well, we didn't have the lights on, and I was careful to block out the candle-light.' Al said.

'I made a bit of a noise when I broke through the fence, but we were inside the house within five minutes. Plus we'd drawn the others out of earshot when we were still in the car.' I smelt my armpit.

'Maybe they can smell our activity – car fumes, milk, dogs. Armpits.'

'Maybe they can smell our flesh, our meat,' Al suggested.

'I can definitely smell theirs.' I said. 'It seems so soon though, for them to be smelling so… off. I know its been a hot day, but still.'

'I've smelt that smell before, when Dmitri dug up a seagull dad had buried in the back garden. They'd been shitting on mum's washing for weeks. I've smelt enough to know they're dead, and there's definitely no cure for dead. Listen, I don't know what I would have thought if you hadn't been jabbering away about zombies all day. I might not have been on my toes so much, so thanks and all that for being irrationally paranoid about the undead.' He looked awkward. 'Never thought I'd say that,' he muttered to himself.

'Actually Lou thanked both of us earlier, you know, for picking her up.' I slapped my forehead. 'Sorry, I forgot to say.'

'Well, that's okay. I did drive exceptionally well.' He yawned.

We didn't talk much more after that, except to briefly discuss how many AA batteries you'd need to run a PlayStation, and then Al fell asleep where he sat. It had been a long, weird day. I curled up on the sofa next to Lou.

[day 0002]

I woke to streaming sunlight and Lou shaking my shoulder.

'Come on baby, we're going.'

'Eh? Where are we going?' I rubbed my belly.

'Anywhere. We've got to go now. They had all disappeared when Al woke me up; now there are three of them at the back door again, and they're trying the handles.'

'You're shitting me.' I held my head. 'Where's Al?'

'He went to his parents' house when it was still dark. He left us two radios and said he'd be back before midday, but its only eight o'clock. There's two more.'

I pulled myself to my feet and stepped over Floyd who was upside down and snoring on the hall carpet. The back door handle was waggling erratically, knocking against the top of the upturned coffee table, and they were doing the same in the dining room to the doors onto the decking. If they could try the handles today, why not chuck rocks through the windows tomorrow - or before midday when Al was due back? I shuddered. My head was throbbing as I walked to the stairs.

'There's more in the garden, they're coming this way,' Lou shouted.

'Get away from that glass. They might have a *2001* moment and start using tools,' I called back to her as I ran up the stairs to my office – really a spare bed-room – at the front of the house. I sidled up to the window and looked up and down the deserted street, then dashed back down to Lou and Floyd, who was now awake and snarling at the door handles in the dining room with his tail between his legs.

I picked up three bottles of wine from the wine rack.

'Get a thing; er, get the lamp or something.' I told her. 'Get ready to paste one of them.'

'What? No, I'm not going to,' she said.

'Look, I'm not asking you to decapitate anyone. I'll do that. Just push them out of the way for me. Don't look at me like that; you wanted to be more in-volved.'

'Even if some of them do move after they're dead you don't know that these particular ones aren't still alive,' she said.

Look,' I said, tucking two of the bottles into my baggy trouser pockets. They started to fall down, so I did my belt up two notches too tight. 'If we're going out on foot, we both need some stuff from the shed. You know - to shoo them away with...'

'Don't be sarcastic,'

'I'm not,' I lied. 'You don't have to disembowel any of them, you don't even have to go outside. Just push one backwards and I'll do the rest.' I said, one hand on the key in the door, the other holding a bottle.

She unplugged the tall standard lamp.

'Okay, I'm ready,' she said, holding the lamp as if guessing its weight.

'What did you do that for?' I asked.

'What?'

'Why did you unplug it? Safety first?'

'Stop having a go at me,' she said hotly.

'The electricity's off anyway.'

'Come on, if we're going to do this,' she hissed, nodding at the door and curling her elbow around the stem of the lamp. Floyd was pawing at the glass and whining.

'Ready?'

I turned the key, opened the door and saw a head right in the path of my swing, so I swung. The bottle fractured, and the impact sent the girl to the ground in a pool of claret as I pulled another bottle out of my pocket. I watched Lou sizing up one of them as he pushed his way towards us, and saw her ram the bulb-end of the lamp into his chest, shoving him away until she was holding the circular base. I watched the shade buckle - I had always assumed it was glass but it was clearly plastic – and heard the bulb's crystalline pop. He fell backwards over the picnic table and down onto the lawn. Floyd had felled the third one, and was working on a fourth, but I couldn't see the last one so I poked my head out. A kid of about fifteen was ambling to the open door, his jaws in motion. I cracked the bottle over the top of his head and he crumpled onto the floor. That was five. I leapt over the bodies, off the decking and onto the lawn, hearing Lou pull the door to and Floyd following on behind me.

I had one bottle left but there were two to go. I took one of them out with a crack across his pus-bloated face, sending him reeling into the bushes, and Floyd flung himself at the throat of the other. I tore through the open work-shop door, turned and whistled. Floyd, possibly because Dmitri wasn't there, satisfied himself with just some simple face-work before leaving the corpse writhing on my garden path. As I slammed the door shut behind the hound I caught sight of my neighbour Bill laying in the bushes, still in his pants, with his neck bent backwards so his head faced behind him. His throat had no broken skin except for the network of red sores but I could clearly see the hollow break in his neck above his Adam's apple. I ducked down and crept along the work-bench to the window, slowly lifting myself up so I could see outside. On the decking only one was getting to his feet; the others lolled uselessly on the ground.

I turned around to my tools. The list, which I had mentally prepared long before that day:

>1 x garden spade
>1 x garden fork
>1 x pressure sprayer, with white spirit
>1 x wooden mallet
>2 x claw hammers
>2 x circular saw blades
>1 x 24 inch hand saw
>1 x cordless drill

I decided that some of this was now redundant, especially if we were to escape the house on foot. The garden spade I could sling through the shoulder straps of my backpack if I had room, and Lou could do the same with the garden fork; I was quite set on the flame-thrower idea; a mallet we'd have needed if we were going camping anyway, and one of the hammers was definitely in; the impractical circular saw blades went, even though they were cool; I wouldn't have time to use the hand saw effectively; and the cordless drill was just simply gratuitous.

I filled the sprayer with the white spirit and hauled it over my shoulders, tucking the spade down between the sprayer tank and my back which worked well but wasn't comfortable. I pushed the mallet and hammer into my belt, then opened up our chest freezer (now starting to give off a whiff of stale cheese), and pulled out two carrier bags full of portions of chilli and Bolognese sauce, as well as some bread rolls and a carton of orange juice. I had got into the habit of cooking up batches of chilli and Bolognese in a huge pot ten litres at a time and freezing it. It meant I would double the cooking but get fifty meals out of it, meaning more time on the sofa. Then I had a brainwave. I picked up a roll of parcel tape and a small pot of red gloss paint, together with a half-inch paintbrush.

I wanted to get back into the relative safety of the house, but I felt that I wasn't properly armed yet. Everything I'd gathered so far had a drawback; the sprayer would need igniting; the mallet required a short swing and contact would be too close for comfort. I needed something like a club, a baseball bat or even cricket bat, but I was no sportsman and had nothing of the sort. I did, however, have lots of wood. I turned to my pile of timber off-cuts and pulled out a couple of three-foot lengths of two-inch by two-inch wooden post, and a box of barbed four-inch wood screws. I set about screwing them straight into one end of each post, so they both looked like angry toilet brushes when I was done. I pushed one of the clubs down the back of my trousers with the screws pointing away from my arse, held the other in my left hand and made for the door.

I didn't think I had made too much noise until I heard something heavy thud against the door. Floyd's immediate high decibel reaction would only begin to attract more attention so I had to move quickly, and tapped the alarm's keypad to start the beeping. Pressure.

I tested the door with my foot but it offered no resistance and opened to reveal a fat bloke on his knees facing towards me. He must have gone for the door and knocked himself over but he was about to get to his feet. Resisting the temptation to growl a cheesy Hollywood-style one-liner, such as 'Confession time, punk!', I instead conducted an immediate field-test of my DIY mace by bringing the useful end cracking onto the back of his head. I had to work to get it free, but he was out for the count. A design fault, I thought, watching Floyd run up to the others bumbling about on the decking and mindful of the two sprawled out on the lawn. I turned and closed the shed door nicely within the alarm's beeping time, and jumbled up the numbers on the padlock.

As I strode back towards the house I tested the weight of my club. One of the ones on the grass in front of me stood up and pointed his face into the air, nostrils twitching. He turned on the spot and levelled his nose at me, then bared his teeth and gurgled. I walked up to him and slammed the club upwards into the soft flesh underneath his chin. It was effective enough. I could see Lou watching me through the blinds as I stepped up onto the decking, catching one of them on the side of the head as he got too close. The three others trying the kitchen door had spotted me, but I was a bit disappointed to see that Floyd was more interested in ripping to shreds a pair of trousers he'd torn off one of the creeps. I kept facing them as Lou held the door open and I backed into the dining room. She looked at me.

'Blimey!'

I got her to pull out the spade and her club before hauling the sprayer from over my shoulders.

'Who are you supposed to be, *Shaun of the Dead*?'

FLOYD
THE BEAGLE

'That's yours.' I explained, pointing at the improvised club I'd made. Mine was dripping with jet fat.

'Okay,' her brow furrowed. 'Can I take the screws out?'

'No. Empty the fridge; I'll throw down the cool bag from the loft. Bung these in it, along with those ice-packs.' I handed her the carrier bag of slowly thawing food, and pulled a big bag of cat biscuits from the cupboard. 'Grab some knives, cutlery, half a dozen plates, and some mugs – you know, like we were camping but more permanent.'

'Will we be expecting anyone? And where are we going?'

'Camping.'

In the loft I started hauling out the gear. The previous owner had boarded and carpeted the loft and installed a couple of windows. It was nice enough, but it was a drag getting cups of tea up the steep staircase so we didn't use it that much. Now it was a place for Maui to take refuge from an over-inquisitive puppy who wanted to sniff her backside like his life depended on it. She was up there now, licking her paws and washing her face in the morning sun. She mewed at me and sprawled out on her back. Happy days.

I split open the bag of cat food so she wouldn't get her head stuck in there. You couldn't do that with a dog; the whole lot would be gone in minutes, and you'd be clearing up puke for days. A cat - especially Maui - would make it last. I knew she'd be okay; she was a smart cat, a survivor. Years ago when she was a kitten and we had lived on the seafront a stray greyhound had caught her and ripped her side open in the front garden. I found her under one of the arm-chairs in the living room, soaking wet through slobber and all her muscles showing down one side. I also found greyhound hair and bloody rolls of skin stuck under her claws when we were driving her to the vet. She'd be fine with zombies.

I started ferreting under the eaves for the camping gear; the camping stove, kettle and gas lamp were all downstairs already. What else would we need? I settled for the following:

> 1 x four-man tent
>
> 1 x twelve-litre plastic water container
>
> 2 x mess tins
>
> 1 x cooking ring adapter for gas lamp
>
> 6 x spare small blue gas bottles
>
> 1 x 20ft corkscrew dog tether

1 x four-inch lock-knife (illegal in UK, bought by my brother-in-law
        Mike in a high-street French pharmacy)
1 x pair binoculars
2 x vacuum flask beakers
1 x foldaway aluminium table
2 x foldaway chairs, single
1 x foldaway chair, double
2 x maggot/mummy convertible sleeping bags
1 x inflatable double air bed
1 x car lighter powered air bed pump
1 x washing-up bowl
2 x tea towels
1 x small bottle washing-up liquid

I'd often wondered how resilient the tents, table and chairs were, all folded up and stored away in their bags with shoulder straps, so I took the opportunity to find out and started to drop them through the hatch. Lou couldn't have a go at me, it was an emergency. Some of them fell all the way to the bottom of the stairs, and I could hear Floyd barking and Lou shushing him. I was quieter with the pots and pans and gas canisters, then slung the binoculars around my neck and made my way down the stairs. Lou was at the bottom, arms folded.

'We can't take that much.'

'I know, we'll have to cull it but at least it'll all be by the front door when we've got a car again.'

We decided to ditch the chairs, airbed and pump but not the table, and Lou insisted on the washing-up stuff. She'd found two rucksacks and found two of our holiday suitcases 'just in case'.

'We can do this easily,' I said as I went to the sink for water, trying not to look into the back garden. Lou had taken all the food we weren't carrying with us out of the fridge and kitchen freezer and into two bin bags. She'd unplugged them and propped their doors open, and even cleaned up the black sludge from around the cat-flap. I loved her with a powerful fire in my belly. The plastic water container was about two-thirds full when the tap gave a splutter, and I heard the plumbing kicking itself behind the walls. I pulled the container away and watched the flow of water - after five seconds and some more spluttering it ran cloudy, then rust red, then brown, then trickled, and then it just stopped.

'Water's gone.' I shouted
'No.'
'It's fine; I got loads out before it went.'

We packed up my survival kit which came in a rolling tin with electrician's tape around it and boasted a flint; fishing line; hooks and weights; waterproof matches; a button compass; a wire saw; a Morse code sheet for people who hadn't bothered to learn it; and some other stuff like swabs and eyewash. Lou had got a small first aid kit from the bathroom and we started to pack the rucksacks. The two medical kits went in my outside pocket, and I estimated that the tent would take up the bulk of the inside of mine. I peered in.

'There's some stuff from holiday still in mine.'

'No its not,' Lou explained efficiently. 'I packed you some trousers and pants and a towel and some highlights from your frankly grotty wash-bag.'

I was peering into my bag still.

'I love you.' It was muffled.

'What?'

I bent down to grab the tent up. 'I love you', I said, straining to pick it up with one hand.

'I love you too baby.' She helped me put the tent into my backpack. She seemed quite cheerful.

Everything else fitted fairly well. Mine was heavier than Lou's which I was pleased with, and I used garden string to attach some of our smaller Le Creuset saucepans and a frying pan to Lou's back pack, which she had put on already.

'Fucking hell.'

The cast iron pans were heavy, and according to the leaflet they were so resilient you could sit them on hot coals to cook on. We'd never taken them camping, they were wedding presents and Lou thought they were too nice, but I'd been intrigued by the thought of sticking them straight onto a bonfire to cook with. Now was my chance.

I hadn't thought about wearing a backpack when I'd grabbed the pressure sprayer, but there was no reason it couldn't be worn on my front. I took my pack off again and set up the sprayer tank on my chest like a papoose. At least the fumes would be fun, I thought. I pulled the rucksack back on and, in a flash of inspiration, picked up our mini kitchen blowtorch – also a wedding present – and stuffed it into my pocket.

I was forgetting things I needed, but remembering other things too fast to remember them. This was classic key-forgetting territory. I went to the front room and picked up my Zippo lighter and tobacco. I was overloaded. Floyd had sensed something was afoot a while ago and was hopping round us and whining, his head occasionally making contact with Lou's dangling pans as she strapped the spade to my back.

'Like a soldier,' she said.

'Dog food. Oh nuts, and his lead,' I sighed but Lou was there already, stuffing them into the top of my rucksack. Floyd had smelt the kibble and was jumping up.

'Down Floyd! You ready Lou?'

'If you've got your keys?' she smiled, smacking the back of her club into her palm.

'Yep.' I patted my pocket. 'Radios!'

'They're here. Al's set ours and one of his to the same frequency, but he'll be well out of range at his parent's house.'

I helped Lou fit hers onto the belt of her jeans. She had hiking boots on.

'Where are we going, by the way?' she asked me, putting Floyd on his lead.

I clipped the radio onto my shoulder strap and looked at her.

'Cissbury Ring.'

As we stepped out of the front door I popped the lid off the red paint with a pound coin and dipped the little brush.

'What the fuck are you doing?' Lou hissed, looking up and down the road.

'Hang on woman.' It was only when I knew the outcome of what I was doing would be triumphant and victorious that I spoke to her like that. Sometimes it backfired, but I was confident as I started to paint on the front door: "WALKING THE DOG". I had to go onto the wall, and the "G" of dog was on the bay window, but it did the job. I put the lid back on and stuffed the tin and brush into a side pocket of Lou's backpack, very pleased with myself.

'Why didn't you just write "UP CISSBURY"?'

'Al needs to know where to go, and everyone else that we know will understand exactly where we are. But we can't make it easy for other people - even if there are survivors, the stupid ones will get us killed. Anyway, we've got to get up there ourselves first.' I scratched my head. 'We're taking the same track up that we drove down last night, but then cutting across the golf course. We drove down from the car park last night, not from the centre of the Ring.'

'Of course,' Lou said as she headed out onto the pavement.

'Keep to the middle of the road. You'll be easier to see but so will they. I don't fancy getting pulled into a garden hedge right now. Take this.' I handed her the mini-blowtorch.

'You've really, actually, seriously thought about this day, haven't you?' she asked.

'Yep.' I said, pumping the T-handle on my pressure sprayer tank up and down. I held the thin metal wand in my left hand and the club in my right. We moved up the street cautiously but without dithering, Floyd's lead pushed up my arm to my elbow joint as he trotted along behind us. We'd got half-way to the end of the street when a hunched man limped out of a front garden on our right, his ankle dangling uselessly at the joint, and his dressing gown stained black. I wondered what yesterday had been like for him; was that his house? I hadn't seen him before - at least I didn't think I had. The few infected that I had recognised looked nothing like themselves; instead the illness gave them the appearance of a caricature, or a cheap horror mask. The man had a dressing gown on so maybe he'd been ill and infected other people. Maybe he'd been in bed and answered the door to one of them. That was unlikely, unless they'd worked out doorbells. He might have answered the door to someone fleeing though, someone looking for a safe haven - someone who had already been infected.

As we drew up alongside him I could hear the wet crunch as he kept putting weight onto his snapped ankle. I heard a rustle up ahead, and a young woman fell from a bush and slapped face-first onto the pavement. She was wearing a ripped England football shirt, and lifted herself up as we drew closer. White dotted lines now marked our path down the centre of the street onto the T-junction with the A27 as we passed the man. His eyes followed us, his arms stretched out towards us and his ankle squelching moistly.

'He's okay; he'll never catch us up at this pace but watch out for Waynetta Rooney up ahead.' We drew closer to her. 'Light me.'

'What?' Lou asked.

'The blowtorch...'

She was there already, almost over-efficiently, blue flame licking my nozzle. I squeezed the trigger.

'That's it, back away.'

I squeezed harder, and the *whump* of the orange jet made my face hot. I'd got her, the shiny material of her football strip blackening and shrinking around her torso. She didn't react as it bubbled into her flesh, but it seemed to send her muscles into involuntary spasm. She went down to the sound of spitting fat and popping tendons and began to arch her limbs wildly as Floyd strained to get to the smell of cooking. I spotted another three up ahead and went to pull Floyd away to face them; but I caught my breath when I saw the girl in the football strip's steady gaze through the flames, as her muscles thrashed her around on the tarmac. She was looking straight at me when her eyes boiled.

We heard a thump on a car we'd passed. I wheeled round to see another one alerted by our activity.

'Take this dog and light me!'

Lou did the business and a plume of flame leapt away from the nozzle, dousing him as well as a clearly quite dry privet hedge.

'Let's jog.' Lou suggested.

As we yomped up to the three creeps at the junction with the A27, I kept the fire going by dousing the barbed tip of my club with spirit, dripping flames onto the street. I let out a searing arc in front of us as we sped up towards them. The pressure on the sprayer was dropping so I only hit the two at the front, who lit up like torches and dropped to the tarmac. The third one proceeded to stumble towards us over the others who were now writhing on the ground. His clothes caught fire, spreading quickly up man-made fibre, soon licking at his chin. He continued towards us undaunted for a few paces, then finally collapsed in a twist of muscle and taught limbs. We were running as we turned left towards the bridleway up the Downs, and I pumped my handle. The rucksacks were heavy - I was obviously not as fit as I used to be and I slowed down, grimacing. Lou sprang ahead, eager to show she wasn't short of breath yet, approaching a series of wrecked vehicles dotting the middle of the road.

'Wait!' I had a stitch.

She stopped. A man sprang up from behind a car and stood with his back arched, gawking at my wife. I could see the entrance to the track up to Cissbury just off the road to our right, past the wrecked cars.

'I don't want them to see us going up that path.' I yelled, fighting for breath.

Lou backtracked to where I was now doubled up but eyeing the man who now took juddering steps towards us, and I saw her swinging her club in readiness.

'There's too many of them,' I pointed to a house on the corner of the road and the path. 'Let's get to that garden.'

Their numbers were swelling all the time, some appearing from behind the cars, others out of a nearby garden. I saw a block of flats fifty feet away with people standing in the car park, staring at us with slack mouths. We all ran, Floyd twice as fast as us.

'How do they know we're here? We've been quiet,' Lou had a note of exasperation in her voice. 'It's not like they're communicating with each other.'

Good, I thought. She's not thinking in human terms.

'I think I stink.' I explained, clambering over the garden gate and opening it for Lou. We ran up a driveway to a garage extension at the side of the house where I grabbed Lou's arm to stop her running in front.

'Hang on a sec. You wait here, I'll go on ahead.' I said, and shushed Lou's tutting noises. I crept to one side of the driveway to keep out of view behind a parked Jaguar, and jumped out holding my club high. I saw something which made the bile rise in my throat.

A man sat cross-legged on the back doorstep just like the sheep-eater on the Downs, but instead of a lamb's ribcage he was burying his head into a pair of toddler's denim trousers with a sew-on patch of a strawberry on the back pocket. It almost looked at first like he was hugging a reminder of someone he wanted to be close to. Then I saw the scarlet blood, as he lifted his face up with the sound of wet suction and I saw a pair of little legs in the trousers as he literally growled at me.

'I can see them coming up to the gate!' Lou hissed, still mercifully out of sight. 'What the fuck are you doing?'

I was frozen, staring at the man and trying to process too much information. Long seconds passed before I snapped to, bringing the club down onto his head - but it glanced off onto his right shoulder and stuck in. He looked at it; then looked back at me with something close to disappointment in his eyes. He started gnashing, dropping the child's corpse and trying to stand up but my club was stuck fast and acting as a handle to keep him at bay.

'Lou, chuck me your club,' I yelled over my shoulder. 'I've got my hands full here.'

'But they're getting closer. One's just fallen over the gate.'

'Quickly!'

The club clattered to my feet.

'Sorry. Hang on.' She was coming to pick it up.

'No, wait there!' I barked. I bent down, but the handle was just out of my reach. I tried another way, and dropped to one knee, constantly keeping my eyes on the bloodstained freak on the end of my two-by-two. He worked to free the club stuck in his shoulder, the skin on his fingers getting stripped away by the screws. I swapped the stuck club to my other hand, still keeping him at a distance, and picked Lou's up with my right. I lifted it high and swung it straight down onto his forehead, but he looked upwards just as it made contact so he got the barbed wood screws in the face instead. I saw them embedded to the hilt into the bone of his forehead, piercing his cheeks and flattening his nose. One of his eyes was spitting dark juice.

He slumped with the blow but was still going, so I used the head-handle as a lever to work the first club free from his shoulder, and swapped hands for a second time. I turned him away from me and brought the club down onto the side of his head. It didn't glance off this time, instead the screws sunk into his temple. That did it. I was now holding two bits of wood which were both firmly attached to a man's head, and I had to take his weight as he dropped to his knees, nearly falling on top of him. I hauled him backwards onto the door-step and on top of the child's corpse, which I didn't want to touch, and called out for Lou.

'Help me get these out.'

She grimaced when she saw the man and his punctured scalp, but couldn't see the grim truth underneath him. We wriggled our sticks as if trying to get axes out of a tree stump. They each worked free with butcher's shop noises.

'They're coming; three of them are over the gate now,' Lou whispered. I stood up and looked over the roof of the Jaguar.

'Four of them.'

'Do you actually know if there's a way out of this garden?' she asked.

'No, but I assumed there would be a back gate or something.' I gesticulated. 'Why wouldn't there be?'

'Maybe they nailed it shut when the bin men stopped coming round. We'd better get looking.'

There was a thick, high hedge running along the large back garden's perimeter. I made my way to the side of the garden closest to the bridleway and after a moment of sweaty panic I found a gate which was hidden from view by the bush.

'They're all through now.' Lou said, staring back down the side of the house to the road - I didn't want to know that. I quietly twisted the handle - willing it to be unlocked and discovering that it was, with a joyful rush - and poked my head out to look up and down the leafy lane. It was clear, so I ushered Lou and Floyd through. Lou had to drag him, as he'd seen the approaching figures and seemed keen to get stuck in.

'Come on, boy.' She hauled him through the gate. It was a tight squeeze with my backpack and the sprayer tank, but Lou guided me through and I clicked the deadlock behind us.

'If there's any more on the road, hopefully they'll follow the others into the garden and not come up here.' I looked back down onto the A27. 'Keep to the sides until we're over the prow of the hill. I'll take the lead.'

Lou handed me the dog.

'No, I mean I'll go first. We might as well let him off now anyway.'

I used indents in the hedgerow as cover from the road behind us, sometimes creeping between the foliage and the back garden fences of the expensive houses to stay out of sight. We both relaxed a little when we lost sight of the road, and saw no-one up ahead until we reached the old golf course.

'Shh... look!' I pulled Lou down beside me and locked my fingers round Floyd's collar, thankful he was examining horse dung and not paying attention. Ready to tee off just ahead was a man in torn clothes and dusty white golf shoes, with a bag of clubs strewn at his feet. We watched through the long summer grass.

'What's he doing?'

I hushed Lou, fearful that he might hear us - I was confident he wouldn't catch sight or smell of us as we were well covered from view, and downwind. However he was standing right next to the path we needed to take across the golf course, an alleyway which ran along the back of all those houses that had crept furthest up the Downs. A long stand of trees made for excellent cover, but he'd still be far too close for comfort.

It was fascinating to watch him though; I'd seen the phenomenon before, most memorably in *Day of the Dead* when all the zombies head towards the shopping mall. It was like a fragment of memory left behind, as if they were on autopilot. Maybe that's what the zombies gathering at the door of Lou's office in Crawley were doing: unthinking, repetitive behaviour, as if acting out habits even death couldn't break.

The skin over his face was pinched tight and you could see cracks in the surface of his forehead. It looked like he'd been in the sun a while. He rasped as he took a clumsy backswing, before letting fly, spinning on the spot and falling to the ground. We watched his awkward routine for a while – he'd take a swing and either fall flat onto his parched head or lose grip and send his club arcing away into the bushes.

'This is really fucked up.' Lou said.

'He's got full motor function still; isn't that mad?' I grinned. 'It's not just grabbing, biting and walking. Watch; he even goes for another club when he loses one.'

'We should cut across whilst he's still busy.' Lou was getting anxious. It would be a close call, but he had his back to us as he crouched down to his jumble of golf clubs. Sure enough, when he was happy with his choice he carried on swinging as we edged our way along the cool, leafy path, strewn with brown fir needles from the trees above our heads. Floyd was good, I kept him on the lead but I don't think he wanted to bother much with this one; he'd seen living people in that same position, in identical clothes, teeing off from that spot not a week before. I noticed that not once was he putting a golf ball in front of him. He always bent down, but only ever just pinched lightly at the air an inch above the ground before standing up and surveying the horizon with glassy eyes.

The path dips at the half-way mark, and soon we were at a sand pit and a lush green oval with a flag. I wondered if he'd been thinking about his handicap all week, before he caught zombie 'flu. What was the story of his death? Had he been infected up here, bitten as he sized up the ninth? I wondered if his car was still in the car park, or if he'd walked. He might have even walked here after he died. Had he eaten already, and the brief satisfaction of appetite allowed him to turn to patterns of his former life; or was the need to play golf stronger than the bloodlust?

The path led past the green and up to a stile and an old flint barn, then out onto the track which would eventually take us up to the centre of Cissbury

Ring. As we got out onto the more open grass I checked behind us, but Lou gripped my arm.

'Fuck, don't do that!' I exhaled. 'You scared the hell out of me!'

'There!' she hissed. My guts twisted at the word. At first I couldn't see what she was pointing at, until a bloody face appeared in the long grass. Floyd howled, straining on his leash until it slipped from Lou's grip and sent her into splits with a grassy skid. I helped her up as the man's huge frame lumbered out onto the green.

'Come on, we need to get to the stile.'

True to form, Floyd was barking and growling around his feet, circling until he was behind him.

'Let's just get some distance between us and him. Floyd's keeping him at bay.'

He was doing more than that. He jumped up onto the man's back and tugged at some scalp, using his weight to bring the oaf down onto his knees and backwards, grabbing at the air behind his head. Floyd bounded round to face him, protecting us. When we were at the stile I whistled for Floyd and was pleased to see him following, tail wagging in self-congratulation. We continued for a few metres up the track, before I held up my hands.

'I want to stop him. He'll just follow us all the way up there. Grab the mutt.'

My wife said nothing. I thumbed at my spade on my back. I didn't want to use the sprayer; the grass was as dry as I'd ever seen it, golden in the blazing sun. The big freak had stopped at the stile and was now pawing at an imaginary latch as Lou handed me the spade. I held it differently to when I was about to dig over the vegetable patch or bury a bird that Maui had given me, weighing it up in both hands as I strode up to the big guy. This one's for *Shaun*.

I heaved the spade over my right shoulder and panged it hard into the side of his head with a satisfactory ring. As I jumped over the stile he collapsed to the ground, not unconscious but stunned, as if his limbs weren't responding. I stood over him. Teeth gnashing he looked up at me through eyelashes glued up with some kind of dried seepage, presumably from his puffed-up eyes. His face looked as broiled from the sun as the golfer's.

Now I did hold my spade like I was about to dig, placing my right foot on the top of the blade. I hovered over his neck, eager to make a clean break, and then drove my foot down. It came off in one go with a gristly crunch, his head rolling cut side up, his body motionless. I peered down onto his neck wound. It was clean, and I had even dug three or four inches into the turf below. There was no blood, certainly no squirting, but through the splinters of bone and bubbles of yellow fat I could see the meat of his neck, dark and marbled like well-aged beef. I retched a little, not from the sight or the thought of what I'd just done, but from the egg-smell which hit me like a slap. I wiped what little black oil there was from the spade on the long grass by the fence and walked back up the path to Lou.

Floyd was panting in the heat, his tongue lolling around his chops, so I checked up and down the path and kicked out a deep dimmock in the dry ground with my heel. I poured some water into it from the container which he drank in gulps as Lou reattached my spade. After a three minute breather we headed onwards and upwards. The climb got steeper in the beating sun but we met no more of them on the path. We reached the prow of a hill after another twenty minutes, so we took another break.

Lou pointed out two figures far away below us on the golf course. I freed up the binoculars from straps of the pressure sprayer - they used to belong to my granddad, a leaving present from when he worked on the factory floor of an aviation company at Shoreham Airport. They were made by Bosch, but were so old it was spelt Bosh. I used a dark, tall tree on the horizon line as a reference point and followed the curve of the hillside until I had them in my sights. They were a man and a woman, and she had long black hair matted to her face and neck. She was bare-breasted, and from their angle I estimated she was late forties, both of them just staring up into the sky. It looked like their eyes had rolled back in their heads. Did they know each other two days ago? Where they a couple, or had they been united through newfound common pursuits?

I turned and looked up the hill, towards the mound of Cissbury with its steep fortified earth trenches ringing the smooth, wide plateau which was dotted with trees. It was close now, half a mile away or so - but the steepest climb was to come.

'I can't see anyone up there. Let's do it.' I said, helping Lou to her feet. She'd been stripping grasses of their feathery heads and had stuck a stem between her teeth like she would when she walked the dog. I usually told her that she looked like a yokel, but right then I was just pleased to see her enjoying the hike. We forced ourselves up the increasing incline, Lou watching me to see if I'd noticed her walking backwards.

'It helps' she explained. 'Try it.' I did try it and it didn't help, although I had told myself any perceived benefit would be purely psychological before I'd even tried it. I wished I didn't do that so often, any help would have been welcome in the ever-increasing heat. Facing backwards, though, and with the height we'd gained, I could see hundreds of ribbons of smoke pouring up from the surrounding towns. They hung in the sky before dissolving into watery, nicotine-yellow smog. The constant arid buzz of the crickets was deliciously lubricated by birdsong. Small blue butterflies burst up from the tall stems at the sides of the path, and I saw a kestrel hovering stock-still in the cobalt air. We soon reached a point where higher vegetation lined the track, and I got edgy so we moved on cautiously to the sound of Floyd panting. A dark, dense wood closed in on our right and I constantly squinted into the gloom, trying to see shapes that weren't there. We passed some old water tanks on the ground, like coffins.

We could see the oldest, most forbidding tree standing like a sentinel on the corner of the woods closest to the Ring, its tangle of branches overlooking a large V-shaped notch cut into the steep earth ramparts to mark an entrance to the hill fort. Our path led straight through this gap up and onto the centre of the Ring. We climbed and climbed, fighting the weight of our kit before finally flopping under a couple of low trees, panting.

We lay on our backpacks, watching the sky through the twisted boughs of the wind-stunted trees. Lou unclipped Floyd's lead as he lay sprawled out in a patch of long, cool grass, before starting to take off her backpack. I could have done with a spliff and an icy beer at that point but I didn't have either, and anyway I couldn't just sit there watching Lou unpack. I sighed, stretched and rolled onto my front; delaying the inevitable tent erection indignity by faking death for no-one in particular - Lou had seen all of my comedy faces and visual illusions plenty of times before, so she wasn't obliged to comment. I enjoyed the cool grass on my face though, and thought how clever my young pup was. I felt sleepy.

The level plateau sustained a hundred trees by my reckoning, although most of it was open; covered in long grasses or bare patches of chalky earth and criss-crossed with pathways. We stood on the southernmost tip of Cissbury Ring and it made a perfect natural camp – flat ground, rich topsoil for digging and pegging-in tents, and for cover a stand of low trees. I estimated roughly

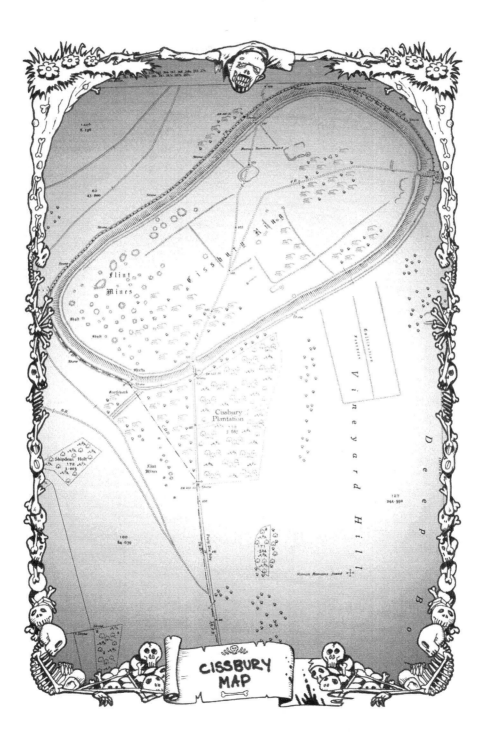

CISSBURY
MAP

where the tree shadows would fall in the early morning sun, a trick I'd learnt from years of camping. I hated waking up sweating in a tent, it was highly unpleasant. So we put the tent up right where the shadows would be, with little trouble, away from the tree's overhang so we wouldn't get wet – if it ever rained again. Our tent had a four-man side-pod for sleeping, off a central section that you could stand up in. One whole side of the tent could be unzipped and put out on poles like a canopy. The top foot and a half of the structure also unpeeled like a banana to reveal clear plastic windows - perfect for seeing the starlight at night, and for confusing trapped insects by day.

Whilst I sorted out our fold-up aluminium table Lou set up the sleeping area and put in it all the clothes, washing stuff and what little valuables we had with us, and then started unpacking the cooking items onto the table. The table came in a thin bag, but when its top and legs were unfurled and the thing was clipped together it made a very sturdy surface, around three feet square.

She started to make tea on the little gas stove, but I wanted to get a fire going. After a bit of an argument about whether it was too hot for a fire and whether that mattered anyway I won by default after suggesting it was a.) good camp craft, and b.) we could save the gas. Ray Mears would be watching over us like Yoda.

I decided against getting fuel for the fire from the dark woods below. I could find all the types of firewood that I needed, from kindling up to logs, right here on top of the Ring. I'd also found a long log for both of us to sit on, and scraped off a circle of turf about four feet wide around the fire, to create a ring of bare earth so it couldn't spread. I laid down a row of thumb-thick sticks like a raft to start with. I built a tripod of the three longest lengths I had, and hooked the kettle over the centre so it dangled about a foot and a half over my first camp fire in years. I remembered then how much I'd enjoyed the Cub Scouts. I never rose to the heady rank of Sixer though.

I pulled my lighter out and the flames took quickly. Lou made a great cup of steaming hot tea and gave Floyd some more water and a handful of biscuits. I unhooked the red-hot kettle, swapped it for the biggest pan we had with us and poured one of our bags of chilli into it. Refreshed and unpacked, we took our tall flask mugs and set off for a wander, Floyd weaving between us. We found the triangulation pillar and I told Lou about the men who had positioned these all around the country; the network of volunteers who, in the 1930s or something like that, dragged bags of sand and cement up every mountain and across every moor in the country, working to a specific set of instructions to create thousands and thousands of pillars all exactly the same as the one Floyd was pissing up against. By looking for the nearest other two trig points with a special telescope we made the first accurate map of anywhere in the world, triangle by triangle, working in blazing sun, driving snow and howling winds.

The thing that always got me about that story was that they obviously had no cement mixers, no radios, and no four-wheel drive vehicles to get them there. Of course they had no accurate maps either, and instead had to rely on the combined guile, hardiness and cunning that blessed the gaggle of ex-Army types, amateur ramblers and sporty chaps who volunteered for the task from all around the country. Even if you found the volunteers, nowadays they'd drown in Health and Safety red tape before they'd even pulled on their hiking socks.

The flat top of the Ring always appeared much larger than I had remembered, but the biggest bonus was the ancient fortifications. Earth and chalk had been dug from a deep ditch which circled the whole structure, and piled up at the edge of the plateau creating a steep drop-off away from the edge of the Ring. The outer rim had also been built up to form a narrow walkway all round Cissbury Ring, separated by the deep ditch.

Floyd was constantly nose-to-the-ground, working in curves and sometimes doubling back. We walked slowly; I had taken on the gait of a country gent, whilst Lou had found another stalk to chew. We found lots of depressions and hollows in the ground – the remains of the ancient flint mines, I guessed – some with trees growing in them, some deep and fenced off. The views were awesome up there, five-hundred feet above the gentle swell of the surrounding countryside, even through the thin veil of smoke above the roads and the more built-up areas. On the South side we could see Beachy Head and the Seven Sisters looking left and the Isle of Wight looking right, possibly sixty miles apart. We could see Devil's Dyke above Brighton and what I assumed was as far as Surrey when we looked north, although the smoke on the horizon there was thicker and darker. Lou counted ten windmills but I think she must have double up on some. In one of the back fields was a huge combine harvester, pointing an angled tube down into the open top of a lorry next to it. The scene looked frozen in time, with the flow of grain stopped dead and the blades still. Where were the drivers? Had they been infected sitting in their cabs; or had they fled the scene across the open fields, screaming for loved ones?

After reaching the northernmost point of the ancient structure we sat down, and I made farting noises with a long piece of grass. When I got bored, which was quite quickly, I laid back and let the sounds of the glorious English summer refuel my heart and soul. Soon I could smell something familiar, which made me salivate and realise how hungry I was - chilli. Floyd smelt it too, and started to whine. As he led us in a straight line back to the camp, Lou and I walked hand-in-hand, soaking in the calm, restoring our nerves and making some sense of the crazy couple of days we'd been through.

The pot was bubbling furiously, so I ripped a couple of bread rolls from the packet and handed one to Lou, who had laid out our mess tins on the ground. She used the tea towel to pour the chilli, giving me more than her. We sat and ate in silence, occasionally grinning at each other, and relishing the moment. I used a second bread roll to make a 'sloppy Joe' out of the last of my chilli, and also to mop up my tin. Lou put the kettle on for another cup of tea, and I grabbed my home-made club and fetched my knife from the tent. I sat back on my log after taking off my vest and wrapping it around my head, and made a start on shaping the handle so it was a bit more comfortable to grip.

I was beginning to worry about Al. It was mid-afternoon, and we hadn't heard from him, even though I'd been intermittently turning the radio on to check. I was about to say something to Lou when we heard a huge thump, like a cross between thunder and someone flicking a giant towel. I stood and whirled around me, unable to pinpoint the noise – but I had to do a double-take when I saw a black globe hundreds of feet across growing like bubblegum above the centre of Worthing. I couldn't work out what I was seeing for what seemed like an age as it grew and grew; only when I saw its deep buttercup yellow underbelly when it started to rise into the air did I realise that it was the gas tank in the town centre exploding. It blossomed into a crimson ball, its surface like those close-up photos of the sun. We felt the heat on our cheeks, even though we were two or three miles away. As the vast fireball lifted up it cast a shadow which travelled eastwards, seeming to suck in the rows of terraces and plunging the green parks into darkness.

'Well at least that'll get a few of them.' I said.

'I hope no-one we know was left alive in there before that went off.'

I got my binoculars out and saw a river of fire from the town centre leading up to the hospital. The huge gas container which had stood between the two was now an open spray of twisted blackened metal. The wall of flame had left fires dotted all around the town, catching the oldest buildings first, turning into a blazing fury, creating its own wind which whipped up the flaming debris. Trees shrivelled and warped, sending dry leaves into the vortex like fireworks, settling on hot roofs and soft tarmac. Cars popped like bright yellow corn; offices and shops spewed fire from blackened windows; the smoke rose higher.

We watched for as long as the fading light would let us, sipping our tea and taking turns on the binoculars. I managed to pull myself away before the sun went down completely and gathered four loads of firewood which stacked together so high I could only just see over the top. Floyd had whined at me to come with me each time I returned to dump it at camp, but I wanted him to stay with Lou whilst she neatly sorted and stacked the wood. We had seen no other soul, living or otherwise since that morning, so I felt confident going alone. I still made sure I was back well before the darkness came and shrouded the camp.

Al still hadn't turned up by the time night came. I knew his parent's house was well away from the gas tank, and he had no reason to head into the madness of town. I couldn't think about Al though, because if I did I would start to think about Jay and Vaughan; my parents and my brother; all the other people we had left behind. If we had survived that day, there was no reason why there wouldn't be others.

A patchwork of flaming buildings across the towns lit up in the night like lava on the slopes of a volcano. They were linked by blazing roads; the intense vehicle fires looking like psychedelic dew on cobwebs. The brightest flames of all were in the middle of Worthing, spreading unavoidably until they hit the sea. I hate to say it, but it looked beautiful.

We heard a plane that night, probably a passenger jet by the heavy sound of its engines, and clearly in trouble going by the erratic changes in pitch, but we couldn't see it anywhere above us. We listened breathlessly as the whine of the engines dropped, struggling, and then stopped dead with a series of muffled crumps.

Lou sobbed, so I stroked her hair. We turned to our campfire, sipped our tea and lost an hour or two watching the fleeting sparks lifting from the embers, relishing the cooling balm of the night breeze. We decided to turn in early; well, early for me, but late for Lou for a weekday. Not that that mattered much now. We'd brought a twenty-foot steel dog tether with us, which we secured to a tree away from the fire but so Floyd could keep warm in its glow. We made a fuss of him before zipping up the tent behind us. He was quiet at first and I thought he'd be okay until we heard him whining for us. This was the first night in his life he'd not slept in the same space as us, but I wanted him to keep watch on the camp and it was best to get him used to the situation. He'd have to grow up fast. Eventually he was dozing, and I could hear his soft snores above the crackle of the fire. But gradually, as our ears became used to the quiet, we started to hear noises. Rasping, hoarse moans and, once, the blood-curdling scream of a real living human carried faintly to us on the breeze. I sat bolt upright at the sound of it, but Lou gripped my arm and begged me not to go outside. As if I would. I was too scared to make a joke, too scared to even pretend I would. We gripped each other tightly; the droning of the crickets peppered with the groaning of the undead thousands that surrounded our little plastic tent on a hill in the middle of the night.

[day 0003]

There are not many fears that bright sunshine cannot melt. I was pleased to find that my estimated position of the shade from the morning sun was spot-on. Lou was up already and I could hear the dog noisily slurping water outside the tent.

'How long have you been up?' I blinked in the sun.

'Good morning grumpy. I've been up for about twenty minutes.' She yawned and stretched. I clambered out of the tent and stood in my pants looking out to sea – what I could see of it. The fires were really taking hold, and some pockets had spread out to the terraced houses and leafy streets of the suburbs. The smoke tainted the crisp freshness of the morning air even up on top of the Ring. I got my binoculars, walked to the triangulation point - officially now the tallest thing around, except for the odd tree - and stood on it, scanning the area surrounding the Ring from the fields to the woods. No zombies, so I peered through the infernos in the town to try to find any familiar landmarks. The only structures that weren't twisted and flattened to the ground were church spires. In the chaotic, spark-spinning winds some of their bells were sounding with a heavy ring through the scorched stonework, the muffled sound reaching us warped by the heat and setting my teeth on edge.

We could see that our road hadn't been caught up in the inferno even without the binoculars; the nearest flames were patchy and at least a dozen streets away. I could only make out the back of our house pretty much looking straight down our street from where we were. I couldn't quite see the workshop but it looked like the ladder was still against the side of the house. I was about to pull the binoculars away when I saw movement - a car, driving from the middle of our street northwards.

I couldn't make out the colour but it was dark like Al's. I wondered for a moment if he'd even understand my message, but quickly scolded myself for underestimating him. I tracked the car to the end of the road, and saw it turning left onto the A27, before I lost it behind the trees lining the road. It might not even be him, I thought as I ran back to the camp - what if it wasn't him? What if someone else had understood my message, and was coming up here?

'Lou! A car!' I panted.

'Really?' she was pegging the bottom of the tent up, to get air flowing through it. Floyd jumped up at me, wagging his tail like I'd been gone for a year.

'Where are the radios?'

'Here, on the table,' she was on her feet and into the tent, eagerly snatching both radios up and tuning into the sound of static on one of them. She handed me the other.

'He said he'd be on that preset.' She pointed. 'We can go on this one if we want to talk to each other.'

'Okay, but let's not waste the battery. I'll keep mine on standby,' I said generously, thinking that really I should be in charge of the radios. 'He was going up the A27 coming this way.'

'Do you think it is Al then?'

'I saw him coming out of our street. I'll bet a fiver it's him.'

I checked out what I could see of the route up to the Ring. Given that there was absolutely nothing on the roads except car wrecks and walking corpses, I scanned our usual route through Findon Valley and up to the Cissbury Ring car park, wherever the view was unbroken by trees or houses.

'How long does it take us to drive up here, on a quiet day?' I asked. Lou usually drove; it was her car, although I had been driving for thirteen years. I had no points, never had a speeding ticket and only ever had one parking ticket. I didn't drive much.

'About ten minutes.'

I waited and watched. Ten minutes came and went, and turned into twenty.

'Maybe it wasn't him, Sweetpea.' She kissed my cheek and rubbed the small of my back, and made my helmet tingle. I turned and kissed her on the forehead, and she leaned up to my lips. We hugged.

Lou filled the kettle as I fetched some small fuel to put on the embers from last night, which were still kicking out a fair amount of heat. I stacked some big fuel straight on top of the dry twigs and the fire spat into life. I hung the kettle from the tripod, the three sticks scorched now but still holding true as the green, wet insides resisted the heat. As I went to sit in the shade where Floyd sensibly lay panting, I heard the radio.

At first I thought Lou's radio was burping up some static indigestion, but it was a voice, broken and garbled. I turned up the volume and searched the Findon road again with my binoculars. I saw nothing, but the stuttering voice continued, getting stronger and more frequent, until I heard, as clear as a bell:

'Hang on...'

The radio fell silent but then, through the binoculars, I caught sight of a magnificent thing; an old estate with a buckled bonnet, coursing in and out of the burnt-out traffic at a terrific pace. Al had a clear run for a few hundred feet and no zombies in the road.

'Anyone there, over?'

'Yes we are, matey!' I exclaimed.

'Are you there chums, over?' Al crackled.

'You've got to press the button on the side, darling.' Lou was pointing to the handset, but was too far away to be specific. I found a button, and tried that.

'Yes we are, matey!'

'Wicked! Are you walking the dog where I think you are, over?'

'We are indeed! Did you see your old folks?'

Silence, even though he still had a clear stretch, as far as I could see.

'It's Al!' I turned to Lou.

'I heard, Sweetpea. Let's have a quick cuddle before he gets here. I won't get a look-in as soon as you two start talking camp-craft.'

I was so glad we were going through this together; I dreaded to think what my life would be like without her on a normal day, let alone now.

'There, by the garage.'

I handed Lou the binoculars, and watched her as she tracked the car, turning off into the little flint-knapped hamlet. When it was my go on the binoculars I saw the Audi kicking up dust as Al wound through the narrow streets, deserted and dotted with clothes, cars and bodies stripped to the bone. He kept disappearing from view behind houses, walls and lines of trees, until we eventually saw him coming out of the coppice at the bottom of the hill, and thundering up the single tarmac track which led to the car park.

When Al and I would drive up here to walk Floyd and Dmitri he'd always take it at a cracking pace. You could see all the way up the hill, and as it was a single track with passing places, cars coming down would usually do so cautiously. I would shout 'Left left over crest', and we'd laugh. It could get hairy if we'd been playing PlayStation that morning and Al's eyes were tuned in.

Al parked up and pulled a big rucksack from the back seat, along with what looked like a tent bag and a plastic carrier bag. He also wielded an aluminium baseball bat and had a huge hunting knife on his belt.

'You alright mate?' I shouted, cupping my hands.

'Shush!' Lou prodded me. 'You've got the radio, you donut.'

'Al, we're up here, we can see you,' I said into the hand-set. 'Do you want us to come down?'

'No, mate - just keep an eye on my back,' Al said, springing the boot for Dmitri who knew exactly where he was. 'I haven't seen anyone since Findon anyway. Are you alone up there, over?'

'Yeah, it's just me, Lou and the dog. Oh, I think he's coming down to see you.'

Floyd had seen the bobbing white flag that is the tip of another beagle's tail, and with his own wagging furiously Floyd half-tumbled, half-sprinted his way down the slope, ignoring the steep wood-and-gravel steps. A light stand of trees covered the bottom of the slope, and for a minute or two we'd lost sight of all three of them.

'Al, we can't see you.'

'Over,' said Lou, even though she wasn't holding the radio and I wasn't pressing the button. I knew her well enough to know that she wasn't commanding me to say 'over', it was just a subconscious acknowledgement of protocol voiced at no-one in particular.

'It looks clear, and I can't hear anything,' Al replied. 'The dogs would know if there were any about long before us anyway.'

'Over,' said Lou again, watching the dogs burst out from under the cover of the trees and up the open chalk and flint path, followed soon by Al, pushing down on his legs for extra lift. Before long the dogs were upon us, and Lou dropped to the floor giggling as they both bounded around her enthusiastically. As Al reached the final few steps I turned the radio off. He did the same, nodding but silent. He sat down cross legged, catching his breath as beads of sweat pierced his beetroot forehead.

'Room for a brave one?' he panted. I laughed.

'How are your folks?' I asked.

'Dead.' he said, plainly, his eyes closed. I shot Lou a glance, who was sitting up, a dog under each arm.

'What happened?' Lou asked.

'They're both dead, I've seen both of them, and buried them in the back garden. I spent the night there, packed a few things, and then came here. My mum died peacefully, I'm sure of that and I'm glad of that, but I don't want to say any more,' he sat up and looked at me. 'Okay chum? I don't want to talk about it, ever, and that's that. Okay?' Lou looked glum. I took him at his word.

'Kettle's on.'

Breaking Through
[day 0003]

Al was obviously ready for a fight. The tent bag turned out to be full of clothes, but he'd brought a load of useful equipment from his parent's house too, which we unloaded from the Audi. First to come out was a brand new set of kitchen knives, the same set I had at home.

'That's not for slicing and dicing those zombie fuckers, they're for you. I take it you'll be doing all the cooking?' He had a spliff between his gritted teeth. We took armfuls of stuff from the car up to the camp, along with more water and – lucky Floyd – two big bags of dog biscuits. Next came some heavy white canvas.

'It's my dad's sail. I've got the mainsail, the jib and the spinnaker,' he said. It meant nothing to me.

'We're not going sailing, chum.' I was confused.

'No, you dick, I figured we'd be camping and I haven't got a tent. I didn't want to impose on you guys, even though yours sleeps about twenty. I'll Ray Mears it, it'll be fine.' He had some rope too, and we hiked it all up to the top of the ring. Lou was feeding the dogs and getting another cuppa on the go.

'I've got some more teabags and coffee in the car.' Al said

'You hate coffee.' I said.

'Yes, but you two don't. I didn't know if you'd brought any.'

'Thanks, man.'

I could tell he was pleased to see us. We were pleased to see him, and Floyd was certainly pleased to see Dmitri. On the whole, Al's choice of luggage could be summed up by the phrase 'practical hardware', except for the clothes. Al's impeccable sense of style was a mystery to me. He'd even brought the Nike Jordan No. 4's still in their box. A much-visited topic of conversation was what we'd take with us in a crisis – zombie or otherwise – and he'd clearly been thinking about it. I saw a pad and pen in the front (why hadn't I thought of that?), so I got Lou to start an inventory as everything was brought up to the camp. By the time his car was empty, we had added to the camp's stores:

1 x baseball bat (aluminium)
1 x billy-club (his dad's)
2 x garden spades
1 x pitch fork
1 x scythe
1 x hand saw
1 x curved tree saw
1 x hatchet
1 x axe
2 x petrol cans (empty)
1 x tool box (also his dad's)
300 x DVD envelopes (?)
1 x *The Nuclear Survival Handbook* - Barry Popkess
12 x candles
2 x towels
1 x pack antibacterial handwipes-
1 x lock-picking set
1 x first aid kit
50m fishing line
2 x maps West Sussex
Tinned food (various – Lou started a separate list of the food)
4 x pints milk

Al's personal possessions totalled:

1 x ground mat
1 x sleeping bag
1 x pillow
1 x rucksack full of clothes
1 x pair walking boots (Timberland)
1 x *Blackstar* vinyl LP

He'd also brought some other bits up from his car, which included:

1 x mains spotlight
1 x box matches

1 x roll bin bags
1 x tin opener
1 x knife and fork set.

'Where did you get the lock-picks from?' I asked Al.

'My dad,' he said grimly. I asked Al whether his dad being a jeweller actually justified him owning a lock-picking set. He shrugged, saying nothing. I tried to be light-hearted, but gave up. I was on unfamiliar territory here – no-one I knew other than grandparents had died before, and they had done so when I was much younger when you just got extra pocket money and pats on the head. Right then it felt like not knowing whether or not your parents were alive was much easier than knowing for sure they were dead.

After a while I got Al to tell us of his journey. He steered clear of mentioning his parents, describing what he'd seen driving through Worthing the morning before. He didn't tell us what he'd found in the house, but told us that he had fought off attacks throughout the night, and in the morning had reversed through the garden fence so he could back the car right up to their living room doors. He'd packed the car up, raiding the larder for food, which was in a cupboard which joined the house to their garage. He hadn't realised the gas tank in Worthing had blown up, thinking the noise was thunder, but had seen a lot of fires driving back to our house that morning. He'd seen my note I had painted on the front door and driven straight up here on a dangerously empty petrol tank. I told him I had been tracking his progress from the house, not knowing if it was him or another survivor. Like us, apart from the old vicar in Upper Beeding two nights before, he'd not seen any human activity.

'I saw one getting into his car. He had no keys – or trousers for that matter – but he knew where the ignition was. I was watching him, it was fucking creepy.'

I told him about the golfer we'd seen as we started to unfurl the sails. They were old and had a faint yellow tint; probably from some waterproof coating rather than neglect. His dad was meticulous about everything; he'd laid real wooden floorboards all through the ground floor of his house, cutting and staining all the wood himself, even leaving it all stacked up inside to acclimatise for a year before he started work. When he'd finished though, he found that he still couldn't sit down to enjoy his handiwork – there were two holes at each end of every plank, where he'd screwed them down. They bugged him so much he ended up carving metres and metres of doweling exactly the same diameter as the holes, staining it to exactly the same hue as the floorboards, and then set about plugging up all the holes. All seven thousand one hundred and forty-four of them, and yes, he'd counted. Al was the same, but he was also a stoner, so the special guilt that laziness brings tended to drive him even further than his father would go.

Al was about to prove that point. I'd imagined slinging the biggest sail over a branch of a tree, pegging it out and being done with it. That's certainly what I would have done, but Al had far grander plans. We worked through the day, laying out the canvas on his preferred bit of ground, next to the sturdy tree he'd chosen to form the central support. We'd found a stand of young, whippy saplings to the north of the Ring and sawed them through, about a foot from the ground. They were strong and straight. Al knifed a small circle like a dinner plate in the centre of the canvas to accommodate the tree trunk, and then from that cut a straight line to one edge of the sail. He crawled underneath it and dragged it around the base of the old tree, then lifted the canvas up above his head to where the lowest branches of the tree met the trunk. It would be like a tepee with a tree growing out of it.

'The top will be up here; then it'll drop outwards to the ground.' His voice was muffled.

'What about the rain?' I asked.

'Aha!' his head emerged from the hole. 'I've got a plan for that!'

I hadn't thought about bringing any screws or nails from my workshop, and the only ones we did have were the two dozen or so in the end of the makeshift clubs I'd made for me and Lou. I told him I could spare eight of them, which would be fine because it might make them less prone to getting stuck in skulls. He wanted to make the inside of the structure rigid using the young trees we'd cut down - I did think the whole thing was a bit over-ambitious but I kept quiet, pleased to be doing something active. We used the eight long wood screws to attach the hole in the centre of the sail around the tree trunk. He'd got the diameter just right, so it was a nice fit when we screwed them in.

'I'll get some sap to waterproof that,' he said.

As we laid out all the sapling poles in order of length, Al got Lou to whittle sharp little pegs about two inches long out of the green wood left over from making the internal support branches. I'd take a post inside the canvas structure and hold it in place whilst he used a very sharp, thick needle from the lock-picking set to bore holes through the canvas and into the erected poles. We worked on each pole one by one - I stood sweating on the inside of the canvas in the yellow glare, holding them in place. After Al had bored a hole – about six per post - he inserted one of Lou's pegs, gently tapping it in with a hammer. Half way in he would twist each peg, gathering up some canvas and hammering harder, until the pegs were flush with each pole, and a pinch of canvas secured each peg in place. When we were done it was strong, and it got stronger when we pinned the edges of the canvas to the ground with some tent pegs left over from our own primary-coloured synthetic construction, which by now looked positively primitive.

The long cut in the sail acted as an opening which would flap back onto itself for ventilation, and the cone-shape of the canvas meant that there was an overlap of material when it was shut. Al used some rope and made a couple of tie-offs on either side to tether the flap open or shut, and he even made another canopy above the opening, so he had a covered porch area, still seated nicely under the shade of the tree but free from any rain that would filter through its leaves.

'What about rain coming down the trunk?' I asked him. 'You might not be able to get any sap until spring-time.'

'Alright, Nature-boy. That's where this comes in.' He began to attach a bin-bag to the top of the trunk inside his tent, wrapping the opening all the way around it.

'I don't think I'll get too much water coming in anyway,' he said, 'but if I do this'll collect it and I'll wake up to a nice big bag of fresh water.'

He tucked the excess into the top of the tent, took the smallest sail which looked like a little parachute, and laid it down to cover the ground. By the time we had finished, it would have been dark outside if it wasn't for a nearly full moon and our gas lamp, as well as the fires still roaring in the town below us. Al unpacked his stuff and laid out his sleeping mat, pillow and bag. It was huge inside, and seemed much bigger than our tent. I was jealous. Lou had put on a pot and filled it almost to the brim with two bags of Bolognese sauce.

'It'll only go off in the sun; plus I'm starving.'

We talked long into the night eating sloppy Joes and drinking tea, tending to the fire and telling tales of the day before; of the couple I'd seen staring at the sun, and of the zombies trying the door handles. Al had seen many bodies; people who, it seemed, had been killed for their flesh and never made the transition to zombie, people with no faces, plucked throats and open chests.

The dogs snored by the fire, Floyd occasionally twitching at his dreams and giving off a subsonic yelp. Full of hot food and stories, and tired from the day's building, we all turned in. Floyd stayed outside with Dmitri, and we didn't hear a squeak from him all night.

[day 0004]

When I woke up, once again Lou was awake and had already begun her day. Al was asleep still, and everything around us was very quiet. Occasionally you'd get a throat-catching gasp of acrid smoke poisoning the summer air, as a great dark cloud would listlessly drift our way, but on the whole it was bright and hot. The fires in town had got much worse now, spreading westwards; so hot in places it was twisting metal, but I couldn't see that much through the binoculars. Sometimes I could smell sulphur, but it was somehow drier than the rotten stink from the zombies. When he woke, Al accepted a cup of tea and began using the scythe to mow down some of the longer grass so the campfire didn't spread.

Lou took the dogs around the lower walkway which encircled the perimeter of Cissbury Ring. I didn't like it, as we still didn't know whether they would – or could - come up to the top of the Ring. Lou had shushed my worries confidently, somehow assured by the lazy haze of summer all around us. The dogs were probably the best early-warning system we could hope for though, and no doubt I could hear them from anywhere on the Ring if something happened to Lou. To take my mind away from picturing painful deaths my wife might suffer, I compiled a list of things I wanted to bring from the house. The food wouldn't last long, and Al had only brought a few tins and some biscuits with him. Even the lack of water had to be addressed - the South Downs has no water at all on it, there are no cool streams or trickling brooks up here. Any water that falls just soaks straight through the ground, which is why shepherds had built scores of clay-lined dew-ponds in the crooks of the valleys on the Downs, to condense the morning dew into recurring pools of water for the flocks to drink from. None of them were close enough to serve our purposes though.

I thought of the two survival books I had, and I was even thinking longer-term about the books I had on growing vegetables. I wasn't sure help would be coming - I wasn't sure we weren't the last three people left on earth.

'Hello Mr. Frodo sir!' It was a man's voice but it hadn't come from Al, who stood and peered over the V-shaped notch and down the chalky path to Worthing. If a human's ears could ever look pricked, Al's did. I squinted through the smoke filtering up through the trees, and caught sight of two figures. I froze.

'Hello Mr. Frodo, sir! It's Samwise Gamgee!' It was our friend Jay.

'What the fuck about me?' The second voice was quieter, mumbling. That was Vaughan. 'Who am I supposed to be?'

'You can be Merry, or Pippin. They're both gay.' Jay snapped. I could tell they had had enough of each other to be pleasant. I stood up as Al belted over the prow of the ramparts towards them. Jay had a huge backpack – good lad – Vaughan carried a couple of Tesco carrier bags.

'Chums! We thought you lot might be up here!' A huge grin spread across Jay's chops. His bulky frame was topped with a shaven scalp. They made their way up the final steep incline and into the camp, and after we exchanged much back-slapping and derogatory comments about each other's sexual preferences we all slumped onto the cool grass under the two trees at the entrance – they both sweated profusely and were grateful of the shade. I handed the water to Vaughan, who looked the worse for wear. He blinked the salt sweat away from his squinting eyes but seemed to make it worse, so he had to prod a couple of fingers under his glasses to wipe them instead. He was shorter than the rest of us, without one ounce of spite in him, which made him an easy target for our often cruel jibes as he wouldn't answer back, he'd just laugh and shrug it off. Jay wore his emotions on his sleeve, and as he was telling us about their day his mean exterior was betrayed by a child-like excitement.

'I said to Vaughan, "let's get up Cissbury Ring", didn't I Vaughan? Then we realised you might be up here. It's perfect!'

'Very handy if you need to fend off advancing hordes,' I said. 'We've hardly seen any of them since the golf course though. We don't know if they can come up here or not.' I turned to Vaughan. 'You've come prepared!'

'This is all Jay's stuff,' Vaughan said, nodding towards the carrier bags. 'I got caught short a bit - I knew something was up, but I hadn't seen the news. It was nuts - I saw four car crashes.' He took a draft of water then handed it to Jay.

'I saw a bloke's guts fall out of his belly, onto the pavement, and he kept going.' Jay was gasping for breath between gulps. 'He didn't even break his step. Fuck only knows what the fucking fuck is going on.' He drank some more.

'They're slow though, aren't they,' I said.

'Yeah,' Jay answered in a Deep South drawl, 'they're dead... they're all messed-up.'

'*Night of the Living Dead?*' I enquired with a grin.

'Well spotted,' Jay said, handing me the water.

'Zombies.' Vaughan was beaming at me. 'How do you feel?'

'A bit sick, if I'm honest.'

'It's not right, is it?' Al said.

'Nope.' Jay replied. 'Luckily we only had to deal with a few at a time. I took two of their heads off, they stopped then. "If you kill the brain, you kill the ghoul".'

'*Night of the Living Dead* again,' I whispered to Vaughan.

'I know,' he sighed, 'he's been talking about nothing else since we left his house.'

'You were staying at your parents' house this week weren't you?' I asked Jay tentatively, subconsciously observing Al's reaction to the word "parents".

'Yeah, mum was doing my washing. They're both fine,' he said, 'although mum was a bit freaked out. We barricaded them in their cellar with all the food. They'll be okay until some help comes. What about you lot?'

'One time we took out - what was it, five of them? That was in Brighton,' Al explained. 'But there were three of us, plus the dogs.'

'You've been all the way to Brighton?' Jay's voice was muffled as he dragged his sodden T-shirt over his head.

'We went all the way to fucking Crawley mate, to pick Lou up. Her car got nicked, so Al drove up there.'

'How did you manage that?' Vaughan was incredulous. 'We only met them in groups of two or three at most. But you had five of them?'

'Yeah, we saw them off. There wasn't too many of them for us.' Al was puffing his chest out. 'We got some tools.' He grinned.

'You want to avoid the point of critical mass,' I said to three pairs of rolling eyes, but I had a captive audience. 'It's crucial to all zombie action. The tipping point, I think it's called too. The more of them obviously the worse it gets, but you'll get to a certain number of zombies when even though you can out-run them, it will be impossible to get away. You're herd-feed.'

'But what about *28 Days Later*? They can run in that.' Vaughan asked.

'No mate - that was fucking rubbish. They really spoilt it all. Zombies don't run. I'd rather watch *Aliens* or *Zulu*. Zombie films are all about the creeping advance, the slow menace, the inevitable point of absorption. If one of them goes for you its easy to fend him off; two's fine with a spade...'

'*Shaun of the Dead*.' Jay ventured.

'...exactly. But if there are three of them you're pushing it a bit, especially if you let one grab your sleeve or your foot.'

'But if there's two of you?'

'With two people you can see off four, five, six of them even - they're that slow. If one of you has a firearm, keep working the heads, the other gets busy with a spade...'

'Or axe,' Al suggested.

'...or axe, yes, but long-handled. Keep plugging away at the neck. No, mate, as soon as they start running everyone's had it. There's no point fighting, just line up. Running zombies are for the birds mate. Your Romero zombie is the blueprint.'

'Someone once said "you never have to reload a spade, and they never get jammed". Who was that?' Jay asked. It was a genuine question, as opposed to an impromptu zombie cinema pop-quiz. 'And where is Lou?'

'Oh, shit, I'd forgotten about the wife. She's taken a walk. Al, which way round the ring did the missus go?'

'That way,' he pointed, 'she's got the dogs mate, she'll be fine!'

'Of course, Floyd and Dmitri are here!' Vaughan loved the dogs. 'Have they been useful?'

'Mate, they go ape-shit for the freaks,' I laughed. 'Floyd's got really good at sniffing them out, and both dogs howl when they sense they're close. They definitely know something's up.'

'They've both been biting loads of infected people, and they don't seem to be affected at all,' Al said. 'They do have to chew a bit on the more sunburnt zombies.'

'Walkers.' Jay said.

'Stinkers.' Vaughan added, and Jay almost muttered something under his breath. There was obviously some conflict here, and I could guess what it was. There were obvious points to be scored in coming up with a word or phrase that everyone ended up using - even in a crisis. However, we were all aware that using someone else's word for something would indicate an opponent's vernacular victory, so we'd each invent our own word, and as a result our collective slang vocabulary tended to be rather diverse. It had been moulded over a decade by such verbal battles, resulting in some great words for joints and bongs, nicknames and insults. We'd also enjoy Spoonerising pairs of words or phrases at each other in a never-ending joust, so "Take a shit" would become "Shake a tit"; "You spilt my beer" became, tentatively: "You built my spear". All of us knew who "Mary Huff" was. We nurtured a playful attitude towards our own language, from word-games to quoting movie dialogue and TV comedy at each other. Jay loved zombie movies as much as he did war films; Al was a fan of American goofball comedy; and we all loved *Alan Partridge*. Lou gawped in awestruck wonderment (at least, that's what I told myself it was - it was probably closer to sceptical exasperation) as we reeled off whole tracts of dialogue word-for-word. The bog-standard phrase "Tough shit, mate", with enough viewings of *Aces High* and *The Battle of Britain*, had slowly morphed into "Hard lines old chap!".

A howl split the air; a long, baying throaty tone, deep and peppered with shorter bursts of barking. It was Dmitri. We looked in the direction, and saw Lou running. We stood frozen for a moment but soon saw that Lou was smiling. She ran down the outer rampart and into the ditch, and then clambered up the steep bank to greet Jay and Vaughan with hugs and kisses. Dmitri was just barking at the presence of new people, not zombies, and soon started wagging when he recognised the newcomers.

'Where's Floyd?' I asked her, and she thumbed over her shoulder breathlessly. I could see him now in the distance, weaving in and out of the clumps of grass. He jumped off the ground, snapping at the air. Oblivious to any kind of panic, he was chasing a fucking butterfly.

We sat in a ring around the fire, seven living things. Jay sat cross-legged and began unpacking his tent in a fairly disorganized manner, as Lou retrieved the last two bags of chilli from the cool-bag and filled the pot again. The one-man tent was up in a matter of minutes, and it was only then that Vaughan wondered where he was going to be sleeping. Jay told us how he had been playing back-gammon with his dad Jerry when they heard a hullabaloo outside. Jerry had been chuckling as the pub over the road had only just opened its doors, but they soon realised the noise was not coming from daytime drunkards but the victims of vicious attacks, right there in the street below. His mum Jinny had tried to get them both to go outside and help people, but alarm bells must have been ringing in Jay's head because after a few minutes of listening to the radio he had persuaded them both to hole up in their cellar. Jay had helped them barricade themselves in from the outside, leaving them with the tools to get themselves out again and all the food in the house. Jay packed up some things, climbed out of one of the top windows and onto the roof, and painted 'IN HERE' in white gloss paint onto the tiles. Then he headed out into the fray.

He tried to help a few people at first, nearly getting bitten in the process, and had soon changed tactic and started running. However, once he'd caught sight of a woman laid out on the bonnet of a car parked in a driveway, he couldn't walk away. She was unconscious, but two men stood over her, one of them scrabbling at her torn dress with his trousers round his ankles, the other one watching as his friend ground away at her limp frame. Jay had taken a sword from his dad's study so he could really go to town on the self-defence front, but decided to put it to good use on those two. He shouted to get their attention, and the one who was watching walked right up to Jay and pulled out a knife. Jay told us that before he had even had time to pull his sword out, the woman sat upright on the car bonnet. She put her hands into the other man's mouth and ripped his cheeks clean away from his face. As she began to chew on the fatty flaps her rapist disengaged and ran past Jay screaming, his skeletal face bubbling scarlet. Jay laughed as he told us that his accomplice had ran after his mate shouting 'Graham - you alright?' Jay hadn't helped the woman.

He fought his way across half a mile of madness to his house, and had been almost scared to death by Vaughan leaping out from behind the bushes where he'd been hiding, waiting for Jay and keeping very still. Together they had shored up their defences as more stinkers gathered round the outside of the house, but a window got smashed and they had started to come in. Throughout the day Jay and Vaughan worked their way from room to room, moving or fighting when it became necessary. When the gas tank in town blew it took all the windows out, and that's when Jay decided to move to the high ground of Cissbury Ring. As soon as it got dark they tooled-up and ran for the Downs, becoming so exhausted that they had climbed into separate trees at the other end of the woods below us, and slept the night up there. As soon as day broke, they walked the last mile up to the ring. Jay had seen us through his binoculars.

'Have one of these,' Al said, handing them a radio each and demonstrating how to talk to just one other radio or all of the units in range. Talk soon turned to the camp, and both newcomers admired Al's tepee-like construction. He said Vaughan could stay on the floor until he had built himself something substantial to sleep in.

'We need to get a patrol going on the perimeter wall. You know, in case they come.' Jay suggested, swatting a fly away.

'Yes, definitely, but first we've got to get some extra stuff.' I pulled out the pad and flipped over to my wish-list.

'Where from?' Al asked.

'B&Q I reckon,' I motioned down the hill to the town. 'If there's any of it left. I want to see if I can get down to our house too, it's so close.'

'We could see Sainsbury's on the way up here,' Vaughan said. 'It was trashed.'

'Well, that was for food I should think. We saw looters in Crawley too.'

'Why don't we just load the car up?' Vaughan asked.

'No petrol,' Al and I both said simultaneously, so we linked little fingers and said 'Voodoo.' We all brainstormed for half an hour and came up with the best list so far. It was designed to plug the defensive gap which we faced, mainly because everyone had grabbed things to fight the undead with, and didn't bother with the things we'd actually need to last the week.

'If we were in the US, we'd all have brought our guns with us,' Jay said.

'Yeah, and we'd be counting until the ammo ran out.' added Al.

'…if we hadn't already shot each other,' Vaughan chipped in.

'We could try nail-guns,' Al suggested. 'They'll be useful for any building we do too. We'll have to tamper with them so they fire even when they're not pressed up against something.'

'It's worth a go,' I agreed, 'but only if they're not too heavy.' A chainsaw made the list too, but not for wantonly violent purposes and only if we had room.

10ft of 4in diameter plastic drainpipe
4 x nail guns and nails
1 x Water butt
Tarpaulin
Bin bags
Gaffer tape
6 x hand axes
6 x hand saws
1 x pick-axe
8 x litres white spirit or similar
As much rope as we can carry
At least 1000 screws
At least 5000 nails
1 x petrol chainsaw (small)
12 x pairs gardening gloves
4 x pairs chemical protective gauntlet gloves
12 x pairs protective goggles
1 x petrol generator (if there is one)

Vaughan suggested the drainpipe, to cut into lengths to cover our forearms from teeth, and also to make them difficult to grip. We thought the protective goggles and chemical gloves would also be good for any close-up work we might have to engage in. I liked the idea of the gaffer tape so we could bind our trousers closer to our legs; mindful of the handful of clothing I let the cat-flap chap get hold of.

'Did I tell you about the one who came in through our cat-flap?' I asked to nods and grunts. The tarpaulin and water butt were my rather pensive attempt to plan for the water situation, which I knew was woefully inadequate now there were seven of us, including the dogs who would drink a cool Alpine lake each if you let them. With the stuff on the list and any bonus items we might find we would need at least four people to do the trip. I asked Lou if she minded staying put with the dogs, and she rolled her eyes and said that she didn't, that she'd be safer up there and knew the camp needed supplies. I kissed her. She gave Vaughan her empty rucksack, and I joined Al who was listening to Jay as they contemplated the weapons stacked up under a tree.

'We need light and efficient ones. Whatever we take down we'll need to bring back up with us.'

Al was especially taken with Jay's sword, and began negotiations along the lines of swapping it with his baseball bat. The negotiations broke down because one or other of the parties was nominated as being too gay. Jay's dad's sword was ceremonial, but he'd been using the sharpstone from Al's survival kit and had got a good edge to it. Al was huffily 'okay' with using his baseball bat, forcing a grin and explaining that his billy-club was too short for comfort if we ended up in the thick of it. Vaughan wanted to use the pitchfork as a purely manipulative tool, and I could see the attraction - to prong one in the chest and either shift him to a safe distance or use him to fend off others, but I told him about the trouble I'd had working my screw-laden club free of bone, and it put him off. He settled for the long-handled axe, deciding it was worth it the extra weight in order to keep a good distance.

'That's good - now both you and Jay can take heads off,' I said. I really wanted to take the pressure sprayer (I'll admit, for show more than anything), but it was heavy; took up space; needed constant pumping and was running out of white spirit. In the end I went for my club, the handle now reassuringly comfortable in my grip after more earnest whittling. I had also taken out all of the wood screws when Al needed some, and put them all back in so they were pointing the same way, now more toothbrush than toilet brush - I thought it might make it easier to pull out of skulls.

We took two radios. Al was pretty sure we'd be out of range from Lou, but nonetheless she said she'd keep hers on, just until we'd got back. We decided Al should go with Vaughan, and I would go with Jay, so that if we needed to fight on two fronts each team had one clubber and one cutter. I had binoculars, so Jay took the radio. Al and Vaughan fought over who had the radios but of course Al won because they were officially his. I made Vaughan take a pack of antibacterial wipes as his secondary item, but he looked too glum so I gave him the smallest first aid kit too.

'Now you're the medic chum,' I said.

Happy with our roles we set off, and I gave Lou a lingering kiss goodbye.

'Go!' she said, wafting me away.

'Stay out of sight, and don't turn the radio off.'

'I won't,' she smiled at me. Then she handed me my house keys. 'Don't forget these, dumb-arse.'

'You'll have to name your club,' Jay and I were ahead of Vaughan and Al.

'Let's wait for them,' I said, lifting my binoculars to see the first good view of the industrial estate we were heading for.

'What about "Fah-Q"?' he said, giggling.

'That's *Dazed and Confused*, isn't it?' Mindful of a *Simpsons* I'd seen recently, I put on my best Patrick Stewart. '...and now for the Paddling of the Swollen Ass.'

Jay laughed. Vaughan wanted to know what was so funny.

'Nothing,' Jay sighed.

I could see smoke curling up from under the corrugated roof of the supermarket. I saw cars in the car park, but no movement.

'It looks clear.'

'What's that though?' Al was pointing down the trail. Two 'stinkers' as Vaughan would have it were stumbling along the hedgerow towards us. Tattered clothes and dusty hair, one of them had black blood caked down one side of his body from a massive head wound, and his trousers practically round his ankles.

'Okay chaps, here comes some target practice to help get your eye in,' Jay was swinging the sword, taking the feathery heads off the grass by the wayside. We organised into our teams, each naturally focussing on the stinkers on our own side of the track. Al and I were eager to get stuck in, but Jay and Vaughan were equally so, and we all ended up charging them. I got the first crack in with my club, but true to form it just sat there fixed in the top of our freak's head.

'Here you go chum!' I wheeled round, dodging the arms that were thrashing at me, and placed the walking corpse between Jay and I, holding the head still right in front of him. As Jay raised his blade I looked into dead eyes. This one's eyeballs looked cooked, like when you steam fish. I could still see the pupil, with a grey shadow where the iris should be. That's what makes their eyes go white, I thought, they're not rolled back into their heads at all. With a sound like sweeping grass Jay swung the sword and the body collapsed to the floor.

The sudden loss of weight made the severed head on the end of my club lift up above my own head, which was still mercifully attached to my shoulders.

'Cool!' Jay was impressed. We watched as Vaughan cleaved the head off the shoulders of their one – Al had floored him already with one satisfying swing.

Vaughan looked up and sniffed.

'Well, that was easy.'

'Let's not get complacent,' I said. 'We should get going.' I pushed the head off my stick with my foot.

'How about "Pin-head"?' I asked Jay.

We saw two more single walkers, coming up the hill and dispatched them quickly, even though the second one was a little girl of about ten. She was vicious - more mobile than the others, and it took three goes to get her as the only course of action if she came for you was to turn and run. You would outrun her over the space of just a few feet, but her movements were unpredictable. She was hungry, you could tell. Vaughan got her eventually, bringing the axe down at an angle on her neck and spinning her head away over the hedgerow. I could hear him recounting to Al how much her head span as we trudged down the dusty path. Not once did we let the humanity cloud our judgement: we'd seen the movies, there was no cure. I remembered what Jay had said about his parents being okay in the cellar until help was coming, and wondered where he thought it would be coming from.

We were closer to the industrial park now, and decided to cut through the fields to the back of the units, avoiding the road. We found one of them with her foot trapped under what I assumed was a horse feeder. She'd got herself in a right mess, and must have been thrashing about for a while as her limbs where shredded to the muscle where they met the sharp metal edges of the covered trough. Jay took her head off 'to put her out of her misery,' but I suspected he wanted the practice.

We clambered over the fences and onto some waste ground at the back of the store where we saw two dogs. I think they were both border collies, but it was hard to tell because their fur was matted and strung with oily black guts as they fed on the open chest of a fat old man. They didn't even see us - it must have been better than Christmas Day for them. We soon got to the outer edge of the buildings, where there was a low wall onto a path which led all the way around to the front entrance.

TARGET
PRACTICE

'Let's split up,' Al suggested, eager to use the radios. 'You go that way, we'll go this way.'

'Okay, but stop at each corner to report,' Jay said. 'Mistakes at this stage would be unforgivable. First one of us to make a mistake is a gay-lord.'

'First one of us to make a mistake will be dead I should think,' I said as we headed in the opposite direction to Al and Vaughan.

'Okay then, a dead gay-lord.'

We walked around the outside perimeter, creeping silently in the shadow of the tin and breezeblock monstrosity. It was huge on the outside, and the others got to their waypoint first.

'We're in place, it's clear. Over,' Al crackled.

Jay and I didn't hurry. When we got to the end I motioned to Jay who nod-ded and I poked my head round the side. I'd forgotten about the Halfords which was joined at the hip to the DIY store.

'It's clear,' I said to Jay.

'We're here, it's clear, my dear…' Jay was doing his Mick Jagger.

'Say "over", over,' Al hissed.

'Sorry,' Jay was giggling, '"Over", over, over.'

For all his military pretensions, Jay was riddled with an endearing streak of irresponsibility, and had the most infectious laugh I'd ever heard. Al laughed back, to show he wasn't that bothered, but I swear I heard him say "over" be-fore he clicked off. We sidled down the edge of the shop, which sold car and bike parts supermarket-style. I wasn't sure if we could salvage anything from there or if indeed any of it would be useful, except maybe the car air fresheners. I had the list; we'd stick to that for now, we could always come back down here for more.

'Okay, we're at the front corner of the building. The entrance is forty feet away from our current position, over,' Al crackled.

'Hold your horses,' Jay said into the radio. 'I'm starting to see the flaw in splitting up, we're miles away. We can't see anyone though.' We walked quickly across the car park to the corner of the store. I could see Vaughan's head pok-ing out from the other side, and gave the thumbs-up.

'I can see them,' I said to Jay.

'We can see you, over,' Jay relayed.

'I know, Vaughan's just told me,' Al said. They were both laughing. 'Meet you in the middle, over.'

We walked quickly until we all met up at the front entrance. The doors were locked, no-one had forced entry and no alarms were going off. Vaughan had grabbed one of those low trolleys you only get in DIY places and tried nudging the doors with it, but it was too low. It wasn't long before we had sat a second trolley on top of it with its nose jutting over the front end of the one underneath, like a low battering ram. Vaughan backed it up, then he and Al powered towards the glass door, accelerating with each step. It frosted on contact and fell out of its frame in tiny cubes. There was another door inside, but Jay found a fire extinguisher and hoofed it through the glass to the inside of the shop. Still no alarms, probably due to the power cut, although I'd always assumed that alarms were on their own power supply just in case society broke down. We climbed over the twisted door frame and into the cool darkness of the store. It was pitch black, which I hadn't anticipated.

'Fuck. I can't see anything.' We were totally blind – there were no windows anywhere at all in the building and our eyes were more in tune with the blazing sunlight from outside.

'What if there are some in here?' Vaughan sounded worried.

'There shouldn't be; we didn't see any doors open on the way in,' Al said.

'But what if they were in here when it all kicked off?' No-one had any suggestions about that, although I did think someone should stay by the door as a lookout whilst we looked for a torch.

'Don't forget batteries,' said Jay, who had taken up position, sword at the ready. We started out into the cavernous gloom of the store in a group of three, but we lost Al and soon Vaughan trailed off too - so much for safety in numbers.

'I'll look down here,' he yelled, far too loudly for my liking.

I found the torches where I thought they'd be, down by the tape measures and spirit levels. My eyes were slowly getting used to the murk, so soon I could see that only one of the torches on the shelf came with its own batteries – not pre-installed, I was disappointed to see. I burst a packet open, but the batteries skittered away under the shelving at the bottom of the display. I opened another one, more carefully this time, and inserted the batteries. Light.

'Here you go lads!' I shouted confidently. I shone the beam up and down the aisle, the sound of my own voice and the thought of a hand on my shoulder giving me goose-bumps. I saw packs of batteries though, and took four of the biggest style of torch down, took them to the batteries at the end of the aisle and selected the appropriate size. I propped the first one on the shelf and used its beam to kit all the torches out with some power. More light. Vaughan was behind me, and I handed him two of the torches.

'One's for Al.' I walked back down the central aisle to Jay, who was still standing guard.

'I've seen no-one,' he told me. I gave him his torch as Vaughan and Al turned up, heaving a bit of eight-foot by four-foot plywood, which they propped up against the shattered glass door.

'At least we'll hear them coming in.'

I showed them the list, ripped off the bottom of it and sent Jay off to get the small bits like the binbags, screws, and gloves. Al didn't hang around to be issued with a task, and went to look for the chainsaw and the nail guns. I told Vaughan I wanted to sort out the bits we needed to collect water, and he was happy with finding the axes and saws and other stuff we'd need for building shelters.

I found the water butts, and decided on two of the smaller ones instead of one big one of the same capacity in case of accidental tipping or contamination, as well as ease of actually getting them back up to the top of Cissbury Ring. I put one inside the other and unhooked a few bags of extra water butt-related guff it looked like I might need. I walked to the guttering and downpipes – I knew where these were as I'd only just fitted guttering to the pent roof of my workshop – and selected a good fifteen feet of round pipes the right width, and another fifteen feet of normal guttering. The tarpaulin was flimsier than I'd have liked, but it did mean I could get a better ratio of water-collecting surface area to weight. Jay soon appeared behind me with his rucksack bulging.

'I've got all the bits, plus rope and white spirit.'

'We should all carry some rope.'

'I've already got all of the good stuff; I just took the whole reel. There's some chain there too.'

I got Jay to show me what screws he'd picked up, then filled the extra space in my rucksack with screws of different length and purposes, and thinner rope. When I was done we went to find Al, and met Vaughan who was after some chain to attach all the axes and saws to his belt. We took a reel of chain each and moved on. Al was in the power tools section, a large bay overlooking the cash tills and the front doors beyond. He'd found a compact chainsaw, petrol-driven and about a foot long.

'We won't need one that's any bigger than this for the trees up there, but I don't know whether to get the petrol one or the longer electric one.'

'We've got no way of charging it up,' I said.

'Yeah, but I've got fuck-all petrol to salvage from the car,' he said, rubbing his chin.

'There's a combine harvester in one of the fields below the Ring. Maybe we can get some fuel out of it.'

'Okay, petrol it is. I got those,' he nodded to a stack of four boxes. 'Nail guns. They take gas canisters.'

I sat on the ground to strip the guns of their packaging. Al had also found several drums of plastic nail strips, so we started to pack them and the chainsaw into his rucksack. Al couldn't use the saw on the way back up, so he kept back one of the nail guns and filled it with ammo.

'Now, where's the safety mechanism?' He inspected the front of the nail gun whilst I shone my torch at it. There was a metal plate which pushed into the body when it was pressed up against something, which made sure you couldn't fire nails through the air irresponsibly. Jay got out a roll of gaffer tape and ripped off a few strips, and Al ended up laying the tape crossways over the muzzle, pinning the plate in place.

'You've blocked the end off,' Jay was prodding the gaff.

'Watch,' Al said, as he raised the nail gun and fired twice. The nails burst through the tape and thudded into a chipboard display stand boasting empty plastic tool boxes to many 'oohs' and 'aahs'. We gathered round, poking the heads of the nails which had sunk into the display a good two inches or more. Al showed us the tape on the end of the gun, which now had a neat little hole blown out of the centre.

'Cool.'

'Nice one.'

'Gig buns.'

'Right, who wants to volunteer for a mission to destroy the denizens of the undead?' I shone the torch under my chin and pulled a Boris Karloff face, '…and to pick up a few bits from my house. I only need one of you; the rest can wait here inside. Keep the radios on; my house is well within range from here.'

'What do you need from the house chum?' Jay asked. I showed him my salvage list.

Ordnance Survey Explorer Maps 121 & 122
Ray Mears' Book of Outdoor Survival
'Lofty' Wiseman – *SAS Survival Handbook*
David Bellamy's Eye-Spy book of birds
David Bellamy's Eye-Spy book of trees
Reader's Digest – *The Ever-changing Woodlands*
Hugh Fearnly-Whittingstall – *The River Cottage Year*
Charles Dickens – *A Child's History of England*
Bill Bryson – *A Short History of Nearly Everything*
Collins Paperback English Dictionary
JRR Tolkein – *Lord of the Rings* Trilogy
Shakespeare – Complete works
John Wyndham – *The Day of the Triffids*
Big first aid kit
Toilet paper
Antibacterial hand gel
iPod
All TV comedy DVDs

'That's a back-pack full in itself!' Al snorted.

'I know, but we need all of it. Except maybe the iPod I suppose. I've got room in my pack; the water butts won't fit.' I was sensing some resistance to my plan.

'I can see the use of the survival books, and maybe the dictionary and I could do with reading *Triffids* again,' Jay mumbled, 'but what about the DVDs? What are we going to do, hew a flatscreen TV out of chalk?'

'It's *Partridge*.' I frowned, and then added: 'Al brought a vinyl LP with him.'

'I'll go with you chum.' Vaughan said, heaving off his rucksack.

'Okay, well, let's do it now. Got your axe?' I asked him.

'Check.' Vaughan grinned.

'Bye,' someone said it first, but soon we were all sarcastically cackling the two-tone 'by-eee' that people do at each other.

Vaughan and I reached the house without seeing anyone. The fires were close now, we could smell them. I still fumbled for my keys at the front door like an idiot, before stepping into the cool dark. I was pleased the fridge didn't reek, but I could smell something from next door leaching through the walls as I split the list in two.

'I'll do the books; the DVDs are all upstairs, but they're in no order. Get, all the British TV comedy of course, but only on DVD; make sure you pick up *Spinal Tap* and *Ghostbusters* though.' He laughed then saw I was serious.

'Ooh, and *Withnail*,' I said, '…and *Shaun of the Dead*, and *Austin Powers*. Oh, and *Threads*. Any Coen brothers. The Romero boxed set, obviously. Just grab a load, but make sure you…'

'Get the British TV comedy DVDs, I know. Anything else?'

He was being sarcastic now. I worked through the titles on the bookcase, getting half way through my list before I peered into the back garden. I could see no-one out there, although the ladder was now on the ground, having split next door's fence in two. Maui curled around my legs, and yawned. She'd probably had a fantastic few days. I contemplated bringing her, but decided more weight was not needed. I had already underestimated the amount of stuff I wanted to salvage, and had to add the last minute additions of toilet paper and antibacterial hand gel to what I had already.

Vaughan appeared as I sorted the rest of the books out. We packed them neatly into my rucksack along with the DVDs and other bits. I ditched some of the extraneous stuff Vaughan had chosen - like obviously the remastered *Star Wars* trilogy - and replaced them with some of my prized VHS tapes. I had inherited my dad's habit of hitting the record button on significant news days, much to my mother's – and more recently Lou's – discontent. I had recorded a 'live' mix of the BBC News 24 and Sky News when the attacks on the World Trade Centre happened (I only got home after the second plane had hit though), and a few years later during the London bombings. I had also got some of the various colourful revolutions that had happened in Eastern Europe, and the eve of Blair and Bush's Gulf War. I had the original transmission of *Live Aid*, and a fair amount of the first UK series of *Big Brother*. There were sixteen tapes in all, which I wrapped in carrier bags. Vaughan had to take them.

'I always end up with carrier bags,' he said.

I kissed Maui's soft little head and we made our way back out onto my drive, to the sight of a stinker right in front of us. Vaughan split her head as I locked the door. We made our way back to the A27, picking through the wreckage. A group of them were up the road, stumbling into front gardens, and when we reached the car park in the industrial estate we saw four more.

'What do you reckon chum?' I asked Vaughan.

'Fuck it; let's just chicken it,' he said.

'Okay, after you,' I started, but he was gone before I'd finished the sentence. I didn't hang about. I sprinted after him, my rucksack pounding my kidneys. Vaughan was surprisingly light on his feet. We sprinted past the freaks and up to the doors of the DIY store. Jay and Al pulled the plywood from the doors, and we stepped once more into the gloom.

'Right, is everything packed up? There's four of them out there.' I was also eager to get back to Lou – we'd been nearly three hours, according to Vaughan's watch. Whilst my rucksack of DVDs and books was still on my shoulders I got Jay to sit it inside the water butts as best he could, and gaffer tape their rims to my straps. Hilarious jokes were made about Jay inserting things into my butt. We all made some last minute adjustments to each others' backpacks, Vaughan tightened his chain belt after I grabbed one of the short-handled axes off him, and Jay bound up our trouser legs with gaffer tape. Al actually tightened his belt – I don't think I'd ever seen him without his pants showing – and tucked the nail gun he'd been practising with down the back of his trousers.

'We need to secure this entrance – make it so we can get inside quickly and safely in the future,' he suggested.

Whilst Jay and I cautiously made our way into the car park, Vaughan and Al briefly discussed angles then took an end of plywood each and hauled it through to the other side of the store entrance. They placed it flush up against the outside of the door frame – it was a perfect fit – and Vaughan leaned up against it whilst Al shot six nails through the wood along each edge and deep into the metal door frame. Vaughan did an amusing face of terror whilst the nails went in around him.

'You two could have been on *Paul Daniels*,' Jay suggested.

We laughed as we trudged across the car park. There was a distinct breeze in the air, for the first time in what seemed like weeks. It was a hot wind, and when we hit the first patch of grass after the tarmac sprawl of the industrial estate I picked up a handful and threw it into the air. It was going north to south – I never knew if that was a southerly or a northerly.

'At least that'll blow the smoke from the town out to sea,' I ventured.

'Let's just attack the journey back,' Al said as we traced our way across the field and back onto the track up to Cissbury. I swept the long grass with my fingers, plucking one out and chewing the stalk. I thought of Lou. Al reached the path first and I saw him look up it and stop dead. I quickened my pace joining him and Vaughan with Jay on my heels. We all stood and stared at the figures dotting the path, shuffling their way up towards the Downs. There were dozens of them.

'Fuck. That's more than I've seen up here.' Al said.

'The wind must be carrying the smell of the camp down here.' I stuttered, the words catching in my throat. 'Lou.'

I looked at Jay. 'Right,' he said, 'we've got to move. We'll have to keep moving too, or we'll get bogged down. Run up behind them quickly, take one each, and keep going after the initial blow. We'll outrun them, but we've got to keep going.'

Al had the first contact, quick to respond, sending a young woman reeling into the bushes with a sideways swing of his bat and a healthy crunch. He moved on to two men, one in what looked like a fast food uniform, the other naked but covered in wheals and sores. He'd been so quick neither creep had noticed him, but he hesitated behind Burger King, bat raised. The temptation was too great - he pulled the nail gun from his belt as Vaughan appeared next to him, raining the long handled axe down again and again on the top of Nature Boy's head. Jay and I breezed past them, and as Al unloaded three or four nails into the top of the Burger King's spine, felling him instantly, I heard him congratulate Vaughan with a 'Dude! G'work!'

I had the edge on Jay even with my heavy backpack, but I stumbled to the floor and the creep I'd singled out turned to face me. Why did I always get them head-on? He was tubby with a goatee beard and a faded *Wings* T-shirt stained black down the front. I leapt away from him as if I'd been stung, scratching a foothold on the chalky path. I could feel his fingers on my shoulder as I got to my feet and whirled around, flinging my club upwards towards his head. A very lucky shot - I shattered his jaw and sent black-rooted teeth skittering into the dust. The club came cleanly out of the other side, ripping a cheek off which hung loosely from the screws at the end. He was still coming at me, arms wild, when Jay's sword came over the top of my head and into the top of the stinker's. As the impact cleanly sliced off a four-inch deep bowl of skull-top he simply fell backwards a few steps, then started coming for me again. He had about a quarter of his head left - the middle section with his eyes and ears - but nothing above his eyebrows and nothing below his nose, except for the other cheek which flapped around the bubbling vent left open at the top of his windpipe. I backed up, colliding with Jay, and pulled out the axe I'd taken off Vaughan. His eyes flickered, looking uncooked in the sun, and the stumps of his jawbone ground away at the air. I took careful aim at the bone and cartilage exposed at the back of his throat and, just as he grabbed a handful of my shirt, I swung.

The axe - still factory-sharp - cracked into his two visible inches of spinal cord and he fell, his grip loosening instantly. I exhaled, looking up the track where the others were getting stuck in, felling freaks at a good rate. I dared myself to look behind me, and saw all the ones we'd passed still flat on the ground, except for the first one who was on his knees but fighting the inside of the bush Al had put him in.

We hacked and thumped and swung and sliced and felled, pushing up towards Cissbury Ring. I remember my backpack feeling lighter than air and my legs bubbling with might as we made steady progress. The zombies went down silently one by one, so that only our own heavy-footedness would alert them to our presence – the wind was in our favour. We ran the gauntlet through the more open spaces, dodging arms and hopping over the zombies which were rolling around on the ground even before we'd had a pop at them.

After a steady mile and a half of yomping I was starting to panic – they were growing in numbers the further up the track we reached, but we were up high enough now to clearly see the Ring over the tops of the surrounding vegetation. I saw Al cupping his ears before the radios crackled into life.

'Dogs.'

Carried on the wind was a twin baying noise sounding not dissimilar to the jet engine going down that Lou and I had heard on the first night. Then both radios clicked and sputtered. We listened, keeping still, until quite plainly we heard Lou's voice cut through the static.

'...dogs but... you there... come...' followed by silence. Everyone was looking at me, and I started to feel my throat closing up again. Then, mercifully, we heard '...much longer. They're in the camp. Hello?' We all sprang into life, heels digging into the chalk. Jay was on the radio.

'Lou I don't know if you can hear us, but we're on our way, we can hear you. We can hear the dogs. Keep doing whatever it is you're doing, we'll be there soon!'

'Just keep ploughing through them!' I shouted to the others. They could climb the slopes and get into the camp. I was angry with myself, and my ears became very hot. We hit the first wave of ten or so, running straight past them. The last one caught Vaughan's rucksack and pulled him to the ground. He managed to jam the top of the axe head under the woman's chin, keeping him clear of her gnashing teeth but the handle was wedged into his chest, pinning him to the ground. He roared with pain as I ran back to him, seeing other freaks were nearly onto him, and slammed my club into her back with a snap. She went limp, and Vaughan heaved her off with the axe. Al was next to us now, and popped nail after nail into the faces of the three closest ones. One of them dropped, but the others merely slowed down slightly as their heads were jerked back with each shot.

I helped Vaughan up and we turned on our heels, Al following and firing with a pinging sound. Up ahead I could see Jay in trouble, backing up as two creeps bore down on him from the higher ground. Vaughan and I sprinted either side of Jay in a pincer movement on the group and taking out the outer cadavers, allowing him to vent his frustration on the one in the middle. He brought his sword down plumb in the centre of the chap's head, cleaving off a slice like a water melon, but also unmistakably severing his spinal cord.

Al joined us, firing ahead before reloading on the move. There was an all-too-small gap until the next wave, which was still mercifully oblivious to our approach and stumbling up to the irresistible aromas of the camp, the dogs – and my wife. The path up to the Ring was in sight, the ancient woods standing dark and uninviting on our right. I could just about make out the V-shaped notch. It looked like it was ablaze – had the campfire got out of control? I couldn't see for sure, but it looked like a bonfire had been piled up onto the chalk in the centre of it, and several creeps had caught light and were stumbling about. I could see perhaps two or three hundred figures lining our route up to the top.

'Let's dump the bags were we can see them from the Ring. We'll have to break through,' I panted. We could hear the dogs plainly now as Jay got back on the radio.

'Lou, are you there?' he was breathless. There was no reply. 'Lou, are you there, over?' Al was trying too. Vaughan put his backpack on the ground, and I watched him help Jay as I levered my own off. Al was looking at me, waving the radio.

'Nothing,' he said.

'Let's do it,' Jay said eagerly.

'Wait,' I stood in front of them. 'Just wait a sec. We need to do this right. Al, your bag's got the nail guns in, right?' Al nodded. 'Okay Jay, cut off a length of rope a bit wider than the path is. Al, we'll take one end, Jay you take the other. These cock-ends don't look too nimble on their feet; so we'll just trip them all up. We hold the rope across the path and charge them from behind. We'll tip them over. Vaughan, take the bag with the nail guns and mop them up any stragglers with your axe.'

Vaughan looked gutted to put a backpack on. Jay handed us one end of the rope and we all started off up the hill. We thrashed through the grass verges either side of the track, trailing the rope between us. The first four went down a treat, heads thudding into the dirt, but the fifth one was a heavy-set bloke and we ended up just moving him up the hill. He even turned and looked at me before we stopped, his head lolling with every thundering step he took. Vaughan caught up, puffing life a steam engine, and axed the fat zombie full in the face. Jay threw him his radio.

'Get on that chum, see if you can reach her.' He turned to Al and I. 'Some of them are too fat to trip up, so when I shout 'up', just lift the rope over their heads. Vaughan can deal with the ones we leave.'

We sprinted off again, sending a pack of shuffling figures toppling. Jay would pre-warn us of a fat one every so often, and we'd leave them alone. We could hear Vaughan on the radio, pausing to dispatch the waifs and strays. The Ring was close, obscured from view by a densely packed thicket. Soon we hit our first flaming zombie, staggering about as if drunk, and hissing like a potato in a microwave. We saw more on the ground, charred and thrashing as we forged on, and soon Cissbury Ring was in sight. There was indeed a roaring bonfire in the V-shaped notch, spewing out flaming, flailing bodies as fast as they stumbled into it. It was made from gorse bushes. Clever girl, I thought. I just hope you're still there.

I left Al and Jay to pull more of them to the floor as I thumped my way through the hordes ahead. There were fifty or more of them heading for the fire, and I could see hundreds of others stretching around the bottom of the earth ramparts. To my horror I saw several clambering up the slopes, dead fingers gripping clumps of dry grass, feet scrabbling on the chalk.

'They're in the camp; let's get a move-on!' I yelled behind me.

Vaughan had joined the others, holding the nail guns from Al's backpack to arm us with, but they had to be adapted first. Jay was ripping up gaffer tape and they both worked on each nail gun in turn, quickly placing a cross of tape over the safety plate. When they were done Jay held one in his left and his sword in his right, and Vaughan weighed up his axe as he ran to hand me my nail gun. I took it and turned to scale the hill, avoiding the inferno in the middle of the footpath. I could hear both dogs howling, and Jay shouting 'Stick together', as I ran to the bottom of the first slope. The heat from the blaze was fierce but I ploughed headlong through the freaks and started to monkey my way up the outer perimeter rampart. I used the screws on my club to pull at their clothes, clearing a path above me by sending them flailing down the hill. I lost my footing once and nearly ended up in the unappealing pile of twisted, fidgeting corpses below me. When I finally stood on the top of the chalk walkway I could see down into the secondary ditch, curving away around the Ring either side of me. The hollow was dotted with figures, some immobile, some gathering themselves up to scale the secondary, inner slope; steeper and less forgiving. One or two fell from the top ring and back into the ditch. I jumped in, firing my nail gun at the heads of those who spotted me. The nail gun was effective as a distracter, and Al would be the first to admit that a clean kill was rare. If you hit roughly the right spot at the back of the neck – always fire off at least three nails at a time – it either felled them instantly or most often twisted them to face a different direction. Sometimes it even sent them to the ground with the impact.

I chose a path up to the top of the Ring which was relatively free of scrabbling stinkers and began to scale the inner hill. I had got half way up when I was struck by something heavy from above. I had been scanning the ground for a hand grip and hadn't seen the corpse stumble to the edge of the Ring and then over it. He fell on top of me, grabbing at my clothes and trying to bite me as we both fell, his nail-stripped fingers finding a grip on my boot. I kicked at his face with my free leg but his grasp never weakened. I kept kicking, desperately looking around the ditch for help, my nail gun on the ground a few feet above me. There was no-one, but I could hear the warped pinging of nails through the gorse blaze.

But I could also hear the dogs. I whistled the friendly, not-a-care-in-the-world whistle I did when I wanted Floyd to come to me. I kept booting the bloke's head, confident he couldn't bite me, but I was absolutely pinned to the floor by his hunger-powered strength. Our struggle had caught the attention of more peckish walkers, too. I whistled again.

Floyd skittered down the chalk towards us, black blood covering his head and chest. His tail was wagging, and he licked me, seemingly ignoring the fellow trying to consume my foot. He soon got the idea though, turning away from me and slamming his jaws shut either side of the stinker's face, sinking them in and determinedly twisting his head to an impossible angle with an impressive low grumbling sound. The grip on my foot loosened and I got to my feet, grabbed my nail gun and began firing at the others who had got far too close for comfort. I whistled again and Floyd let go instantly, following me up the chalky scree and over the top. I ran towards the first few stunted trees where I could hear Dmitri but see neither him nor Lou. I turned back to the prow of the hill to face a line of tattered figures, one far less hunched than the others and with something in his hand. On hearing a metallic 'pop-pop-pop' I realised it was Al. When he saw me he shouted 'Where's Lou?', but I could only shrug before sprinting onto the plateau of the Ring, Floyd bounding around my feet.

'Where's mummy?' I asked him. He ducked and barrelled off like he really had just understood me. Toward the middle, beyond the camp I could see a tree, windswept but taller than the others. Gathered around its base were twenty or thirty of them, arms clutching at the lowest branches with a collective murmur as Floyd stood to one side and barked at the tree-top. I kept my distance and yelled Lou's name into the leaves. Dmitri appeared, bouncing up to greet me but hauling one stinker to the ground in the process. Floyd took his cue and they both worked the face. I could see the radio sitting on the ground at the foot of the trunk.

'Lou?' I yelled, checking over my shoulder. 'Lou, you up there?'

'Yes. I'm in the tree thanks.'

'Hang on baby,' I swung at a freak that had lumbered up to me. 'She's here!' I yelled at my three chums, all of whom were now in the camp, hacking away. They ran to the tree, screaming to divert the freaks' attention. It worked, and they started to drift towards us. We picked out our targets and worked our way through the throng methodically.

As Al and Jay finished off the final few I looked up to see Lou's leg rustle out of the lowest bough.

'Can you get down?'

'I think so. Hang on.'

Vaughan joined me, standing against the tree trunk and holding a hand up for Lou to step onto. I guided her as she jumped the last few feet. Jay and Al were standing with their backs to us, ready for some fresh zombies who had managed to stumble up to the top of the Ring and now had us in their sightless eyes. Lou thumped me in the chest.

'You took your fucking time!' She was fuming. Al handed her his nail gun, and, seeing that she had nothing at all I gave her mine too.

'I like the bonfire. Where's your club?'

'It was cutting into my hand.'

'Sorry baby.' I turned and faced the strange. 'Spread out. Take one at a time and only advance when they've stopped moving. Be methodical. Push them to the edges.'

We all got stuck in, pounding away, raining blows even when they were on the ground, sidestepping their slow advance and severing heads whenever it was feasible.

Al reached the edge of the ring first having retrieved his scythe from the armoury. He stood and swung like he was deadheading roses. Jay was also whisking off heads with his sword as soon as they appeared. Vaughan just hacked and hacked with the axe, and still they came. Al tried using the pressure sprayer in short bursts, trying not to increase the grass fires that had sprung up all around us but soon gave up, beating at the ground with his towel. Jay and Vaughan tried a new angle with the rope, running rings around groups of five or more with an end each like the Rebel Alliance around an AT-AT's legs, before tightening the loop and felling them, whereupon Al would step in and take off their heads.

I saw Lou with her jet-black hair whipping around her face, both nail guns raised, taking alternate shots in quick succession before reloading in a heartbeat. That's my girl. My girl…

Breaking Up
[day 0005]

We fought into the night, taking it in turns in teams of two to mop up any freaks that had made their way into the camp. The dogs were crucial, and would alert us and fight at the same time. We couldn't see how many more of them were shuffling their way up from the town, but in the brief lulls between waves we stopped, listening to the hoarse moaning and whispering that carried on the breeze. Lou had told us in breathless episodes about the last two hours. After we had started off down the hill she had busied herself collecting wood and clearing more of the long grass with the scythe. But she'd got freaked out when the birds and insects stopped chattering, just after the wind had picked up. She had thought she could see shapes in the woodland below and the dogs had been acting up, growling and drooling. She'd seen that the main weak point was the V-shape through which the footpath led up to the centre of the camp, and had started to hack down the gorse and broom bushes, piling them up in the gap. It was then that she'd seen the first one coming. The dogs ran down to inspect him and had quickly dismembered the threat, but were soon overwhelmed. Lou had been sure her impromptu defences would block their way but they started to thrash through the gorse.

She had called the dogs to her and set the whole lot alight with the pressure sprayer. She'd had to put out some fires but the tactic had bought her some time. Soon enough though they had started to come over the top, seeming to either avoid the flames or, as Jay suggested, learning from the mistakes of the others. I couldn't help suggesting that there were enough of them to spread themselves out randomly. Lou had fought for as long as she could with both dogs staying by her side to defend her. She'd tried the radio – which we heard – but eventually she'd had enough and climbed into the tree, dropping the radio in her exhaustion.

Yet here she was; twice as exhausted as the rest of us but invigorated by new energy for the fight. We were all running on vapours, and Al had brought the

LOU,
WARRIOR

water container round to each of us. We had the southernmost quarter of Cissbury Ring pretty well covered, and luckily for us they seemed to all be taking the most direct route up. Gasping for air, we breathed in the foul sulphurous vapours like we were drinking the purest well water. But blinded by sweat and gagging with every breath we fought on, lopping heads and severing spines. It was worth relighting the bracken every so often, when it got clogged up with corpses and their crackling, withering rasps carried away on the air like ghosts. Flies droned around our heads, settling in our eyes and ears. The fires spread down the slopes and onto the fields, broken up by pathways and patches of bare earth and chalk. Al's nonchalant, absent-minded early-morning clearance of the long grass in camp probably saved our lives.

Lou was the first to say it, in the rests we took in pairs; she was the first to actually say what the others were apparently thinking. She said she wanted to go.

'Go where?' I asked sarcastically, to no answer. But even Al was worried, about our vulnerability on top of the Ring as much as the fires all around us.

'But where will you go?'

Dawn broke, splitting the horizon with slivers of rose and gold. The smoke hung blue over Worthing town, and still they came. We could see them coming through the woods, across the char-streaked fields and up the parched golf course. We saw zombies who couldn't make the slope any more though loss of limb or shredded muscle, and just scrabbled at the chalk and brush in the ditch, sometimes standing on bodies three deep and clutching at the sky with stripped fingers and broiled eyeballs. There were more who could still make it, slithering over the prow of the hill toward the camp with that fixed stare, the gurning jaws and in some cases clothes still in one piece. These fresh ones were noticeably faster, but still we could outrun them and dispatch them quickly if we kept our heads. But we were getting increasingly tired, the adrenaline only going so far when the bursts did come. We had kept each other going with encouraging words like 'nice shot' and 'keep on rolling', but they seemed meaningless now I had the thought in my head we weren't actually defending anything. But I remember becoming steadily less bothered, laughing uncontrollably as I fought, to the point where Jay had to come and help me out.

'You alright chum?' he asked.

'Yeah,' I tried to take a breath. 'They look so funny!'

They did look funny; like broken humans. Social niceties had all gone out of the window. All that scrabbling around and moaning seemed such an obviously un-English things to do. The one thing that stuck in my mind was the fact that none of them were bothering to queue for their food.

'Where's the water?' Lou looked haggard, but I was thirsty too. I was too impatient to be gentlemanly, and took a swig before I passed it to her. There wasn't much left; I had removed the stopper. I'm not sure what happened – I thought Lou had hold of it, and I'm sure she thought I had hold of it too. It fell anyway, water spouting from the container and rolling like mercury on the parched ground.

'What the fuck did you do that for?' I roared. I took myself by surprise, but Lou positively crumpled. The water ran to a dribble.

'Easy chum,' said Jay

'Fuck you, I'll talk how I want,' I rounded on Lou. 'Why did you drop it? The boys hadn't had a drink yet!'

'It was an accident, don't worry,' Al looked uncomfortable. My friends who had known Lou longer than I had hated even being near our arguments, let alone being used in them as guilt leverage. We rarely fought, but when we did it was fierce – Lou could more than stand up for herself, but now she just sat there, motionless, unable to even look at me.

The bodies piled up. I should have been wishing we had the respirators and chemical gloves that we'd left down the path. I should have been wishing we had some water. I should have been wishing I hadn't shouted at Lou, who had picked herself up and kept on fighting although she still hadn't looked at me. I just carried on silently, grimly. The zombie advance thinned during the midday heat, allowing the others sometimes as much as ten minutes to cat-nap in shifts. The flies were getting worse in the heat as Jay opened two tins of plum tomatoes for fluid and shared them out. Al declined the warm watery pulp and even Lou thought twice about it when she started dry heaving at her first gulp. I wordlessly opened some sweet corn which they both took a sip from. Then we all saw something which stopped us in our tracks.

Lumbering towards Lou was a traffic warden, his clothing almost complete if a little dusty. He had no obvious injuries, and even had his radio still attached to his belt. At first I thought – we all thought – he was still alive, and needed help. Vaughan even cried out for Lou to stop when she raised her nail guns and

unloaded them into his face and neck, but he stumbled and just carried on undaunted, although Lou's reaction was enough to spur us all toward him.

I don't know who got to him first, but there was little left when we were
done. Jay puked, and we all stopped and looked at each other. Such a minor
authority figure would have been a source of laughter to us, even treated with
mild contempt. Now, though, the raw sight of a uniformed human we'd bludg-
eoned to paste laying at our feet made us all sick. We had to carry on without
the renewable vigour that made possible our efforts of the previous day and
mistakes were made: Jay nearly took off my ear when taking a swing with his
sword, and Al had been hit in the calf with a stray nail. All of us were in tears
at some stage after that; Lou in the shade of the tree, knees to her forehead; Jay
as he fought; Al quietly, choked; and Vaughan openly and wetly, his round face
to the sun. I was shuddering constantly, great waves of sickness pushing tears
to my cheeks and hot coals to the back of my throat. It began to make less and
less sense. In the old zombie movies, that was the time and the mental place in
which the principal characters usually got eaten.

As sunset reached across the blue sky the wind started to drop. No bird
sang as the stench of rotten eggs built in the stillness, and we battled on. Less
of them seemed able to make the climb at that point, but that didn't stop some
lucky freaks and a few of the fresher ones. We must have destroyed a thousand
of them between the five of us and the two dogs. Lou fed them biscuits from
her hand, still muted, drained. We were all however, united in trying not to con-
template the dry, salty dog food we'd inevitably have to tuck into ourselves.
Vaughan's nail gun had jammed, so Al and I busied ourselves with that, happy
to get lost in something technical and coolly inorganic - something which didn't
require a decision.

The dogs were resting. Looking back on why they failed to warn us, their
noses must have been confused by the fug of double death that cloaked us all,
as well as their own fur which was matted with black tar. Either way the dogs
didn't alert us to the advancing threat. We were all in the shade of the tree, and
it was only the second time since we'd got back from B&Q that we were all resting together. I was now obstinately ignoring my wife back, and I closed my
stupid fucking eyes. The first I heard was Vaughan shouting next to me. He'd
been resting against the tree's thick trunk, and Lou and Al had their backs to the
camp entrance and the edge of the Ring. I suppose they assumed that between
Vaughan and me we had their backs covered. Jay was taking a piss in a bush.

I squinted in the gloom to see Vaughan scrabbling to his feet. He had no weapon - nothing except his open arms. He ran as if herding an animal, and at first I couldn't see what he was running towards. Then Lou was pulled backwards onto the ground, as a heavy-looking bloke grabbed her hair. There were two of the filthy fuckers, and the second was about to lunge at Lou when Vaughan scooped them both up, practically off their feet, propelling them towards the edge. As the fat man's legs tried to get used to running backwards, I saw that he held a clump of Lou's hair in his hand. He refocused his hollow eyes onto Vaughan, who was just facing the ground as he ran, driving his heels into the grass. I don't know what he hoped would happen; whether they'd fall to the ground or whether we'd back him up, but he kept pushing and pushing. We just stood and stared.

It was only when all three of them tipped over the side and out of sight that we ran, in stuttering slow motion, to the edge of the Ring to be met by the vision of our friend at the bottom of the ditch. Fresh meat, he lay on his back looking up at us for a few seconds before his scent hit them. He was pulled apart like a chicken wing, tensing up and fixing my gaze before closing his eyes. He never screamed once.

Al jumped straight in, hacking and slicing, but Vaughan had been absorbed by the mass of arms and jaws. We had no option but to follow Al, but I had no weapon in my hand. I ran back to the fire, now dangerously low, and picked up the pressure sprayer, pumping the handle as I ran and igniting the first dribble of white spirit on the last embers of the camp fire.

'Get down!' I shouted. They stood back-to-back in a tight triangle and lashed outwards. Al was screaming, a deep angry wail which cut straight through me.

'Get the fuck up against the bank, now!'

Lou flattened herself against the grass bank beneath me, Jay pulling Al down next to him. I let off a blazing stream of flame into the bank of white faces, warping in its own heat. Heads spat and fizzed as I helped Lou onto the top. I squeezed the trigger for another burst, with Al and Jay scrambling up the bank under the flames.

There were three of them in the camp, and Al screamed from the back of his throat as he quickly burst their skulls like fruit. Lou was bawling, her head in her hands. Jay just sat down, blankly staring into the lifeless embers of the camp fire.

'Come on, we can't stop. Vaughan's gone, we can't stop. We've got to keep going.'

'Why?' Jay looked at me without expression.

'For fuck's sake, it was inevitable. He went out like a light.'

'But he's dead,' Lou wailed.

'At least he's not going to turn into one of them. There wasn't enough left,' I said. Lou stood, fire in her eyes.

'This isn't a game; it's not PlayStation. If you'd been looking out for me and Al he would never have had to do that. How can you be so cold?'

'I've got to be cold. I have to think like that – how the fuck can you think any of this is real? Anyway, if Vaughan hadn't put down his weapon he wouldn't have had to push them.'

'He saved you wife, mate,' Al was looking at me coldly. He and Vaughan went back a long way, further than the others.

'And your life, probably,' added Jay. He turned on his heels, swatting at the grass.

'Look, Vaughan was always going to be the one out of all of us who got it. He was like the one in *Star Trek* with the different coloured jumper.'

I don't know why I expected a laugh, but one certainly didn't come. I couldn't think of it in real terms. I can honestly say I don't think I would have batted an eyelid if Vaughan had appeared right there in front of us; a cheesy grin on his face, rubbing his belly and asking me what was for dinner. Instead Al was sobbing, Jay was nowhere to be seen and I couldn't even go to my own wife for a hug. I was right – none of it seemed real.

The wind had picked up, a great swell from the west which prickled my tongue with the faintest yet freshest hint of ozone I'd ever tasted. Al and Jay were talking to each other over the cooling ashes of the fire.

'We're going.' Al said to me, simply. His cheeks were wet, and tears gathered at the base of his goatee.

'What? We've done it.' I waved my arms. 'The wind's changed; they're not getting up the slope as much. We're nearly there.'

'Nearly where?' Jay asked, his mouth tight. 'I'm going to see my parents. At least they're safe in there, and they've got water.'

'What are we going to do about water?' Lou looked like a rag, so small and frail.

'Lou doesn't know what happened to her parents.' Jay said, his eyes piercing mine so I had to look away. 'We might be able to get there. Al says he's got just enough petrol to get back to my house, and there's petrol in our garage.'

'Al?' I couldn't comprehend what they were saying to me.

'We're going,' he repeated, and turned on his heels.

I saw the two freaks before the others - a man and a woman bedraggled and dusty, stumbling into the camp with faces like ash. I was behind them and hidden by the tree, so I raised my nail gun, walked briskly up to the nearest one and squeezed the trigger. It gave a hollow click, which was enough to make her turn to me. She screamed.

The sound shook me to my boots, and I stepped back. The others turned, agog. I don't know why I tried to shoot again, but I did. I can never forgive myself, even if she has since forgiven me, but I can blame exhaustion, sleep deprivation, dehydration, or confusion at the others' plan to leave. I could use some emotional psychobabble to explain my behaviour after so many hours of seeing faces torn apart in front of me by my own hand. I don't; I blame myself. Anyway, the nail gun was still empty. She screamed again, and then Jay's hand was over mine, lowering my arm firmly. The man spoke first.

'You've got to help us.'

His voice betrayed his worn, frail appearance – he sounded young, but I wasn't taking any chances. They're almost certainly infected, I thought. I dropped the nail gun, and ripped off the girl's shirt down to her waist. She screamed again.

'Are you bitten?' I screamed. 'Are you scratched? Show me!'

The kid was trying to stop me as I ripped off the girl's skirt. He was fumbling at me, so I snapped, felling him with one sharp crack to the jaw. She was still screaming, and looking at Lou with pleading eyes, but I didn't stop until she was naked in the moonlight. I turned her round.

'Mate, take it easy.' Jay said quietly.

'Fuck off. We've got to be sure,' I stood up, in his face. He was taller than me, but I was screaming, flecks of spittle hitting his stubble. 'We've got to be so fucking sure, get it?'

'Please, stop it,' Lou was sniveling, but not even close to touching me. The girl's milky skin was free from any marks, so I turned to the man who was still out cold and pulled all his clothes off, rolling him over in the dust with the end of my club. He had no marks on him either.

'Pick him up and take him over there, prop him up against the tree,' I ordered to young woman. She did so, cradling his head as it lolled on his shoulders. She moaned quietly. Al tried to help her.

'Fucking leave her!' I screamed. Al walked away, grabbing his bat as he passed his tent. I picked up the rope and threw it at the girl.

'You - stand next to him, backs against the tree. And keep him upright.'

She did so, shivering, and I put the middle of the rope at her feet and took one end round the back of the tree. I picked up the other end – keeping my distance – and pulled it taught. I wrapped it round them a couple of times and tied it at the back, pinning them both to the trunk.

'It's too tight,' she was saying, but I wasn't listening.

'Just fucking stop it!' Lou was in my face now, red with rage, quivering and clenching her fists. 'Who do you think you are?'

She slapped me hard across the face, and I saw a blinding white light. I thought it was my eyes, but a second great flash of lightning picked out the underbelly of the rolling black clouds on the horizon. She slapped me again, then pulled her wedding ring off and slapped me a third time with it in her open palm.

'Cunt!'

'Please help us,' the girl was sobbing but Lou was gone, following Al to the car with Jay's arm around her shoulder. They disappeared into the darkness, and I cried.

Breaking Down
[day 0006]

I broke down, sinking to my knees and falling face-first onto the chalk. My hands clawed the earth, and my mouth opened to scream. No sound came out.

I am crunching chalk, standing, swaying. My throat feels as if is being crushed by the weight of tears which won't come. The crunching sound doesn't cease when my jaws stop grinding. It isn't the sound of chalk anymore; it is wet gristle and dry bone.

Shielding my head from imaginary blows I fall again, eyes shut, trying to stop the sight playing out in front of me. Fearful human faces cower from my relentless clubbing, skulls splitting, voices screaming. Living voices shrieking and bawling as I take swing after swing after swing.

My hands are turned upwards towards the moonlight, beads of sweat pricking through oily pores. I am not wearing my wedding ring. Intricate cobweb patterns offer themselves up amongst the miniscule fissures of my palm print, tracing upwards to my fingertips, shooting sparks into the hot night sky. I run.

I have no weapon. I stand in a field of stubble; new, unfamiliar smells joining the sharp ozone of the gathering clouds. I wheel around and around, collapsing dizzy as the moon is obscured I catch sight of Cissbury Ring on the upside-down horizon a mile away. But closer, and in their droves, dark silhouettes creep towards me.

I am flat on my back, with earth on me. It fills my ears and my nose and I splutter and claw my way into a sitting position as a silent purple crack splits the sky into two. Then I am running again, stumbling through flames, spittle

BREAKING
DOWN

streaming down my chin as claws and arms catch my tattered clothing. A thousand eyeless faces turn to me, stretching away into the distance.

Every limb aches with a deep thud, every joint on fire. I am laying on my front on familiar ground. Everything is quiet. A little dog runs up to me. Arcs of lightning scorch the sky, but there is no thunder. Floyd is standing above me, looking down into my face, jaws hammering away in ceaseless, noiseless barking. Everything is silent, and my eyes are closing.

I look up, and see horses.

Making Sense
[day 0006]

When I regained consciousness Floyd was nowhere to be seen and my head and limbs were pounding. I drifted in and out, sobbing uncontrollably, helpless and alone. My friends were gone. My wife was gone. The only two other survivors we'd seen since the priest on the way back from Brighton I had left helpless. In my waking moments, thoughts focussed on the others; on why they'd gone and whether they were alive. But it hurt. It hurt so much that my mind grew too active to fall unconscious again. This was real, I remember thinking. This is all real, and I am still alive. It was only at that point that I realised how prone I was, lying face down in the dirt, with the scent of my sweat and tears carrying on the air. I had no clue how long I had been there for, unarmed and undiscovered. What about the two survivors who had approached us for help? Maybe they had escaped the teeming, stinking hordes too. The power of my responsibility to them was the first positive reflection I had since daring to think we could survive up here. That was what dragged me to my feet.

I tried to find the tree I had tied them to, but I was disorientated. I looked down and saw that I was naked, except for one shredded leg of my jeans rucked around my ankle. After a second or two of staring down, confused at the sight of my own blue-white flesh, I begin to check myself for cuts, bites and scratches. There were none.

And then I felt my first raindrop in a month. The last time I felt a raindrop on my face, I could tell a man that someone had died and he would come and put them in a wooden box which was then put into a metal box on wheels, which moved slowly to the place where the body would be burnt, and people would cry. I could pick up a plastic box, press three numbered buttons and people would come to help me. I could push a strip of plastic into a wall and paper would come out, which I could exchange for goods and services. I could sit in a dark cavernous space with other humans and watch light playing out images on a huge white cloth whilst boxes made sounds to go along with it, and it would be fun whilst we ate popped kernels of corn. I could even watch a box of my own, and see a man tell me when the rain would come. Would I need a brolly?

Now it was just water, just one drop, big and cool. After a minute of breathlessly waiting another came, splitting apart on the end of my nose and stinging my gritty eyes. Another. The rain fell and I sat, cross-legged and arms outstretched in the mud, mouth open, catching fat drops on my tongue. Thunder rolled, and crisp slivers of purple lightning cut across the clouds and etched into my eyes.

I ran to find the source of the shouting and saw the tree. The rope was loose, but I still could not see the couple.

'Where are you?' I yelled.

'We're in the tree you fucking absolute arsehole! Arsehole!'

The words were comforting to me, and I found myself smiling at the fact that I had not killed them. I walked to the trunk and tried not to look up as I helped the girl down first. I gathered their clothes, sodden and heavy, and began to help them but was waved away. I saw my own nakedness again – I had absolutely no idea where my clothes were – and scampered to my tent to haul on some trousers. They stuck on my soaking wet legs, and I lost my balance and fell over. Where was Lou? When I wrestled my way out of the tent, I could see that their clothes looked old, almost like antiques – certainly second-hand. She wore a net skirt over black trousers, and he had much more trouble pulling on his sodden black drainpipe jeans than I had. They are Goths, I thought to myself. That's just what I need to cheer me up.

'Look, mate,' the man was gesturing at the bodies littering the ground, black oily pools collecting around them in the torrent. 'We can both see you've had a bit of a day of it. Don't worry about anything, okay? It's cool.'

I nodded, dumbly. The girl remained silent.

'Plus, we're both well - all things considered. I understand why you wanted to make sure we hadn't been bitten. But we're fine. Very much alive – look.' He started to do a little jig for me, stamping about in the wet mud and waving his arms. I laughed, but it hurt my ribs. The girl had still said nothing, and I could see she was wary of me by the distance she kept. She did, though, shake my hand when I introduced myself.

'I'm Dawn,' she offered. The chap told me he was David. He had a gaunt face and was a thin streak of a lad, but taller than me. She had frizzy dyed black hair and a fat face. She was quite sweet-looking, under the streaks of white that ran down both their faces, and the black rims around their eyes.

'I saw your white makeup and... I got confused. Sorry I tried to nail you. Sorry I tied you up, too'

'S'okay. It won't be the first time I've been tied to a tree up here. Naked, too, but it's usually Dawn who does the...' He stopped, sensing her discomfort as she shuffled her feet and coughed. 'Look, have you got water?' he asked. I began to explain that we'd run out, but as the rain was still coming down in stair rods, I giggled and pointed upwards.

'Give me a hand with this.' I pulled Al's canvas canopy from the front of his tent, being careful not to rip anything, but not dawdling either in case the rain stopped. David held one end as I sized up the lowest branches of a nearby tree. I tied it off around the trunk then we spread it outwards and lowered it at one end. David grabbed the rope we'd used to fell the zombies on the way up, but I insisted we used a fresh length as we were collecting water to drink.

'Why, what are you thinking?' David quizzed.

'Well, we can't be too careful. I don't know what the threat of contamination is from some guts on a bit of rope, but we should take no chances.'

We tied the two loose corners to another tree with the new rope and I set up a line of pots and pans underneath the low end of the overhang. The rain was already starting to collect. I held a couple of the cups Lou had brought with us under the trickle and made them drink first – a kind of peace offering I suppose. Dawn shivered, even though I could feel the intense thunder-heat underneath the deceptive cool of the rainstorm. Steam came off our clothes as we sat, and soon Floyd joined us.

'Bloody hell,' I murmured, 'I wasn't imagining it. Hello boy!'

I got a good solid licking; the warm familiar contact was like a mother's hug. The fur on his chest was white again, if a little muddy. As he stood proudly facing down the hill his tail wagged frantically. I told David and Dawn how important the dogs had been as early warning systems, and whilst the rain or the change in wind direction seemed to be keeping the zombies away David recounted their story to me.

They'd been in their bed-sit in the middle of town when their neighbour called round. His elderly mum was sick, and he knew Dawn was training to be a nurse so he asked for their help. She had done as much as she could - mainly trying to make the old dear comfortable - but she'd turned on her son and pulled the flesh from his fingers with her teeth. That's when they'd first tried to escape; but the stairwell was full of them. When they started to break through the door into their flat they'd barricaded themselves into their bathroom. David had climbed out of the bathroom window three storeys up and jumped onto the flat roof next door, but he'd nearly fallen through the gap and down into the street. Dawn shuddered when he said that bit. She still hadn't said a thing to me except her name.

They'd jumped onto a fire escape, but their route to ground level was blocked as more of the zombies caught their scent and gathered below — he used the word 'zombie' I was pleased to hear. They'd sat on the roof for hours, listening to the sounds of screaming and ripping, watching the fires taking hold of the town centre. Then the gas tank blew up. It splintered all of the windows around them, covering them with glass. He said they'd been deaf for a full ten minutes, and the heat made every breath feel like fire. They had to move as the heat got more intense, so David bravely jumped the gap back into their little bathroom, soaked some towels and wrapped themselves up before risking the fire escape, clambering down to street level and working their way up through town. Hiding didn't work — they soon found that their combined scent of coconut oil and joss sticks betrayed their location and proved mouth-watering to the less healthy sections of society. They'd outrun everyone they met, paused for breath when they could, and spent two nights in a fenced-off electricity substation, and one night on top of a bus shelter.

Dawn had pleaded with David to end their lives together, so they could be in control. But they had no guns, or any sure-fire way of dispatching themselves safely so they had headed to Cissbury Ring, the one place they would feel most at home. They regularly came up here at night he said, to smoke pot, listen to music and fuck. They'd been running for too long. I let them use Al's tent to catch some sleep as I sat with Floyd, wrapped in bin bags and trying not to fall asleep myself.

Floyd woke me three times in the night, and I used Vaughan's discarded axe to defend the camp. These were fresh ones; lively and quick, but I could see the ditch was still filled with bodies. Some were still, bloodied or charred; others clutched and gnawed at the ground, aroused by the smells of human activity above.

Day came grey and sodden; weak yellow light fighting for space with the rolling pewter clouds. Floyd ate, and I contemplated the stores. I was starving. There was only tinned food really, nothing fresh, and no meat, although I found some rice and pasta and some basics Lou had packed. At least now I had time to make something hot instead of glugging it back straight from the tin. I got the fire going – the pile of wood was still tinder-dry a few layers down - and poured two tins of tomatoes into the pot. I added salt, sugar and couple of handfuls of rice. I'd seen a bay tree up near the camp too, so I stripped off three or four young leaves, pounded them between a couple of flat stones, and threw them in.

David was out of the tent first, stretching, scratching and sniffing.

'That smells great.'

'I wasn't sure if you guys were vegetarian, so I left out the pancetta and pan-seared calf's liver,' I said.

He grinned. 'I'm a vegetarian; Dawn's not. She likes her cheeseburgers too much.'

'Well, this'll be another half an hour. Oh, look out.' I stood.

A stinker had stumbled onto the Ring and was making for the camp fire. I picked up my club and prodded him hard in the chest until he'd stumbled backwards to the edge of the Ring then swung at his head, cracking it in two and sending him reeling into the ditch.

'Eurgh. You've done that before,' he said. I sensed a morbid fascination in this one.

'David, you'll have to do it too.' I said. 'I can't believe you didn't do any of them on your way up.'

'I'm a vegetarian,' he repeated hesitantly, unsure of his argument.

'You'll be a dead one unless you're prepared to stop one of those bad boys. The only way you can do it permanently is to take their heads off, or sever this bit,' I pointed to the back of my neck.

'You're basically talking about killing sick people. What if there's a cure?' he asked. This was no time for playing Devil's Advocate, Goth or not.

'There is no cure.' I said firmly. 'They're dead. There is no cure for dead.' He sat, staring glumly into the fire.

'I thought you'd be into this, all these corpses.' I said, in an attempt to be light-hearted. It didn't work.

'Oh, you mean because we're Goths? Mate, it's more about getting other people to fucking leave you alone for a bit than it is about dancing round graveyards.'

'But it is about dancing round graveyards too, right?' I was being flippant now. This is where I needed Lou to reign me in, to make me put the feelings of others before my own self-gratifying comedy.

'Did I tell you we saw an old man sitting with someone's head, chewing on it like it was an apple?' he asked. 'I know there's no cure. You just seem so... used to it. It's freaky.'

'I'm not used to it. I'm realistic, and I want to protect what's mine.' I tried not to think about Lou. I rubbed my naked ring finger. 'You want to protect Dawn, right?' I asked him. 'You don't want to see her become one of them.'

'I don't,' David kicked at the dirt.

'We lost a friend here last night, just before you came. He was called Vaughan.'

'Have you buried him?' David asked me.

'No, there wasn't enough left of him.'

'Well, you can still build a cross or a pile of stones or something.'

'Ah, a grave you mean? David, are you feeling like doing another little jig? Sorry, I'm... I use humour to make myself feel better. I don't always think about other people though. Sorry. Let's build my mate a grave.'

All I had left of Vaughan was a long-sleeved T-shirt he'd had tied around his waist when he arrived, and then discarded when we went to B&Q. I picked up my trusty spade. David asked me if Dawn would be okay.

'She'll be fine. If one of those things gets into the camp my dog will bark like a maniac, or just destroy it straight away. Or do both. He's a good guard dog at night too. He saved all of us three times last night. Dawn will be okay, anyway most of them seem to have given up for now. We were up here for a few days before you came and we didn't see a single one of them up here. Then the wind changed.'

I realised I'd been subconsciously walking towards the trig point pillar. It seemed as good a place as any, so when we got there I started to dig a shallow trench next to it, about four feet long.

'I feel stupid.' I said.

'If your mate saw to just one of those zombies he deserves a good send-off.'

I laid Vaughan's T-shirt out in the upper half of the trench, smoothing out the creases. When I was satisfied, we pulled back the bracken from one of the numerous hollows dotted around the top of the Ring, and started to uncover stones. We prised them up, loose from the sudden drenching, the damp earth eager to give them up like rotten teeth. We laid them out in the trench. David found a couple of branches.

'For the cross,' he said.

'Vaughan wasn't religious,' I said.

'Oh. I didn't think of that,' he shrugged. 'Well, it makes it look like a grave anyway. At least other people will know what it is if it looks the part.' When we were done, David asked me if I should say something.

'Okay. Er. Vaughan was a good bloke, and a good friend of mine. Of ours. We all loved him, and he went out saving the rest of us, so there you go. Good bloke.' My throat caught the last few words, and I could feel the lump coming again, so I shut up. I shrugged at David, and we walked off. I had a pang of doubt that I should have waited for the others before doing what we'd just done, but I didn't even know if they were coming back. When we got back to the camp, Floyd was inspecting Dawn's skirt. She was sitting by the fire, stirring the pot.

'Hi cuteness!' David said to her. She wrinkled her nose at him before levelling her eyes towards me coolly.

'Thank you for letting us stay here last night.' She said to me.

'This is yours as much as it is mine,' I motioned around me. 'I was glad to see someone else.' There was a pause.

'What, after you tried to shoot me? Sorry, I'm being a bitch. If I'm honest I haven't felt this safe for a good few days. If that's how you're going to treat anyone else who finds their way up here, I'll feel even safer. Anyway, where did your friends go?'

'Oh, fuck knows,' I said, my voice over-loud. 'That was my wife, who slapped me. Fuck knows. Brrr.'

I didn't want to talk about it, so I suggested we ate what was in the pot - it was gone in minutes. After picking some bay leaf from my teeth, I turned to Dawn.

'There's a washing-up bowl over there.'

I didn't even think about it. Maybe some archetype of what a man expects a woman's work to be influenced me, possibly, but I was just projecting the ar-

rangement that Lou and I had worked with for nearly a decade onto Dawn –
me cook, woman wash up.

'What the fuck are you saying?' She was indignant, little lights burning in her
eyes like embers.

'Oh, no, I'm not suggesting…'

'It's okay,' Dave said calmly, 'I'll wash up. You do it next time though cuteness, yeah?'

'Don't use too much water,' I called after him, before turning to Dawn.

'Look,' I said, 'I've just buried my mate. My mate's T-shirt, anyway. I didn't
mean to offend you, but if I'm honest, there's not going to be much room for
getting upset up here. Like earlier, when I tied you both to the tree.'

'And left us for dead,' she jutted her jaw at me.

'Yeah, well. Level heads, stiff upper lips and that. Best of British. Am I being patronising?'

'Yeah,' she smiled a small smile. 'But I get your point though. You won't
get any trouble from me, I have to change shitty old men's pants and mop up
piss every Friday night.'

'Oh, that reminds me,' I waggled a finger at her and she frowned. 'I want to
go over some stuff with you – medicine and that, you know, from herbs and
berries and stuff. It's in a survival book I brought with me – we brought with
us. Well, we nicked a lot of it really, from B&Q, but the book's mine. Anyway,
it's all down there.' I stood and stretched, pointing down the track into town.
'It's only about a half-mile ramble.'

'What? We've only just got here!' David was in earshot, sluicing the water
out of the bowl.

'It's alright mate, we'll all go, and play it by ear. I'm not leaving anyone alone
up here again.' I pulled my binoculars from the tent and scanned the length of
the track. There were no figures standing or walking along the route, just felled
bodies from when we broke through. I spotted the rucksacks, untouched where
I'd left them.

'Here,' I handed Dawn the binoculars. 'See them? Each one's chock-full of
bits from B&Q. We broke in yesterday, all kinds of stuff's in there, mainly defensive.'

When I heard Floyd break into his long baying howl my stomach flipped.
When I saw the horse, I thought I was losing it again. But there it was in front

of us, complete with all its riding tackle or whatever its called. Dawn let out a gasp and thrust the binoculars back at me.

'Well, she'll be happy then. She had a horse when she was a kid.' David looked at me and whispered 'Bit of a daddy's girl really.'

'I thought I'd imagined horses last night. Look, there's another. Floyd hates horses with a passion.'

For whatever reason - lack of food, lack of human contact – the horses had found us. The bravest one let me rub his nose. There were five of them in total, including a much younger one that nuzzled the side of one of the big ones. It didn't seem too bothered about the responsibility, and would butt the little one away from time to time. Two of them had saddles and leads, or leashes or whatever. I hated horses as much as Floyd - I'd been forced to go on an adventure holiday in Wales when I was a school kid, and when we went trekking up the Breacon Beacons on one dismal day, I ended up with the biggest pony out of the lot. It kept nipping the arse of the one in front and eventually got bored and galloped up the steep wet scree to the front of the queue. I didn't have fun.

I wasn't too sure about Dawn's suggestion of using the animals to fetch the backpacks one bit. But after a while, and seeing how confident she was with them, it made sense. She seemed filled with a spark I'd not seen before as she told me how much quicker it would be, and how it meant we'd be above any zombies we came across. It was good timing. Dawn laughed again as she showed me how to get on. These were real horses, nothing like the *Thelwell* mules I'd been on before. David said she had made him ride on a few before.

'Just don't give him any reason to doubt you,' she said. 'Imagine you're riding Floyd.' That made sense to me, and I must admit during some of my heavier smoking sessions I'd had full-on daydreams about me and Al, miniaturised to the size of Action Men and scooting about the living room on the backs of our dogs. I showed Floyd no fear, and as a result he thought I was leader of the pack. How little he knew.

She showed me how to get him going, but it was like showing a driving student the accelerator before the brake. I worked it out myself eventually, after picking up some hair-raising speed.

'He's probably eager for a canter,' Dawn said. 'I wonder whose they are. Were.'

I showed them both the armoury. Al and Jay had taken their weapons with them, so choice was more limited than I'd have liked. Dawn reluctantly took Vaughan's axe, claiming she wouldn't be using it, and David took a fancy to the nail guns.

'I can at least keep my distance with these,' he said.

'I think I'll be keeping my distance from you – do you know what you're doing?'

'X-Box,' he said simply. I understood, but couldn't approve. X-Box indeed.

Dawn was confident enough to take one of the horses without a saddle and, after tethering the others and helping David onto his, she clambered up swiftly, using the mane as a grip. The horse stood still for her, before setting off at a trot on her command. Ours followed hers to the whinnying of those left behind.

'Dawn, do you know where we're going?' I yelled.

'Think so,' she shouted back. Even though she was ahead, I could tell she was smiling. 'Just keep going down, I'll shout when we're there.'

The horses waded through the corpses at the bottom of the trench and around the brittle remnants of Lou's gorse-fire protection. We picked our way through the fallen freaks scattered around the top of the path, with Floyd running ahead, and started south towards Worthing. I couldn't see any stinkers. The town centre was still dotted with fires - many less than before the rain - and the smoke spread out on the wind instead of climbing into the sky. I tried to make out landmarks with my binoculars, but the ride was bumpy. I could smell charred metal and molten plastic above the reek of eggs.

We all had to slide to a stop before we were at the rucksacks, as Dawn's horse reared up and threw her to the ground. She rubbed her elbow, and was about to mount again with a breezy grin when she shrieked. The horse had seen one of the bodies on the ground moving. I dismounted – well, fell off really – and ran up to her.

'Do you want to do one?' I asked her. 'You're going to have to at some stage.' The woman on the ground was young, about thirty. She had a massive head wound opening up her forehead, oily scum building up along its edges. One eye had been dislodged. She seemed to only have movement above her neck. Her eye twitched and her jaws chomped on the damp air.

Dawn had wrapped Vaughan's axe into the folds on her net skirt. She felt the handle tentatively.

'I can't. What if they come with a cure?'

'Who is this 'they' everyone's wishing will arrive?' I gesticulated. 'No-one's coming,' I said more softly to her as David joined us. Dawn stood over the corpse reluctantly.

'I don't want to.'

'She'd dead already.' I said. I was happy for Dawn to do it in her own time, and I knew it would be better for her to do one before David. That way, neither of them would have any excuse not to dispatch one when it was coming up behind me. After raising the axe a few times and checking with me where she was aiming for, she cracked it down at right angles to the woman's neck, sending the head rolling down the track. She sniffed, grimaced and folded the axe back into her skirt. She helped me back on my horse and we carried on. David saw one in the trees. The first I knew of it he had popped some nails into the man's head, but he still lumbered toward us.

'The nail guns are tricky; you've got to be spot-on.' I took it from him and put three or four into his neck, felling him. At least now David had got his hands dirty.

We were soon by the backpacks. The first one I checked was the one with all my books and DVDs, which had let some water in, but on the whole was fine. The VHS tapes hadn't crinkled up, I was delighted to see. I wondered if I should half-inch a TV/DVD combo from Sainsbury's and a generator from B&Q. It was risky, but it would be worth it, I thought - I could do with a laugh, but I did have other slightly more pressing priorities though. I loosened the straps on the rucksacks and tied them together in pairs, so I could sling them over the horse's backs like saddle-bags. Dawn helped me tie the water butts to my own back, like a low-budget Ninja Turtle, before we set back off up the path. We saw two up ahead when we were close to Cissbury Ring.

'Now have a proper go,' I said, dismounting uniquely.

David joined me as I swung my club.

'Just go for the head; this is really what you've got to do to any that have got into the camp, when you've got to finish them off. We left a lot of them alone coming up here – it slows you down if you think you've got to get them all. Going by the amount of survivors I've seen, there could be sixty million of them crawling over the country, so it's usually better to do what you two did, and run.' I struck the first one in a downwards blow to the forehead, and then dislodged my club with a gristly sucking noise. Before he could get up I broke his neck. I handed it to David as the next one shuffled up. He had a gash opening up his leg, and no left arm.

'Use my club for the time being. I'm good with the nail gun.'

'Cool. What have you called it?'

'Haven't decided yet. Club Med. Club Head. Club Dead. I dunno. Go on.'

David was less reluctant now that the man's good arm was nearly at his throat. He rained five or six blows onto his face.

'Aim for the important bits.' I suggested. He struck the man sideways across the neck with an impressive blow, seeming to loosen the chap's head from its moorings as he crumpled to the rain-soaked path.

'He was harmless,' he giggled to himself. He turned to Dawn. 'Armless.'

She rolled her eyes, and breathed out a deep breath. I saw she wasn't looking at David's handiwork. We followed Floyd back into camp – the little pup seemed well at home now. Dawn tended to the animals whilst David and I unpacked the booty.

The first thing we set up was the tarpaulin. It would be far more economical than Al's dad's sail, as it was much bigger. I dismantled our impromptu rain collector and used the same tree to stretch out the much larger sheet of blue plastic. I put a rock onto a raft of short sticks in the middle of it, weighing it down to form a point and also hopefully keeping the wind from tipping it up. I put one of the water butts underneath and cut a small hole in the sheeting – around an inch in diameter and as circular as I could get it, as a lot of weight would be on it and I didn't want it to split. It was still raining, albeit lighter than during the night before, yet it worked well, making a constant trickling sound echo inside the container.

Next we unpacked Jay's bag, with all the small bits. I put all of the screws, nails and chain into Jay's tent, and then David and I silently pulled on the chemical gauntlets and face masks. We knew what had to be done, and worked for the rest of the day grimly clearing the camp of bodies and body parts, and hauling them over the sides into the ditch. When we sat for a rest, we discussed ways to get rid of the corpses below us. They stank, and the flies were starting to reappear as the rain slowed.

'If it wasn't so damp I'd incinerate them down there where they lay, you know; torch them in small batches so as not to cause a massive fuckup,' I said.

'It would be too risky with the hot weather.' David was leaning back on his elbows.

'Yeah, I suppose. But we could dig fire breaks in the grass on the edges so it didn't spread up here.'

'It's too wet anyway,' he said. 'We could make quicklime.' David's eyes showed eagerness. I knew quicklime decomposed things quicker, that they used it in mass graves; and that they put the stuff into cigarettes - but that was about it. I had no idea how to actually make it.

'How the fuck are we going to make quicklime up here?' I asked.

'Chalk!' He spread his arms out to demonstrate the undeniable excess of chalk. 'You just burn it. You get quick lime from burning chalk.'

'How do you know that?' I asked incredulously.

'Dawn's favourite song. It's about a high school massacre, and the kid makes quicklime to decompose the corpses of his fallen victims.' He looked serious, contemplative.

'We could give it a go. We'll dig a trench on the side with the least wind – that side.' I pointed. 'Prevailing winds almost always go from west to east in England. We can get a load of chalk and burn it on the embers. Will that work?'

'I dunno, I'm not a quicklime expert.'

'How hot does it have to get?' I asked.

'I'll refer the speaker to my previous answer.'

'We need more logs, more than we've got here. Try under the trees, and any dead wood off the ground. Do you watch Ray Mears?'

'Yeah, of course,' David said. 'That canoe was awesome.'

We gathered wood and piled it up on the east side of the Ring. I dug a trench in the shelter of a low, long bush, first of all breaking through the dense weather-beaten turf and then hacking up the chalk which lay below that. Dawn had been seeing to the horses, but now she picked up the pick-axe Vaughan had lifted from the DIY store and joined in. We broke the chalk up into fist-sized lumps and piled it up by the side of the pit. David followed our progress on hands and knees, lining the bottom of the trench we were creating with flat rocks from the same place where we'd found the stones for Vaughan's grave. When we were done, backs aching and sweat dripping into our eyes it looked like a fifteen-foot long strip of perfectly excavated Roman road.

We began carrying the wood over, putting about a quarter of the thinner stuff onto David's orderly flagstones. Then we kicked, dug and pushed all the chalk back into the hole on top of the sticks. After this the rest of the wood went in, until it stood three feet high and not quite fifteen feet long. It was mid-afternoon and the sun glimmered weakly through the rain, which was easing all the time but still ever-present, soaking our clothes through from the outside whilst the toil did the same from the inside. I put three long staffs into our campfire and sat next to it, rotating each one until they were well alight.

'Ready?' I asked the two Goths at either end of the pyre. I stood in the middle, and when they nodded, we rammed our firewood into the thick mass of sticks. It took quickly, even in the drizzle. We hadn't seen a zombie since we'd gone for the backpacks, so we'd been able to work carefully and steadily enough to keep everything dry, and soon the blaze was raging.

'Well, we'll just have to wait and see,' I said.

'What did we do all that for?' Dawn asked.

'Quick lime,' David said, pulling her closer to him.

'Oh, cool.'

Making Up
[day 0007]

Dmitri woke me up. It confused me at first - I though Floyd's voice had broken or something. Night had crept up on us quickly, and the last thing I could remember was being by the campfire, drinking mug after mug of tea with no milk. But here I was in my tent; boots off, dead to the world. At least, that was until Dmitri started waking up the neighbours. I scrambled out of the tent, getting the zip caught and fumbling at the Velcro. My socks soaked up the damp from the earth. Both dogs were in front of me, so I definitely wasn't imagining it. But he was alone, which meant the others were out there somewhere in the night. Floyd was trying to get Dmitri to play, but that hadn't worked and he was now biting at his back legs. The usually tolerant older beagle snapped at Floyd, then persisted in barking at me. My skull felt like it had a crack in it, and my back, arms and legs ached from the previous day's digging. As soon as I walked a few step towards him in an effort to shut him up he ran away, then stopped, turned back to me and started barking again. David's dream-creased features emerged from Al's tent.

'What's the noise? Oh look, that's your mate's dog.'

'Yeah, but no mates. Or Lou.' I scratched my backside, yawned, and tried to shake myself awake. I walked towards Dmitri again. He did the same thing. Each time he kept going in the same direction, towards the back of the ring, then stopping and barking until I caught up.

'Car park', I said to no-one in particular. I ran back to the tent and hunted for my binoculars, then pulled my boots on. Dawn was next to David, rubbing her eyes.

'I think they're down there,' I nodded, 'in the car park. I'm going to have a look.'

The moon, fat and buttery, was dodging the scudding clouds. I ran north, both dogs disappearing ahead. I kept to the straight line they took, and after a heart-pounding five minutes I stopped, breathless. I could see the car park, and

I tracked the grey line of the road until I could see Al's Audi, headlights fading, and hear the slur of a struggling starter motor and someone's scream carrying up to me on the breeze. Dmitri was giving me full volume now. I could see five or six figures crowding the car, and more in the fields either side of the road. I tore myself away and sprinted back to the camp.

'Dawn!' I collapsed onto the cool grass. 'Dawn, you've got to help them. Get a pony. They're all down there.' I waved north, my face crumpled by a stitch in my side.

'How many are there?' She was kneeling next to me with water.

'It looked like all three of them. Lou was screaming. Al's car's not working.'

'Well, I'll need more than one horse. You ride one down and I'll lead a third one alongside mine. Get up then!'

'No, David's got to come with us,' I panted.

'It'll be quicker without him.' Dawn said.

'I'll stay here, get on the radio.' David offered. I had no time to discuss it.

'It's in my tent, they're on channel two,' I panted, 'so keep on it, tell them we're coming. Dawn, have you got a weapon?' She showed me a glint of metal in the folds of her skirt and beamed.

She was fast, even when she was in charge of two of the bastards. I was bouncing about all over the place and nearly came a cropper several times, and that was on the calm flat top of the Ring. Hammering down the slope I just grabbed some mane and shut my eyes.

'You go first!' Dawn was at the bottom, nodding at the gate. I didn't muck about; I could see a freak coming towards us from the undergrowth. The dogs set about him. Dawn had to wrestle two horses through the gap, so I dug my heels in, eager to get out of her way. I tore through the open gate and onto the road. The hooves on the tarmac made a noise that made me think of family holidays in other seaside towns, and the wind whipped my hair around my face as I guided the horse towards the fading headlamps of Al's Audi. I could hear Lou screaming quite clearly now. As I pulled alongside them and lashed out at the nearest member of what was now a twenty-strong swarm of freaks, I could hear Jay inside the car shouting 'What the fuck is that?'

I worked solidly, patiently; the animal keeping a good distance for me. The dogs had kept up with my horse and were getting stuck in. Dawn was soon beside me, and I could hear the steady crunch of her axe-work. When we'd cleared them away from one side of the car, I leant down on the horse's foot-holder-thingy and peered in through the window.

'Alright?'

'Fuck me. Are you riding a horse?' Jay sounded a bit drunk.

'Yep. Get out; one of you is going to have to ride one on your own. Dawn'll take the whichever one of you is left. Lou, you're with me. Hop on.' Lou was out of the car already, making a fuss of Floyd. She obviously hadn't seen him in a while, even though I was sure she'd taken him when she'd left. I noticed she was wearing one of Jay's big coats.

'Have any of you ridden a horse before?' Dawn asked, but none of them had. 'Right, you,' she pointed at Jay, 'you're more... substantial. Take this one. She's got everything you need to ride her. Just hold on, she'll follow us. Quick!' Jay took the horse, looking pale.

'You - Al, is it?' Dawn pointed. 'We're bareback, so hold on tight,' he was getting a licking from Dmitri, but he stood up and did as he was told. She sounded like a schoolteacher. 'Jay, help him on, we'll wait for you.'

After much potential for comedy, including me falling off in order to help my wife onto the back of our horse, we were all set. Lou had looked me in the eye briefly, and that was good enough for the moment, I thought. The zombies had gathered themselves up and were getting too close. I started to take a couple of lively ones down again, but Dawn was off already. Lou's grip tightened around my waist and I kicked my heels. I could hear Jay following behind us, screaming for his mother. Hooves clattered, and a few walkers span into the bushes as we rode into them. Dense, cold bubbles of rain started to hit my face. Al yelped as Dawn's steed jumped straight over the fence next to the open gate. Ours was less adventurous but soon we were all at the base of the Ring.

'Dawn, was this gate open when you came up here?' I shouted.

'Think so.'

'Nuts.' I didn't want to delay our escape, but equally I didn't want to increase the number of undead walking the base of the Ring, especially now they seemed to be spread out all around us and not just approaching from Worthing. We trotted back, and I booted the wide gate. It took a few goes, catching in the grass, but soon it swung home and clicked shut.

'Lean forwards, it'll help the horse get up the slope,' Dawn yelled over her shoulder.

We all scrabbled upwards, the horses seeming to relish the task, even though we were now out of immediate danger and onto the relative safety of the plateau above the South Downs. Soon we saw the glow of the freshly stoked camp fire, and David's white face as he shook the radio.

'I think the battery's dead,' he said, looking up. 'Hello. Home safe and sound!'

The dawn sun hung low and feeble on the horizon, dull through the milky clouds. Lou had still not said anything to me, but I was quietly delighted to find her small cold hand finding mine and gripping tight, as the six of us stood around the campfire. We'd lost one, but gained two, Al said. They had thought they'd lost Floyd as well, soon after they set out into the night. Apparently Floyd had jumped out when Al stopped to check his tyres in Worthing after failing to negotiate some broken glass in the road. He'd bounded north, towards the Downs, and they'd not seen him since. He'd come to find me. Now we had a full brace of hounds again and a small herd of horses, now safely tethered and chewing at the grass. Al told us how they had driven Lou to her mum's place, a mid-terraced house in West Worthing, but they'd found it completely empty and lifeless. Lou had let herself in, but there was no note, no clues as to her mum's whereabouts. Lou had assumed the worst, and sat silently in the back of the Audi whilst Jay and Al raided the larder. They'd tried to keep Lou's spirits up – at least she hadn't found what Al had seen at his parents' house, but she was beyond consolation. I loved Lou's mum, but without any proof of her demise I kept an open mind.

I was right, Jay was drunk – they'd driven onwards to his parents' house in Tarring, breaking through the defences he'd left them sheltering behind as quietly as possible. His mother - a large lady with a shock of black hair - had the same filthy, infectious laugh that Jay had. She had a kind heart but an evil sense of humour, a deeply unsettling combination. His dad Jerry was quieter; small, stout and achingly funny, with little round glasses and a snow-white beard. They had only moved in recently, trading in a huge house on a leafy street for a tiny one, hundreds of years old with doorframes that would knock you out unless you ducked your head. Jerry, an accountant, had done some maths about their new house, measuring and mapping all the rooms but something didn't add up: even taking into account the foot-thick walls, there was a void in the centre of the house, behind a fireplace. The few original houses that remained along their row had been built by a Roman Catholic landowner, and Jerry put two and two together and suggested that it was a priest-hole, designed to quickly hide outlawed priests away from the religiously oppressive laws of the time. He'd never found it, and was unwilling to smash the place up in order to do so.

The house also had a cellar, where Jay had barricaded them in from the outside. The one thing they hadn't taken enough of with them was water, and they'd gone thirsty until – another bizarre feature of the house – the underground stream which trickled beneath the foundations welled up. It was swollen with the rains and ran crystal clear and cold. They had enough tinned food from their emergency stores – yes, memories of Cold War civil defence advice had left them *that* prepared – to last them for months. They were raucous with laughter to see the three travellers, and even helped restock Jay with UHT milk and tins of spam and rice pudding as Al kept watch. On the whole they'd seen very few zombies and absolutely no other survivors. Jinny spoke comforting words to Lou who had been in hysterics, having as good as lost her mother that night, as well as her husband and her dog. Jerry and Jay were keen musicians, Jay going all Dylan and taking his dad's love of folk music into new, more electric directions from an early age. There they'd sat, drinking Jerry's home brew and playing Jay's guitar and his dad's banjo and sitar, sitting under the foundations of an ancient house whilst a stream flowed by their feet and the world raged above them.

Jinny and Jerry were fascinated to hear of our attempts to set up a camp, and wondered at the lack of other survivors. They'd both shot glances at each other at the news, as they'd always assumed some sort of help would be coming. Jay told them about Vaughan and about what I'd done, how I'd been with Lou, and the relentless onslaught we'd all endured. They were still dumbfounded that I had been left up there, and persuaded the others to get back to the Ring – Jerry even suggested they may follow them up in their battered Citroen 2CV. Al and Jay agreed to leave at first light, and enjoyed the last of Al's skunk as Jerry told old stories and legends till they'd fallen asleep. So up they'd come at the break of day - at least until Al's car had spluttered to a halt on the outskirts of town. They'd obviously started it again in order to make it as far as the bottom of Cissbury Ring, so I asked him if he'd found the problem.

'Guts,' he said simply.

'Eh?'

'Guts. In the radiator. Compacted bone, caked blood. Rancid. I had to work it out with a stick, but there's still loads in there. It smells like the worst barbecue you've ever been to.'

'Plus there's a ton of food in the back,' Jay said. 'What my folks gave to me and what we took from Lou's mum's house.' He stopped, and looked at Lou, who tightened her grip on my hand. I looked into her beautiful eyes – forget-me-not blue today - her face puffy with tears. I remembered what she'd told me one argument; about how men always want to fix things, but that's not necessarily what a woman wants to hear from a shoulder she's crying on. I decided not to tell her that it didn't mean her mum was dead, so instead I wrapped my arms around her and squeezed her tightly, making farting noises with each squeeze until eventually I could hear muffled, sob-staggered giggling coming from within my clothes. Al said that they'd been heartened on the way up by the sight of the blazing pyre David and I had built, and assumed I was still alive and kicking. I explained about David's plan for the quick lime.

'I don't think we've been introduced. Well, not properly, anyway.' David was grinning, his hand outstretched.

'I'm Al, pleased to meet you. Have you been treated well?' Jay collapsed into a fit of giggles, rolling around on the floor. Soon they were all introduced, and it felt good again. My stomach eased, and I hugged Lou even tighter.

'What on fuck are you doing with those horses?' Jay asked when he'd caught his breath.

'They just turned up on the night that… you left.' I explained. 'We used them to pick up the rucksacks the next day.'

'Really?' Al was impressed.

'Yeah, I've put all the supplies we haven't used yet in your tent Jay.' I showed them the water collector and offered to show them the pyre.

'What's that for again?' Jay asked.

'Quick lime,' said David, 'it's to decompose the corpses quicker.'

'I see you've cleaned the place up.' Jay said, waving his arms behind him.

'Yeah, we threw them all over the side,' I explained.

'Where did they all go? The live ones I mean.' Lou snivelled. This was the first time she'd spoken to me since she slapped me.

'I don't know baby. The wind's changed, but I'm sure the rain had something to do with it too. None of them are alive though.' I stopped trying to fix her opinion on the effects of the illness. The fierce heat from the trench greeted us.

'There's still thousands of them, but the ones we saw on the way up here were all really spread out.' Al said, absently poking at the white-hot embers with a long stick. 'There were no real groups of them. They're slower too, I'm sure.'

'I thought that – they've stopped climbing up the slope too. We only see one or two up here now, it's like they're running out of steam.' I said.

'Yeah, up here maybe – but town is still chock-full.' Jay was pissing in a bush, yelling over his shoulder. It felt good that Jay was pissing in a bush, and Al was setting light to stuff, and Lou was holding my hand. I gazed south, over the trees onto the coast. Worthing was not burning any more, yet a slate-grey curtain of smoke still sat above the twisted wreckage of the town. Lou and I left the warm chatter of the others and walked slowly, arm-in-arm, until we were back at the camp. We kissed, long and slow, before holding each other tight as Lou buried her snotty nose into my beard. How did her hair still smell so sweet? Lou spoke first.

'I was glad when they decided to come back. I missed you. I haven't got my wedding ring,' she started sobbing again.

'Nor have I baby, I... lost it.'

'What?' she looked hurt, even though she'd practically chucked hers away and called me a very bad word, but I bit my lip. I didn't know; maybe I'd chucked mine away too.

'I woke up and I didn't have it on my finger. I don't know how, no-one nicked it that's for sure. There are a lot of things about that night I haven't worked out yet.' I said, staring into the fire.

'What are we going to do?' I knew what she meant, and it wasn't the breakdown of society. Those rings meant a lot. We'd not even been married a year, but even after living under the same roof for the previous seven years and just shagging once in a while for a further three years before that, it felt horrible without them. We'd always insisted it would be just a piece of paper – we didn't need it, but we felt it was the way to make our relationship official before we started a family of our own. We were wrong – it made such an awesome difference. Even simply by the act of me proposing, we laughed more, she felt safer and more secure, and the sex was like we'd just met that night, wild and electric.

When we were finally married fourteen months later, it was like we were living a whole new life. We were enjoying ourselves so much the plans for a new family got put on the back-burner and we'd decided to get a puppy. You know, so Lou could cuddle something small and warm in the meantime. It led to a few accusations of my bollocks not working properly, but being ginger-haired and therefore branded a 'Jaffa' since my first day at school I could draw upon years of imaginative playground banter to counter any verbal attack within nanoseconds.

'I'll get us new rings,' I said hopefully. I was sure there were lots of jeweller's shops still left unplundered. I knew, though, that at least Lou's was somewhere up here, on top of Cissbury Ring. I was poking at the fire with a stick, when Lou let out a delighted 'Ooh!' and pulled from the pocket of Jay's coat a red carton of UHT milk.

'I forgot about the cow juice! Shall I put the kettle on?' she beamed triumphantly.

A light drizzle had drifted over the camp, possibly due to our height above sea level; it might well have been the base of a low-flying cloud. Either way it clung to my clothes and made me shiver. I built the fire up, and soon it was crackling away, but the woodpile was getting dangerously low. I could hear voices approaching above the whistling of the kettle, and the smell of damp wood smoke caught deliciously in the back of my throat. The horses murmured to each other, and soon the others were around us, licking their lips at the sight of the seven mugs laid out on the ground and firing banter into the dank air.

'The quick lime's nearly done,' David said to me.

'Yeah, we still don't know if we got it hot enough,' I said, not wanting to spoil anyone's fun.

'True. That's the downside of not having broadband any more.' He chuckled.

'Oh, yeah, I wonder what's happened to the Internet?' Al said.

'S'probably still there. I suppose if bits of it have still got power that would all still be up and running.' Jay pondered.

'I don't know enough about it,' I admitted, 'I thought it was powered by voodoo.'

It was only after Lou and I had finished off the teas to everyone's specifications that we realised we'd made one for Vaughan too. Heavy silence. I broke it by telling them all about the grave David and I had built to bury Vaughan's T-shirt. Al wanted to see it, so we took our mugs to the mound of rocks and the little cross. I gave him a bit of a back-slapping hug, and he sniffed into his steamy tea. He was carrying Vaughan's cup of tea with him too, and he set it down at the head-end. I stood with him for a bit, and pretty soon everyone else was gathered around. No-one said anything. No-one needed to. He'd saved us all. When we started to make our way back to the camp, I walked next to Al. I still wasn't sure if I'd done the right thing by making the grave, and I didn't know how such a concrete reminder of it, after all Al had seen in the last week, would sit with him. It soon became clear though.

'Thanks for doing that chum,' he said, the tears forced dry once more.

'Well, it was David's idea really.' I was being honest. 'I hadn't thought about it, but I suppose it makes sense.'

'I like it. It's like we've got him up here still. With us, not with them.'

'He won't be one of them, chum.' I said. 'How are you feeling?'

'Tired. Very tired,' he replied

'Oh, you've got some house-guests by the way - the Goths.' I did a zombie walk to illustrate. 'Jay's tent was full, and I didn't think you'd mind. They don't have a tent of their own, plus I didn't actually know if you'd be coming back.'

'No, I'm sorry about that. It seemed like a good idea, and Lou was upset.' Al turned to me. 'You asked me to protect her when you weren't around. It really didn't feel like you were around that night. I'm glad you're back,' he said.

I fell quiet.

'So how many of us are there?' he asked. 'Six? But we've got tents for five. Halfords is down in the business park. I'm sure they sell – sold - tents.'

'Yep, that's true. But how about we build them something?' I suggested. 'It'd show them they were both welcome.'

'I like that. We will. We should build a shelter for all the stores too. Got any ideas?' Al asked me.

'I'm sure there's something in one of the survival books I've got. It's pretty simple with this many of us I should think. It's not like we're short of water or anything.'

'Or wood,' Al shrugged. 'You can suggest it to them. It'll keep everyone occupied too.'

[day 0008]

The next day we began to build what would become the first permanent structure on top of Cissbury Ring for a long, long time. We started out by prepping the small chainsaw, filling it with petrol from a can Al had relieved from Jay's garage. It worked after a few pulls, so we set about finding some suitable wood. We weren't eager to take any of the old trees down – they were too thick and gnarly anyway. After consulting the *SAS Survival Handbook* I saw that we should be looking for young trees, like those in a coppice, long and tall with no branches until the whippy ones right at the tip. I jotted down some plans, and realised the few young trees up here would never be enough to build what I had in mind. I wanted any buildings we put up to be substantial – I felt Dawn and David deserved to feel at home up here, and I didn't want them living in a pig shed. It would be good practice to build a shelter for the Goths.

'We could build the stores under the same roof – if you guys are up for that?' I suggested. The Goths nodded agreement. We did have a lot of stuff between all of us, and there were still more edible supplies in Al's car. All of our tents were crammed full of all the bits we'd managed to salvage so far.

I seemed to have been nominated as foreman by default, so I suggested we started with the thicket at the northern, car park end of the site.

'The one you walk up from the back of the Ring. There's a load of young trees there. It's covered and it's on a slope.' Al thumbed his agreement, thrilled to be doing something constructive. 'Dawn, can you and David make something safe for the horses to use with the chain over there? We'll get them to tow the logs up here if you think they can.'

'Possibly,' Dawn rubbed her chin. 'It usually takes quite a while to train a horse to haul stuff. They get freaked out pretty easily.'

'We'll take it nice and slow. There's a hand drill in my dad's toolkit.' Al said. 'We can drill a hole at each end of the poles and thread the chain through.'

'I like it. Jay - I know you've got a bit of a hangover, but you're on security. Lou and I will help you out; we are at your service. Tool us up. Al - you'll be felling trees with the chainsaw and drilling the holes. David - when we're down there, all you have to concern yourself with is making sure none of us get brained by a tree. That's it. Oh, and Dawn - you'll be on the horses and will probably have the best view, so keep in touch with Jay as a lookout. We won't take the radios, it will be too noisy with the saw and we should all be pretty close to each other anyway.' I took a breath. I was relishing the prospect of getting something done. We all hurried to get what we needed. The prospect of working in the damp grey air, which breezed cool on our necks, was especially appealing after the heat of recent days. I scanned from the horizon down to the path below us, and counted no more than a hundred freaks as far as I could see. They were spread out, but nonetheless we had to keep on our toes. I offered Jay the binoculars, but he pulled out a pair of his own – they were lighter than my old ones and more powerful too.

Jay helped us wrap our legs in gaffer tape and cut lengths of drainpipe for our forearms. The three of us on defensive duties also wore chemical gauntlets, and lightweight clear plastic safety goggles. We all made our way towards the back of the Ring, and the slope down to the woods, after Dawn and David had sorted out the tow chain. She'd lashed two of the horses together and neatly linked each end of the chain to the back edge of each mule's head-gear. The chain clanked as it trailed behind us, Al and I leading the party into the woods, with the Goths on horseback and Lou and Jay walking backwards downhill. 'It helps,' I heard Lou explaining to Jay, and I laughed.

Al worked fast, David whistling low and loud before each tree came down. The hounds soon worked it out, although Floyd had a couple of lucky escapes. The logs were rolled into place alongside each other and Al knelt to drill through the base of each one as David held them steady. Jay, Lou and I were spaced out, walking around the perimeter of the work as we moved from tree to tree. We'd stop each time we heard the whistle, and either watched the tree fall or ran out of the way. Jay had the axe as a backup in case the chainsaw failed, and would hack away at the leafy ends of the logs whenever his circular route let him. We were all listening for any warning from Dawn, who had my binoculars and sat astride one of the horses keeping watch, calming the animals when the chainsaw started its rattling drone. She only yelled once, as a corpse appeared, dragging his feet through the leaves and stumbling up the slope. Jay had already spotted him and felled him quickly, then rolled the headless body downhill with his foot. It had been impossible to tell how old he was. His face seemed blackened as if burnt, but his limbs were all there and his clothes were intact. I only guessed he was a he.

When Al had felled thirty or so trees - all at least twenty feet long - Dawn reversed the horses into the clearing and David helped Al thread the chain through the neat hole in each log. We started back up the slope in the same formation as before. The horses had no problem on the level bits; it was like they could have carried ten times as much wood, but on the steepest part of the track they struggled. Any leaves and branches Jay had missed soon got ripped off on the stony path, and we made steady progress.

'Look at that,' Al pointed. A stinker had started to climb up the base of the slope, but was now laying face-first in the dirt at a steep angle, his legs working away at the grass. He didn't seem to be using his arms at all.

'Now, has he forgotten how to climb, or are his arms broken?' Al wondered.

I pointed. 'His arms are still moving. Maybe they're all just running out of energy.'

'Maybe he was just as thick as pig-shit when he was alive,' Al chuckled.

When we got back to the camp I smoothed out the plans I'd drawn out onto a bit of lined A4 paper, and spread the book out on the ground.

'This is what we're making.' I explained. 'It's basically a log cabin. It says here to use the length of the logs to dictate the size. I think we might have to get some more for the roof, but we can do that tomorrow.'

'I got some really long ones, maybe thirty feet or so. Why don't we halve them or even cut them into thirds, and have one side shorter?' Al was eager. 'We should clear the ground too, make sure its solid.'

We all kitted ourselves out with hand saws, and Al and I went round each log with two rope markers to mark the cutting points, so we were sure we were making the most of the timber - one length of rope was around eight or nine feet long, the other eighteen or nineteen. Soon we had twenty-two long ones and twenty-four short ones, as regular as telegraph poles. Any off-cuts went on the log pile to dry out.

It was invigorating work, but soon we were all hungry. Al took the empty backpacks and went with Dawn and Dmitri down to his car, taking a radio. He was eager to try out a horse for himself, and he was a natural. They didn't need to use the radio though, and soon returned with bulging bags. Lou looked a bit sick when we started to pull out the things that she recognised from her mum's larder, so I suggested she put the kettle on whilst I set about some food. There were two big white onions, loads of tins of tomatoes and some tuna and sardines. There was more salt and pepper, and – genius Jay – Lou's mum's spice rack. There was a kilo of dried spaghetti. Tuna bolognaise. As the mixture sat bubbling next to the big pot of pasta on the campfire (now made wider to accommodate two tripods and two pots), I joined the others.

They were hacking notches into each log with the hand-axes, about six inches from the end, so we could slot the poles on top of each other precisely. Some were better at it than others, being more skilled with their hands naturally or by experience. By mutual agreement these people took over the work, increasing the time needed to finish the job but vastly improving the potential for solid joints. David and Dawn chose their plot, level and facing the fire, a polite distance away from the other structures already erected. The camp already sat in a good spot, in the lee of some trees which should act to break up and soften even the strongest winds.

As there were to be no windows in the structure, the Goths suggested a south-facing door to catch the most light in the morning. The ten foot by twenty foot strip was cleared of turf quickly, and levelled by whacking it with the flat end of a spade. We laid out the first layer of four logs flat on the ground in a rectangle, following the shape of the exposed earth and scraping away even more soil at the edges so each log sat halfway down into the ground. When that first layer of logs was laid out we could see the actual size and shape of the building for the first time. The notches hacked into each end allowed them to lie together more snugly, making a tighter seal with the next layer of logs, but as more were added it became clear that our measurements had to be spot on. It took a bit of juggling, trying two or three different logs in the same place before we found a good enough fit, with Jay and Al lifting each one into place and me chipping final adjustments out of the notches with one of the hand-axes.

'We need my brother here,' Lou said wistfully. Mike had been a carpenter and joiner since he left school but had a lively passion for photography, so whenever he could afford to do so he jetted off to the other side of the world to take pictures of interesting stuff. That's why he was in Thailand. I wondered what the rest of the world thought, if indeed there was anyone left - we certainly hadn't seen any contrails, or even any planes in the air since the jet we'd heard crumpling into the countryside. Mike would never have the benefit of air travel again. He was trapped alive, effectively, if indeed he was alive. Nice place to be trapped though, I'd seen his photos.

We worked on the cabin until bad light stopped play, the structure standing chest-high. It all fitted together pretty well, and we'd not even used all of the logs yet.

'Nuts!' David spurted. 'We've forgotten to put the door in.'

We had indeed, but as this was everyone's first attempt at building a log cabin I thought we had done well. Laughing, Al came up with a plan. We lashed two of the eight foot logs upright and next to each other tightly to the outside of the structure - about the right width apart for a modest door. Then he just used the chainsaw to cut out the gap between them, saving the excess for the wood pile. The next day we could work up the door frame until we'd hit the right height to start building a roof. David was eager to spend the night in the unfinished building, laying one tarpaulin out on the ground and stretching another over the top of the half-built walls as cover from the rain.

'It's alright!' he exclaimed. 'It's homely, if a little draughty.' Dawn wasn't as impressed by the lack of roof, and opted to stay in Al's tepee for the night. David shrugged, and said he'd enjoy keeping the dogs warm. After some pre-dictable banter about how David felt about animals we all settled in for the night. As Lou snuggled into my chest I stroked her hair, she soon dropped off, and I began to think about the progress we'd made, and planning how our own house would look. House. I'd never thought of it like that. I contemplated the notion that we might be up here for longer than even I'd thought.

As I drifted, my eyelids heavy, Lou let out a piercing scream. I've heard people say the hair on their head stood on end, but this was the closest I'd ever come to it. It might have had something to do with the proximity of Lou's vo-cal chords to my ear; the back of my neck began crawling with electricity and every follicle ached in time with my pulse. The dogs began barking. I sat bolt upright, but my arm was trapped under Lou's head. I couldn't hear anything, until Al shouted 'Chum?'

Lou screamed again, and I looked around the inside of the tent. There were no claws ripping through plastic, no fingers scrabbling under the sides. Lou's eyes were still tight shut.

'I think Lou's having a bad dream,' I shouted. I tried to wake her but she was out cold, breathing heavily, her forehead creasing. She thrashed her head from side to side and let out a gasp. I shook her, until her eyes sprang open. She took a breath, locking my eyes with her gaze, but not seeing me. Her hands clutched my arms.

'Lou, you're having a dream.'

'Oh. Sorry.' She closed her eyes, but looked drained. 'Really sorry.'

'It's okay baby,' I stroked her head again. 'It's okay.'

I stayed up most of that night, waking Lou when she screamed. I left the door-flap open a crack so Floyd could poke his head in and check on us. When he'd started to scrabble at the outside of tent I'd really nearly shat myself. I could have done with a spliff after that, and remembered our first few camping trips, smoking under the stars listening to John Peel on the radio. I was woken once more in the early hours when the dogs started to howl. I heaved myself outside into the hazy dawn, and found Al and David standing over a headless body. David was still fully dressed, but Al was wearing just his pants and some walking boots. He was holding Jay's sword.

'This is spot-on,' he said to me, swinging the blade in an arc.

I donned the gloves, grabbed a twisted leg and dragged the body to the edge. Al wrestled the chap's head from the dogs and drop-kicked it over the edge with a crunch, before looking with dismay at his right boot. It was slicked in a gloss-black sheen.

'That's rotten,' he said. 'It sounded like his head was hollow; it split when I hoofed it.'

I filled the washing-up bowl with water and carried it to Al at the edge of the Ring. I sluiced the water over his boots, taking care not to splash any back on us or into the bowl. I mumbled my goodnights and stumbled back into my tent.

[day 0009]

The others had let me stay in bed; Lou was up before anyone else. She and Dawn had set about tidying the camp up, and made a big pot of porridge with half water, half UHT milk. Mine was like dry sponge when I finally got to it, but it tasted amazing dipped in sugar. It was a hot day, but the others had made an early start and finished off the logs from yesterday, adding another foot to the height, and were eager to get back into the woods to fetch more. I pulled my shoes on whilst Dawn got the horses ready and Jay and David discussed security. They showed me a quick-release thingy they had worked out for the chain, in case they needed to dump the wood and get the horses away from danger quickly. The plan was to have the Goths continually tow sets of ten logs up the steep track from the coppice to the camp, making several journeys slowly and steadily. It would keep the horses busy and out of the way of the noise the saw made; but would mean we'd have to be on our toes in the woods, and would lack the higher vantage-point afforded from horseback. We could also fetch a lot more wood this way, and if we had to abandon the woods we'd have at least some materials in camp to work with.

We hiked down first to make a start on the felling, and to see how we fared on our own. We almost felt more mobile without the horses, and were especially heartened when we saw another two zombies failing miserably to scale the side of the hill fort. Al took responsibility for safety, and worked out a system of warning based on the hours on a clock face. We all knew roughly where each tree would fall by now anyway, but we could have done with David's warning whistles. When we had eight or so logs cut and drilled, Lou radioed up to the Goths. We rolled the logs into place next to each other, and soon we heard horse's hooves as Dawn picked her route through the coppice. David sat atop the other horse, carrying the chain. They set down, and we loaded them up. They were in and out in just four and a half minutes.

We carried on through the morning, the heat building with each hour, Al stopping after each tree to quaff the water David had brought down with them. We walked our circle, and picked off just two walkers that had ambled into the clearing, both apparently uninjured. I found I was being almost over-cautious since nearly pasting Dawn, and I actually thought they might be survivors at first. Their clothes were stained – red not black - but not tattered, and it was only their gurning jaws and bared teeth that gave their game away. They were quicker than the one we'd seen the day before, and had no problem with the slighter slope of the mulch-strewn floor. Seeing their split skulls spilling healthy pink globes of fatty matter onto the leafy ground made me think of the difference between these fresher ones and the hollow-sounding head that Al had put his foot through, with its black, rotten core. They were definitely slowing down, perhaps even decaying. We left them where they landed, at the edge of the trees - we were felling in the other direction. But just before we radioed to the top for what must have been the fifth or sixth load, Lou saw more movement through the trees, down towards the car park. We saw it was the shape of a man, and then we heard a voice.

'You have to help us. My daughter.' He was sobbing.

There were two little figures alongside him, but he was carrying something too, which hung limp from his arms like a sack. They all burst into the clearing and the man stumbled, falling to his knees. He was holding a young girl. Soon another little girl and a slightly older boy were at his side, with black hair and nut-brown eyes, clutching at the man's clothes - their dad I assumed. The littlest one's face was streaming with tears whilst the older one, still no more than eight, stood with his jaw out and a determined look in his eye. The dad had a bandaged head and a beard, and it was only when he started speaking more slowly that I realised from his accent that it was a turban, clawed loose by the branches.

'My daughter has been bitten,' he sobbed. 'We were in the car and we got a flat tyre, we tried to fix it. Sachbir, she's only fourteen. Sirs, you must help us.'

We were dumbfounded, but Lou was the first to act. She walked forward cautiously, and asked the man to lay her onto the ground. He seemed to crumple as he let her free from his grip. She seemed wilted and grey, her clothes sodden from sweat. A great long gash lay open on her calf, one edge serrated as if torn. She moaned.

'Oh great, she's still alive.' I murmured.

'How did it happen?' Lou asked him.

'Has anyone else been bitten?' I was keeping my distance.

'No, none of us have, except Sachbir. She was helping me find the place to put the jack underneath. It is my brother's car, an unfamiliar one, but she is smaller than me you see? I took my eyes off her and a young man just bit her in the leg. He was one of them.'

'One of them?' I asked.

'One of those fucking filthy dead bastards!' He sputtered. That was that, then; it wasn't just me and my stoner, zombie-movie fan chums. With everything out in the open I thought it was best to cut to the quick.

'You know she's gone, don't you?' I asked quietly. Lou shot me a glance. 'Mate? You know that she'll be one of them? Sachbir is dead.'

His face seemed to collapse into his beard, and great fat tears rolled into his lap. He spoke after a minute.

TREE
FELLING

'I know, I know. I have lost my wife and my father this week. The very same happened to them, I tried to nurse them, but they turned onto me, onto the children. We were escaping yesterday night when we broke down and...' He heaved great juddering sobs, and his smallest daughter buried her head into the folds of his jacket. The little boy still stood stock-still, only his chin now quivering.

'We have walked here,' the boy offered quietly.

'Okay, we've got a little more way to walk, up that hill, you see it?' Lou was bending down to the little boy, taking charge. 'I'll take you and your sister up there, we can have some tea. Would you like to do that?'

'I'll come with you,' Al said, pulling the chainsaw to life. 'You'll be safe here, with us.'

'Will Sachbir be well again?' the little lad shouted to Lou over the two-stroke rattle of the saw. She said nothing; I wondered if she was choking up. I stood next to his father, who was built like a bear. I could feel the soft ground shaking with every judder of his shoulders. I put a hand on one.

'Mate, you know what we've got to do, don't you? You know why you were escaping?'

'Yes,' he said softly.

'Well, age is no barrier for whatever this disease is.' I said. 'She's dead already, and we have to do this now.'

He threw his head back and let off a long wail. My neck-hairs stood dutifully to attention. Jay got on the radio – he was getting jumpy too. Lou and Al had already headed up the slope with the kids and now it was just the three of us standing round just the one of them. One was enough. It felt like it was all starting to unravel.

'Dawn, David – we've got some survivors here. Lou and Al are coming up with two kids, and we're with another one now. Can you come down to meet them, over?' A whoop sounded from the radio.

'You have radios?' he sniffed moistly.

'We've got lots of things. You'll all be safe here,' I told him. 'But I'm afraid Sachbir can't come. You go on ahead with the kids, Jay and I will follow you, but you have to leave her here with us.'

'No!' he roared as he pulled himself to his feet. He was massive - I wasn't going to argue, even before I noticed the long curved sword at his side. Then the girl groaned and sat up.

'No, you two go. I will follow you. First I will kill this thing that has taken my daughter,' he hissed.

'Make sure you get this bit,' I said, pointing at the back of my neck, but Jay was pulling me away by my arm.

We left him in the woods with his daughter's corpse. After a minute we heard a dry crack ring out followed by another wail, then nothing. We waited where we were, halfway up to the top of the Ring. We'd heard Dawn's horse trotting to meet the others, just out of sight at the top. Soon the man appeared behind us, with his turban restored to shape, carrying his daughter in his arms just like before, but this time her head sat on her lap, facing the sky, lips apart. He looked half the size as we walked in silence next to him.

'I'll radio ahead; to get the kids out of sight.' Jay said.

'No,' the man said sharply. 'They have to see.'

Tough love, I thought. It was true, they had to be careful, and demonstration was the best education - if they were to survive, that is. When we'd got him back to camp and we'd laid his daughter under some trees, he wiped his eyes and told us his name was Daltegh Singh. The boy was called Patveer, and the little girl Janam. He told us to call him Dal. They all lived in Worthing and had holed up in their house when the virus hit, turning the streets into a frenzy and blocking the roads with traffic. He thought they were safe after the third day, and they all walked out of the house to get help. They hadn't got far before Dal's father had fallen and been bitten by a girl in a bush. Dal ran back to fetch his sword, but his wife had been attacked by the time he returned. He had got angry with her, he said, looking apologetic. I tried to tell him it wasn't his fault, but he wasn't having it. He'd carried his wife and father back to the house, and nursed them as best he could until they'd turned. Then they ran for the safety of the children. Sachbir had been infected on the way.

'I had seen your fire from the town,' he said to me. 'Sir, I will need to use that fire,'

'Oh, for a pyre,' I said. Al was looking at me.

'We do not have to,' Dal said, 'but I would like to do so.'

'Some council up north got done for letting a Sikh family burn a relative's body in a public park last year,' I explained to anyone in earshot. 'It was the first open pyre in Britain since the 1930's. It looks like we're going to have another one. What do you need us to do?' I asked him.

He told us, and I explained that we needed to get the quicklime we'd made out of the pit, and then build the firewood up again. Dal nodded, and we all set-to, raking away the charcoal to reveal the grey powder underneath. The quicklime process had certainly seemed to work, but whether or not it would do the job of breaking down the corpses any quicker was another matter. We piled the finished product up onto the tarpaulin and took it to the V-shaped notch, the centre of the most activity over the past few days. The corpses – three deep in places - stank in the heat, a thick black cloud of flies ever present. Gagging, we used spades to fling the claggy powder into the ditch, as evenly as we could. We got a thin coating over most of them with the amount we'd made, and wherever they were still moving but unable to walk, the contact of the grey dust would make them squirm like salted slugs.

'If we do this once a week, we'll soon be able to cover them quite well.' Al said, firing nails into the faces of any that were still moving. It wasn't very efficient, but no-one was volunteering to jump in to do a neater job.

'It's supposed to halve the decomposition time David says.' I told him. 'I suppose we've got all the time we need.'

We built an awesome pyre; chest-high with straight sides, just like Vader's at the end of *Return of the Jedi*. We topped it off with the shorter, thicker off-cuts from the building work, making a level platform that Dal rested Sachbir's corpse onto. He spent a while resting her head in place on top of her shoulders, but it kept rolling to one side.

Al and Jay had made six torches, four of which they handed out to David, me, Dal and little Patveer (already nicknamed 'Paddy' by Jay). But Dal shook his head, and gave his to Lou and told the kids to share theirs. I guess they'd assumed he wasn't into women doing things, but from what I'd seen he'd not got many hang-ups. He certainly was eager for the kids, snot-faced and small, to get involved. Patveer had stood with him as he prepared the body, wrapping it in the canopy Al had given him from his tent. The girl had taken a shine to Dawn and they'd both made a fuss of the horses, watching us prepare the fire.

I asked Dal if he wanted to say anything but he didn't, so we all leant our torches at the base of the structure. We all stood for a few minutes. I watched as the flames played around the girl, melting her hair to her scalp and sucking her cheeks around her teeth. We left silently, leaving Dal clutching what was left of his family.

'We've got to get a treaty going, or a pact, or an agreement or whatever.' I was sat with the others around the campfire, sipping Lou's mum's vegetable soup.

'Rules you mean?' Lou asked.

'Yeah, but rules that mean something – they'd be rules that are too deadly to be broken,' I replied. 'We've got to establish a system; something that people can rely on, and that we can use without any sense of guilt or remorse. You know, to make it as difficult as possible for newcomers to put the rest of the camp in danger.'

'Like what though?' Lou quizzed.

'I dunno. It won't be pleasant. To guard against exactly what happens in the movies when someone gets bitten. You know the sort of thing; hoping their loved ones will recover, looking after them but also spelling Game Over for everyone else.'

'Take the bull by the horns. I agree; there should be absolutely no fucking about.' Al was sitting up. 'Zero tolerance on foolishness, no question - if someone gets bitten, that's it. Even if you love them there's no option. Especially if you love them, you've got to put them out of their misery.' I wondered what exactly Al had seen at his parent's house. He was so sure of the point I was making, and I appreciated the backup.

'It is fucking miserable. It has to be done humanely, as it were.' Jay scratched his nose.

'Like Dal, in the woods.' I said 'He knew he had to do it, I think he just wanted to hear someone else say it. He did it without questioning it really, as soon as he found us. He did it for the other two kids too. But the truth is we can probably expect more survivors to come, as their food runs out or as they see that there are signs of life up here. I would suggest that most of them won't be as quick to reach to the conclusion that Dal did, and time is of the essence.'

'Also,' Al chipped in, 'If they see any movement after they've become zombified that'll just add to the illusion that there's some hope of a recovery.'

'Very true,' I said.

'But won't they have seen what these things are like over the past week? Won't they know what they're dealing with?' Jay was playing Devil's Advocate, which was good, it was what we needed.

'Some people might have been holed up since the outbreak.' Al suggested. 'They might not have seen anything really serious happen, and now they could easily make it all the way up here without seeing what this disease can do.'

'Plus, some people are just idiots with their eyes permanently shut anyway. I don't want those idiots putting anyone up here in danger. We deserve to be here, we deserve to have survived. We're not idiots; should decide how best to survive from now on.' I said.

'Yeah, I'm not too sure about this,' David admitted. 'This was your site, you were here first. If you want to do anything like that I'll definitely support you, but I don't want the responsibility of making up the new law of the land.' Dawn nodded her agreement.

'Fair enough,' I said. 'So that's that. If we're all agreed, the four of us – me, Lou, Al and Jay - then we're making the law.'

We the undersigned hereby state that we will abide by the following rules of the camp at Cissbury Ring under penalty of complete and permanent expulsion, imposable by force and decided by the common consent of the first four to strike camp there (hereafter referred to as the Group of Four):

I am a free human being, of sound mind, and understand that I am entirely responsible for my own actions

I understand a highly infectious disease has spread throughout the country

My skin has not been broken by or near an infected person

I have not, to my knowledge, ingested, inhaled or consumed anything that may be infected, including: blood; spittle; mucus; flesh; skin; bone; semen; menstrual fluid; vomit; bile; urine; faeces; breast milk; tears; or any other potentially infectious material not mentioned

If my skin has been broken by an infected person I will be decapitated without question or compassion by the person closest to me at the time of infection
(If decapitation is not an option, the top of my spinal chord must be severed)

If the skin of someone next to me is broken by an infected person I will immediately decapitate them without question or compassion
(If decapitation is not an option, the top of their spinal chord will be severed)

I understand that my responsibility to other survivors goes beyond family, love, friendship or any other human compulsion

I understand that if I need help, assistance or support at any time I will ask a fellow member of the camp

I will arm myself and be prepared to use my weapon to protect myself and other members of the camp, and will help keep the camp secure in any way seen fit by the common consent of the Group of Four

Only specific camp members agreed by the common consent of the Group of Four may interact with the water storage and water collection equipment (hereafter referred to as Representatives)

Only Representatives will be responsible for the horses; the armoury or the stores or anything else deemed appropriate by the common consent of the Group of Four

I am free to put myself forward for consideration by the Group of Four to be a Representative responsible for the horses; the armoury or the stores (or anything else deemed appropriate for protection by the common consent of the Group of Four as they arise)

I am free to use a horse or anything in the armoury or the stores, but I will give as much notice as possible to the Representative responsible

I will not collect water

I will not leave the camp without someone else

I will not leave the camp without telling a member of the Group of Four or a Representative

By using the camp's supplies (firewood; building wood; water; food), I am bound to replenish them as I can

I understand the Group of Four is not exempt from any of the above, nor should be afforded any special or favourable treatment or bias of any kind

As the four of us were signing our names I'll admit I did wonder briefly if we were doing the right thing, but I quickly told myself it would be preferable to have set up the laws before any other survivors might arrive. The decapitation was a bit harsh – I hoped I'd never have to do to Lou what Dal had done to Sachbir. I also wondered if the pact would ever mean anything, even in a year - for the time being at least it could just keep us alive. Anyway, deep down English people liked rules, I told myself. I just never thought I'd be making them up on a bit of A4 with my chums.

Dal was impressed with the camp. He said he'd ridden horses before, but that ours were far too weedy to be good in battle (his phrase). He loved Al's tent, and told us of the tents he'd seen when he was living in India. He'd described them like ships, with great white sails flapping against the horizon. He had no shelter, but was happy to sleep by the fire if the kids could bed down somewhere under cover. We showed him the cabin, and for the first time I saw the fruits of our labour in the woods. In a neat pile there was about three or four times as much timber as we'd collected the day before, so I was confident we could house the new arrivals, even if it was in temporary lean-to shelters. David had numbered each log with Al's knife, and kept notes of the amount and size of the timber. He'd also written a complete inventory of the equipment, consumables and weaponry that we had amassed in the camp. I even watched David scrambling for his notes when he first spotted Dal's Sinbad-style scimitar, which he'd let Al and Jamie play with. Dal sat cross-legged on a log as his children played with Floyd and Dmitri, and he told us that he knew a way to make the horses far more efficient. He talked about making a yoke for them to push against, instead of pulling the weight of the logs.

He had already signed the bit of paper we'd thrust at him without question, and got the kids to sign their names under Dawn and David's. I rolled it up carefully and put it back in my tent, then returned to the others. I caught the tail-end of a rhyme or something that Janam had wanted to sing to people for ages, but my ears pricked when I heard a woman wailing. Janam stopped singing and ran to Dal's arms. Patveer demanded the sword from Al and handed it to his father, who stood to join Jay and I as we searched the horizon.

'I'll check it out,' Jay said, and walked to the sound, swinging his axe. Al followed, and Patveer went too but his father called him back, much to his disappointment.

'What do you want me to do?' Dal asked.

'Chill,' I said. 'Jay's pretty handy, but that sounds like a survivor to me.'

Sure enough, a woman was being hauled up the slope by a sweaty man, as tall as me but wider, with short curly hair and jewellery. They were red faced; her from crying, him from a painful-looking suntan. The woman moaned and wailed, trying to flop to the floor as the high heel of her single shoe caught in the thick tussocks of grass at the edge of the Ring.

'Stop there,' Jay had his axe lowered yet visible, but Al openly slipped a strip of nails into his nail-gun in front of them. The man looked at them both, but continued dragging the woman towards our camp.

'Have either of you been bitten?' Jay was shouting now, and held his axe up. We all waited for a response, but none came.

'Look, mate,' Jay said, 'I need to know if you've been bitten or scratched or...'

'Fuck off, sunbeam. I got the missus in one ear; I don't need you on at me too.'

Al turned to look at me and I nodded. I didn't really know what I was nodding for, but it soon became apparent as Al popped three nails into the man's foot. He promptly dropped the woman and they both fell to the ground, screaming.

'You fucking twat! What did you do that for?' he demanded of Al, who was airily unsympathetic. I walked up to them. Jay looked ready to take his head off, and I puffed up my chest and stood over the man. I hated confrontations, they made me shake and my eyes go blurry. My heart felt like it was going to burst into my mouth.

'My man here asked you to stop.' I said. 'We've got people up here, children too. None of us are infected. You were asked to stop because you might be infected. What's wrong with her?' I pointed at the woman.

'Oh, she's as useless as arseholes, there's nothing wrong with her.'

'Oi, fuck off!' The woman's fall had brought her round from her wailing stupor, and now she was simply indignant.

'She's not been bitten, or scratched? You've not been bitten or scratched?' I demanded.

'Nah, mate, she's fine, I'm fine. We just got pissed off waiting around. Help me with my fucking foot.' He was clutching it and wincing. I looked behind me, to see the others who were now making their way towards us.

'You were at home when it all kicked off then?' I asked.

'Look mate, what's it to you? Who the fuck are you anyway?' he stuck his chin out at me. I was getting a bit fed up with him.

'I'm going to have to ask you both to take your clothes off and sign a list of the camp rules.' I said, unable to stop a big grin from spreading across my chops. As he began to splutter insults at us, Jay turned to me, lowering his voice.

'What do you want to do with them?' he asked me.

'Dig a pit.'

Making Friends
[days 0010 – 0015]

More survivors turned up over the next few days but we'd only dug two pits. True to form Jay and Dal worked pretty much constantly with pick-axes and spades. Every new arrival went in for four days, unless they were willing to show us they had no breaks in their skin by stripping off, in which case they came out after twenty-four hours to sign the agreement and help with the digging. Each pit was impressive - at least ten feet deep but they could only hold three or four people standing up. They were like vertical graves really, and pretty inhumane if I'm honest. A family of four were in one of the pits; sunburnt, hobbling Brian and his gobshite girlfriend Jenna were in the other, along with two people who hadn't met each other. We'd only had one major scare; a woman who had refused to show us a wound on her leg promptly fainted and puked black slush down herself. I took her head off. Her husband Paul was one of the people in the second pit, and the other was Jez, a student who had spent a week and a half up a tree in a park before running here simply because it was the highest point he could see. No-one had a problem with the procedure except Brian and Jenna, who were still refusing to prove they'd not been bitten. The others all showed their unbroken skin and seemed glad to let someone else defend them for a while.

The family of four were nice. I made sure I sat and talked to them all for at least half an hour each day. Jez was funny too – he was a chronic piss-taker and never let up on Brian, who nearly thumped him on several occasions. Jay, who had taken on the pits as part of his security duties, had to lasso Brian one time to keep him from fighting. Paul, however, was inconsolable after I'd decapitated his missus. I tried to explain that his wife had been doomed from the moment she'd got bitten, but he couldn't see it - he didn't really have a clue what was going on. I wasn't very good at being comforting to people, so I gave up after a bit. Glyn, the father of the family, was very understanding about the quarantine pits, and he had shown us that they had no scratches or cuts even before they'd got into their pit, which meant that they were only in for a day.

He had a key to a mechanics in Findon, and he'd barricaded his family inside the inspection pit and toughed it out. The garage door was still open onto the street, so they had freaks coming in and scrabbling at the heavy steel plate he'd pulled over his family. They had no food or water and the gas lamp ran out on the second day, so they'd been in total darkness too. They'd broken out one night and started to fight their way up to Cissbury Ring with crowbars and spanners. He'd joked that it was nice to have the fresh air, even in the dank pit. We fed and watered everyone, and used tarpaulin to cover the tops of the pits at night. The rain still got in though, and rats too. We'd seen rats in the camp, as the flesh got stripped from the corpses in the ditch around the base of the Ring and they began to look elsewhere for their food. Al had got his eye in with the nail gun, but everyone had their own weapons, so they didn't last long if you could catch them. The dogs found the rats very amusing indeed.

I divided my time between cooking, felling, building and foraging. Most other people seemed to settle into routines, sticking to their tasks but being on hand to help out anyone else. David and I knew the food was running low but said nothing, eking out the last of the supplies as best we could. I'd dug a latrine – a deep ditch which led over the back edge of the Ring. It sloped slightly, allowing urine to trickle away (piss was pretty neutral anyway – I'd heard of people using their own on their vegetable patches). Turds just sat there, and as people's guts started to complain about the change in their diet, it got pretty stinky. Dal had crushed a load of chalk into powder, and we encouraged people to throw on a handful after each visit to keep the smell down. Every time we finished washing clothes or cooking equipment, the water would be carried to the back of the Ring, and get sluiced down the trench. Someone built a couple of little seats, like decorator's trestles, which you perched on if you needed to. Several people's guts went the other way and just got bunged up in the change of circumstance, so some of them fell ill, getting pale and sweaty. Only Dawn had any kind of medical training, but was lost without pharmaceuticals, so we consulted the survival books, already looking well thumbed and worn. We got two cooking pots and soaked, then stewed any dandelions that we could find, reducing the green-brown liquor by a third and giving it to those with constipation. It worked almost too well. I picked blackberries and crushed some hazel leaves and elm bark, then poured boiling water on it. Dawn did this once a day for those who had the squirts, and pretty soon there were far fewer complaints.

We worked solidly on building at the same time and started using the yoke Dal had made. It meant we could bring up twice as much wood. By the time we'd finished, the stand of trees between the Ring and the car park had been completely levelled, and we had two huge stacks of timber posts in the camp. David told me there were one hundred and twelve twenty-foot posts, and one hundred and seventy six eight-foot posts. Al had felled nearly two hundred trees in a week, and slept for a whole day when he'd finished. There was also now a clear view from the back of the Ring down the path to the car park, which would prove useful when we made forays away from camp.

The first objective was to get more fuel. We'd already used up the petrol we'd salvaged from Jay's garage, and he couldn't finish cutting the timber until we found some more. David, Al and I plundered the fuel tanks of the two empty cars that had been left in the car park, presumably by dog walkers on the day the virus hit. We even ventured out into the fields - the vast combine harvester in the northern field was too tempting, its elephantine grain pipe angled into the top of a truck next to it. We'd approached cautiously; the human activity needed to work the two huge machines had obviously been interrupted mid-flow, but we'd found no-one; no blood or signs of struggle. There was a pack of rolling tobacco in the cab, and there we'd sat, on comfortable seats for the first time in two weeks, fifteen feet above a half-mown field, sucking on our roll-ups, eyes closed, smiling serenely. None of us had smoked anything in a while, but even just with tobacco the smoke made us light-headed and giggly. The truck's top was open to the rain and sun so the grain inside had spoilt, but some of the ducting in the harvester had loads of completely dry wheat packed into it. We filled up two bin bags.

On the way back a dozen or so sheep, straggly and damp, had flocked around us. They were probably hungry, but so were we; so we set about the youngest looking ones with our weapons. We only got two cleanly before the rest fled, so we radioed for a horse to come down to help take the grain and the meat back to camp.

Jay and Dal had got into a rhythm of taking turns to walk the perimeter of the Ring during the day – a mile round, according to the National Trust information board at the entrance to the car park. We generally let the dogs use their noses at night, but the infiltrations were getting fewer and fewer. Jay had grand plans; as soon as there were enough people available he planned to have two walking the perimeter in opposite directions, working in shifts all day and night. We could cope with whatever freaks made their way up into the ring, and we'd certainly not seen anything like the attacking hordes we'd fought off in the first week.

David had some great ideas too – he'd thought up a 'pungee-pit' design for the V-shaped notch – the widest and most accessible entrance up to the camp from below. It was basically sharpened poles stuck into the ground, pointing outwards like a hedgehog's spines to block the gap. He thought we'd need around a hundred to make it effective, and we could string brambles between the poles to catch the skin of any stinkers trying to get into camp. We needed a fat masonry drill the same width as the poles, so I added that to my new salvage list for Sainsbury's and B&Q, both of which we planned to hit on the next expedition. As for the poles themselves, we had plenty of straight, strong branches from the coppice, each about the width of a broom handle. David said they'd be perfect, and he earmarked about a hundred and piled them next to the stores, spending his spare time whittling each end to a sharp point with Al's knife.

After we had finished the Goth's cabin earlier that week we'd all helped Dal to make a start on one for his family. Next to be built after Dawn and David's should have been mine and Lou's new house, but we wanted to get a roof over the kid's heads as soon as possible. David and Dawn were a bit tearful when they saw the cabin with its roof on; it certainly looked good enough to call 'home'.

Dawn and Lou had packed any gaps between the logs with moss and mud, and made a tie-off for the horses around the back. Inside, the cabin was split into two; around half for their bed and a place to sit, and half for the food, equipment and other supplies we'd all accumulated. David was now officially the camp quartermaster. He had to get good at shooting rats with the nail-gun. I added Maui to the new salvage list. I hoped she'd made it.

First out of quarantine were Glyn and his family. The kids - twins Danny and Anthony - got on well with Dal's children, even though they were older, and the dogs loved having them around to burn off their extra energy. His wife Debbie was small and fragile-looking, but she had complained furiously when I demanded that the children sign the agreement too. I explained that if she wanted them to stay, they'd have to be prepared to stop the zombies as much as the next person. She'd questioned the word 'zombie', asking me if I was out of my tiny mind, and I was a bit disappointed to see Glyn kept quiet. I didn't want to get into a debate about it, so I just repeated myself, saying that they were welcome to leave. Eventually Glyn talked quietly to her, and Danny and Anthony had signed on the dotted line. They were only ten or so but they were both eager to muck in, and after getting some inspiration from our makeshift armoury, were also keen to start making their own weapons. Glyn was a fan of archery and mentioned getting a few longbows made from the wood. Debbie still wasn't happy.

'How come you lot are so cheerful about it? I've lost some of my family you know,' she said, rather pompously. Al's hackles had risen at that, and Lou explained that we'd lost several people. She shut up when she saw Vaughan's grave and the little headstone we'd made for Sachbir.

'I still don't get how you can be so up for it,' she said glumly.

'What do you suggest we do?' Lou asked her. 'Roll over and die?'

[days 0016 – 0030]

Brian's face was a picture when he finally got out. Jenna had stripped off the day before to prove she'd not been infected, and joined the rest of us in camp. He was right; she was as useless as arseholes, and sat moaning that we couldn't supply her with a tent. She just kept on and on, and when that got her nowhere she'd tried to be funny, or cute, or endearing or whatever. Lou and Dawn took a dislike to her, but remained polite and as helpful as they could stomach, watching her as she lounged about and refused to get her hands 'filthy'. She'd signed the agreement though, and I asked David to note her intake of water and food. I made sure Lou checked her out for bite marks and not one of the lads, but Brian was still fuming. He'd got a case of the squits pretty bad, and Dal had laughed at his weak European gut system. Jez had been mercilessly cruel to Brian, having done his stint and been released, and the first thing Brian did when he got out was to lamp him one. I'd made them shake hands when Jez came round again, but Brian still hadn't been that sporting about it.

'Why'd you have to be such a cheeky little twat?'

'I'm not the only cheeky little twat around here – I spent last night with Jenna when you were stuck in your little grief-hole.' He'd smirked. Maybe that was going a little far, I thought, but I couldn't keep myself from laughing all the same.

'Right you smug fuck,' he said as he lunged at Jez, but Jay batted him away like a moth. 'Are you being clever?' he spat.

'Why, are you being stupid?' Jez snapped back.

'Okay, fellas, that's enough. I think we need some time out.' I sent Brian off with Jay to sign the Agreement, before starting to help Dal with the work on his cabin. I took Jez to one side.

'It's funny and that, I mean we all laughed; but he's gone through the ringer like the rest of us. Give his little brain a break, eh?'

'Yeah, I suppose,' he dabbed at his split lip. 'Stupid people should shut up more, but they're always the loudest.'

There were now seventeen of us. Seventeen survivors up there on that old hill fort, which seemed to take on a new life as it surrendered to its ages-old duty of protecting those that fought for survival from the safety of its green plateau. Seventeen signatures on a bit of crumpled A4.

We worked on, perfecting our building techniques, finding novel ways to cook lamb, and telling stories. One day amongst the tattered figures on the golf course I saw through my binoculars a man walking a flyblown dog carcass on a lead. None of the other stinkers were bothering him, so I assumed he was dead and not just mental. It sent shivers down me, the raw link between a man and his habits laid bare in front of me. Some of the others had laughed at him, but it made me cry in great heaving sobs. I didn't let anyone see though, and I had found Lou who wrapped me up in her coat and squeezed me.

Late one evening, when the fire was roaring and the sound of laughter rippled through the camp, someone gave out a squeal. It wasn't the sound of fear though – the dogs weren't barking - it sounded like someone had seen an old friend. We tore off to find the sound and found Dawn on one of the horses by the trig pillar. She was looking north-east with binoculars, but you didn't need

DOG
WALKER

any help to see what she had found. On the horizon was a bright orange pin-prick of fire, on the black silhouette of a hill.

'Where's that?' someone shouted.

'I think it's Steyning way. Steyning Bowl, maybe, or Bramber Castle.' I said. We'd driven through there on our way back from Brighton on that first evening.

'I can see people in front of it,' gasped Dawn. We were not alone, and a day or so after that we saw another fire, further away to our north.

'That's definitely Chanctonbury Ring.' I said. Chanctonbury was another, smaller hill fort, probably made at the same time as Cissbury. By day, of course, we saw nothing other than a thin wisp of smoke from each camp curling into the air, but by night we would gaze in wonder and break out into spontaneous rounds of applause for our fellow survivors, even though we knew we may never meet them.

Every new arrival seemed mostly happy to sign the code of conduct we asked them to abide by - everyone except Brian that is, who by now was really grating on everyone. Even Jenna had stopped talking to him, and frankly rubbed it in by spending a lot of her time with Jez. We had a meeting and decided the best thing was to get the bull by the horns and force them to work together, so Jay – whose plan for patrolling the ring was now in full swing - put them on the same shift, walking in opposite directions around the perimeter. True to form Jez put the effort in, but he would meet up with Brian earlier and earlier each time round due to Brian's sluggish walking speed.

Brian had been slack during the building work too, often taking off completely to walk on his own around the Ring. He'd laughed in my face when I'd asked him to tell someone where he was going. Jay had bristled up and stood shouting down at him, purple-faced, but he'd only laughed harder. Jay, like the rest of us, was a lover not a fighter, but he could barely keep from rabbit-punching him.

One evening Dawn kneed him square in the bollocks near where the horses were tethered because he'd told her he'd 'always wanted to fuck a Goth,' and that Dawn might be his last chance. Dal had overheard, walked up to them, obviously taken Dawn's side and promptly got called a paki, which was wrong on quite a few different levels. I'd told Brian not to be so spiky but he thought I'd called him a pikey, and it all got a bit heated. I had to hold back from twatting him myself.

Jez didn't hold back from taunting him though, and would often relieve the tension with a cutting one-liner, sending Brian into fits of spitting rage as if he held the copyright on all forms of taking-the-piss. Still we made them work together, and Jez even seemed to soften towards Brian, actually sticking up for him once when he'd had a second helping from the pot, finishing the last of that evening's meal before Dal and David had finished their shifts and eaten themselves. Of course they both insisted it wasn't a problem, and shared a tin of beans Jez heated up in the fire for them. Jez was proving popular amongst the camp, and never seemed to let the situation weigh him down.

One day though, Brian came back from their shift alone.

'Where's Jez?' Dawn asked him.

'Oh, he got bit.'

'What?' I demanded. This was the first time someone had been infected after they had signed up.

'Yeah, it was some stinky fucker over the back. I got to Jez and he was sort of laying there, white as a sheet. He'd been bit in the leg, so I...' He made 'chop-chop' actions with the hand-axe he'd chosen as his weapon.

'What, he hadn't been eaten?' Jay quizzed.

'No, I scared them off, you know. I dunno, they might have come back for him by now.' The grin had all but gone.

'Alright Brian, you've done your shift. You did the right thing.' I said. Jay shot me a glance.

'Yeah, well it's your rules mate, not mine.' He sauntered off, and I turned to Jay.

'Shall we go and have a look?'

We hiked to the north edge of the fort, saying nothing. We were eager to see for ourselves what had happened. I certainly wasn't in any frame of mind for bullshit. I'd had very little sleep; Lou's nightmares seemed to be getting worse and I was spending half the night up with her. She seemed too scared to drop off, and the exhaustion would often send her into sobbing fits. When we got to the back edge of the Ring we saw nothing. No stinkers, no Jez.

'Maybe he was telling the truth.' Jay said.

'Well - innocent until proven guilty and all that, eh? Let's have a gander down there.'

There were no bodies in the ditch there at the car park end, at the opposite end to the V-shaped entrance and the 'Battle of the Stinkers' as Jay had named it. We clambered into the dip and up onto the chalky ramparts of the outer ring, watchful for any movement, then searched along the walkway until we were practically on the easternmost side. We were about to retrace our steps when Jay saw something in a gorse bush. It was a trainer. On the end of it was Jez, upside-down and headless.

'Well, they haven't come back for him.' I said.

'What was he saying about scaring them off?' Jay raised an eyebrow at me. 'Have you ever seen any of them get scared off?'

'No,' I pursed my lips. 'Just hungry.'

'Where did he say he'd been bitten?' Jay asked me.

'In the leg, wasn't it?'

We hauled him up onto the path. I pulled his trousers off as Jay kept watch.

'Nothing. No bites, no scratches.' I rubbed my eyes.

'Right. What do we do now?' Jay asked.

'I need to have a little chat with Brian, I suppose.'

Jay said nothing, which usually meant he agreed. We looked for Jez's head, and found it wedged under a thicket. Brian had really gone to town with the axe, Jez's face was almost unrecognisable. We trudged back up the slope, pulling the decapitated Jez with his head pushed down his T-shirt. Once on top, I suggested we said nothing to the others in the camp, at least until I'd had a chat with Brian. We stashed Jez in the shade of an old tree – a yew I think – and set off back to camp with a determined stride. When we reached the quarantine pits, Jay handed me his sword.

'Brian, can I have a word?' I asked politely.

'Piss. Ha ha. Will that one do?

'No, Brian, I need to have a little chat with you. We'd best go for a walk,' I called out where we were going to David, who did an annoying little salute. I really wasn't in the mood for any of this. When we were out of sight, I asked Brian where he'd last seen Jez.

'I fucking told you, round the back,' he pointed.

'Let's go then. We'd like to bury him, if there's anything left.' I said.

'I told you, he's probably not there any more.'

'Well, let's look anyway. Satisfy my curiosity.' I said. We walked in silence, Brian leading the way. I made sure we walked right past the spot where we'd found Jez, and I clocked Brian looking down towards the gorse bush.

'Getting warmer?' I asked.

'Nah, it's further on. Much further on,' his voice sounded edgier.

'Brian,' I said.

'Yes?' he turned to face me. 'What is it now?'

'Don't imagine for one fucking millisecond you can get one over on me. Jez had survived whatever this mess is. He had survived. I'm going to give you a choice. Either fuck off down there to where I'm never going to see you again, or I'll take your head off right now.'

'Go on then you little prick,' he said, squaring up. 'Take my head off!'

So I did. The arterial squirt of bright fresh blood which soared away from his neck really took me by surprise.

When I got back to camp, lugging Jez over my shoulders in a fireman's lift, word had spread. Jenna was in my face, screeching like a banshee. She soon shut up when she saw who I was carrying. I considered telling her I'd sent Brian away, but instead I told her in earshot of the others what he'd done; that I gave him a clear choice, and that I had executed him. She went pale. I didn't hear much from her after that. No-one else said anything except Glyn, who asked if I was alright with a trembling hand on my shoulder. We buried Jez, and Patveer made up a poem for him which she recited. Dal made a cross. Dawn, Al and Lou cried. In the middle of the night I woke Jay up, told David where we were going, and trudged to the back of the Ring. We found Brian, and buried him where we lay, with no headstone. It weighed heavily on me – I'd never killed anything bigger than a rat before I extinguished Brian, but on the whole everyone was very supportive. Al said he would have done it in a flash, Lou said it was a situation I shouldn't have been put in. Her nightmares were still bad, and she'd recently tried sleeping through the daytime, tending to the fire and doing her security shift at night. Floyd would follow her, wagging proudly with his chin up. We saw less of each other, but she slept better to the sounds of the camp's activities. We had sex for the first time in too long, one misty morning when she was coming to bed and I was waking up. She just kissed me, lingering long and warm, and I ended up late starting work.

Over the next three weeks or so we got at least one new person a day coming up to the camp, hungry, battered and bruised. No-one opted for our alternative to getting into the quarantine pit, which was to fuck off. Jay and Dal had dug four more; wider, with wooden platforms raised off the damp floor. As they dug deeper into the new pits, they'd shown me around a dozen flint arrowheads they had uncovered, sharp and gleaming black. By the time they had finished there were over a hundred of them, of varying weights and sizes. Glyn and his wife took over the logistics of the pits – I think he was eager to get her involved as she was constantly miserable, to the bemusement of the twins who were having the time of their lives. By now all of the children had dispatched at least one zombie by themselves, and proved sharp-eyed and quick, not usually batting an eyelid. I didn't have much contact with children before the virus had broken out that summer, but I was amazed by their resilience and adaptability.

The new arrivals - some of whom brought dogs or kids with them - were generally practical people; the outbreak had seemed to siphon off most of the lazy, stupid or feckless members of the public. Almost all of them had taken refuge in their own houses, and used their own supplies and resourcefulness until the situation got truly unbearable. For many, the treks up to Cissbury Ring were a last-ditch stab at survival, drawn toward the three huge quick-lime fires that now blazed twenty-four hours a day. Most of them seemed more than delighted to strip off and clamber into the pits. Those who didn't - either through stubbornness or as a reaction to the sudden imposition of rules after such anarchy - stayed in for the four days and emerged eager to help. On the whole, though, there seemed to be a distinct air of gloom about the place, as people mourned loved ones and friends, and wondered at the hopelessness of it all. They accused us of not thinking about the future, but that was exactly what we were thinking of. Whether it would be a future with or without fake tan spray pods, or adverts, or mobile phone ring tones, was another matter.

You could tell who was up for the challenge laid out in front of all of us – generally those who jumped at the chance to work on the shelters, and who would encourage the listless ones to be active. Some had brought food with them which got commandeered and added to the stores, and whatever examples of the increasingly rarer perishable items they may have brought with them were consumed the same day. I was getting into the logistics of the field kitchen, and relished the chance to be as thrifty as possible. The supplies were running low until we'd caught more sheep and even found a few chickens, but the situation couldn't last for much longer. We hadn't been into the business park at the bottom of the Downs since Vaughan was alive, but now was the time, and we certainly had the manpower. My list of things likely to still be edible, as well as some practical cooking equipment, ran to three sides of A4.

Al led the foray. Dal took Patveer, who was eager to get out of the camp and see new things. David was now almost as accomplished on horseback as Dawn. They and Dal took all four adult horses with them, as well as a team of six of the fittest and strongest people, including Lou. Eight of them split up when they got down there, half on lookout, half plundering the giant Sainsbury's of tinned and powdered goods, gagging at the stench of rotten meat and mouldy produce. The air had been swarming with bluebottles, even with the recent colder weather. Lou and Al went back to our house, which had had its windows smashed in. There had been two zombies in there, feeble and hungry, but no threat. Lou found Maui after what seemed like an age. She had recognised Lou straight away, and jumped into her arms. Lou said there were feathers in the loft, and some bones.

On the way back up to camp each horse pulled four shopping trolleys full whilst the others stopped them from tipping on the rough ground and kept watch. The few walkers they had encountered never got further than Dal who led the way on horseback, swinging his sword. The party entered the camp to rapturous applause, and the children handed out sweets and chocolate to everyone, although by the state of their guts afterwards I should think they ate as many as they distributed. There was powdered and UHT milk (at last - milky tea), literally thousands of teabags, coffee, loads of rice and pasta, and pasteurised fruit juice. They brought tinned tomatoes, sweetcorn, soup, potatoes, rice pudding, spam and baked beans. They brought four large cooking pots and hundreds of plastic cutlery sets, as well as yeast, jelly, sugar, salt, cooking oil and about a hundred different spices. The camp now had bleach, disinfectant, five more first aid kits: even toilet roll, although this was kept aside for those who had got diarrhoea. In fact they brought everything on my list, as well as some things I'd not thought of, including a fire extinguisher, dog food, crossword books and batteries. They said the only thing that had been looted before they got there was the pharmacy, as well as all the tobacco and alcohol.

David had his work cut out for him, logging everything as it went into the stores. Lou and I had to keep some of the items – all the non-edible things we decided – in our cabin, which was the third one we had all built and frankly embarrassingly larger than the others. We used the extra space to house new arrivals just out of quarantine, as their shelters were put up. Before long they only tended to stay one or two nights, as more and more people became available to help with the building, until eventually there were spare buildings awaiting new tenants, and Lou and I had the place to ourselves for the first time. Maui settled in, and we decided not to feed her but to let her do her natural job of keeping the vermin to a minimum. She did us proud, but still refused to make friends with Floyd, who insisted on trying to lick her backside before receiving a face-full of blurred claws.

That evening we all gathered around the main campfire which was now sited a good distance away from the original one we had set up. That first fire now burned on the southernmost tip of the ever-growing site, but still in the middle of the rustic cul-de-sac which housed the first nine of us to set camp at Cissbury Ring. Al and Dal told us of their trip, whilst we tucked into the tomato pasta I'd made. Apparently they'd seen a car in motion in the car park, and thought it was a fellow survivor. But it was going round and round in a circle, its steering locked. In it they could see a man and a woman, decaying flesh flapping in the breeze, staring at each other. They'd also seen two people, their disease and decay disguising any signs of sex or age, pushing shopping trolleys. Dawn and David then regaled the wide-eyed children with stories of the Battle of the Stinkers, now a fully-fledged fable, whilst Lou, Al, Jay and I chuckled to ourselves. The kids fell asleep one by one. Patveer was the first to drop off - even though he loved stories - having taken to carrying a bundle of straw around with him in the evening as an instant bed. He usually slept where he fell, until Dal wrapped him up like a parcel and carried him off to their cabin.

I wasn't a huge fan of children; they could be ear-splittingly noisy and in my experience were often pukey. But these ones were good ones. They were kind, attentive, intelligent, and readily understood the seriousness of the situation we were all in. They were quiet now, asleep around the fire; unlike in the daytime when they hared around like little tribesmen, brandishing the 'junior' bows and arrows Glyn had made as practice for the longbows. He'd made just one longbow before, with his brother, and was unsure of how he'd get on doing one without many tools. He soon found out that it was just a question of adapting what he already knew. After Glyn had made – and promptly snapped – two perfectly finished bows, he decided to check that they could draw cleanly before spending any time really refining them.

He used the tendons from the sheep's legs for the string, pounding them into individual fibres between two rocks before soaking them and hanging them out to dry. He'd perfected a method of extracting a four-foot strip of tree with young, green, elastic wood down one side and tougher, older more resistant wood down the other. He'd worked and worked on the design, drying and shaping the wood, until he was producing about one full-sized classic English longbow every two weeks. He'd given the first one to me, and had kept the second one to be made. Jay had the third, and he'd stifled tears when Glyn presented it to him. Right now Glyn was working on Al's bow, and Dal had expressed an interest too. He taught the twins how to make arrows, how to choose the long stems with the right diameter, and how to hold them in the fire to soften out any bends and kinks in the wood using their teeth. The girls worked on the flights, made from the feathers of some particularly stupid pheasants we'd found in the woods, and of the pigeons we trapped in the trees. We utilised the ancient arrowheads Dal and Jay had unearthed, binding them to the shafts with tar scorched from the car park asphalt.

The armoury swelled each day, and the kids got pretty good at arrow-making. I slept with my bow - it was a real masterpiece. I'd seen Ray Mears using an English longbow on TV, when he'd had one made and taken it to a tribe in Africa. It felt totally instinctive as we formed a tightening circle around our quarry, each of us firing on signal, reloading and firing again so, if we were lucky, two or three arrows in the neck or head brought the animal down quickly. The best time was first thing in the morning when the mists lay thick in the valleys and the first tendrils of daylight curled across the hills. We'd go for live-stock mostly, left to fend for themselves in their bedraggled coats, but they were getting thinner on the ground. By now other creatures were venturing forth in their search for food, unfettered by men living or dead. We even came across two young deer, their ears pricked in the rose-pink haze – and bagged them both. After a week of hanging the meat in my cabin the camp feasted on venison with a blackcurrant and sweet chestnut glaze, and I had been pleased to finally produce something to eat that didn't rely on Sainsbury's.

One day I was preparing that evening's meal – curried lamb and rice, one of Dal's most popular recipes – when Jay appeared, beaming from ear to ear.

'Look who's just turned up!'

It was his parents, Jinny and Jerry. Jerry carried a tangle of tubing and flasks (I assumed the remnants of his home brew kit), as well as his banjo and Jay's steel string guitar. Jinny lugged two heavy-looking suitcases and a bag with two of her favourite cats in it.

'Hello!' Jinny shrieked. 'Bloody hell, you need a haircut!' Jerry giggled into his beard. We hugged, and Jerry shook my hand.

'Alright Rasputin?' he asked me. 'Where can I dump this?' Some of the tubing uncoiled and sprang around him, falling to the floor like a tangle of snakes. Floyd eyed Maui as she set about the apparatus. Chuckling, I pointed him towards our cabin.

'Sling it in there if you like. Hold on,' I said. 'You haven't been in quarantine, have you?'

'It's alright, mate, they're clean. They haven't been bitten.' Jay said.

'Oh, I believe them, but we've got to put them in. Think of how it would look if we didn't,' I said.

'That's fine,' said Jinny, 'you little fascist.'

'It's for the safety of the camp,' I began, but she cut me short, smiling. It was only then that I saw who was with them, and it completely span me out. He was one of the local weirdoes you see in town and generally try not to interact with. This one, Rockin' Johnny, Horace, Pint-talking Man and Polish Lec were the five main local nutters. Every town should have at least one. We used to see him when Jay had a cramped flat in Broadwater, dressed in combats and webbing with a cumbersome-looking field radio on his back. We'd named him 'Keep-fit Man' as he always ran everywhere, the ten-foot aerial whipping the air above his head. He hadn't changed, he appeared a little smaller perhaps, but still carried the radio. He also had what I guessed was a film prop, possibly a Klingon or other *Star Trek*-related weapon, with an elaborate pewter-coloured blade on the end of a gnarled, jet-black pole. I could see that he'd carved about thirty little notches in it.

'I'm Mark,' he explained, extending a grimy hand for me to shake.

'We found him on the way up here. The 2CV made it all the way to the car park. It started first time.' Jinny said. She extended her compassion for waifs and strays beyond cats. He might be a real asset though, and the radio intrigued me.

They all stripped, and Glyn and his wife checked them over before putting the three of them in the only available pit, one of the original ones. Keep-fit Man had been reluctant to hand over his radio, but I'd told him I would keep it safely in my own cabin. When their quarantine was up he hugged it like an old friend.

'Can you pick anything up on that?' I asked him as he was unpacking his rather eclectic possessions.

'Noo, battery's dead, innit?' He had a tick which forced a grimacing smile to break out every so often. He smelt a bit of piss. 'I did speak to someone though. They were on Harrow Hill, about six clicks west of here. That means 'kilometres', when I say 'clicks'.'

'How long ago did you last speak to them?' I probed.

'Last week. Perhaps a couple of days ago. I dunno, I don't do time,' he said, sounding irritated and baring his teeth.

'What did they say?' I asked him. 'What was their 'sit-rep'?'

'Well, I gave them my location and they suggested I did a recce up here, to Cissbury.'

'Up here?' I asked. 'Why didn't they invite you up to Harrow Hill?'

'Well, they'd just received someone who'd escaped, from Chanctonbury Ring,' he pointed north. 'The survivor told them he was heading for you lot, up here at Cissbury. They said you'd be a better bet.'

'Hold on – they'd escaped from zombies in general, or they were escaping from zombies up at Chanctonbury?' I quizzed him, knowing the answer already.

'What?' he asked, head cocked.

'That bloke who went up Harrow Hill - do you mean that he was escaping from the zombies in the general countryside; or do you mean the survivor was escaping from an infestation of zombies in the Chanctonbury camp?'

'That one,' he said. 'They were escaping from the Chanctonbury zombies,' he said, matter-of-factly.

'We've seen they've got a camp up at Chanctonbury. What was the problem?' I pressed.

'Apparently,' he was drawing his words out, relishing the moment, 'the virus got into the Chanctonbury camp. Bad camp-craft. Got into the water. This bloke escaped and tried to head down here, to Cissbury, along the South Downs Way. I've walked that.' He said to Lou.

'I bet you have,' she smiled at him.

'Well, he took a wrong turn and headed up Harrow Hill towards their fire instead. He'd been bitten, so they eliminated him after they'd extracted the intelligence,' he said.

'Well, Chanctonbury obviously weren't as strict as we are.' I said, quite smugly. Night time had crept up on us, and looking north we could see that the fire wasn't burning on Chanctonbury any more. Sure enough though, further west, two orange dots glowed dimly.

'There's two camps up there,' Keep-Fit Man said. 'That other one's Black-patch Hill'

We couldn't mourn people we hadn't known, even though we had made some sort of connection. After ten minutes of 'bet you're glad we didn't listen to you and go up to Chanctonbury instead,' and 'well, what can you do?' the crowd dissolved, leaving just Lou and I. The air had turned colder recently, and that night was crisp and fresh, with a beautiful canvas of stars strung across the sky. No streetlamps meant that the view was incredible, and we could see the wispy end of the Milky Way stretching out above us. I realised this was the freshest air I'd tasted in months. As Lou and I hugged, staring up at the empty space, I felt a sense of union, a sense of place. Usually the sight of the stars just reminded me that we were all simply carbon lumps, scrabbling around on a mould-stained rock which was hurtling through nothing. Now I felt at home, possibly for the first time in my life. Cheesily, that was also the moment Jay and his dad chose to start playing, and the sound of *Across the Universe* came drifting towards us from the camp. We laughed, and ran. Some of the people who were sat around the fire sang along; I was just happy to fill my ears with something familiar.

The aroma of the lamb curry was thick in the air, and stomachs rumbled audibly as I slopped it out into bowls or onto plates. Jerry came and stood in front of me with his back to everyone else. He wordlessly showed me a bottle of rum, twenty years old. I grabbed a few cups and he set about pouring an inch into each, understandably out of sight. He poured six or seven little tots as well as our own, leaving the rest for those cunning, sharp-eyed or fortunate enough to cotton on. The rum and the curry made me so hot I broke out into a sweat. It was a hearty meal, and there was even second helpings. No pud though; not yet. Maybe when the fruit's out next year, I thought.

Someone laughed and said 'Oh, how cute!' as Floyd started howling. The sound chased the heat from my bones and filled my stomach with dread. Dmitri's low rumbling growl mingled with a woman's screams and carried on the night air. I stood, sending my plate clattering onto the chalk. I couldn't see Lou.

'Watch it!' One of the new arrivals shouted at me, brushing imaginary flecks of lamb curry off his grass-stained trousers.

'Everybody! Stinkers in camp! Get up, they're coming from the north!' Jay screamed. Al was already on the case, halfway to the armoury. No-one else around us seemed too bothered, like we were disturbing their evening. As Al tried to hand weapons out, people just looked at him, bemused. The woman whose screams we'd heard then stumbled into view. She was young, with long hair, impractical earrings and plastic nails - I'd only spoken to her a couple of times since she'd come out of quarantine. Now she was sobbing quietly, like she was tired, and I had to look twice at her midriff, at the stomach that just wasn't there. Strings of severed gut hung limply within the cavity made by her stripped ribcage, and I could see the underside of her lungs heaving silvery in the firelight. She was close to us, and I could see her eyes were rolling in her head. I whistled to Al but he had already sent the long axe sailing through the air and into the ground in front of me. I loosened it, stepped up, and took her head off. It took two goes, and in the moment between strikes her eyes met mine and she gurgled the words 'I'm alright'. Her head rolled onto the hot stones around the campfire and sizzled, hair curling tight to her scalp. More screaming. My actions – as well as Patveer hollering at them to help – seemed to spur people into life. I'd not heard everyone's stories of how they came to be atop Cissbury Ring in West Sussex that clear autumn night, but it occurred to me that any number of them might have never had to fight like we were about to.

'They must be from Chanctonbury – they're lively!' David was shouting over his shoulder as he knocked heads together. I looked for Lou again, but had to help out a bloke who was cornered by two stinkers. He had no weapon. I swung down hard on the closest, cleaving off one side of his head. The other one – a young boy – was fast, and sunk his teeth into the man's forearm as he shielded himself. He shrieked as the boy wrenched his head back, taking muscles and tendons away in his jaws and stood munching with stuffed animal eyes, before the urge took him over again and he made a second lunge. As he was a lot smaller than me I had to strike downwards at an angle, and his head actually flew off the edge of the Ring a good twenty feet away, as if I'd chipped a golf ball. The man sat quietly now, pale and sweaty as he looked down at the mess of his arm. He turned to face me, shivering. He knew what was about to happen, he'd signed the contract. I was wondering whether or not I should say anything when the man spoke himself.

'What do I do now?'

'I'm sorry,' I said, and his shoulders slumped. My ears roared with the pumping of blood. He closed his eyes; I found my footing, raised the axe and let it fall under its own weight. I looked up to see four of them advancing on me. Four vs. one is not good zombie-mathematics - the ratio is definitely not in my favour. I started to backtrack towards the campfire when an air-expanding crump of flame jetted into them. Lou was beside me, my pressure sprayer loaded, pumped, and on her shoulders.

She had a torch; I guessed pulled from the quick-lime fire pits where the sprayer had also been kept for quick ignition of the trenches. The quick-lime was an ongoing industry now, a production line of chalk- and wood-collecting; pyre building; chalk-burning; and finally the collection of the quick-lime itself. Then the pit would be raked over and the process began again. We had five pits now, and the quick lime lay an inch deep all around the ditches below. New arrivals had unquestioningly completed shift after shift at the pits, some not even knowing what they were making. Some were inquisitive; others positively enthusiastic. They seemed to be eager to help on the whole; eager to work for the good of the camp. This would be the acid-test of teamwork, though.

I kissed Lou's head before dispatching the four creeps that lay thrashing and spitting on the ground, then we both ran to our cabin where I collected my bow and arrows, together with a long sheepskin quiver for the arrows that Dawn and Lou had helped Janam to sew for me. David was right: these ones were obviously from the Chanctonbury encampment, as they were coming into the north end of our site and were very fresh. The big giveaway was that their clothes were relatively intact but adapted and modified like our own. The shelters for the new arrivals had spread northwards to the back of the Ring, so they were the first to be confronted by the freaks. Their collective inexperience meant they were all vulnerable, and the scene was devastating.

Several huddled walkers sat feasting on our fallen camp members. Lou lit them all up with the sprayer, as Al and Jay worked to protect those caught unawares with axe and nail gun, and we all shouted at people to get to the armoury. Glyn started to help but I got him to release everyone in quarantine so they could at least defend themselves. The kids were true to form; brutal and efficient. Dal and Dawn rode through the throng on horseback, lopping heads. I stood on the edge looking down - there must have been forty or so scrabbling up the sides of the outer ring. I saw David, who had been keeping watch, now running along the path, swinging a sword and yelling to attract their attention.

I picked one out, drew my bow, fired - and missed. I stopped, taking a breath, trying to relax. I pulled again, picked out the same chap and sent the ancient flint arrowhead through one eye and out the other side, thumping into the neck of one behind him. Two for the price of one made up for the crap shot. I drew again.

I heard Al yelling, and turned to see him on the floor being pulled by the trouser leg by two women stinkers. They scratched and scrabbled at him, and he kicked out, making contact with one and snapping her jaw. Jay ran up to Al and started to pull him the other way, but Al shouted at him to stop the freaks instead. He was laughing, and soon Jay started too. I caught sight of a couple of our camp members fall off the edge of the Ring into the ditch, and I thought of Vaughan.

Pretty soon the top of the Ring was clear, as far as we could tell. There were less of them and more of us this time, and it felt almost too easy. Dal had felled half a dozen on his way up to the top, and we were soon joined by Glyn and Jay, their bows at the ready. In all I think there must have been close to eighty living dead coming our way from the Chanctonbury camp, and we'd seen off maybe a third of them by that point. We spread out in a line on the Ring's perimeter and were soon bolstered by the more willing newcomers, their newly chosen weapons at the ready.

'Don't shoot 'till you see the whites of their eyes,' Jay shouted, only half joking. Dawn and David trotted down the slope, followed by Floyd and Dmitri who quickly disappeared from view into the approaching morass of limbs and teeth. You could make out where the dogs where as the odd creep seemed to get sucked out of sight, like cartoon carrots pulled underground by cartoon gophers. The Goths hacked and sliced, and we picked out ones starting to scramble up the base of the slope with bow and arrow. Any zombies that were closer we let come to the top, to the waiting clubs and sticks and blades. Dal thundered past us, on one of the horses with no saddle. Patveer clung onto his shirt with one arm, looking tiny as he bounced dangerously into the air but swinging his weapon with gusto. The week before, he had unearthed a sharp flint rock - only a little smaller than his own head - and lashed it to the end of a length of heavy duty rope, making a fearsome Indian club. He caved heads in, not flinching from the task at hand. He looked terrified, but his face was the only thing that gave him away. He was a fierce fighter like his father who, grim-faced, set about the advance. Lou sent arcs of flame into pale faces. Jerry had a long pole and was jabbing at heads with one end of it, herding them towards those with more effective weapons. I heard a throaty gurgling sound on my right and turned, expecting to see one coming for me, but it was Keep-Fit Man. He was doing some crazy moves with his bladed *Star Trek* stick, the guttural noises he made presumably Klingon fighting-talk.

Slowly but surely the advance thinned, and the pace of fighting eased. Some of the new people collapsed, puking and wailing. Jay and Al walked around them, checking for wounds, as those on horseback saw to the last few stinkers below. The Chanctonbury Assault was nearly over. Only the dull crunch of Al's axe and the light whip of Jay's sword pierced the sound of sobbing and dry heaving, and pretty soon Al came up to me with a sober look on his face.

'One of them has got a leg wound. He says it was a blade,' he whispered. 'I must admit it doesn't look like a bite but I thought I'd check with you before doing him.'

'Get him in the pit. Everyone's got to strip, now.' I turned to the campers. 'We need to check you all out for wounds again. Take your clothes off. Anyone not willing to do so goes back in the pit. Anyone with a wound – even if it doesn't look like a bite or a scratch - goes back in the pit. Anyone bitten, well...'

No-one moved. I sensed their disbelief. I was being ruthless and cold, but I was determined not to muck about. We'd got this far. Still no-one moved, as Dal, David and Dawn trotted up to join us. I saw Jay talking to Dal, who motioned to the Goths, before they made their way back down the slope to keep watch. I put my bow and arrow on the floor and undid my trousers. Lou began to remove hers, and Jay and Al weren't far behind as I pulled off the last of

DAL,
HORSEMAN

my clothes. Soon the four of us stood side-by-side, naked and defenceless, looking around us. If ever there was a time for a mutiny, this was it, but Glyn stood up and started to take off his clothes, hauling Debbie to her feet who started to make complaining noises. A few more took their cues. The kids threw their clothes into the air, whooping, burning off adrenalin. Lou, Al, Jay and I picked our weapons up and started to move amongst people. I got accusing looks, as some of the less useful children cowered in their mother's arms. We weren't sorting people out into male and female for the benefit of people's dignity, either.

'Pit!' I heard Al say, levelling his baseball bat at a woman with a strip missing from her arm. 'We'll patch you up when you're in. Go!' he prodded the woman, who winced her way to the west side of the camp towards the quarantine pits.

'You too,' Al was saying to a middle-aged man.

'Nah, it's a fuckin' graze. I slipped yesterday.' He protested.

'That looks as fresh as a daisy to me,' Al snorted. 'Pit. Now!'

The man turned to walk in the opposite direction to the pits, so Al cracked the back of his head with his bat. With a metallic ping he fell to the ground. Al called to the woman with the flesh wound to take him down with her. A few campers stood to help her, but Al told them to sit back down. One woman was screaming, her leg open to the air. She was fully clothed still, her trouser leg in shreds. Her husband had pulled her away from the freaks that had set upon her, but he just watched now as Jay raised his sword above her head.

Glyn called me over to the pits. They were all full again now; five of them with naked and wounded campers, but the sixth one had a fully-formed zombie in it, lashing out at the chalky walls and gurgling. The urge to feed made him scrabble up the walls, his fingernails stripping away to black stumps. He wasn't getting out though.

'We'll leave him in there if we can. It might give us the chance to see if they ever fucking stop. Have we actually got enough room for the wounded?' I asked Glyn.

'Sure, there's five each in A, B and D, six in C and E,' He said. 'That one's pretty much spare.'

'Give them all the full four days,' I told him, and then turned to look into the pits. 'We'll bring you the first-aid kits. You all know why you're in here, so I'll not apologise. You'll be out before you know it.'

The rest of the week was sober, with many people mourning relatives or new friends, but we saw no more stinkers on the top, just the usual squirming barricade of weaker ones rasping and scratching at the steep sides of the earth embankments. On the sixth day Lou ran to save a woman who stood at the edge of the ring with arms outstretched, before dropping with a sense of purpose face-first into the heaving ditch. Someone who knew her told me that she had been wracked with guilt, even though she'd saved three other people the day the virus had hit.

Two people in quarantine had been infected after all, seemingly okay until they had fainted and hawked the black sludge down themselves to the screeches of the others in the pits. We'd lassoed them by the necks, thrown axes to the others in the pits, and buried them headless in the graveyard alongside the eighteen citizens who had not survived the Chanctonbury Assault.

[days 0093 – 0098]

It had snowed. It was early October, but usually - even in the depths of winter - we hardly ever got snow this far south. The weather had been weird recently, with mists and sea fog rolling in out of nowhere even on bright, sunny days; and powerful lightning storms, splitting the sky without thunder. There had been sharp frosts too, glistening crystals clinging heavily to the trees and bushes, but this was proper snow, lying thick on the ground. We'd kept the skins of the two-dozen or so animals we'd found and slaughtered, but it would never be enough to keep everyone warm. Ray Mears' book detailed how to prepare skins properly, and even before it had got really cold we'd made frames and done it all properly; using lime to soften the hair and even mashing the animal's brains up, and diluting them to treat the skins which made them pliable enough to be used like cloth.

As the temperature traced out the shape of our breath like ghosts and left crystal pearls on cobwebs, we had built heat-reflecting fences on the windward side of all the camp fires and fitted simple chimneys to the roofs of the more substantial buildings so we could actually light fires inside. We'd plugged all the gaps between the logs with mud and moss. We'd also gathered as much hay as we could from a nearby field, for the horses, so a great mound of it sat under the tarpaulin behind the camp. I'd got everyone to take as much as they needed for the floor of their shelters after drying it out by the fire, as it was a little damp even under cover. Around half the forty-four survivors left in the camp had managed to grab sleeping bags or duvets before fleeing, during the scorching weeks after the outbreak hit. No-one had any form of winter clothing with them, but the supplies of those camp members who were killed during The Chanctonbury Assault were plundered for protection against the cold. The kids felt it most, so they got the sheepskins, which only added to their tribal appearance.

The snow did not bode well – we had potentially a further five or six months of this - although the children loved it and soon set about making igloos. They took their time - I suppose the lack of Dick and Dom or X-box, together with the hard work they'd all put into developing the camp, had stretched their attention spans – and they had built three child-sized structures. They'd tried to persuade their parents to let them sleep in them, but they had been told the igloos would be too cold to be safe. I had to disagree, and it was only when I got Glyn's wife to stick her head inside one of them that she agreed they were much warmer even than the log cabins. To Debbie's disappointment, the twins now had no excuse not to stay the night in them, so they did so with glee.

After one unsuccessful hunting trip, we all gathered round the fire as night closed in. An earlier snowstorm had fallen thickly from the parchment skies, clouding everything around us in deathly silence, and we could see more dense clouds gathering to the north just as the light failed. Then the dogs howled long and low - I jumped to my feet, awaiting confirmation of an infiltration from someone on security before spurring into action. None came, but the dogs got louder. Right then, as the fresh snowflakes started to fall I saw my parents - dressed in furs and sporting what can only be described as umbrella hats. My parents.

'Fucking hell!' I spluttered.

'Language, honestly.' My mother said.

'You were swearing like a dock-worker when you put your ankle out,' my dad said. Then he turned to me casually. 'Hullo son.'

'What are you doing here? Where did you come from? Where's Philip?' I stammered. Lou had stepped up and gave them both a hug.

'Hello!' Lou said. 'It's nice to see you. Let me make you both a nice cup of tea.'

'Ooh, lovely,' my mum began, fumbling about inside her battered handbag. 'I've got my special teabags somewhere, hang on.'

Making Contact
[days 0098 – C153]

My parents were both retired teachers. My mum was head of the science department at one of the ancient private schools dotted around the Downs, whilst my old man taught Graphic Design at the local sixth form college in town. He had even ended up teaching me, to my unfolding horror, and I had met some kids at my own school that had been taught by my mum. They didn't like her much; they said she was too strict and 'a cow', which was about as insulting as children at my school got about each other's mothers. The kids in the camp, however, found them both highly amusing, and had fallen about laughing at the adapted umbrellas they wore strapped to the top of their hats. My dad made them worse by performing a little tap dance for them, whilst I wished the ground would open up and take me away from the hot-cheeked embarrassment. They were delighted to see Jay's folks, who they had befriended at our wedding, and my mum declined a dash of Jerry's rum for her 'special' tea (I've never asked), which she sipped still steaming. Dad nodded a tot into his, and they sat back to regale everyone with their story. They were arguing briefly about what point to start the story at, but my mother won by beginning the story where she thought best with a sharp 'shush'.

'When they first said some kind of virus had broken out we were already visiting our other son Philip in Bristol - who is fine by the way darling and says 'hullo' - when it started to get quite fraught right outside,' she began, clutching her hair with both hands to illustrate exasperation.

'They said it was a biological attack didn't they at first, then that it was avian influenza! I knew it wasn't that because my old friend Edie caught it and Edie hates birds; she's not been near one since her wedding. I won't bore you with all the gory details but we had to defend St. Ethel's. What a blooming hoo-ha it all was. Golly.'

St. Ethel's was a little church tucked away in a forgotten corner of Bristol. My older brother was the caretaker, and he stayed rent-free in a draughty room above the vestry. That way he and his wife could save up for a deposit on a place of their own whilst looking after the creepy old building. He was a fearsomely intelligent man; but gentle, meek and kind with it.

My dad was quite happy to bore us with all the gory details. They'd been in my brother's flat waiting to go out for lunch when the streets outside erupted. Of course they had begun to let people into the church to seek shelter, find relatives, or to wait for medical treatment; the vicar was nowhere to be seen. Naturally they had let the wounded in too, and the virus had taken hold inside the church. As people had started to get bitten my brother led my parents up the organist's stairs to the rooms at the top. There they'd stayed, watching the carnage from the upper balconies, letting people up who could prove they hadn't been bitten. My dad had been the one to realise that the dead were walking first – he'd pushed a chap down the stairs, breaking his neck, but he'd got straight up and come at him again.

They'd been under siege for weeks when the church finally emptied and they had closed the heavy oak doors for the first time. They'd even looted a local store – my parents, looting – so they could restock my brother's larders. When they decided to leave for home, Philip opted to stay boarded up in the church with his wife, telling my mum and dad that it would give him a good opportunity to finish two of the books he was writing. My parents ventured out into the country, going by car as far as Wiltshire where their petrol ran out. They'd walked the other hundred-odd miles to Worthing. I couldn't believe what they were telling me.

'What do you mean you walked the last hundred miles?' I demanded.

'Well, we put one foot in front of the other in succession. You should try it.' I was disappointed to hear people laughing – I knew from experience my dad needed no encouragement.

'But what did you do about all the walking dead that happened to be roaming about?'

'We adapted to the circumstances,' My old man said sniffily, as if I should have given them more credit. I probably should have, as they had obviously adapted to the circumstances well. He showed me his shooting stick - like a walking stick, but with a fold-out seat for a handle. The other end was pointed, with a collar of metal to prevent you sinking too far into the ground. But, like his hat, he'd decided that some modification would prove useful so he'd sharpened the point and fitted a much wider diameter metal disk. My dad used the point to pierce the breast-plates of advancing stinkers and push them towards the nearest immovable object. Meanwhile my mother – a champion of dissection in the classroom – would push a garden hoe she had found and sharpened into their open mouths and through the backs of their necks, severing the spinal cord. Simple but effective, and their golden rule was, apparently: 'if there's more than one - run'. They told me they'd dispatched five hundred on the walk between Stonehenge and Cissbury. My mum accepted her second cup of tea whilst my dad waved the dogs away, who seemed particularly interested in his trousers.

'What do you think it is, mum?' I asked, eager to hear her take on the outbreak.

'Well it's undoubtedly a virus - the transmission happens through blood I should think, suggesting also through saliva in bite-wounds, but we've heard people talking about it spreading like a cold too. There are similarities to other viruses as well. We know rapacious appetites can occur with certain diseases, so that's fair enough. The closest thing to the bad attitude that seems to go with it would be rabies or something similar, although I've never heard of anything like this.'

'No. But they're dead, mum.' I said, still none the wiser.

'Yes they are - completely dead. Which is, of course, impossible. There's certainly nothing I've heard of which is able to reanimate the dead. But I'm just a science teacher,' she laughed.

'Christ only knows what they're concocting in these labs, though,' my dad only noticed his profanity when my mother placed a hand on his arm. 'I've heard some right horror stories. Don't forget, Porton Down is just over there,' he pointed. Porton Down, the government's chemical warfare lab, was in fact many miles away, back in Wiltshire.

'Yeah, but they said this started in Sheffield,' I told him. 'That's way up north.' I realised I was pointing too.

'Exactly,' he said triumphantly. 'If we know about Porton Down, what about the ones we don't know about?' he asked. He had an annoying habit of subverting anything correct that you'd countered his argument with, by absorbing it into his own as if he'd proved you wrong.

'The Thames had flooded. We saw pirates,' my mother said proudly, seeing my face and trying to diffuse a scene.

'They weren't pirates,' my dad scoffed.

'They were; they were hippy pirates. That's a type of pirate,' she refused to be deflated. 'You'd have loved it, they had a house boat.'

'Nice,' I said. 'So how are they walking about, if they're dead?'

'Well, technically they're not "walking about",' she did the air-quote sign with her fingers, which I'd never seen her do before. 'That's a human function. They're simply seeking fuel.' My mother explained.

'Technically, bumble bees cannot fly,' my dad said randomly but utterly confidently. I had heard this one many times before, but some around the fire hadn't, which gave the old man the opportunity to break down some principles of aeronautics to those who would listen.

'Seeking fuel...' I pondered. 'They slowed down loads after a few weeks. Presumably there's not enough 'fuel' to go around forever?'

'No, well even then they don't seem to actually stop going. We've seen ones that are almost skeletons, no real muscle mass left at all. They're still at it, even if it's just their eyes rolling in their sockets,' she said. 'I take it you've seen them expel?' she asked.

'Seen them what?'

'Expel,' she said simply. 'They seem to be ejecting all the waste products from inside them in one go. They don't defecate or urinate, so their bellies swell. If they can't get any fuel they seem to start living off the dead host's stores of body fat and whatever food is left in the gut, but after a few weeks they blow it all out of both ends. Excuse the phrase,' she said to Lou, anxious she'd upset her with the idea of a human body having two ends.

'But how are they still going after they're dead?' I asked, getting exasperated. She obviously didn't know.

'I don't know, really. Terry, what do you think?'

'Lots of theories, but nothing that really sticks,' he said, scratching his ample beard. 'Scientifically, it can only be a very economical use of small amounts of energy which is just enough to power one train of thought, and I suppose the limbs and jaws follow. Electric impulses, you know. Impulsive behaviour. I'm sure you're mother's right about drawing on the energy reserves, and they do seem to slow down if they run out of fresh flesh. They soon perk up when they've had a bite though, I can tell you.'

'Yes,' my mum continued for him, 'it's funny. Looking at them as a new sort of species, they seem to have the instinct to survive. Reproduction's a dead fish, obviously. We have seen some of them acting out routines though, as if there's some semblance of thought process left. Patterns, habits - you know. Probably just crumbs of human action rattling about.'

'We've seen them playing golf, and driving,' I told them. 'I've even seen one walking a dead dog.'

'Oh, shush,' she said, as if I was lowering the tone.

'You know its zombies, don't you?' I probed.

'What, from your horrible films?' mum sneered. 'Don't be so stupid.'

Dad said they'd had to walk for miles picking through the strewn luggage of a passenger plane. He'd found – and kept – one of those laminated safety procedure cards with the cartoons of people putting on lifejackets. They didn't see the plane itself, just a charred scar seared into a nearby hilltop. They said they'd been in many camps on their way home. Some were as rigorous as ours, others even more so. They'd been resting at one of the less thorough sites when the virus had broken out all over again, and my parents had to fight their way out. They came across one encampment in the walled garden of a stately home in Hampshire, and the guards refused my parents entry because it had already broken out in their camp and they had sealed themselves in.

'Like they did in Eyam in Derbyshire, during the plague,' she explained.

'How many people are left, do you think?' Lou asked quietly.

'Well,' said my dad, 'we came across one encampment every, ooh, five miles or so. Average of a fifty people in each camp, some were big, some were smaller. Say a hundred people for every fifty square miles, fifty thousand square miles in England, er...' he pulled his beard. 'A hundred-odd thousand? That's in England, mind. I can't work out the rest of the UK because of the difference in the original population densities, and I'm tired.'

'Fucking hell,' I said.

'Language, for pity's sakes!' my mother had her hands over her ears, as if the swearing would curdle her brain.

'Mum, a bit of perspective, please.' I said.

'Still no excuse to swear,' she pursed her lips.

'Okay,' Jay said, stretching his arms out behind him. 'We'd better get you in the pit,' he grinned.

'Oh, you've got pits? We've been in lots of those,' mum said, ramming her hat back on her head. 'Cages too.'

I swear Jay looked mildly disappointed. As we guided my parents towards Glyn at the quarantine area my mum walked arm-in-arm with Lou, and I heard them talking about Lou's mum. My dad stopped suddenly, and reached into his bag.

'I brought these for you,' he said, holding out a carrier bag. I rattled it – VHS.

'No. You didn't?' I jumped up and down, unwrapping them like it was Christmas.

'I did. Right - they're yours now,' he said. 'I know you'll give them a good home. You've got the Berlin Wall coming down somewhere in there; all that Perestroika; Concorde's last flight; the Pope and Reagan getting done, not at the same time I'm sorry to say; the Brighton bomb; Torville and Dean; the Libyan Embassy siege; erm, Charles and Diana's wedding and her car crash – irony they're both on the same tape; a few *Comic Reliefs*. What else? Oh, the Channel Tunnel opening; the Mary Rose salvage; Thatcher crying when she got the boot. Happy now?' he asked with a smile. I was – I'd always badgered him for them, and he'd always maintained he'd burn them onto DVD for me.

'How have you even got these with you?' I asked.

'Oh, thank goodness, you've offloaded those horrible things onto your son. Sorry Lou,' mum looked exasperated. 'We went back to our house when we got back into Worthing, I couldn't believe it when his-nibs went straight for those,' she continued as dad rolled his eyes. 'He's been hoiking them around ever since. We went for a stroll on the seafront, and made our way up to your house.' She made it sound like they'd been on a day trip. 'We thought you'd be walking the dog up here.'

I'd forgotten about the sign I'd painted on my front door.

'Horrible things. A catalogue of doom.'

'This is bits of our history on these tapes,' I said.

'If you can get hold of any electricity to play them,' she said smugly, before catching sight of the stinker we still kept in the end pit. 'Ooh, you've got one in there,' she said, pointing at him. 'Is he for experiments?'

'Oh, him - he fell in there during the Chanctonbury Attack,' I explained. 'We haven't cleared him out; I was keen to see if they ever stop. Obviously he hasn't.' Jay had named him 'Bub', like the one they'd experimented on in *Day of the Dead*, with the headphones and the gun, but we hadn't kept him in there out of morbid curiosity. The children had wanted to keep him anyway, and by then there were less and less survivors coming up to the Ring so we only ever needed two of the quarantine pits at any one time.

'Well, you're welcome to dissect him,' I told my mother. 'You'll have to be careful though.'

'Teach your grandmother to suck eggs,' mum mumbled as dad helped her into their pit, as far away from Bub as possible.

'How long in here?' he asked.

'Twenty-four hours,' I replied.

'Bring me a good book, son,' he whispered.

When they came out of quarantine mum started work on her research, whilst Dad had been happy to join Jerry with the plans for a new building. He'd already marked out a pretty large plot in the middle of the camp. We'd never suggested a maximum size for the shelters - in fact mine and Lou's was still the largest cabin - no-one had really made anything this big yet, but space was not really a problem. New arrivals in the camp had so far been either too polite to ask how big they could build their new shelters, not wanting to appear greedy; or they assumed from the size of every other structure bar ours that a maximum size of domicile had been stipulated by some imaginary bureaucrats.

I'd asked Jerry what he was building – it was at least four times the size of our cabin – but he'd just winked and tapped his nose with a chuckle. He and Jinny slept in one of the open-sided lean-to shelters by the main campfire at night, and he used the stock of timber and the building crew by day. The ingenuity and enthusiasm he displayed seemed to have an inspiring effect on other people, and soon many houses were customised with little fences marking out plots, front gardens and even rockeries and garden paths.

When he rested Jerry had started to build a chess set. He had carved about a dozen or so pieces by now, which he'd made to look like the Lewis chessmen, to replace the chalk and flint counters we'd been using to play draughts. In the evening the children would gather around him, and between Jerry's banjo and my dad's Münchausian tales they would keep the kids rapt until they fell asleep at their feet. The children all loved camping up here still and each had their own preferred aspect of the situation.

Patveer loved the fighting and 'protecting the womenfolk.' Janam loved the animals. Danny and Anthony were agreed that not having to clean their teeth did it for them. The general consensus, they timidly admitted, was not having lessons. I smiled at the thought that they were learning lessons but just didn't know it.

'So I know you don't miss school,' I asked them one night, after my mother had announced she had come to the end of her conclusions about Bub, 'but do you want a lesson in zombie physiology from a real, old-fashioned teacher?'

'Yay!' they squealed, before double-checking what 'physiology' meant.

'Guts and that.' I explained.

'Yay!'

Mum had set up a shelter overlooking the pit, where she kept notes and sometimes slept. Even though she insisted she was 'a dab-hand at all this' I made her wear a rope around her waist which was tied to a stake in the ground above, whenever she worked in the pit. Glyn had agreed to keep an eye on her whenever she was in with Bub, whose hands and feet were each restrained by the wrists and ankles with rope. We'd also slotted a wooden lattice down one side of the pit and threaded Bub's ropes against the framework and up over a bar wedged into the ground above, then back into the pit. This meant my mum could work him like a puppet. We had knocked his teeth out with Al's bat, but even then I had insisted his head be tied back too. Mum kept his teeth, as well as anything else that fell off him, in snow-packed jars, using a field microscope she had produced from her handbag to peer at thin slivers of his meat. Glyn always had his hands on Bub's head-rope, but he never had to use it.

The children peered into the pit excitedly, usually not even allowed to lean over, and especially not allowed to throw rocks, mud, quick lime, fire or dogs in with Bub. They were as excited to hear what my mum had to say as we were. Patveer made them all sit in a half-circle round one end of the pit, whilst my mother stood over the other side. Several adults, including the Goths and Jinny and Jerry, joined Al, Lou, Dal, Jay and I cross-legged at my mum's impromptu lecture. It was morning, and I had set a fire roaring to one side, as the snow clouds sat low in the sky, edged with crimson from the weak winter sun.

'Right,' my mum began, peering over the top of her spectacles. My mouth felt dry. I hoped there wouldn't be a test. 'Incredibly strange creatures.' I sniggered, knowing she hadn't got her own reference to the bad 1960's film. She stopped, and gave me a withering stare.

'Would you like to come up here?' she enquired. I shook my head.

'Alright then. When it started it was difficult to know what the disease would do. We certainly didn't know what it was, some said rabies, some small-pox, others suggested a strain of Q-fever. We even heard people on the news, who thought it was influenza of some sort, or even bird 'flu,' she snorted. 'Anyway, 'flu symptoms certainly, such as shivering, fever, pallid skin, cold to the touch, erm, streaming noses, red eyes, that sort of thing – did manifest them-selves. The people we saw infected, and I've spoken to several of you to con-firm this, seemed to pass out for at least an hour during the height of the fever.

'Some sort of early attack-response is usually triggered, which is when a lot of other people first got scratched or bitten, but this seems to wake the subject from unconsciousness too. They seem perfectly ordinary at this stage, but it's only a brief window of sentience - around a minute or two - and it will be the last you'll see of them. Then they're usually sick during the second bout of unconsciousness. This vomiting seems to be the virus making its first inroads into the intestines and the bloodstream. The vomit is usually black, indicating an early rejection of toxins, and probably toxins quite natural in healthy hu-mans. Then they seem to come round again, but the person you knew has gone for good by now. This is a crux point, as the subject is still alive but actually unconscious, and whatever primal response supplies motor-function to the corpse seems to briefly take over here, before death. Then they die. No spasms, no bowel movements, nothing. To a bystander they're still alive, but get any closer to check and you will end up bitten and metamorphosing, transform-ing, whatever you wish to call it. Responses that would be negative would be pupil and knee reflexes, I suppose. There's a bigger indicator obviously, and that's... anyone?

No-one spoke.

'...no heartbeat, hence the lack of arterial blood when they're cut, and no breathing either,' she finished for herself.

'But I've heard them moaning,' someone said.

'Aah,' mum countered, 'that's interesting. That is, I believe, muscles around the chest-plate and back which end up responding to the same impulses that power the limbs, pushing or pulling the lungs open. This air passes past their vocal chords, giving the impression of noise, but it's not a choice, and it cer-tainly isn't oxygenating the blood or anything.

'Poison present in the host corpse not only escapes as fluid from the mouth but also pushed up to the surface of the skin, which breaks out in pustules.

This occurs where the vessels are close to the skin, and also in similar places to where the herpes virus typically shows on the skin. The groin, the lips, the nasal area. A terrible stink is given off, like sulphur or eggs. This is a smell commonly associated with the final stages of biological breakdown. We'd normally associate that rather sweet smell, like rotting meat, to be given off this soon after death, but these chaps seem to want to do things the other way around, almost like from the inside out. The insides seem to get putrefied, and all sorts of things are forced through the surface of the skin, from fat to faecal matter. All very nasty.

'That's poo,' I whispered to Danny, who giggled.

'Yes, that's right, poo,' mum said with another withering stare. 'Full motor function is apparent straight after death, but it seems to be driven by something other than the things we draw energy from. Their fuel is, of course, the flesh of humans. This cannibalism seems to be the only choice as they seem not to want to touch animals much.'

'We saw one eat a lamb,' Al said.

'Okay, but I'd suggest that was an exception. They'll use up whatever reserves of human-favoured energy are left – and remember, they're not human any more, so it's not ideal – such as fat reserves, food in the guts, and I think they even absorb the congealed blood left in their own venal system. All the while they're driven to seek out fresh flesh. It seems for all the world that they're sense of smell has also vastly improved, but this is unlikely. More probable is the suggestion that the same, unimproved human olfactory organs are simply given a far higher preference in the brain's input. This, coupled with the remnants of human memories they clearly possess, leads them to fresh food via the smells they remember – sweat, car fumes, woodsmoke, anything really, that might find them a hearty meal. The appetite will be eating them up at this stage, possessing their every movement.

'If they don't get food, and therefore energy, they slow down. If they eat, they simply pick up speed again. We saw ones who definitely hadn't eaten since the day it broke out – infected people stuck under the wheels of cars in the middle of traffic jams – who are still trying to eat, so it seems as long as there's a scrap of muscle on them, they can keep going. The active ones change appearance. The vitreous humour inside the eye breaks down, reacting almost like how vinegar cooks things without heat. They end up like eyes in a steamed fish head. If they could see - and by that I mean process images in the brain - before that point, they certainly can't now. Teeth sharpen after so much contact with bone, making the jaws and cutting action more efficient. The skin breaks down and falls off, accelerated by any wounds they may have sustained, which attract flies and encourages maggot laying, which gets rid of the flesh quicker. That might be what will finish them off in the end - the common bluebottle.

'It is, of course, an unsustainable way of existing: soon a point comes where there is no more food – the incubation period of a week or so means that it is most likely that the flesh of anyone still undergoing transformation would have time to be consumed by those already changed, hence there aren't sixty-five-odd million of them, ha-ha!'

'If you are bitten, you catch the virus. If it is allowed to incubate inside you - which it can only do if you remain alive - you have well under a week of life left. Then the transformation takes place and death occurs. Your corpse simply will not get up and walk around if you die by any means other than the virus itself. Therefore if you are partly eaten but your heart stops during the attack, you have died by other means and will never become one of them. This disease, as my son's horrible films would have it, will not reanimate entire graveyards, turning long-dead corpses into... zombies.'

She had said it. I breathed out.

'Why don't they eat themselves?' Patveer asked, wide-eyed.

'Well, I don't know really. I assume the response to eat is a response to prolong existence, so maybe that overrides the craving of their own flesh.' She said, matter-of-factly.

'Tell us about the expelling!' Jerry called out.

'Well, that seems to be jettisoning useless human by-products out of any available orifice. We've only seen a few ourselves. It's not pretty. Bub hasn't got rid of his yet; his belly's nice and swollen though, so it shouldn't be long. I'd get some sort of lid on that pit, frankly. By the way, he's also frozen up a few times, once completely, but I have thawed him out again and he's been only a little less functional than he was before.

'Some of you have been asking about a cure, and, well, even if there was a cure for the disease, you'd have to somehow find a cure for death too. And if you were so stupid as to do something like that, you'd basically have a rotting person with all their nerve endings suddenly alive again, and I wouldn't wish that on anyone. Whatever it is that makes them appear human still - the moaning noises; the familiar activity - it is highly unlikely, if not impossible, that they would be able to process any rational thought whatsoever.'

Al had his hand up.

'Erm, can I add something?' he asked. 'When I went back to my house and found my parents, I saw something that might change your mind about that.' We all fell silent.

'Go on,' mum said, peering over her glasses again.

'Well, my mum was in the bedroom. She'd not been affected at all, and had… she'd used tablets. She'd died peacefully. But my dad was the other side of the locked door, with bite marks on his foot. He'd worn his fingers down trying to get to my mum, and there were spots, you know, on his face like you said. So he'd been infected and died. My dad was a zombie.'

'Right,' my mum encouraged him to carry on as his voice stumbled.

'Well,' he said, 'you just said they couldn't have any rational thought. No problem-solving, no compassion, nothing like that. No love.'

'Right.'

'Well in his hand was the single-shot .22 calibre air pistol he uses – he used for the seagulls. He'd shot himself in the head.'

'Maybe that was one of the automatic responses I was describing. Maybe it was the last remnants of a sense of duty to your mum.' My mother suggested kindly.

'Maybe,' he said. 'But he'd reloaded it sixteen times. He'd shot himself in the head sixteen times.'

Making Money
[days 0I54 – 0204]

Hard work kept the cold out. The activities had split into what people did for the good of the camp and what people did for themselves. For purely personal reasons I had wanted to put a flag up, so I found myself a long rusty scaffold pole in one of the fields and had worked on rubbing it down, whilst Al had adapted his dad's hand-drill to accommodate the inch-thick, foot-long masonry bit we'd acquired. We had to slowly drill down into the ground around a fifth of the length of the pole. I bartered the use of Al's triangular canvas canopy – originally one of the sails from his dad's boat - by agreeing to help him with his more permanent cabin. I made a paintbrush from horse's hair and some of the tendon twine Glyn had made to string the bows, and used the pot of red paint I had grabbed from my workshop five months earlier. I neatly painted a St. George cross on both sides, so it looked like the old triangular standards you see knights holding in pictures, but much bigger. I used some bits from a fan-belt I'd found in one of the abandoned cars to make a pulley, and soon my flag fluttered in the breeze twenty feet above us.

I'd also made a dry-smoker which I used to preserve a lot of the meat, including what we'd butchered from a pig that the kids had caught. It was basically two old barrels - one an empty metal drum of pig food, ironically; and the other a proper wooden barrel we'd salvaged from a garden. They were linked by a slowly rising ten-foot length of drainpipe, which I'd fitted a metal collar to at one end to stop it melting. The fire – made from oak chippings and set to one side of our cabin – whistled away to itself in the metal drum, whilst the smoke cooled as it drew along to the wooden barrel, in which I hung the butchered game and quarry which arrived almost every day.

There were four main groups out of the fifty-two survivors who would regularly go out into the countryside in fours or sixes to hunt. One of the hunting parties used catapults, another spears, whilst the other loved to trap. Our group was the one with the English longbows though, and our success rate was constantly improving - we'd caught two more deer since the first ones we'd seen and there was no way I could set about preserving all of the meat at the same time. Each batch took a good week or so of constant smoke, so the rest sat frozen in sacks in a mound of snow I'd built up. Lou and I would thaw them out and rub them with salt and some carefully selected dried spices – sage and thyme for the pork, rosemary and black pepper for the venison - and start the process again, whilst the whole camp feasted on the frankly spectacular results from the previous batch.

Al had recently ventured into Findon village with Jay and Dal, where they had broken into a motorcycle shop and Al had taken a few of the all-in-one leather riding suits. I asked him what he was doing as he unpicked its stitching around the campfire one evening, and he wagged a finger at the pile of tanned skins we'd been working on and told me he was designing a zombie protection suit. He had always been fascinated by the relationship between fashion and practicality, often getting hot under the collar about clothes with zips which led nowhere, or the town-centre alcopop-tarts who would wear short skirts in the winter. Now though, he was in his element, carefully following the curves of each dismembered piece of leather and cutting the treated skins to size, talking of embedded cast-iron breast-plates and inset steel elbow blades. It sounded good.

David the quartermaster spent most of his time in the stores whilst Lou and Dawn built a fence for the paddock round the back. When he wasn't charged with retrieving spanners, food or even the books we'd pooled into a meagre library he added more sharpened poles to his pungee pit. Al used his adapted drill to help David to build up the bank of spikes in the V-shaped notch. When he had finished he'd made a start on the other, smaller breaks in the fortifications, which had been cut into the chalk in quieter times and which had steps leading up to them.

In return David had helped Al to build his own permanent shelter whilst he lived out of his original tepee. Al's place was a work of inspired beauty, and only a little smaller than our cabin. He and David had planed each log to a flat side for the internal surfaces, and had calculated a neat, efficient tongue-and-groove system to fit them all together to form the walls. He'd dug downwards too, forming a second, underground living space. They'd kept an overhang of chalk above which supported a beautifully flat wooden floor (or ceiling, depending on where you stood). His sleeping area was almost a third floor by itself, tucked into the crook formed by the pent roof, reached by a stunningly crafted ladder.

Jerry was very taken with the idea of digging downwards into the chalk earth, and before long he had doubled the space inside his construction, which by that time nearly had a roof on it and stood higher than all the other structures around. It was only when he had carefully started to move his stills and demijohns of foaming, sweet-smelling brew from his lean-to into the building that I realised he and my dad had been building a pub.

The process of digging into chalk was easy but messy. We used pick-axes to break it up, and spades to remove the rubble and smooth the surfaces. Walking into the building from the outside would take you down four chalk steps into the cool lower floor, which was around ten by fourteen feet, with enough room for fifteen or so thirsty campers. The wooden ceiling was no more than six feet high, less in some places, but a wooden ladder led up to a snug where that ceiling became the floor. It was more cramped up there, and the sloping roof meant that you could not stand up at the front of the pub. However, Jerry had built the front wall so it could lift up on rope hinges at roof level, which he could then prop open to create a canopy which felt rather like a cosmopolitan veranda. Towards the back of the snug Jerry had made a sleeping quarter for him and Jinny. He and my dad now both worked on making chairs and tables, whilst the first batches of brew bubbled away behind the bar. He intended to get back to their house in Tarring one day and raid their spirits cupboard, but for now he had plenty on his hands. He had lots of help too, as people cottoned on to what was being built.

There were fifty-two of us now, and the new arrivals had eventually slowed to a stop. We had filled three sides of A4 with signatures, and now we only met those who were simply passing through, like my parents had passed through all the camps they'd visited on their journey home. Many were seeking loved ones or just heading for whatever was left of home. Some, though, were keen to take advantage of the situation. The first chap we saw arrived with a heaped wheelbarrow and a backpack, waving away any assistance as he puffed his way up the slope. It was obvious that he hadn't been bitten, and told us that he would just carry on with his journey if we made him get in a pit or anything stupid like that.

He had some serious defences. He too had gaffer-taped his trouser legs, but they were hardly visible under the coils of barbed wire he had strung around his belt - unsurprisingly he didn't want to sit down quickly. He had 'found' a stab-proof vest which he wore under about half a dozen fur coats, a WWII German helmet and a spiked club. As the children gathered round him he handed out sweets to them, to the tutting of some of the parents. Once he had our attention, he began to unpack his wares. Someone, who had seen the packs of tobacco, had ran to their shelter and pulled out a wallet. The traveller laughed in his face.

'Now where the fuck do you think I'm going to spend that?' he roared.

'I dunno. I thought... I thought you were selling stuff.' He looked deflated.

'I am, but not for this. It's useless paper, save it for wiping your red arse with.' There was a slight Irish lilt to his voice, so 'arse' was 'airse'.

'What currency do you take then?' I asked him, eager for a smoke myself.

'Euros are good,' he chuckled. 'Nah, I'm always meeting people who have got things I like the look of. If it's precious to you it may well be just as precious to me. Or less precious of course, I've got a wicked exchange rate,' he chuckled to himself. 'Now what have I got for you? Salt?'

'Got that,' I said, as Lou curled her arm into mine.

'Bullets; cigarettes; whiskey;' he said. Jerry said nothing. 'Furs; some kind of meat. What can I do you for?'

'I'll have some tobacco,' I said. 'But I don't know what you'd want of mine.'

'Use your imagination, lad,' he chuckled. 'Aren't you married?' He asked, nodding to Lou. I bristled at the suggestion I assumed he was making.

'What did you say?' I asked him, my face turning red and my ears warming. Jay was already at the man's side and looking down at him, expressionless and unblinking. The man didn't move his head, but merely looked at Jay through the corner of his good eye. He reached down and slowly drew back one of the animal skins at his side to reveal the dull glint of a gun barrel.

'Do you want to call of your bulldog?' he asked me, but Jay was already backing off, although I watched Al silently moving to stand behind him all the same, one hand on his nail gun.

'I didn't mean I'd like to screw the brains out of your lovely wife's head there, you ignoramus feck. I'm talking jewellery.'

'Oh, I see. No,' I said, rubbing my ring finger, 'we... I lost them both.'

'Has my friend Pat already passed through this way then?' the man asked with a cocked head.

'No, I was just... careless. I've got a meal for you, though. It's hot. The pot's over there.' I nodded. The food, even though it was communal, was mine to barter with I guessed, and no-one objected.

'What, have you got a stew going on there? English stew?' he roared with laughter. 'I'm sure that'd be fine. The last people just had biscuits,' he chuckled. 'You've got a good-looking encampment here, that's for sure. One of the best I've seen. Here. I'll throw in a packet of rolling papers for you too.'

'Two.' I said bluntly. 'Two packets of rolling papers.'

He scratched his head. 'Alright, but my appetite just got bigger,' he said. 'Anyone else for anything else?'

He watched with a beady eye as people rifled through the things he'd laid out. There was some cheap-looking jewellery; watches; women's knickers still in the packet; tins of tuna; even fireworks. He had pencils; paper; condoms; toilet paper; matches; water purification tablets and some medicine. I wondered what he'd charge a sick man for antibiotics. He had a bible and some smoked fish. I saw some people bringing out their jewellery, to which he'd inevitably shake his head and push for more. I watched him thread his latest haul of rings onto a chain around his neck which was positively heaving with others. He tucked into his stew and bartered hard, gaining anything from sunglasses to books people had claimed back from the library. Eventually David had to take up position in the stores with an axe, as people got creative with what was rightfully theirs.

When most were relatively satisfied we all sat back around the fire, sucking sweets or rollups or miniature bottles of spirits. I was keen to get the visitor's take on events, especially if he'd been around the country.

'I've seen the cities. I've seen the filth, the decay, if that's what you're after.' He turned his eye on me. 'There's a pestilence afoot in the cities; a plague, and it won't turn you into anything, it'll make you shit and cough liquid fire for a week then die stone cold dead. If you were in a city on that day – you're fucked now, I tell you. If you went to a medical centre – you're fucked now. If you cared for a loved one who'd passed – you're fucked now. If you thought with any emotions at all, well, God help you.'

He told us of the sounds he had heard coming from an army camp he'd passed one hot night, of men screaming and firing guns. He'd seen the vast hulks of two dozen ships washed up on Dorset beaches, and passenger aircraft which had taken out whole towns when they had come down. He'd seen men kill for water, and women kill for less. He said he had witnessed blood turning the Thames red, and babies turning on their mother's teats.

'I think he's exaggerating, rather,' my mum whispered to me, having dared my father to even think of buying anything from the man. 'He's basically a tinker; a hawker of tat. Leave well alone,' she had advised, but no-one else listened. My dad eyed a tiny die-cast Spitfire, but hadn't been brave enough to make him an offer in front of my mum. I smelt something pungent, a sweet, sickly aroma I hadn't smelt for a while, and Al prodded me on the shoulder holding out a generously packed doobie.

'Bloody hell,' I said. 'That's…' He was offering me a joint – a rare occurrence even before civilisation disappeared - and I accepted. I let the stiffness drain from my limbs and chased the busy thoughts from my brain.

'He's got everything,' Al said. He certainly had enough to net him a fine haul of rings and other shiny things, and I even saw him disappear with Jenna at one point. Slowly people drifted away to their straw beds, and the man began to pack away his goods.

'You've a fine pair of hounds there lads,' he said to me and Al, the last two left around the fire and, if I'm honest, too stoned to actually move if we wanted to.

'Not for sale,' exhaled Al, who was staring at the stars.

'No problem. Nice horses, too. Both useful, dogs and horses. Animals are getting harder to find. No-one's really into feeding anything other than themselves any more. Is your young horse for sale?' he enquired. They say jazz pianists love to get stoned before performing, as the drug opens up all the pathways in the brain at once, allowing for some truly inspired, instinctive decision-making. If he was serious, and it seemed he was, I had an inspired idea of my own. I found Dawn.

'Have we got enough horses?' I asked her.

'Well, yes. There are only three useful horsemen up here, and a few amateurs who could end up being a liability. No offence.'

'None taken, but that's good news - the fifth horse, the youngest one. He's looking good now, isn't he?' I asked.

'The foal, yes, he's looking fine. Why?'

'I think we should let him go.' I said, and then explained what I had in mind. Dawn was all for it. I took the now strapping young horse back to the man, who was waiting for me.

'No tackle, I'm afraid.' I said.

'Tack,' he said. 'What are you asking for him?' I told him what I wanted in exchange for the horse.

'Oh, and that little die-cast Spitfire model you've got.' I said.

'Okay,' he chuckled. 'That actually sounds more than fair, given the circumstances, but I can't exactly give everything back. Know what I mean?' If I didn't know then, I certainly did the next day, when I saw Jenna parading her new fur coat.

Jerry beamed at me, a twinkle in his eye. He had an opening date set for his pub, one week before Christmas. He had gone back down to Tarring with Dawn on horseback, and retrieved every last scrap of alcohol from his house, as well as the houses of those neighbours whose drinks cabinets he knew the location of. He'd returned to stock up the pub, and had also brought a stack of glasses of all shapes and sizes. His three recipes of homebrew were ready and waiting for customers.

'The only thing I haven't got is a sign,' he said. 'Know any good pub sign painters?'

'I think I know one. I laughed, and scratched my beard. 'I've even got a half-finished one in my workshop. Dawn'll have to drive me down there.'

'Drive you?' Jerry chuckled.

'Well, you know. Horse me.'

'Okay. In return for painting me a sign, you can drink at The Cissbury Ring for free for one whole year,' he told me.

'What happens after a year?' I asked him.

'I'll settle for extra dumplings whenever you cook them,' he said pensively.

'Sounds like a very good deal. Is that what you're calling it then?' I asked.

'Yeah, it makes sense to call it that - at least people can remember where they are when they leave!'

Dawn and I went to the house the next day to find it completely gutted; a gas pipe had split in the house next door, but I don't know what ignited it. Many of the houses in my street were burnt out, some with windows or whole walls blown out. Wooden beams splayed open like ribs, soaked and warped by the rain and fire. Roofs lay in the streets, and the tarmac on long lengths of the roads themselves had melted, along with the car wrecks they now seemed to have absorbed. Some of the cars jutted out at an angle, as if sinking into a tar pit.

Dawn had selected her favourite horse, and we moved at some speed. The few, weak stinkers we met were swatted away with little effort. Once inside (we were actually able to get the horse into the kitchen at the back of the house) I did a quick search. Snow and ice had made the stairs one flat slope, and all of the books were ruined by their exposure to the moisture. I grabbed the photo I had taken of me proposing to Lou, stuffed it in my bag and went upstairs. I took every coat we had, including a thirty year old duffle coat that I had inherited from my dad with fake animal tooth buttons, before making my way out to the shed and my half-finished pub sign.

It was still intact – luckily Lou had given my keys to Dawn as we left – and I set about gathering what I needed. I took one of the cast iron brackets I had commissioned from a chap with a forge up north, as well as all the acrylic paints I used for the illustrations. I grabbed some black and white gloss paints and all my brushes. Finally, I took the half-finished Royal Oak sign, mercifully smaller than the traditional three feet wide by four foot high, but nonetheless thickly framed and heavy. Dawn helped me to load the horse up, and we started up the road back home to Cissbury Ring. Back home.

When we were approaching camp we met up with Dal who was just finishing two people's shifts patrolling the lower ring on his own, at speed on horseback. He waved to us, his long black hair flowing behind him – lately he had taken to leaving off his turban. When I'd asked him why, he had mysteriously said that he'd always been told that there were many paths to God, but he had not understood the phrase until now. Others, too, had recently expressed some reluctance to follow the familiar paths of their own religion. Even Glyn and his wife had stopped going to the weekly bible and prayer meetings someone had set up. People were drifting away from what they knew in the face of lots of things they didn't.

When we reached camp, the children ran to see what we'd brought back with us.

'What is it?' an indignant sounding Patveer asked me.

'It's a pub sign,' I said.

'No, I know what the sign is, not the sign stupid,' he was pointing, 'what's your picture supposed to be?' he quizzed.

'Its an oak tree with a crown on it,' I said.

'Why?'

As we unpacked, I told them about Charles II who, in sixteen-hundred-and-something, had climbed up an oak tree to escape. I promised myself I would look it up in the Dickens' *Child's History of England*.

'Zombies?' asked his sister Janam, wide-eyed.

'Roundheads,' Dal said. 'That was when you folk had other things to worry about, I think,' he boomed from within his beard, and started to tell the children about the English Civil War. Jerry let me paint sitting on the veranda of his pub in the quiet sunlight, the heavy wooden shutter propped up to let the fumes out. There were enough fumes coming from his eye-watering stills in the chalk-walled room below, and when Jerry gave me a nip of his Sussex Moonshine for lunch I thought my head had caught fire. I sanded back the sign writing, and guessed that the shape of the oak tree would easily be adapted to become the top of Cissbury Ring. Jerry had left the design up to me, and I decided to do a slightly different image on each side.

On the first, the profile of the Ring stood out against a thunderous sky, the trenches below filled with dancing skeletons. On the summit I painted Lou, Jay, Al and I, weapons drawn. The second side was exactly the same view, but in summer sunshine, with meadow flowers in the ditch, and a curl of wood smoke rising from the camp on top. Jerry loved it, and we put it up the night before he was due to open. He'd covered it with a cloth which he intended to remove dramatically at the opening ceremony, but it blew off about midday so he just opened up early and we abandoned the ceremony. The place was heaving within minutes, and Jerry simply kept a tab of who had drunk what, presumably to wave at people when he needed their assistance.

He had already spoken to David as quartermaster and me as one of the Group of Four, to arrange some sort of exchange system so customers who didn't make stuff but could offer their own manpower had something to barter for drinks with. If, for example, you could only offer extra shifts on things like the security detail or mucking out the poo-trench which everyone was expected to do, then you could swap one of Jerry's shifts for a strong drink. But if Jerry likes the sheepskin purses your friend makes, you could do two of your friends' "shit-shifts", as they had become known, and get two strong drinks from Jerry.

Or if you'd helped design and build the pub with Jerry you could get free drinks for the foreseeable future and prop up the end of the bar, regaling those in earshot (everyone) with tales of derring-do.

The pub was already a hub of activity, as people swapped shifts and possessions in order to get a round in. Before long hearty bales of laughter rang out, which were soon joined by the crackly sounds of an old jazz record on the gramophone Jerry had brought up from his house.

The presence of a public house up there on Cissbury Ring suggested that all the other houses were private, and that was certainly the case. Before long, the exchange of services had become accepted and practised enough by the majority for it to be perfectly feasible for someone to get a house built and then starve to death in it if they didn't carry on pulling their weight. Many people opted out of the communal food and foraged for themselves. Sometimes they would go hungry; sometimes they would have a glut of provisions with which to barter. It was all about striking a personal balance, and as I had to say to several of the newcomers who had pissed and moaned about the smell, the mud or a hundred other things; 'Muck in, build your own house, then I don't care what you do with your time.'

Christmas was the best Christmas I'd ever had. Jerry organised a Wassail for everyone, toasting bread and dipping it in mead made from the honey of a hive he and Jay had plundered, and hanging it in the branches of what we had worked out was probably the oldest tree on Cissbury Ring. We banged pots and pans to chase away bad spirits, apparently. The fun was facilitated by more of Jerry's brew, but the children just got high on sweets that Dawn had been saving for them. My big plan, the stoned one I had come up with when I'd swapped the horse, paid off. I took two bulging potato sacks around the camp and proudly handed back everything that people had swapped with the 'travelling tinker', as my mum insisted on calling him.

Rings, chains, watches, glasses, prescribed medicine, books, lighters, binoculars – all were returned to their previous owners to gawping mouths and much disbelief. Jenna looked sick, but Lou had let me have her old mascara for Jenna, and she had cried when I gave it to her. I had also painted house signs for each of my friends, and my dad had blubbed like a girl when I gave him the little Spitfire model. I was tempted to tell mum she'd not behaved enough to get a present, but I didn't have the heart and presented her with some flowers Lou had pressed at the end of summer, folded into a little square of oven paper. Dal and Glyn had bartered some of the flint arrowheads from the pits for a travel Scrabble with the visitor, and they both gave it to me 'from the children'. Al had saved me, Jay and Lou a spliff each, but he had been impatient and had smoked all his own already, so we agreed we'd share ours with him - it was a close call but it seemed only fair. Jay had got Al a miniature bottle of Malibu from his dad, and Al had made Jay a wooden scabbard for his sword. Secret Santa had visited again.

I definitely got the best present – Lou woke me up on Christmas morning with a kiss, sat down in front of me and pulled two wedding rings out from inside one of her snotty tissues. I hadn't been able to leave the cabin for an hour after she told me how she'd come by them.

It was an odd tale indeed - the hounds had been quite content to scratch out a general bed and lounging area under the gnarled low boughs of one of the older trees on the Ring, behind our house so the general wind direction would carry early warnings and the smell of camp cooking to their eager muzzles. It provided welcome shelter from the sun on the exposed hilltop, but in winter it formed a natural igloo as the ice bound the knotted branches together and the hard-driven snow filled the cracks. Their combined body heat did the rest, but on the coldest nights I'd put a soft-glowing log under there on the chalkiest scrap of earth as a treat.

David regularly had to check the odd little nest for things that had gone missing from the quartermaster's stores which now doubled as a sort of general store crossed with a lending library of tools and talents. Like all dogs I knew they collected - and fought over - favourite sticks or scraps of cloth, or a lamb bone with the faintest smell of cooking still on it. The den was their canine quartermaster's store. Treasures or memories; only they know what significance such crap possesses. Floyd had taken a fancy to these little carved bone handles for walking sticks and knives that some old chap was making, and several had gone missing from the stores where he was offering them for swap. After some enquiries, David checked in the hounds' shrub-kennel and found the two wedding rings. He took them to Lou to see if they would stand as a substitute for the ones we had lost. It was only after washing them and checking the hallmarks that Lou realised that they were our actual wedding rings.

Making Amends
[days 0205 – 0345]

At its peak the ice had formed thickly on the stony tracks across the Downs, making foraging slippery and dangerous - even the horses had trouble getting up and down the slopes of the Ring. Lou had started to remember some of her dreams when she woke and, whilst she found it hard to talk about them, she had recounted some of her fiercest nightmares to me. Just after Christmas she kept having one recurring dream about her work colleague Susie. She described walking in the moonlight along the Downs, brushing closed flower buds with her fingers, drinking in the cool, still air. The path crunched, crystalline under her feet, and she said barn owls would silently swoop past her like ghosts. Then she'd stop, and turn, seeing what she had been distracted from seeing before. Impaled on a sharpened fence post was Susie, leaning back with her bra in the air, talking to Lou about work, her boyfriend she was thinking of dumping, and about getting her nails done. Then she would stop, in silent, gaping mouthed spasm, and her flesh would peel away to the bone. Teeth and hair fell out, jelly dropped to the floor, and bones sighed into dust. Lou would wake when she looked down to see the crushed skulls littering the path.

'How many times have you had this dream?' I asked her one frosty morning.

'Loads,' she yawned, tired from her fitful sleep. 'It's starting to take over from the others I think. I definitely had it last night too. It's because I know she's still there.'

I stroked her head. 'Susie's dead sweetpea. Anyway, she might not even be there anymore.'

'What if she's cold?' Lou asked.

I had got into the habit of baking bread, slowly in a second drum fitted to the top of my oak smoker fire can. I cut Lou a piece of hot, fresh bread, still doughy and moist, and spooned some rosehip jam onto it. I took it back to my wife with a cup of tea before setting off to work painting Al's cabin walls. Lou had taken to sleeping at night again when it got really bitterly cold, but she would still have terrible nightmares, jerking our bed with their powerful grip. I hated to see Lou in this state, and was constantly thinking about how – or even if – I could help her. It turns out I had already voiced the answer, months before: to go and get Susie, and bury her. Give her a good send-off.

'Maybe we could go and fetch her back,' I said to Lou that evening. She hugged me, but slept no sounder.

Winter had melted into spring, and the air was fresh. The snow had thawed, and the ice had finally disappeared. We could see hares still brilliant white in their winter coats as they got hungry and a bit too confident against the green hills. They spurred us into action, and it was after Al and I returned with the dogs from our first proper hunting expedition of the New Year that I decided to have a chat with Dawn. I told her wanted to take two horses over to the track north of Southwick with Lou to bring Susie's corpse back. She wouldn't let us go by ourselves but did say she'd take Lou on the back of her horse, and help me not kill myself when riding a mule of my own.

I showed Lou the map, and told her of my plan to take a horse track east, then up to meet the South Downs Way and over the footbridge at Bramber, whereupon we'd join up with Monarch's Way down to the Southwick tunnel to get Susie. She agreed with some trepidation, but the next day the three of us set off with Lou on Dawn's horse and me bouncing along behind them. I had brought Jay's sword, the long-handled axe, wire cutters and some thick bleach, as well as the canvas sail Al had been using on the floor of his tepee.

We stared down at the devastation in the towns, at the impassable roads, strewn with the molten hulks of thousands upon thousands of cars. We saw the glass shattered by fire and ice, and the steel twisted to the ground. We came upon the ivory skeletons of stricken people, ripped of almost all skin and flesh by scavengers or the weather or both. Woven into the earth by the first eager shoots of spring they lay, often with their jaws gurning, their limbs still imperceptibly resisting nature's grasp, as they returned to the earth in super slow-motion. We saw three stinkers which must have survived the winter as humans before turning recently, their thick coats and shredded winter gloves betraying their season of infection. They were easy, and went down hard as we struck at their heads and necks from horseback.

Bodies were piled high on the river bank, squirming in the mud or in the reeds, their bellies swollen and their faces blistered. We stopped to speak to a man who was fishing off the footbridge. He said his friend had got infected from eating the fish, as the bodies were piled up in the river for too long, but he was just fishing for fun. He seemed relaxed enough, and patted his dog, a border collie, who he told us was an excellent look-out. He was from the camp up at Bramber Castle, and said we should drop by when we passed back through. He said they'd seen our fires at Cissbury Ring, and were intending to send a party out to greet us, so we should definitely pop our heads in on our way back.

'What are you doing out here?' he asked.

'Collecting one of our colleagues. We left them over that way on the day it broke out,' I said.

'I don't fancy there'll be too much left of them by now,' he said, rubbing his cheeks. 'Still, good luck, eh?'

We said our goodbyes and made our way east. Dawn could gather a substantial pace when she wanted the horses to, and soon we were approaching Shoreham and the Southwick Tunnel. When the copse with Susie's corpse in stood in view at the bottom of the hill, Lou asked Dawn to stop. She wanted to walk the rest of the way, to do in the sunshine what her dreams only let her do at night. Dawn and I watched as she approached the edge of the woods and the fence we had impaled her workmate on. Dawn led the horses slowly behind Lou, so we were never more than twenty feet away, and we watched as Lou stopped and held her hands to her face.

For a moment I thought someone had come and swapped Susie for someone else – she was unrecognisable. After a while though, I saw that the clothes were the same as she'd worn that hot day last year – the pencil skirt, and her bra now grey and tattered, still strung into the air by the splintered fence post. I could see the dry flaps of her breasts, leathery and mildewed. She looked pretty motionless, but as our smells and sounds got more intense she was spurred into action again. She had already 'expelled' - the ground around her was slicked with black, slippery fat. Birds had pecked away most of the skin from her face and shoulders; I suspected rodents had feasted on pretty much everything else.

She stank, and the smell got more intense the more she moved, the sound of popping gristle and grinding bone making me gag. I had to stop it now. I asked Lou to move into the fresh air and let me deal with it but instead she grasped the handle of the long axe. I thought about what Dal had said about killing 'this thing that has taken my daughter', as Lou took Susie's head off fairly cleanly. I cut the barbed wire as close to her body as I could, but most of it had sunk into what little meat was left on her, so I had to snip carefully. The tension in the wires would make them lash out when they became free, and the thought of all the little barbs coated in oily infected scum lead me to wrap myself in the canvas and wish I'd brought the goggles.

I was careful though, and eventually she was free. I had brought some rope, and I set about looping it behind her, spread evenly enough to ensure she stayed in one piece when I lifted her body off the post. A crispy, bubbling suction noise and a whole new stink accompanied her movement as Lou helped me raise her up. We had to stop for two puke-breaks.

I started to roll Susie up in the canvas sail, half of which I'd soaked in the bleach. I placed her head on her shoulders and tucked the fabric around it when I got to the dry end of the cloth. I trussed her up with the rope in the same pattern I used to hang the animal carcasses after they had been gutted. I slung her over the rear of my horse and mounted again. Lou had said nothing, but as she and Dawn rode past, Lou mouthed a 'thank you' at me. My horse followed Dawn's – I hadn't even tried to communicate with the beast - and soon we were galloping across the downs towards Bramber.

Bramber Castle isn't really a castle any more. It's a twenty-foot-wide section of very tall and very thick flint wall, towering alone over the little village of Bramber on a high hill, complete with its own moat - dry now but still deep - with overhanging trees and bramble thickets. On top of the hill there are just one or two flint outlines of rooms and low sections of wall remaining; but on the whole it's just another fortified mound, easily contained and protected. It's much smaller than Cissbury Ring and at most a quarter of its age, with a tiny church positioned halfway up the steep steps which form its only entry point. It was on these steps that the survivors had built a high gate from lashed-together poles, which swung open when we arrived – they were clearly expecting us.

Once the local zombies had slowed down and had stopped scrabbling up the steeply piled earth ramparts, the survivors who had fought their way up there and made it secure settled quickly into a routine. They had a verbal contract instead of the written one we had initiated. Maybe that was a faithful indicator of the more trusting nature of life in a small village, from which surely most of the survivors would have come from - we suspicious townies had to get people to sign on a dotted line. The Bramber contract was surprisingly

SUSIE,
MILDEWED

similar to our own, but I was pleased to hear 'zombies' included in the wording. They had both a St. George Cross and a Union Flag on a proper flagpole, which the oldest camp member Bob said he had taken from the roof of the convent school down the road where he had worked. He'd had to decapitate the headmistress during an emergency staff meeting, and left those who had subsequently tried to detain him to suffer their own fate. He'd been the first up the hill to the castle, and soon he watched the school burn to the ground. We must have driven right underneath him that night. Bob had a mischievous glint in his eye, but clearly didn't suffer fools gladly.

Their camp had pretty much everything ours had: water, food, a graveyard. They had permanent shelters, with walls made from woven sticks and the thick, smooth mud from the banks of the Adur. They didn't, however, have their own pub, and had heard passing travellers tell of The Cissbury Ring, and its banjo-playing landlord who'd get you pissed on a promise. They had also heard about me, and I was stumped to hear people referring to both 'The Battle of the Stinkers', and 'The Chanctonbury Attack'. One kid wanted me to sign his club but I declined, more from confusion than modesty. Some of them nodded wisely when I said we were picking up Susie, and the men wanted to shake my hand. I was, frankly, embarrassed, and Dawn couldn't stop laughing. The camp was united in its disappointment not to be meeting the beagles too, and a man came up to me with a bitch beagle pup, no more than seven months old. He said he'd sheltered in a dog pound in Surrey, and one of the dogs had given birth to a litter whilst he was staying there. He'd taken one pup, and left the others to fend for themselves. Naturally, she would still function as a mate as she still had 'all her bits', he told me earnestly.

Lou had been whisked off by some of the women, and when she returned they had garlanded her hair with the early spring flowers. She looked beautiful. Bob showed me around, and said he wanted me to paint them a pub sign, for when they did get round to finishing their own pub. He pointed to the foundations they had dug on the northern side, for the cellars of what they had in mind. It was big.

'We don't feel so bad, we've got a church just down there if we want to re-pent!' he grinned. 'I feel like we've earned a drink though, don't you?'

'Absolutely,' I said. 'What are you going to call it?'

'The Bramber Castle Inn,' he said triumphantly.

They sat us down and fed us after Dawn had taken the children for a ride on the one horse which didn't have a corpse strapped to it. They'd begged her to accompany them down into the dry moat, and Dawn said they had shown her lots of tiny little holes dug in the side of the hill, many with woven shutters.

'Our kids are the advanced guard,' Bob had twinkled. 'They've got tunnels all over here. They're wily and quick. They've been indispensable,' he said proudly. It seemed at least half a dozen of them were from the school itself, prim convent girls now hardy little warriors. Unlike Dawn, I thought, who had gone from renegade stroppy Goth to responsible young lady just as quickly. I kept my thoughts to myself, though.

'What's this?' I asked, munching on the hearty, herby stew I had been given, dipping grainy unleavened bread into the autumn coloured juices.

'Hare. It's been tough times here over winter, but you tuck in. We're just pleased you could join us!' he beamed. We declined a drink of rum – they only had half a bottle left - but I gladly partook of some of Bob's tobacco. He told us about the poisoned fish they'd caught, and how it had taken six of the women, three men and two children. He told us how, when they'd first been taken ill, the rest of the camp had refused to believe Bob that it could be the same disease. Four more were bitten when the disease finally took them. They'd had to behead all fifteen of their fellow survivors before burying them in the little fenced-in plot under the towering castle remains.

When it was time to go, as the sun started to turn the sky pink, Bob pressed four little twists of paper into my palm.

'What's this?' I asked.

'Seeds,' he said. 'From the school greenhouses. You've got carrots, broccoli, parsnips and tobacco.'

'Tobacco?' I asked.

'Yeah, everyone used to grow it in their back gardens. Gone out of fashion now, but fashion is a funny thing, isn't it? Put them all in now, give the broccoli some space. I'll be over your way soon, and I'll bring a sack of chitted potatoes with me, ready to sow.'

'Well, I don't know what to say. Thank you.' I stuttered, genuinely touched.

'It's nothing. Consider it a down payment on that pub sign,' he grinned.

As we rode down the steps I turned and committed to memory the image of the camp. It would make a good pub sign; the steep hill and the even steeper flint wall of the castle, alone and functionless yet still doing what it was supposed to do, at least in part. It stood proud against the blue sky, and beneath it fluttered the flag of my shattered country.

We buried Susie in the graveyard straight away. Lou had buried her head in my chest when Janam read out her now customary composition. The flag had been put to half-mast, and Lou had gasped when we heard church bells ringing out from the valley below. We'd all gathered around the little grave as Keith - the man who'd agreed to be in charge of the poo-trench in return for a free tab at The Cissbury Ring – finished filling the grave in with his shovel. Now we stood in wonderment at the sound, one we hadn't heard for months; the sound of civilised summers and lazy Sundays, if a little cacophonous.

It was the first time I'd seen my mum cry since they'd come up here. After all she had seen, after all both of them had been through together, church bells made her cry. When the bells finished pealing their uncoordinated racket, we could hear over to the east the faint sound of the bell of the little church at Bramber. As it tolled, dull on the warm spring air, David appeared on horseback breathless and pleased with himself, confessing to being the impromptu bell ringer in a little church he had found just over to our west. As Dawn tried to get him to breathe, he told us that on the hill behind the church were the remains of another, deserted settlement. It was clearly visible from our camp, but I'd never seen so much as a wisp of smoke above it. I left the reprimanding up to Dawn – he should never have left camp on his own, but it was a gesture that didn't go unappreciated.

My mum had recently taken to going on field trips with the children and some of the more curious adults, always accompanied by Jay and at least one other burly tooled-up chap.

'We've never seen a really fresh one,' she told me one day, apparently used to simply avoiding any zombies that were left roaming around. She said they were usually knotted into the chalky earth and 'quite useless', as the brambles and bindweed grew up through their ribs and out of their mouths. They'd still see anything up to fifty in a day, still walking, still ambling in their unmistakeable gait across the South Downs of England and beyond. Mum and the children studied beetles, bugs, butterflies: anything really, that fired up the children's curiosity. She had a vast treasure trove of knowledge about almost anything they could find, from discarded adder skins to the flourishing Downland flowers which grew everywhere on the recently fertilised soil. She'd even brought a few owl pellets back with them, and the children had washed the little pods of regurgitated waste, teasing the rodent fur apart to reveal miniscule little bones and whole mouse skulls.

Over the next few days I set about creating our vegetable patch. It was much larger than the one we'd made back at our old house, so I could give the vegetables more space between the rows. I scraped back a rectangle of turf on the opposite side of our cabin to the oak smoker - the side which would get most light throughout the day but which was still in the lee of our log cabin. I even set up an irrigation system using hosepipe attached to our own water butt, burying it between the drills where the seeds were scattered. I had only used a third of the plot, so it was agreed we would make a trip to the superstores to see if any packets of seeds were left. I couldn't really see seeds getting looted, at least not in the initial rush. Late one night, after Al had seen what we were doing he came up to speak to me with excited eyes, holding out a handful of little seeds of his own.

'Are they what I think they are?'

'Yup,' he grinned. He'd saved them from the pot he had bought from the travelling salesman, and we'd scurried off to my vegetable patch and sowed the seeds, giggling like a pair of twats.

'What are they going to do, arrest us?' Al smirked.

Sure enough the next expedition to Sainsbury's brought back basil, mint and rosemary seeds, as well as more carrot; wild rocket; cauliflower; onion; spring onion; leek; kale and pumpkin seeds. They even brought some sunflower seeds for the children to grow, but I was more eager to get them into the idea of growing the vegetables that we would be eating. The twins Danny and Anthony had already proved useful on several hunting trips; now they could see for themselves the relaxed side of feeding yourself.

The children all found it confusingly simple – no job, no money, no supermarket, no packaging. Just a bit of graft and a jot of teamwork could sustain us all. They had asked me why we adults had decided to change it, to make it all more complicated, and I had to say that I just didn't know why.

Lou had sidled up to me, slipping her hand into mine. She'd seemed much more able to relax since we had retrieved Susie, and had got in three full nights' sleep at least. She said she'd dreamed about chasing rabbits with Floyd. She was much happier, and I once saw her sat by Dawn's grave making daisy chains with Janam. Now we just stood and watched as the children dug the new drills into the freshly exposed topsoil of our further expanded vegetable patch. Janam was chastising Patveer for being too bossy, whilst Danny and Anthony poked the seeds about on their open palms, my mum pointing to the pictures of the finished crop in the *River Cottage Year* book.

Lou stood on tiptoe and whispered 'Wouldn't you like one?' and squeezed my hand. When I knew that I'd heard her correctly, I expected the grip of fear to tighten around my throat, but I was actually quite excited. I was honoured, and at that point in time – for the first time - I knew that I could actually give our child an education, upbringing and environment which finally felt like a life; an existence. The thought of bringing a child into a world of product placement on pre-school toys, a world in which it was considered cruel to bring up your child without the presence of the Disney corporation in their lives, was what had filled me with dread before. But all of that was gone now. We were free. We sent the kids away out of earshot 'for a break' and started trying for the baby straight away.

Before long the first few green shoots poked out from the strong soil, and soon after that, long green rows of young vegetable stood up and identified themselves. We had also worked out how to get baby chickens to come out of eggs – surprisingly simple, again – and they provided the staple meat now, the white meat healthy and firm, and the brown meat somehow herby and earthy. Their eggs were fantastic too, and due to some superhuman abstinence we'd let so many hatch that there was now a full flock panicking around on the top of the Ring. We had found several decapitated, their feathers strewn everywhere but hardly any meat taken, and some carcasses completely untouched.

'That's foxes,' said Jerry, who had kept chickens as a boy.

'Foxes? I didn't think they'd get so close to human activity.' I was puzzled. 'I remember my bins getting done over by the little fuckers, but that was in a deserted street in the middle of the night. The camp's always buzzing.' I said.

'They're vermin, like the rats; the food they usually scavenge down below will be getting scarce, without humans producing it. They're just following us up here.'

'But they haven't even eaten most of them. Just pulled their heads off.'

'They don't need much. They might have been training their pups or something. They're sure to have taken what they need to survive, though. That is, until they need to come back here.'

I wasn't having any of that. I spoke to Al, who suggested what I was thinking; hounds. Over the next week we tried to get the dogs to sleep closer to the chicken's patch, and built a permanent open sided shelter for them, bedded with straw and scattered with some of the rag-and-bone trophies they had kept in their little nest they'd made under the low tree. We sat and kept watch with them for a few nights as Floyd could be spectacularly dippy when chickens were involved, but they soon settled into it. As we sat for the third night without a fire, Al and I talked into the night to keep the cold from our bones. He said the suit was coming along nicely, and that he had transferred the pattern to cloth so he could make more. He'd been using me for measurements, but had kept many of the finer details a secret. He told me how to shoe a horse; Dawn had recently found some stables, with riding equipment and hay, and had plundered the lot. She'd even found some old farrier's equipment in the offices, and loads of horseshoes. Dal had watched his grandfather shoeing horses in India, and was confident he could do it too. Al had been eager to learn and now knew enough himself to while away a night on fox-watch talking about it. He asked me about Bramber Castle, and I told him about the beagle bitch I had been introduced to.

As we were discussing the practicalities of getting bitches pregnant in a survival situation, something caught my eye. Floyd stood motionless, down on his haunches, nose twitching. In the chalky moonlight at the edge of the camp was the distinct outline of two foxes. We soon saw two more join them, smaller and thinner, and they all circled the chickens. Dmitri finally woke up to the lowest growl I'd ever heard Floyd emit - it was barely audible, but it worked for Dmitri who slowly rose with his hackles up. They waited silently for the foxes to get closer than seemed possible without them seeing or smelling us.

Upon some imperceptible signal both dogs flew into the chickens, scattering them clucking and flapping. I saw Floyd lift one of the fox pups into the air and thrash it back onto the ground, limp. Dmitri had one of the adults by the leg, and tumbled in the dust with his quarry. Al and I stood, grim-faced, as the other two foxes fled. Floyd followed, nose to the ground, and Dmitri was soon behind him. Two down.

They were all over the edge of the Ring and out of sight within seconds, leaving Al and I to peer through the settling feathers at the two spittle-soaked bodies of the foxes. Dmitri came back first, with another young fox in his mouth. Floyd had either been outrun by his one or dropped it on the way back – he was no retriever.

'Well, we'll have to see if that stops the senseless violence,' Al said, scratching his dog's back.

'They're pretty territorial, according to Jerry. You get one family working a certain area, so that could well be it.' I said hopefully.

'Well, they won't be missed around here,' Al said, and we certainly didn't have any chickens wasted for a few months after that.

We had all assumed that finding meat would get harder, but we couldn't have been more wrong. None of us knew anything about keeping livestock, except for what we had learnt hit-and-miss about chickens. It seemed logical that without a farmer, animals would just die. In fact as Jeff Goldblum told us all 'Nature will find a way', except we didn't get dinosaurs we got lambs - by the hundred. They gambolled through the fields, oblivious to the grand plan we had for their parents and Sunday lunch a generation previously. We educated a few of them though, but never took more than the now fifty-eight-strong camp could sensibly get through. I grilled six spring lambs whole on my new barbecue pit and we had feasted like kings. I made a rosemary and salt rub, and bashed ten good handfuls of tender young mint leaves together with oil and vinegar for mint sauce.

I was delighted that Bob also decided to visit that day with three of his fellow settlers; Janet and Simon, a married couple; and Graham, the man with the beagle bitch. He had wanted to see our two hounds, which wasn't hard as the smell of cooked lamb drew both of them like sailors onto the rocks. They'd have plenty of juicy, thick bones to get through, because right then I wanted our visitors to eat until they were stuffed senseless. Bob gave me the chitted potatoes he'd promised me – spuds with little black knobbly beginnings of shoots. I had already told the children how we were going to plant them, and we'd marked out a huge area for spuds, so when they had finished fighting with the dogs for an opportunity to play with the puppy bitch (which Graham had called Bramble), I let them get on with it. Bob wanted to see how the sign was progressing, but I told him he'd have to wait – today wasn't a day for working, I had meat to eat.

'Lambs, eh?' Bob had said with a mouthful.

'Yeah, we expected them all to die off, especially in the winter. But they seem to have found food. They kept each other warm and some of them even found a mate at the right time. They've looked after their lambs. There's hundreds of them – round some up and take them back with you.'

'Oh, that'd be great. They are hardy little blighters, South Downs sheep,' he said.

'We expect them to be reliant on us, but they're animals all the same. Their survival instinct keeps them going well enough without us.' I said.

'True,' Graham waved a juicy leg at me, 'and next year, because none of the little boy lambs running about will have been neutered there'll be even more of them to eat!'

That evening, after we had waved the group on their way with full bellies (and throats on fire courtesy of Jerry's latest batch), Dawn and Dal appeared with a bucket. They had been foraging and had stumbled across a smallholding with a nursing cow in an outhouse. They'd mucked her out, replaced the straw and opened the gate to a small enclosed field. She'd been cooped up for too long: her haunches had sores on them, so Dal had applied a poultice - made from his trouser-leg - of mashed-up thyme leaves, a natural antiseptic. In exchange they'd taken some of the milk from her udders which looked fit to burst anyway. They'd carefully carried the milk back over the Downs to the camp in a tin bucket they'd found in the cottage garden, which was overrun and bursting with colour. That night, we had proper, milky tea – no UHT crap, no powdered rubbish, just fresh, proper milk.

Dal and Dawn's tale made me realise that we had a duty to the lambs on the fields surrounding us. None of us were farmers, though, so we had no idea what we were doing. I tried to pool as much knowledge from everyone all the same, anything they knew about sheep or lambs or any other animal. It was scarce, but the next day we rounded up as many of the wriggly little buggers as we could in batches, checked their teeth and hooves, and cut off the dungy clegnuts which dangled around their backsides. It wasn't much, but it felt like we were doing something. We took a few more lambs for the grill for our trouble.

Making History
[days 0346 - 0365]

'I knew it would be you,' the young man said as he walked closer. I recognised the voice but he had the sun behind him so I shielded my eyes, but I still couldn't place him. I knew he hadn't been a stinker when he first approached – we'd not had one actually get up onto Cissbury Ring for a while now.

'Mike?' I scrambled to my feet to look at my brother-in-law, who was heavily tanned and broad-chested. This wasn't the young man who we'd waved off to Thailand a year ago, I thought, with a camera round his neck, bum fluff on his chin and arms like reeds. Mike looked swarthy, like a cartoon sailor – more Bluto than Popeye. He still had his camera with him, which now dangled battered and dusty from a thick strip of leather.

'Your reputation precedes you,' Mike said. 'Your beard's looking well. How have you been then?'

'Fucking hell it is you. Mike, you're looking... leathery.' Lou's brother, standing right there in front of me, was grinning from ear to ear. I hugged him tightly, realising how long it had been already. It only seemed like yesterday when we sat pissed at his birthday barbecue, arguing about whether or not the fact that you could make John McEnroe appear by folding the old ten pound note in the right places had been the deciding factor for them changing its design.

'Well, a few months of sun and salt spray will do that to you,' he said. 'Where's Lou?'

'I think she's working on the classroom,' I replied. 'Have you eaten? It looks like you've eaten well. Let's go and find Lou – walk and talk. How the fuck did you get back here from Thailand?'

'I'll tell you both later, when I've said hello. I knew it would be you,' he said again.

'What do you mean?' I asked.

'I'll tell you that, too,' he grinned.

'You secretive little bugger, tell me.' I was bouncing around him.

'All in good time, brother, all in good time.'

I introduced him to David, who was sat by a fire out the front of the stores making a new handle for his knife. He was heating an antler in the fire then chipping away at it with flint. It turns out Mike recognised David anyway, from drinking in town on a Friday night, but they'd never spoken. They put forward a few possible mutual acquaintances, and found that Mike had dated Dawn's older sister Joy a few years previously. We showed Mike the armoury, now underground and bristling with new additions, plundered from farms and homes. Mike pulled a parang out from his backpack, a curved Malaysian machete. It slid through some of the greener branches drying out for firewood as he hacked downwards at the pile.

'It's for the jungles, really, but it does just as good for the *phee dip*,' he said casually.

'For the what?' I probed.

'Thai for zombie. *Phee dip*.'

'So it got there too?'

'It got everywhere,' he admitted grimly. 'Ah, the famous Chanctonbury Ring Inn,' he said, admiring the pub. Jerry was leaning out of the shutters at the top, cleaning my sign.

'Jerry, it's Mike,' I yelled. 'It's Lou's brother.'

'Time for a drink?' he called back.

'Later. We're going to find Lou.'

'I can't believe you've built a pub,' Mike chuckled.

We walked down the main track with Mike still keeping quiet about his story, instead admiring the houses on either side.

'I take it that was your place, with the flag outside,' he asked.

'Yup. My pub sign on the pub too,' I replied.

'It looks great, what you've done with the place.'

'Thanks, everyone's worked really hard on it. All the building helped us keep warm in the winter – it got pretty tough,' I said.

'I got plenty of bad weather,' he said.

As we reached the end of the row of wooden buildings we came to the site of the classroom. You could see the first three layers of logs that had been put down, like a full-scale floor plan. It had three small rooms and two bigger classrooms. The wall between the two classrooms could be removed, and Al had agreed to lay some sort of flat flooring. My mum saw us first.

'Oh, hello. New bug,' she said, offering a hand.

'Mum, this is Mike. Lou's brother.' I explained.

'Oh, gosh so it is. Grief, how are you? You're looking well!'

Lou had no such problem recognising the newcomer. She ran screaming like a banshee towards him. He looked awkward as she flung herself into his arms, nearly toppling him. He giggled.

'Steady on. How have you been? Has this ginger bastard been looking after you then?'

Neither of us could get any sense out of her for a good fifteen minutes, until she was sat by the main fire, tea shaking in one hand, Mike's hand clasped in the other, with puffy eyes and a snotty nose.

'What happened to you? How did you get back?' she sniffed. Girls were funny. The same stuff leaks out of their faces whether they're deliriously happy or profoundly miserable. Mascara had always struck me as a particularly stupid idea. She told him about their mum but Mike didn't seem too phased and stretched out, loosening his scarred, blackened boots and pulling them off. His feet were as noxious as usual.

'I've learnt not to count anyone dead until you know otherwise,' he exhaled, and clicked his neck. 'It's easier that way. I thought I'd lost Jim, until he turned up one night. He'd been bitten though. Well, I suppose I'd better tell you.'

'Should I get Al?' I asked him, but there was no need. Dmitri appeared, hackles raised, growling at the new face. Floyd had no reservations though, and knocked Mike backwards, pinning him to the ground and giving his face a good scrubbing with his tongue. Dmitri took his cue and joined in. Al peered through the mass of tails and tongues.

'Is that Mike?' Al asked. 'Jay! Mike's here!' Mike tried to sit up, and Al pulled him to his feet, batting away the dogs. Jay ran up, hugging Mike and whooping. It did feel like another triumph, like we'd won all over again.

Are you all here then?' Mike asked, dusting himself off.

'Me, Lou, Jay, Al and Vaughan made it up here… we lost Vaughan though.'

'Well, he was quite small,' Mike twinkled. I nearly pissed myself – it was a release. Even Lou saw the funny side after Mike disarmed her with another hug. Al kicked the dust, mumbling something about bad taste. Mike slapped him on the back, apologised, and showed Al his parang. Soon Al joined us all around the fire, as Mike pretended to sit on Floyd who yelped until he let him go.

'Yeah, sorry about that. No disrespect intended. How did he die?' Mike asked.

'He saved the rest of us.' I explained. 'He pushed a couple of – what was it, *Phee yip*?

'*Phee dip.*'

'He pushed a couple of walkers over the edge. They took him down with them, and there were just too many of them to save him.'

'Was that during the *Battle of the Stinkers*?' Mike asked.

'Jesus, how do you know about that?' Jay demanded.

'Word travels far. In Portsmouth, at the docks, they know about this place. They talk about it, about the camps that people have set up. One thing I have seen lots of is respect when survivors talk about each other. There's about two hundred people in Portsmouth, working out of a luxury liner moored there. It's a pretty rough place; like a trading post I suppose. Dock workers, people from the city, sailors.

'They were totally safe in the ship as there are only three gangways onto it, but it was quite lawless until someone took charge. Filthy Gordon, he's called,' Mike chuckled. 'He really is quite a filthy man. They got by on supplies pillaged from the other ships - the ones that had been abandoned or their crews infected - enforcing maritime law when they had to. There's a lot of drinking and gambling and fighting all the same. Whores too, and bare knuckle boxing. It's great. They were all getting along fine, until the ships started to come in. Then they had to start working again.'

I handed Mike a bowl of lamb and chicken risotto, my favourite since we'd started to collect the cream from the cow, now tethered by the stores. Butter and cream, and some young thyme leaves finished it off. Mike appreciated it, and sucked it hot off the spoon.

'What happened in Thailand?' Lou couldn't hold out any longer. 'How did you get back? By boat?'

'Jesus that's good. Of course by boat, there's no planes any more. Or no jets anyway. I hitched a lift in a seaplane when it all kicked off. I had to trade in my guitar.' He looked gutted. Jay said he could have a go on his, and went to get it until everyone hollered at him not to distract Mike from the story. The kids had gathered round too now, and pleaded to hear something of the world outside.

'I've told this story so many times,' he said wearily. 'I was in a hostel when it hit last summer. I would have been out there for, ooh a week?' he turned to Lou.

'Eight days, when it kicked off,' she told him. 'What happened to Jim?'

'We'd found a nice place in the hills, on Ko Samui. We heard some of the new arrivals in a bar in town talking about being on the last flight out from Britain. They said about the disease, that it had brought London to a standstill. At first we'd all been high-fiving each other, at the thought of being marooned over there, but it turned a bit nasty a few days later when the military came round, separating all the tourists from the locals. All the Thai were put into the grounds of the official buildings, in tent camps. We were left to fend for ourselves outside; I guessed they thought it was easier to seal off the locals, as there were more of us than them. Anyway, after a while we could hear screaming from within the walls of the Thai compounds, and then the gates got opened and they all spilled out. A lot of them were infected already, and that's when Jim and I got separated.

'I pinched a scrambler bike from the hire place, and headed back up into the hills. I found a camp there, locals who hadn't wanted to be trapped in the camps mainly, but a few tourists too. They talked of the spirits of the dead that had yet to be cremated, making corpses walk again. It wasn't a disease for them - it was a war between good and evil in another dimension. They worried about their *phee reuuan* - like amiable house spirits - and they all seemed more concerned that the zombies would eat them rather than actual people. They would tie any newcomers to a tree whilst they proved they weren't bitten.'

I looked at the Goths. David looked at me and winked. Mike took a few mouthfuls of risotto.

'That's really good,' he said to me. 'That was around the time Jim turned up – he had been bitten, and his clothes had been torn off. But he must have fought them off, because it had time to infect him. He stumbled into the camp, probably drawn up by the fire - or the hog-roast come to think of it – and one of the Thai took his head off. They didn't bury him, just sent him and his head downstream. I left soon after that. I used the stream to head to the coast, and found Jim's body. I buried him amongst the mangrove trees, but it didn't feel right, without his head being in the same hole. I never found it. I did find a little dinghy with an outboard motor and headed round the island, and managed to get onto the seaplane with about six other Europeans which took me back to Surat Thani on the mainland. Loads of places were on fire. Someone fell ill whilst we were in the air, so the crew just kicked her out of the door. The man threatened to throw her boyfriend out after her, he was out of control. The pilot tried to calm everyone down, shouting that that was how it had spread so fast, because people weren't quick enough to act.

'It was rough in the town; I didn't see any survivors at all after the plane left again. I holed up in an empty railway carriage, until I plucked up the courage to fight my way out and pinched another boat. I headed down to where I thought the main ferry port was, but I ran out of petrol though, and I hiked the rest of the way along the coast. There was still a government office open in a sealed compound on the docks, next to a huge tanker which had moored there. We stood there in the rain for three days with the military patrolling us at gunpoint. If you looked ill, they'd shoot you and drag you to the edge of the quay. Eventually an Englishman appeared on the ship gangway, who hand-picked a crew of one hundred. It was like a chain gang, but at least I was going somewhere. He'd asked for only British people first, so I suppose I thought I was coming back here. I just wanted to get somewhere else at the time though.

'If I thought it was rough in Thailand it was rougher on the ship. Any sign of illness - which basically meant any sign of slacking off – and you'd be de-capitated and tipped over board, and your head sewn onto a bit of rope around the funnel, slowly cooking along with all the others. There were forty-two of us out of the original hundred left by the time we docked in Portsmouth. The captain, Captain Hammond was a fucking madman, but I got to know him well. He decided I'd be useful when we went through the Malacca Straits and ran into pirates who thought we were carrying fuel. They shot at us with a grenade launcher, but the Captain had mounted some old Gatling guns on the top decks which he ordered me to use. I didn't argue, they were awesome, but didn't half make you shake. The captain strutted around chucking grenades over into the sea, and the pirates soon went away again.

'We ran out of fuel and had to barter for more at Suez, in another fortified compound. We had to stop there for a month. Eventually he won half of their main stores of fuel in a poker game, and said he'd buy up the rest as a goodwill gesture. We all boarded again, and he sent two of his men on shore to settle up - I think they accepted gold bars. Anyway, the captain just sailed off, leaving his mates there and getting us to mount the guns again, firing randomly into the dockside - I made sure I missed. Absolute madman – after that he gave me one of the positions on the bridge that had just become open. I just hoped we wouldn't have to stop for fuel again.'

He went to put his clean bowl down, but Dawn took it off him. Jerry appeared with a few glasses of dark foamy broth, and handed Mike and I one.

'New batch. Bit strong,' Jerry wheezed. I could see his eyes were watering. 'Don't let me interrupt you.' He said. I noticed the eye-watering wasn't letting him stop quaffing. It smelt like nail varnish.

'Bloody hell, Jerry,' Mike wiped his mouth, wincing. 'I can feel the hairs sprouting out of my chest as I speak. Okay, here's where it gets really grim though. Six people fell ill after Suez, so the captain sealed off a whole bit of the ship, trapping eleven healthy people in there with them, who were just looking after the ill ones really. We could hear them banging on the doors at night, shouting for us to let them out. No-one did let them out though - I kept thinking about what the bloke said on the seaplane in Thailand and kept quiet. After a few days the shouting stopped – but the banging never did.

About ten people shuddered in unison.

'It was hot in the Mediterranean, just as hot as it was much further south. We saw lots of wrecked ships, too, sometimes crawling with corpses. They never drown, either. Anyway eventually I recognised the Rock of Gibraltar and even saw the Union Jack flying, but no-one was left there. We didn't dock. One thing about Captain Hammond, was that he loved his food. He'd 'miscounted' some of the cargo when he'd got into Thailand on the day the virus really took hold. No-one noticed. There was loads of livestock on board, which got a bit chewy by the time we'd been sailing for so long, but we still ate well.

'When we pulled into Portsmouth, we were left for a week in quarantine, and then Filthy Gordon came on deck. They'd squared up to each other – too much testosterone, you know? He asked Captain Hammond whether he knew if anyone on board was infected, and he said there wasn't, but when two of Filthy Gordon's men opened up the doors to the end of the ship they got bitten by the *phee dip* that he'd sealed in there.

'Filthy Gordon put a bullet right into Captain Hammond's eye, and then he shot his two men. That's when I first met Filthy Gordon. It's a shame, really, because they would have got on with each other like a house on fire. I worked in the docks for a bit, with a room on Gordon's liner, glad to be home amongst

the rain and the gloom and the piss, you know? But the place had changed...'
People laughed.

'I knew I'd come back to Worthing at some point, I mean it's only sixty miles. But the snow, as well as their stories of what England was like outside the camp put me right off the idea. They said that Portsmouth town centre was piled high with stripped skeletons, and if the ones with any flesh left didn't get you, the rats would. With nothing but marine diesel, they said a group of the men went out of the camp trying to find petrol from a car. They didn't get far, as two of them suffocated from inhaling flies – literally their mouths filled in seconds, and the others had to retreat.

'We'd often get people passing through, and some of them told us of the other camps that survivors had set up. Most of the stories were ones where the camps had been lost to the virus, where they hadn't made it more than a month or two. They said any camp with a doctor in it was doomed, as they just did what they thought best and began on a smaller scale what the rest of the country had done the weeks before: tending to the sick, instead of taking off their heads. Some of the stories were about successes though, and near-misses. There's a camp at Tintagel Castle...'

'Where?' Al asked.

'Tintagel,' I said. 'It's in Cornwall, sticking out into the sea on a little bit of rock. I went there when I was a kid – it's supposed to be where King Arthur had his pad. Sorry Mike, didn't mean to interrupt.'

'Yeah, a camp at Tintagel. A chapter of the Hell's Angels took it over, and took in as many survivors as they could; caring for them, protecting them, feeding them. But if you lied about being infected they'd make you kill the people you'd arrived with, before chucking you off the cliffs. Not many people lied. Also, there was one camp in the caves at Cheddar Gorge where a man killed everyone who believed that a new illness that had broken out in their camp wasn't the virus that started it all. He even killed the ones that weren't sick, even killed his wife.'

The children were goggle-eyed by this point, and I must admit Mike had got better at telling stories. Lou said nothing, and just stared into the fire.

'Anyway, there were other stories, too; far too many to go through now. Filthy Gordon collected information on all the camps they heard from, and had a map set up. He'd put a pin in each, and could reel off a story for every one. The country was dotted with them. When he first heard that I was trying to head back to Worthing he told me about a man with a red beard and two beagles who set up camp with his wife on Cissbury Ring, who'd kill you if you didn't sign his contract.'

'Well, that's not strictly true,' I said.

'One of those beagles is mine,' Al snorted.

'Well, half of its bullshit anyway. It's like these survival tales have become new folk stories, I suppose,' Mike stretched out again. 'To keep the kids quiet, you know. Bullshit or not though, they said you had saved a hundred men women and children, felled a thousand zombies and a thousand trees, and then built a pub because you needed the refreshment!' He beamed. 'The Cissbury Chapter's reputation, as I say, precedes you.'

I didn't know where to put myself.

'That brings me onto my next… well, duty I suppose. When I finally got ready to make the journey back to Sussex, I was given these, one for every camp I would meet on the way.' He pulled a flattened scroll of paper from his jacket pocket. 'A man dropped them off in Portsmouth one night in the winter. A representative of someone important.'

'No.' I said, agog. 'What do you reckon, The Queen, the government or the church?'

'He didn't say who he represented, apparently, but you should read it. I'll bet a tenner Liz got whisked off quick-sharpish when they started puking in the Palace. He didn't have white gloves and a top hat on or anything,' Mike laughed. 'He came in an ancient Land Rover with three soldiers. They stayed for a night, and he explained to Filthy Gordon that they were establishing contact with the surviving citizens of England.

'Get this - there were many survivors in Scotland who had been cut off, where the disease had spread more slowly, and they easily slipped into ancient ways of governing themselves. They had all politely declined the representative's offer, but said if they could help the English in any way they'd be delighted. Gordon loved that - Wales was pretty much the same, apparently. Anyway, the flunky had travelled the country, stopping at obvious centres of activity, areas of life. Walled towns, ports, that sort of thing, you know.

'He was looking for people who'd made maps just like Gordon's. He took careful notes, and then filled out these scrolls, which he left with instructions to distribute them as best he could. Oh, and a map each. That was it. He wanted a representative of Cissbury Ring to have one.' He handed it to me.

'It's like an ambassador. Fuck. Perhaps we should decide who's the leader... you know, who the representative is. We've never decided,' I said to Mike.

'Aren't you the founding member of the Group of Four?' Mike asked me.

'Well, yes,' I replied, 'but its like Al says, one of the beagles is his. Everyone's done something, I mean it's not like I did anything special. Anyone would have done what we've done, wouldn't they? Surely?'

No-one said anything for a while. Lou was smiling at me. Al spoke first.

'I've always said I'm in no doubt I wouldn't be here if it wasn't for you.'

'I don't answer to anyone else up here do I?' Jay shrugged. 'We're all survivors up here, but it's your camp.'

'Dawn and I, well, you know how grateful we are, don't you?' David had his arm round Dawn. 'Credit where it's due and all that.'

'You have looked after my children; your mother has been like a mother to my children too. I am indebted to you and I am also proud of what you have done,' Dal frowned, 'and so you should be too.'

'He is the Messiah!' shouted Jerry in his best *Monty Python* voice.

Raucous laughter joined the murmurs of agreement from those that had gathered by the fire. I was proud, but I was more curious about the scroll.

'Okay then, does that mean I get to read this thing now?' I asked, pulling at the red ribbon.

'Read it!' Jerry hollered, egging the children on to make a noise too.

'It's an invitation,' I was trying to sound relaxed. 'It says "*A special summons to an honourable member of the Cissbury Ring encampment, one of the sixty-five hundredths of Sussex*"...'

'That's some old-school shit,' Al said.

'"...*to a Council of the scattered fragments of our island, on Midsummer's Day this year, for one week at the Windsor Encampment at Windsor Great Park.*" that's right by my old university,' I said. 'Lou and I got lost there once, when it was dark, do you remember sweetpea? I got freaked out and tried to climb a tree, but Lou had hauled me down and made me carry on until we could see the road.' Everyone laughed. Sometimes I wondered why she loved me so much.

'"*You will not be granted entry without this missive and three copies of your local charter,*' I read, '*two duplicates and the original, all signatures included. Make a third copy to stay within your camp. If you have a verbal charter, commit it to paper along with the signatures of all present.*" I wonder if Bob's got one at Bramber?' I asked.

'Bramber Castle?' Mike waved another scroll at me. He had four more.

'I thought you were stopping?' Lou asked.

'Oh, I will for a day. I've got to find Hanna though,' he said. 'I promised her I'd come back to her, before I went.'

'Where is she?' I asked.

'Now? I don't know, but I know she was in Brighton, staying with her parents when it broke out.' he said. 'It was the holidays at university.'

'Oh. Do you think she's alive, Mike?'

'I've got to find out. I'm going in a straight line, that way,' he pointed, squinting. 'I've got to get there before next week.'

'Why, what's next week?' I asked, dumbly.

'Midsummer's Day.' He grinned.

I was getting increasingly nervous – I really wasn't expecting to do much more travelling in my life, before Mike arrived with that scroll. Dawn spent a lot of time with me making me ride on the back of her horse, all over the Downs. She said it was a patient, strong horse which could easily take us the long but relatively safe route recommended on the map Mike had shown us. Cleared or regularly patrolled sections of track which linked known encampments were marked in blue architects' pencil. Red areas were no-go zones, mainly correlating with the densest pre-infection population. We transferred some of the information from Mike's map to a few we'd collected in the library, including an old map of the south of England Jinny had brought with her. It had some really detailed local tracks across the Downs, so we thought it might come in useful further afield too.

Our best route took the South Downs Way west from Cissbury to a place called Lynch Down south of Midhurst, where we could take the old Roman Roads pretty much all the way into Windsor Great Park. It was a bit of a dog-leg but it beat trying to take a more direct asphalt route, and I certainly agreed with the notion of avoiding towns.

As well as a few sacks of quicklime for bartering with I decided to take something with me which might go down quite well – providing they had a generator. Jay lent me his newly sharpened sword, and his scabbard. Patveer lent me his sheepskin - the biggest one yet - and told me not to be cold in the night. Dawn thought we'd be travelling for at least one night, so I packed some smoked ham and butter, and Jerry gave us a pitcher of his latest fire-water. My dad thumped me on the shoulder and wished me all the best. My mum had simply started fretting about anything from underpants to water. I grabbed some bread too, and Jay wrote out three copies of our charter which Lou and Jenna took round for everyone to sign, and lots of people wished me luck.

Al appeared with something dark red draped over his arm. It was his zombie protection suit, and when it was laid out you could see the perfectly stitched patchwork of different material. Around the elbow and knee joints was softer, suppler hide from the bellies of deer, stretched over metal reinforcements which Al had hammered into shape. The main body of the suit was made from thick cow hide, stained a marbled red-black by red onion skins Al had been collecting from the compost heap. A high collar was an addition to the original pattern stolen from the motorcycle suit which covered my throat and halfway up the back of my head. It was stiff, but surprisingly comfortable when I tried it on, and Al said it should loosen up quickly with use. It had been studded with inset flint arrowheads, to strip the teeth from the rotten gums of any stinkers fixated on my neck. He'd got two zips from ruined trousers, which meant I could wear them with any shoes, but Al had also re-upholstered a pair of steel-toed safety shoes he'd found in the same red-black skin. Also inset into the top of the forearms and the shoulder blades, and in a spine effect down the back, were sharpened strips of corrugated iron, stitched and riveted in at a vicious angle. The sewn-in chemical gauntlets were fingerless to allow me to operate the longbow, which was strapped across my back by part of the inbuilt quiver belt. Below the knees was completely solid, with a re-shaped length of drainpipe inbuilt into the material, and a chest-plate made from a cast-iron omelette pan. It looked great, even on me, and Jay laughed when I held my longbow that I looked like a *Marvel* baddie.

'The Bearded Bowman,' he giggled.

Soon — sooner than I'd hoped - it was time to leave. Lou and I tried for a baby for a bit before I really had to go — Al had put in a handy access panel under the steel codpiece. Dawn was getting impatient though, and pointed out that I had been the one that wanted to strike camp before night fell.

Lou and my mum were both crying when I left, and Dal rode with us for at least fifteen miles up until the point where we left the South Downs Way. The Roman road Mike's map suggested stretched out like an arrow in front of us, overgrown in places but passable. We crossed the A272 and the A3, riding past Alton and Basingstoke, through pillowed fields and over teeming hedgerows towards Silchester. We stopped to water the horse three times, and thought we should ride through the night and stop first thing in the morning instead of trying to set up a camp in the dark. The steed was doing well, and was happy to stretch its legs. There was no need to ride through the night as it happened - we were drawn to the smoke of a large encampment as sun set. We trotted down the track towards the camp, lined with flaming torches chained to tree stumps. From the dim glow of its fire we could see it was on flat ground, with high fencing following the surrounds of what we were told by its residents that evening was a Roman town. It made sense – it was at the end of a Roman road. Siclhester was a busy camp, with strict rules, and had great gates that lowered like drawbridges. The quartermaster helped us find a spot to tie the horse and told us they knew about the Council meeting, and they had been working with "the Queen's men" as he put it.

'What have you been doing?' Dawn asked.

'Clearing the forest, yonder.' He pointed at one of the four gates that opened out onto straight, green lanes leading away from the camp. 'We been marking the way through to the Windsor Camp.'

'How far is it?' I asked.

'Ooh, twenty-odd miles. Won't take you long on a mare.'

We thanked him for the straw and the advice, and took in the new sounds and smells. It was basically two playing fields, surrounded on two sides by modern roads, yet totally enclosed by the perimeter which was constructed from a mix of modern fencing, scaffolding poles and sheet metal. We made our way to the largest of the buildings, a wooden barn. Inside was pealing with laughter, and the smell of gin and ale oozed from people's pores. Blazing torches hung from the clay-covered walls, and a hog roasted in a trench at the entrance. Many wore the leathers of people who worked with horses, others wore tweed; and some even denim and trainers. All were ruddy-faced in the glow of the oil lamps. Straw lay on the ground, and a counter top had been made from plywood, which stood in the corner furthest from the open barn wall.

'Can I help dear? Grand Council folk are you? Up to the Great Park?' the old lady asked. I was gawping at some prostitutes, so Dawn spoke to her.

'Yes, we've been summonsed to the Council. I have the papers.'

Z.P.S.

'Oh, that's alright dear, I don't need to see no papers,' she clucked. 'You've a room made upstairs, have a word with Joe at the bar, he'll see you right for a tipple, too. There'll be no charge for either - how about that?'

'That's kind, thank you,' Dawn said, tugging me toward a smoky snug to one side.

'Don't thank me; thank her up at the big house.'

It seemed that the ruddy faced types in the straw-laden hall behind us were just those who couldn't get into the pub, or who had been kicked out. The place has heaving.

'What was the old crone saying?' I hollered in Dawn's ear.

'Don't be rude!' Dawn shouted.

'Sorry. It seemed quite appropriate.'

We fought our way to the bar, apparently ripped out in its entirety from a local pub. After about a twenty minute wait it was our turn, so I showed Joe the scroll and he nodded at us. Dawn had been excitedly reading the labels on the bottles, and wanted a Bacardi Breezer. I rather foolhardily asked for some of the local brew, which seemed to have both bird's nest and egg shell in it. I haggled with a large man for some tobacco, and as he had no use for a sack of lime I ended up doing a fairly merciless caricature of the fat oaf on a square of cloth, which he didn't find funny but his friends did. The bastard refused to pay up so his mates collected a whole pouch of tobacco, and one of them pressed a little green bud into the palm of my hand.

'Don't let the governor catch you with that mate,' he winked.

Joe brought another drink over to us when the queue at the bar was only three deep, and said Rose on the front desk would show us our room when we were ready. Dawn looked embarrassed, and Joe twisted a bar towel, looking anxious.

'Sorry, ma'am, I didn't mean to suggest… it's just we're packed tonight, see?' He turned to me. 'You the 'elp?' he asked gruffly.

'I'm sorry?' I asked.

'Are you 'er 'elp?' he quizzed. 'The baroness?"

'Who?' I asked, genuinely stumped.

'He's talking about me,' Dawn said. 'No, Joe, He's the one that's been invited to Windsor Great Park; I just rode him here. I wasn't expecting to share a room, that's all. We were hoping to camp tonight.'

'Oh, camping's not clever ma'am. The forest's not safe yet, there's plenty of them abroad. They're spread out, see? When it finally took hold in the Bracknell camp – we knew it would, there were hundreds of people camped up there, some said thousands – it got worse all round here, much worse. The forest's no place to camp, if you'll forgive my impertinence,' he laughed awkwardly, and gave the towel another nervous twist.

'Not a problem, Joe and we'll heed your advice with gusto,' I said.

'Very good sir,' he said, and limped off.

We finished our drinks slowly – I didn't need another beer – and I puffed long and slow on a roll-up as Dawn played cat's cradle with one of the barmaid's grubby-faced daughters. We were shown our room, which was really only a wattle and daub partition on a long upper floor. There was one bed - a box with straw piled into it - so we sat on it and, and I rolled a joint as we talked into the night over the stifled giggling and not-so-stifled humping noises.

'Jerry would love that place,' I nodded to downstairs. 'He'd have a fit.'

'You should do them a new sign. Their one was rubbish.' Dawn said. 'You don't mind, do you?' she asked me. 'About me not wanting to share a bed? I don't mind sharing, really I don't, it's just that David and I, well, he'd saved up to take me to a hotel, and it was my birthday the day after... the day after it broke out. I was supposed to be staying in a hotel with David.'

'Aw, bless you.' I said. 'No worries. I'm pretty sure this doesn't count as a hotel, anyway.'

She snorted into the dregs of her Breezer. I eventually stubbed my doobie out and closed my eyes. I heard her get out of her boots and under the furs on the bed. I left my boots and my superhero suit on, and pretty soon I was sleeping like a baby.

Morning came with the smell of wood smoke, eggs and bacon. Dawn was creeping out of the door as I woke.

'Just checking on the horse,' she whispered, and creaked down the narrow stairs to the hallway below. I dozed a while on the bed, then stretched, and rolled onto the floor. I pushed open the tiny shutters and looked into the courtyard below, to the chickens and horses. Muddy cart-tracks collected the morning drizzle which clung to my beard. I could hear a hammer striking an anvil; I caught sight of an open-sided hut, and a man with a beard talking to Dawn, with cartwheels piled up around him. There was a tannery too, and the stench of boiled fat would occasionally hit my nostrils. First and foremost was the question of where the bacon and eggs were.

I collected my stuff, and gathered what little of Dawn's she had left scattered about. I made my way down the stairs to the sound of snoring and farting from the other rooms. It was early. Rose from the barn - reception, I suppose you'd call it - appeared at the end of the stairs and ushered me into the bar. She sat me down and fussed, pouring me a cup of tea.

'Want something stronger?' she asked.

'No, thank you, this is perfect,' I replied, bleary-eyed. 'Rose - where is that smell of bacon coming from?'

'Ooh, that's Joe – he's knocking out egg and bacon sandwiches for England this morning. He's got the kitchens through there, and a little counter-top opening out onto the courtyard. Hang on, I'll grab you a sampler.'

Before I could stop her – which I didn't really try to – she had disappeared in a flurry of apron and the smell of cream. She soon returned with a plate, and I stared in disbelief.

'Two bacon, two egg, sausage – they're my recipe – mushrooms, black pudding, bread and tomatoes, fried. That do you?' Her smile looked like it would split her face.

'That's amazing. What do I owe you?' I asked.

'Don't fancy a shag, do you dearie?' She cocked her head.

'Er, no, thanks, Rose, I'm married. I really can't accept this if you want to…'

'Oh, I'm just messing with you, you daft bastard. Rose's got a wicked sense of humour, that's all,' she giggled. 'No, you tuck in; I'll frig myself off in the cowshed.' I splattered tea onto the table as she disappeared with a demonic cackle. I didn't need to be told to tuck in twice, and demolished my breakfast although I'm sorry to say the old dear did rather put me off my eggs. She wasn't around when I finished, so I licked my plate clean (I couldn't think of anything else to do, I couldn't leave her a tip), pulled on Patveer's sheepskin and walked into the grey morning.

Dawn beckoned me over to the wheelwright's shack.

'This is him,' she beamed at the bearded man. He was huge, and had to stoop to offer me a hand.

'Pleased to meet you,' I said, shooting a glance at Dawn.

'This is John, the wheelwright,' Dawn grinned at me.

'Pleased to meet you, too. Well he looks the part, in that get-up. It's not that red though,' he said, looking disappointingly at my beard, which I self-consciously stroked. 'So you'll be painting me a new sign?' he asked me. Dawn made eyebrows at me as subtly as she could. I took my cue.

'Oh, yes,' I said. 'I take it you've told my, er, my assistant what you need?'

'Yes, it's all up here,' Dawn tapped her head.

'Well I look forward to seeing it anyway. Nice to meet you, Dawn,' he said.

'Nice to meet you too. Are we good to go?' Dawn asked me. I thought we were, so she helped me up onto the horse to much hearty laughter from Huge John the Wheelwright.

'I really should learn how to do that by myself,' I said in her ear.

'I know you should, I've lost count of the number of times I've shown you. We ready?'

She trotted up to the gate.

'Is this the right gate for Windsor Great Park?' she called down to the master of one of the gate crews. He nodded, and waved for his men to lower it. I saw for the first time that they had dug a huge trench as a moat, the skeletal remains of a bright orange JCB digger amongst the mouldering corpses. No wonder they'd agreed to have a tannery in such a small camp – to disguise the stench of the dead. I thought about our overkill on the quicklime production front the year before and stroked my beard.

We thundered over fields and through woodland, past the forty-strong crew that the quartermaster had told us about, hacking back the forest's advance onto the ancient road. Soon we were at the southernmost tip of Windsor Great Park, a huge forest of oaks which some Royal or other had put there just so he could hunt deer. I think it was the same chap who made the New Forest, too, but I'm not sure. Sometimes I still missed the internet.

We were guided by a horseman in a black velvet cloak to the edge of a taped-off but otherwise open area. I heard Dawn gasp when she saw the signs for the minefield. The guide led us onto a track marked out only by strips of yellow plastic tape on sticks, and dotted with the occasional hoof-print, through the minefield and up to a set of huge, ornate tents. On the way up to the first and smallest tent we caught sight of different uniforms from what seemed now like a different world. There were policemen, members of the Horse Guard and the odd normal soldier. There was even a Beefeater. They all had old-issue SA-80 machine guns.

'I bet they've all pledged allegiance to the Queen somewhere in their careers – now the old girl's cashing it in.' I said to Dawn quietly.

Our horse was led inside to be tethered by a waiting chap in white gloves, whilst another asked to see the scroll and the various copies of our charter. He asked if we understood that the wording of our own charter also must also apply to the ground we were about to step foot on, and we said we did. He called to another bloke who got a box and helped us down. I looked around the over-dressed field tent, with its paintings and vases and its carpet laying on what was, essentially a field. They'd even stretched to a chandelier, which I thought was pushing it a bit, not only because they had candles inside a canvas tent.

I was told that quarantine would last for three days, and that Midsummer Night was the day after that. Dawn said she'd be back in exactly five days, and said she wanted to try and get back to Silchester that nightfall. She kissed me on the cheek and wished me luck, and then she was gone. I stripped, had a very hot and quite public bath, and then settled back into three days of what must have been the most luxurious quarantine in world history, zombie virus outbreak or not.

I met people from all over the south of England in that tent. All were headed for Windsor Great Park in the middle of what was proving to be a hot, wet summer. It rained pretty much constantly, but we were confined to the tent anyway. We had beds, and everything was open-planned. There were soldiers inside, and there would be at least two of them posted at all times on both the entrance and the way through to the next tent, which we all eyed with curiosity. Most people came on horses of their own, but a few had made their way up the Thames and accepted one of the steady stream of horse-drawn carriages that waited patiently on the banks of the river, taking guests up to the Royal Park. Someone even arrived by hot air balloon, but he had crash-landed a mile away and they had to send out some horses and men to get him. Arthur, he was called, and had a huge red nose. He was obviously used to better than tents, and had stood scoffing at the chandeliers and tablecloths, shouting about when he would be let out, and that he felt like snot in a bloody giant hankie. He told me he lived in a stately home in Staffordshire, and that the hot air balloon was one of three.

'No, I've left it there. Got plenty. Thought I'd give you johnnies an entrance to remember,' he guffawed.

Not everyone was such a twat; in fact most people were, like me, standing around gawping - pretty normal people, really. Well, as normal as English people get. There were hot baths running constantly behind more private curtains. They had a cooking section going all day and all night, which had a constant supply of roast beef, fresh horseradish and Yorkshire puddings like children's heads. Thick, russet gravy of rosemary and redcurrant, legs of lamb and fluffy roast potatoes. They roasted a suckling pig three times each day and once in the night, as people could arrive at any time. They would pull a round table into the centre of the room and pile it with silver platters of roast chicken in lemon and thyme butter; goose with bacon-wrapped figs in brandy; steaming pies of steak, gravy and mushrooms or game and stuffing. There were whole steamed fish from the uncontaminated ponds and jugged smoked kippers from the pantry. Marzipan cakes, cream-filled biscuits, apple jelly and elderberry ice cream stood next to ice-cold jugs of cider, warm foaming ale and pitcher upon pitcher of wine.

I introduced myself to a lot of people, who like me were staggering about getting slowly drunker and fatter. Julia, a mum-of-four from Brighton, said she used to walk her dog on Cissbury Ring when she had to pick her nephew up. He went to school in Worthing, but she didn't know where her family were now. She had lived the previous year in the system of underground caves and tunnels on Brighton Beach. She was pasty, and looked like she needed feeding. I met Colin, from Glastonbury, who had spent the day on Glastonbury Tor when the virus broke out. A dozen survivors had joined him, but by the time the zombies spread out that far, they could no longer climb the steep walls. Elijah from Southall who had successfully sealed off the tower block he worked in, saving hundreds of residents from the virus, had told me that London was now impenetrable. The Thames barrier, unmanned, had failed, sending spring tides and putrefying, bloated flesh-eating zombies flooding through the streets. The corpses had turned the Thames black, and people had fallen ill just by breathing the air outside. Greg from the Isle of Wight had holed up with forty others in the trees in Shanklin Chine (a chine, he told me, is a fissure of rock that nurtures sheltered, almost jungle-like vegetation usually stretching down to the sea). He was a keen rock climber, and had built a tree-top village with other survivors. Someone said the leader of the hundred-strong Eden Project survivors from Cornwall were here too. It was all getting a bit hectic, so I stood outside to smoke a joint, but a soldier ushered me back in. He stopped, sniffing the air.

'What's that?' he demanded.

'It's a spliff,' I said meekly, feeling the giggles on the horizon.

'Give us a bit. Oi, Eggy,' he called to his mate. 'Come and have a puff on this.'

We finished off my spliff; me, the soldier and Eggy, a policeman from Egham. More people arrived, and the tent filled up, but before I knew it I was being ushered into the bigger tent off to one side, via a clear polythene tunnel lined with eight armed guards. My three-day quarantine was over.

It was dark inside the main tent; the roof stretched above my head and out of the reach of the torches which blazed from high wooden stakes in the ground, and I could see faces in the gloom, reclining on wide chairs. Dead in the centre sat a huge circle of a hundred tables and chairs ringing a low, round fire pit. The tables were lit strongly and artificially by a large theatrical lighting rig suspended up at the pinnacle of the tent, which made the rest of the place appear dark even in the orange flicker of the flaming torches. They did have generators then, I thought, and considered asking someone if they also had a DVD player and television. The lights cut a bright white column through the hazy darkness, and a sense of calm pervaded the place, in contrast to the hub-bub of the smaller quarantine tent.

I found a quiet spot, and laid my sheepskin down to cover a soft, long chair for two. I took my boots off and sprawled out. Lining the vast circumference of the tent behind a long tapestry I could see hundreds of beds, partitioned by curtains and right now looking very tempting. Before long yet another roast dinner was thrust in front of me along with a jug of beer, but I could have slept. A table was pulled up to put my dinner onto, and someone offered me a cigar. I did ask about the DVD player as the sounds of a guitar being played were met with a ripple of approval.

I spent the evening people-watching as they filed in and took up seats on the outer ring of dimly lit chairs. People were wearing a lot of animal skins with huge boots to match. Some had cloaks and wore long hats; others were in more modern dress, one or two even in dinner jackets. I drifted off a few times, and woke to see a man wheeling a television in front of me. He pointed to a DVD player, and I eagerly fished around in my bag.

A slowly growing crowd built up behind me as I watched back-to-back episodes of *I'm Alan Partridge* and *The Day Today* until very early in the morning. The dozen or spectators who were left looked up from the TV to a seemingly empty marquee. I was guided to my own bed – it had 'Cissbury' embroidered on the curtain. I slept that night fully bathed and fed, between crisp, starched sheets on a pillow like a cold cloud, dreaming of another world. I only woke up once, to the sound of a land mine going off outside.

Kedgeree, sunset yellow with saffron; quails egg's omelette with wild mushrooms; Sausage and brown sauce rolls. Cup upon cup of creamy tea. I had to request mine the way I like it, to the befuddlement of a flunky: brick red, two sugars – builder's tea. Fresh fruit and oysters. This was getting silly, I thought, but never objected for long enough to actually decline anything. They even wheeled out a table which groaned with every edible bird you could think of, with golden skin and steaming, juicy meat.

'They've let themselves down a bit here,' I nodded at the table to one bystander. 'The bloody least they could have done is laid on a nice bit of swan.'

Today was turning out to be sunny, and it was only then that I realised there was access to outside, to a fenced off are like a paddock, ringed by armed men. I stretched my legs, looked at the view; then returned to the gloom, eager not to miss anything. Today was the longest day of the year – Midsummer's Day. I had a cracking hangover, but declined the offered painkillers. I had got on fine for a year with no man-made medicine, so why start again?

There were four large, high-backed seats on every table, and I reckoned there must have been five hundred people in the tent. The day's proceedings began, and we were encouraged to take our seats at the brightly-lit tables. My place was marked out with the word 'Cissbury' again, this time sign written in gold leaf italics. Even further toward the centre from where we sat was a long curved table, its linen crisp and white in the piercing light. After what must have been a good hour of reverent coughing, around a dozen people started to shuffle towards their places on the head table, heralded by a rather pompous fanfare.

They looked like us – a haggard gaggle of survivors, scraping out a life in a new, strange England. There weren't many old people, save one or two with wisps of hair and dew-drops on their noses. A few military men appeared, next to a couple of chaps in black coat tails. They all waited for one old lady in a headscarf and a tatty body warmer to sit down before taking their seats. She waved a gloved hand to a ripple of applause and whispering.

'Fuck me sideways. That's the Queen!' someone near me said rather too loudly. I shrank into my seat as one of the old boys in coat tails stood.

'Thank you for joining us in these extraordinary times. My name is George, and I am the Master of the Household. I will be your host. If there is anything you require during your stay here, do not hesitate to ask me or a member of my staff,' he waved all around him. 'I trust you've been looked after well?' A polite murmur rumbled round the cavernous tent. He introduced a fat chap, the Lord Chamberlain, who outlined the day's events.

'If you have any problems; concerns over safety or anything similar, there are representatives from both the Royal Company of Archers and the Gentlemen at Arms, who will assist you. At dusk we will begin to read out your names and your wards. Please come forward when your name is called. I shall now call upon my colleague Field Marshal Chesterton, who will be able to fill you in on the story so far.'

I groaned, as more food was brought out and laid on our table. Trays piled high with clams, oysters and winkles on ice, more game, and a suckling pig on each table, with jugs of mead and bread to rinse it down. The Field Marshal stood, and tapped some papers on his table. He didn't know anything new, really, but told us that the infrastructure of the country broke down quicker than expected. The phones jammed within an hour of what they now called 'Point Zero', when the critical mass of the infected numbers made containment impossible and total infection inevitable. By their best estimates, he said, there were no more than a quarter of a million people left in the whole of England. The disease had torn through schools, hospitals and army bases alike. Only those that had sealed themselves off - or were isolated in the first place - had survived, and only those that had been brutal and without mercy had stopped the spread of infections. The stock market had stopped trading on the same day, and had never reopened. The streets of every major city were overrun with the living dead, the air poisoned by disease.

Another old chap rose to his doddery feet and started to explain about the future of England as they saw it. Taxes were, they insisted, to be an entirely voluntary affair, at least until they could pay for anything tangible.

'Who's paying for the swan roast?' grumbled a man on our table.

'Yeah, they won't be voluntary for long,' another added.

'You are expected to retain your self-governing, self-sufficient statuses for the foreseeable future. If you don't wish to pledge your allegiance to the English Crown,' the old boy mumbled, 'you will be issued with a Care of Sovereign Land Agreement and you can be left to your own devices – we know you've all fought for your individual wards, and they have been earned in blood. Those of you who are willing to take to your breasts this most noble of tasks shall be made Barons by Writ of Summons, and may be required to partake in parliamentary debates on the future direction of our great country. Ladies and Gentlemen, Queen Elizabeth the second is asking for your help to protect the surviving inhabitants of England.'

There was raucous cheering and applause. Whistling and the banging of goblets drowned out the man's words, but he forged on, suggesting that new county borders would be created and new maps drawn; but he also said it was increasingly obvious that ancient infrastructures were cradling life, so it was possible they'd just dust off some old maps and use them instead. He also suggested we write our stories of survival down onto paper, so they would not be lost.

Each ward was to be given a new insignia by something called the Central Chancery of the Orders of Knighthood – a coat-of-arms on a standard to be flown from each settlement. This would not only keep travelers to the right paths and ease the transport of livestock and people, but would also serve to help the two dozen newly appointed Knights of the Crown. They would attempt to stay in every encampment in England at least once a year, which would maintain a unity and sense of connection with the Crown and other camps. There would also be a six-monthly parliament to be held here, in Windsor Great Park. National games were to be organised for two year's time, and we were to take details back to our camps and encourage likely participants to train for the competition. Two royally-appointed theatrical troupes would soon begin touring the country providing entertainment, and a circus would move from district to district at a slower pace.

I got Baronified, or whatever its called. I even got a coronet; a band of silver with six balls. I wore it on my head as I knelt, and one of the old men read out some Latin, and the old lady with the headscarf and tatty body warmer laid a sword on each of my shoulders. Then that was it. I was ushered out into a third tent, as small and crowded as the first, and was handed more beer. England's new Barons chewed on lamb legs and quaffed their ales, and hearty cheers would greet the latest additions as they stumbled bleary-eyed into the tent. Many people were interested in commissioning a pub sign for new inns, and about half of them had even heard of Jerry's pub - I ended up with a list of orders longer than my arm. People drifted off into the night, as their horses arrived or they were taken down to the Thames and their awaiting boats.

I got a tap on the shoulder from a flunky when my horse arrived outside. I stood blinking in the dark still air, finally catching sight of a horse with Dawn on it. I was confused - it seemed to be pulling a cart.

'What's that?' I asked, confused.

'It's a motor home, arse-head. This is what I swapped your sign for – the sign for the wheelwright. I figure we're even for the trip. Anyway, I've brought someone to see you,' she said, and nodded over her shoulder. I rubbed the horse's nose before walking up to the cart. It was a fine thing, with iron bands around the circumference of the wheels and long handles shaped from smooth, golden wood. A bundle of furs lay inside, covering up a layer of straw. Lou whipped off the animal skins and pointed her finger at me.

'Ha, ha! You got turned into a Baron!' She seemed a little drunk.

'Well, you got turned into a Baroness,' I said. 'I've got the papers. Lord and Lady Cissbury. That means you too.' I helped Dawn turn the cart around in a circle to face the way they'd come from.

'Do you want to stop and eat?' I asked. 'There's plenty of food. I've got a sackful with me, though.'

'No, just get in and give me a cuddle. Keep the crown on,' Lou peered out from under the furs.

'It's a coronet, apparently,' I said. Dawn told us we'd be in Silchester before dawn, and grabbed a chicken leg from my sack. I climbed onto the straw floor of the cart next to my wife, and we pulled away.

'The suspension isn't too good,' she grinned.

'Are you pissed?' I asked her.

'No, I'm pregnant,' she whispered. 'I haven't touched a drop. Anyway, I'm sure this thing will shake it out of me before we get home.' She and Dawn laughed. I sat back, drinking in the news. The moon was out, and we were going home – my family were going home.

As I watched the black branches grab at the deep blue sky like fingers, and as the moonlight lay in silver patches on the cool dark ground I remembered a story I'd read the previous summer in the local newspaper. It told of an ancient tree in the middle of a traffic roundabout in Broadwater - near what used to be our house. The council had decided that the tree was too old and it posed a danger to the traffic, so it had to come down.

I didn't know anyone else that was bothered about it, or even heard of the story or noticed the tree. No-one was really too fussed about an old tree on a busy roundabout, but I felt like I knew it. Years before that, when I was a small boy, my dad had always pointed it out as we'd driven past it and I pressed my face against the car window.

'That's the skeleton tree,' he'd told me. 'On midsummer's eve, the dead crawl out from under its roots and dance around in the moonlight.'

'Terry,' my mother had jabbed him with a finger. 'You'll terrify the boy.'

They didn't get to cut down the tree, as the end of the world happened instead. I was glad England's skeletons had something to dance around. They only get one night off a year. I pulled a sheepskin over Lou's shoulders and kissed her forehead, but I kept one hand on my longbow, and both eyes on the ancient green road stretching out ahead of us.

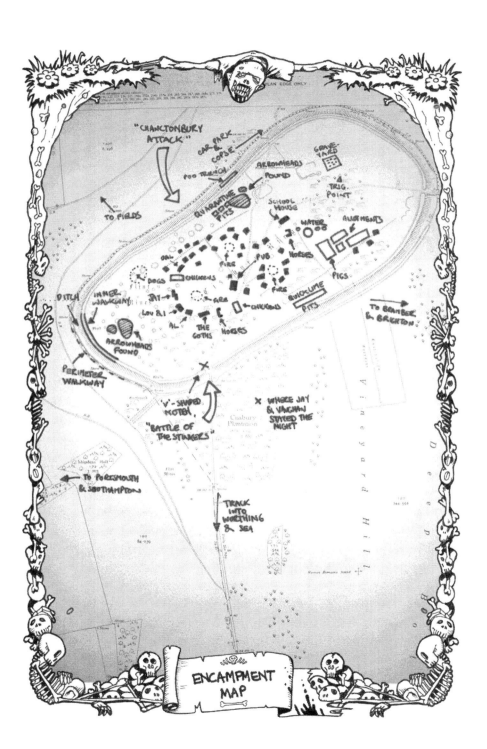

ENCAMPMENT MAP

The Cissbury Ring

The Cissbury Ring

To be continued...

Printed in Great Britain by
Amazon.co.uk, Ltd.,
Marston Gate.